PRAISE FOR

Not Until You

"If you don't want to get hooked, then you shouldn't read [*Not Until You*]. But why would you not want to?"

—*Under the Covers Book Blog*

"Sexual tension that will absolutely stay with me."

—*Fiction Vixen*

"[*Not Until You*] is just fantastic."   —*The Sweet Escape*

"Beautifully written and heartfelt . . . With all the emotion and passion that comes from a love so hard-won and richly deserved . . . Roni Loren has outdone herself with *Not Until You*."

—*Seductive Musings*

"Filled with so much love and so much sadness . . . Satisfying and meaningful."   —*Romantic Book Affairs*

PRAISE FOR RONI LOREN
AND HER NOVELS

"Hot and romantic, with an edge of suspense that will keep you entertained."

—Shayla Black, *New York Times* bestselling author of
Theirs to Cherish

continued . . .

Not Until You

RONI LOREN

BERKLEY BOOKS, NEW YORK

THE BERKLEY PUBLISHING GROUP
Published by the Penguin Group
Penguin Group (USA) LLC
375 Hudson Street, New York, New York 10014

USA • Canada • UK • Ireland • Australia • New Zealand • India • South Africa • China

penguin.com

A Penguin Random House Company

NOT UNTIL YOU

Library of Congress Cataloging-in-Publication Data

Loren, Roni.
Not until you / Roni Loren.—Berkley trade paperback edition.
pages ; cm.—(A loving on the edge novel ; 1)
ISBN 978-0-425-27503-0 (softcover)
1. Women college students—Fiction.   I. Title.
PS3612.O764N68 2014
813'.6—dc23
2014026191

PUBLISHING HISTORY
InterMix serial edition / June-July 2013
Berkley trade paperback edition / November 2014

PRINTED IN THE UNITED STATES OF AMERICA

10 9 8 7 6 5 4 3 2

Cover photo of "Wrought iron door" © Photokin/Shutterstock.
Cover design by Diana Kolsky.
Interior text design by Tiffany Estreicher.

For my NaNa, Kelli. You would've gotten such a kick out of this crazy career of mine. I miss you more than words can say.

CONTENTS

Not Until You

PART I

Not Until You Dare

ONE

"Andre, this isn't a good time. Can I call you back?"

I did my best not to let my cell phone slip from between my ear and shoulder. *Just don't drop the tequila.* I adjusted the enormous bottle that my friend Bailey had given me as a graduation present from my right hand to beneath my left arm and tried to dig my keys out of my purse so I could open the main door to my apartment building.

"I'm so sorry I wasn't able to make it, Cela," my older brother said, his guilt obviously trumping my request to call him later. "I got caught at an investigation site this morning. I thought I'd be able to get there in time, but we had a witness wanting to talk and . . ."

I cursed silently as my keys hit the pavement. I crouched down, doing my best not to flash my underwear to anyone who may be passing by. "Really, it's fine. They called my name. I walked across the stage and got a piece of paper and a sash for being summa cum laude. Papá yelled my name like he was at a baseball game instead of a ceremony. Mamá cried. We all went to lunch at Rosario's and then the two of them headed back to the airport. Not that interesting."

My brother's heavy sigh said everything. I almost felt guilty that *he* felt so guilty. "Before you move back home next month, we're getting together to celebrate. My baby sister, the doctor. I'm so proud I could burst."

I smiled. I did like the sound of that. Dr. Marcela Medina, Doctor of Veterinary Medicine. Seven years of exams and studying and clinics, but it was finally done. Now it was time to leave Dallas and head back home to Verde Pass and take up the slack in my dad's practice.

That last part had my smile faltering a bit. I hooked my key ring with my finger and wobbled back to a stand. "That's sounds great. But I really have to get going. I have my hands full and need to get through the door."

"Cela, you know better than to carry too much. Parking lots at night are one of the most dangerous places for women. Are you holding your mace?" he asked, his voice going into that bossy cop tone I was all too familiar with.

"It's in my hand," I lied, trying to remember where I'd stowed the last little canister he'd given me—probably in my junk drawer. "But I don't have a free hand to pull the door open."

"All right," he said, placated. "Congratulations again. I love you."

"Love you, too."

The call ended but I didn't have a way to take the phone off my ear, so I just shuffled forward in a sideways hunch, trying to juggle everything I was holding to get my key into the door. After two attempts, I got the lock turned and pressed my back against the glass door to push my way into the lobby.

As soon as I'd cleared the entrance and turned toward the stairs, male voices sounded behind me. Of course someone would show up right after I didn't need help anymore. I peeked back to see who it was, Andre's danger warnings still echoing in my head, but found something more distracting than criminals—my neighbors, Foster and Pike.

Foster stepped through the main door first and glanced my way. As usual, everything went melty inside me, his smile like a zap of heat to my system. Ridiculous. "Need some help, neighbor?"

I straightened, but forgot about my phone in the process. My brand new iPhone went sliding off my shoulder.

"Crap!" I lurched forward, trying to save it from its imminent demise, and accidentally dropped my plastic bag of Chinese takeout on the way.

"Whoa, there." Pike, Foster's roommate, was at my side in a second. His hand caught my elbow, saving me from losing the ginormous bottle of liquor along with my balance. But my phone clattered to the ground, the harsh sound mixing with the *splat* of my noodles hitting tile.

I winced, anticipating a broken screen. "Dammit."

Foster bent down, his tie brushing the ground as he swept my phone off the floor. He peered at the screen, dark brows lowering over pale eyes, then he turned the phone toward me—the happy puppy screensaver staring back at me intact. "All is well. Luckily, these things are built to take a licking."

My brain got snagged on the word *lick,* and the back of my neck went hot. My lips parted, but words failed me. *Great, imitate a gaping goldfish—that's cute.*

Pike cleared his throat, easing the tequila from my arms, and then crouched down near the open bag at my feet. He grabbed a noodle from the spilled box of Chinese food, tipped his head back, and dropped the noodle into his mouth, his eyes watching mine. "The lo mein's a loss, though."

I swallowed hard, his gaze even more bad boy than the tattoos peeking out from his open collar. His tongue snaked around the noodle. *Look away.* I forced my face upward, but then ended up focusing on Foster again. *Say something.* God, I was standing there like an idiot. This was why I always avoided these two like they were contagious. They made me go stupid.

Foster held out my phone, and I managed to take it, the slight brush of his fingers against mine hitting the Reset button in my brain. I managed a feeble, "Thank you."

Foster glanced at the mess on the floor. "I'm really sorry I said anything. I didn't mean to distract you from your intricate juggling act."

I shook my head. "No, it's my fault. I shouldn't have been trying to carry everything at once. It's been a long day, and I was hoping to save myself a second trip up the stairs."

"The joys of a walk-up." Pike grabbed a few napkins and started cleaning up the noodles at my feet like it was his mess to worry about.

"Oh, you don't have to do that." I lowered down to my knees. "I'll take care of it."

He grinned over at me, the mirror opposite of his roommate. Ian Foster was all suits and dark looks—a man who preferred to be called by his surname. Whereas Pike didn't seem to even have a last name. He was a drummer in some popular local band—jeans, a sex-on-the-mind smile, and spiked, bleached hair his usual uniform. Not that I had studied either of them. Or listened to their escapades through the wall I shared with them. Not at all.

Keep telling yourself that, Cela.

Despite my protest, Pike helped me finish picking up the mess. "So what's the big-ass bottle of tequila for? No one could've had that bad of a day."

I glanced over at the bottle I'd set on the floor, debating whether I could be trusted to have a normal conversation with these two without sounding like I had a speech impediment. "I, uh, graduated today. It was a gift."

"Oh, right on."

"Congratulations, Cela," Foster said. Just the sound of him saying my name in that smooth, dark voice had my stomach clenching. He was all Southern refinement, but I didn't miss the glimmer of a drawl underneath it all.

Ay dios mío. My body clamored to attention like an eager Labrador ready to be petted. *Down, girl.* These guys were way above my pay grade. I wasn't dumb or delusional. I'd seen/spied on/secretly hated the women who'd passed through their apartment door—women who looked like they'd earned their doctorates in the art of seduction.

I hadn't even reached the kindergarten level in that particular department.

"Thank you."

"You were going to vet school at Dallas U, right?" Foster had tucked his hands in the pockets of his slacks, and though the question was casual, I had the distinct impression he was tense beneath that suit jacket.

Pike handed me a napkin for my hands and stood to toss the food into a nearby trash can.

I wiped off my hands and pushed myself to my feet, trying to do it as gracefully as possible in my restrictive skirt. "Yes, how'd you know that?"

"The scrubs you wear have the school insignia on them," Foster said, as if it was totally normal that he'd looked at me that closely.

"Observant." Especially considering I usually only managed a head-down, mumbled, hey-how-are-ya exchange when we passed each other in the hallway. Secretly listening to one of your hot neighbors having sex had a way of making eye contact a bit uncomfortable the next day—particularly if said eavesdropper had used the soundtrack to fuel her own interlude with her battery-operated boyfriend.

Not that I had. Several times. Whatever.

Pike sidled up next to Foster—a motley pair if there ever was one. "So, doc, now that you've got no dinner and clearly too much liquor on your hands, why don't you join us? We already have pizza on the way, and we can play a drinking game with the tequila. Do college kids still play Never Have I Ever? I was always good at that one."

Kid? Is that what they saw me as? Neither of them could be *that* much older than I was. Though in terms of life experience, I had no doubt they trumped me a few times over.

"Oh, no, that's okay." The refusal was automatic, long practiced. How many times had I turned down such offers—from guys, from friends? My parents had been so strict when I was younger that I almost didn't know how to say yes even after living on my own the last few years. Studies first. Fun later. Yet, there never seemed to be any time for fun after the first one was finished.

"You sure? I don't want you going to bed with no dinner because of us," Foster said, frown lines marring that perfect mouth of his.

Going to bed and *us* was about all I heard. My father's stern voice whispered in my ear. *You don't know these men. You'll be all alone in their apartment. Medina women have more respect for themselves than that.*

"Really, I'm fine. I had a big lunch," I said, my smile brief, plastic. "But thanks."

"Oh, come on," Pike said, his tone cajoling. "We've been neighbors for what, two years? We should at least get to know a little about each other."

Get to know each other? I knew that Foster was loud when he came—even if he was alone. Knew that Pike liked to laugh during sex. Knew the two men shared women. And the other sounds I'd heard over the last two years . . . the smacks, the commands, the erotic screams. My face went as hot as if I'd stuck my head in an oven.

"Y'all just want me for my tequila," I said, attempting to deflect my derailing thoughts.

The corner of Pike's mouth lifted. "Of course that's not all we want you for."

"Uh . . ." *Oh, hell.* Pictures flashed across my brain. Dirty, delicious pictures. I almost dropped my phone again. I had no idea what to do with my hands, my expression.

Foster put a hand on Pike's shoulder. "The lady said no. I think we should let her go celebrate her graduation however she wants."

"All right." Pike's face turned hangdog, but he handed me the tequila bottle. "If you change your mind, we've got big plans. Supreme pizza and a *Star Wars*–themed porn marathon. *The Empire Sucks C—*"

Foster smacked the back of Pike's head, and Pike ducked and laughed.

"Kidding. I mean, a Jane Austen marathon," Pike corrected, his green-gold eyes solemn. *"Pride and Pu—"*

Foster was behind Pike, his hand clamping over his friend's mouth in a flash. "I seriously can't take him out. He's like an untrained puppy. Maybe you can lend me a shock collar or something."

Pike waggled his eyebrows, all playful wickedness.

I laughed, putting my hand to my too hot forehead, and turning toward the stairs. "Yeah, so, I'm going to go now."

"Cela," Foster said as I put my foot onto the first step.

I glanced back. "Yeah?"

His ice-melt eyes flicked downward, his gaze alighting along the length of me before tracing their way upward again in a slow, unashamed perusal. "Promise you won't go to bed hungry."

I wet my lips, my skin suddenly feeling too tight to accommodate the blood pumping beneath it, and nodded.

But it was a lie.

I always went to bed hungry.

And it had nothing to do with a spilled dinner.

T W O

"What the fuck were you thinking?" Foster asked shrugging off his jacket and loosening his tie, annoyance digging at him like a bad case of chiggers.

Pike straddled one of the chairs at their breakfast bar with *Who me?* innocence in his eyes. "What? I'm not allowed to flirt with the neighbor? You certainly can't tear your eyes away from her anytime she's around. I know you time your morning run so that you pass her in the hallway."

Foster groaned. "You invited her over to watch *porn*, Pike. I thought her eyes were going to fall out of her head."

"Oh, come on. I was joking. She knew I was kidding."

Foster wasn't convinced of that. Cela's movements had gone jerky at the suggestion, and her usually imperceptible accent had thickened her words. "You can't joke like that with girls like her. She's not some chick you met after a show."

Pike somehow managed to smirk without his mouth so much as twitching. "Girls like her?"

Foster tossed his jacket across the back of the other chair and opened the button at his neck, his shirt collar feeling nooselike. "Yes, girls like her. You know what I mean."

"Vanilla ones."

Foster rubbed the spot between his eyes with his thumb, trying to chase away the throbbing that had started at the office and had gotten worse downstairs. "She's not just vanilla, she's . . ."

"Hot."

"Innocent." He grabbed two beers from the fridge and plunked one down in front of Pike. "And young."

"She's a doctor." He twisted off the cap and took a sip. "So not that young. She's got to be at least . . ." He paused, apparently counting in his head. "Twenty-four."

Twenty-four. Not a total stretch for Foster's thirty-two, but somehow Cela seemed even younger than that—untouched by the world. Part of it was that sheltered vibe that seemed to waft off her, like she'd been raised in another era. But he knew it was more than her demureness and manners that screamed innocence.

Foster leaned back against the counter, taking a deep pull of his beer, his throat dry and his blood hot from the brief encounter downstairs. The scene replayed in his head—the sound of her breath catching when he'd said her name, the way she'd looked there on her knees, that hint of a blush beneath her honeyed skin. His cock twitched to life. *Fuck.*

Pike rolled his bottle cap between his fingers, walking it over his knuckles in the way that said he'd spent way too much time in bars. "She's interested, you know?"

"Right. She almost vaulted up the stairs to get away from us after your Jane Austen comment. She's probably next door right now googling to see if we're on the sex offender registry."

But despite his protest, Foster knew Pike wasn't far off base. His friend had probably noticed the same signals in Cela that he had. She'd been flustered, maybe even offended, but her nipples had been hard points against her blouse and her pulse had been pounding at her throat like a beacon. He'd wanted to lick the spot. He'd wanted her to say yes.

But maybe Pike's crassness had actually saved them. The last thing Foster needed to be doing was messing with his good-girl neighbor. Women like her were off limits. He'd learned the hard way not to get interested in someone from outside his scene. Once those women got over the excitement of the *ooh, I'm being so scandalous dating a kinky boy* phase, they bailed and went to find someone they actually wanted to be with for the long haul.

And Foster was tired of getting his hopes up and was *really* tired of one-night stands. His interludes at The Ranch, the BDSM resort he belonged to, and the occasional ménage with Pike and one of his band groupies satisfied the physical itch for a while. But the dominant side of him—the part that craved ownership—was shriveling into a desiccated husk.

He was over thirty, had a job that could fund a posh life, and even had a swank home his family had left to him sitting empty. But he was still living like a college kid, rooming with his best friend. Foster had good reasons for setting his life up this way. But on days like this, when he saw glimpses of what else was out there, he found himself wondering if his life was bound to be haunted by *what ifs*.

The doorbell rang and Foster headed over to the door to get the pizza. He paid the delivery guy and took the two large supreme pizzas from him, passing them over to Pike who'd eagerly stepped up behind him. After one furtive glance toward Cela's closed door, Foster stepped back into the apartment.

Pike already had one of the boxes open and a slice in his mouth by the time Foster made it into the living room. Pike pointed to the box. "This one's mine."

Foster snorted and grabbed for a slice from the other box. Some things never changed. Pike could out eat a linebacker, though you'd never guess it looking at him. Apparently, a few hours of banging on drums every night was as effective as running marathons. Plus, Foster wasn't entirely convinced that some part of Pike didn't still worry about not having a next meal. Food hadn't exactly been easy to come by when Pike was a kid.

Foster sank into the love seat and set his beer on the side table.

"You really think she wasn't interested?" Pike asked, propping his feet up on the coffee table. "Anytime you said something to her, she got all tongue-tied. And she shivered when I touched her."

Foster shrugged, trying to appear as if he'd already forgotten about their run-in with their neighbor and wasn't sitting there trying to get the image of her on her knees or those big brown eyes out of his head.

"Maybe she has a boyfriend or something." Pike folded another slice of pizza in half and bit.

"Doubtful. No one ever sleeps over." The words were out before Foster could call them back.

Pike's eyebrow arched. "And you would know this how? Taking up stalking as a hobby?"

Foster tore a bite off his pizza, eyeing Pike, warning him off the topic.

"No way." He pointed the neck of his beer bottle at him. "Don't give me that *eat shit* look. Spill it, dude."

Foster polished off his own beer. He had a feeling this was going to be more than a one-drink night. When he set down the empty bottle, Pike was still watching him, waiting. Foster sighed. "We share a wall—a thin one. I can hear some of what does . . . and doesn't go on in her bedroom. All sex noises have been . . . solo."

And had provided erotic background music to his own solo tours more than once, imagining Cela's hands roaming over her body, her fingers sliding between those pretty legs. He adjusted himself on the couch, his boxer briefs developing a choke hold on his quickly swelling erection.

"Holy shit." Pike's mouth broke into a grin. "You dirty eavesdropping bastard."

Foster looked at the ceiling, wishing he could rewind and take back the admission. "I'm in my own fucking room. It's not like I have a glass up to the wall."

Though he'd considered it.

"Well, no wonder she's so quick to get flustered around us," Pike said, laughing. "If you can hear her, God only knows what she's heard on her end."

Foster cringed. "Tell me about it."

Anytime he and Pike shared a woman, it was in Foster's room. He had the bigger bed and master suite. And neither he nor Pike were quiet. Fucking was noisy business.

He'd considered moving things to Pike's room once he'd realized how thin the walls were, but then he hadn't been able to bring himself to do it. Knowing that Cela could be on the other side, listening to them, had only served to turn Foster on more. He'd found himself talking louder, issuing his commands in a voice that he knew would carry, and he hadn't held back his own sounds of pleasure. She'd become the focus of Foster's attention, an unknowing part of a foursome.

He figured if she was bothered by it, she'd complain to the office. She'd reported the couple across the hall who couldn't seem to keep their shitty music to a non-earsplitting level, so she wasn't afraid to speak up. But as the months had gone on, no word had come. And when he'd pass her in the hall, arm full of books, scrubs hiding that cute little body, he'd catch her sideways glances, the way she held her breath when they passed each other. He scared her on some level, set her off balance, which only served to prod his dominant side, tease it. It'd turned into one tortuous exercise in restraint.

"You think she's going to get herself off tonight?" Pike asked, shifting on the couch and peering in the direction of Foster's bedroom. "She looked pretty keyed up."

There it was again—illicit images of Cela on her knees before him, those wanting eyes locking with his as she unzipped his pants and wrapped those plush lips around . . . "Ah, hell, we have to stop talking about this. I'm getting a headache and a hard-on. And aspirin's only going to help one of those."

Pike chuckled. "So go bring her a couple of slices of pizza. Maybe you'll catch her at the right moment."

"No." Foster undid his tie fully now and untucked his shirttails, everything irritating him at the moment. "She's not our type."

"She's not *your* type. I have no problem introducing a good girl to the dark side." Pike swigged his beer. "Sometimes the quiet ones turn out to be the dirtiest of them all. All that pent-up frustration, digging up those repressed fantasies and making them happen for her."

"And then they freak out, blame you, and bail the minute the guilt catches up with them," Foster said darkly. He'd been on the receiving end of that dynamic before, and had no intention of taking that not-so-scenic tour again.

Pike frowned over at him. "Of course they all leave eventually. Good girl or not. Women don't come to guys like us for an I-do, my friend. Thank God for that."

"Right." 'Cause having someone to come home to besides your pizza-inhaling best friend would just be the most horrible thing imaginable. Foster's appetite left him, and he lost a taste for the beer. "I need a shower before the movie."

Pike snorted. "Sure you do. Extra lube is in the hall closet. Just don't call out her name too loud when you blow."

"Fuck off."

Pike smacked his lips in an air kiss. "Love you too, pumpkin."

THREE

I stood in front of my freezer, contemplating the uninspiring microwaveable meals and letting the frosty air wash over my still-burning skin. I'd changed out of my graduation outfit into a tank top and pajama bottoms, but I couldn't seem to cool my temperature or get my heart to stop pounding. My two hot-as-sin neighbors had *flirted* with me, invited me over.

I hadn't imagined that, right?

Maybe I had. Picking up the signals when a guy was interested had never been my strong suit. My *stay away from boys at all costs* rules as a teenager along with my all-girls Catholic high school had left me with an emaciated female intuition. And any boys that came around the house were scared off by either my father or brother.

Maybe Foster and Pike had just been joking around—or worse, teasing me. They had called me a college kid after all. I'd seen some of the girls who'd made the walk of shame out of their apartment. They certainly didn't look anything like me. Maybe all the innuendo I'd read into the brief conversation had been my hormones inserting my own hopes into their words.

I groaned and slammed the freezer door. Like I'd act on a sexual invitation anyway. I hadn't done anything more than kiss someone since starting grad school. And I didn't even know these guys, not really. And there were *two* of them.

My body quivered at the thought, and a hot ache pulsed between my thighs. I collapsed onto one of the stools lining the breakfast bar. "Good Lord, what is wrong with me?"

I uncapped the bottle of tequila I'd left on the counter and poured a shot into a juice glass, then lifted it. "Happy graduation to me."

I kicked back the shot, the alcohol burning like liquid lightning on the way down. My face scrunched up as I tried not to cough. *Wow.* Maybe that's why you were supposed to do those with salt and lime.

As the fire cooled in my throat, I looked around my empty apartment, wondering what to do for the next few hours, because I sure as hell was too wired to go to bed. Every night was usually spent in front of my books, eating takeout, and studying. But now every test had been passed, every class completed. This chapter of my life was done.

Sadness flickered through me.

The "find yourself" years were rolling in my rearview. Real life was here, waiting for me to claim my spot as a responsible adult.

In a few weeks I'd be back in the vet office I'd grown up in, but now my name would be on the placard next to my father's. I'd get my own patients, my own house. I'd eat dinner with my parents a few nights a week and probably date Michael Ruiz. My former high school boyfriend had been the only one to make it past the test with my father, and that was only because my family had been friends with his since the beginning of time. Michael had made it no secret that he was happily awaiting my return to Verde Pass. He'd even sent me a bouquet of daisies for graduation. Such a nice guy.

Nice. Polite. Just like the rest of my life.

I traced her finger around the rim of my glass, the droning hum of the freezer a mind-numbing soundtrack to my thoughts. My whole future was stretched out before me—a dot-to-dot picture with a set path I'd known I would follow for as long as I could remember. One I'd never thought to question growing up. But now that it was staring me in the face, a ribbon of regret threaded through my already melancholy mood, darkening the trajectory of my thoughts.

Grad school was supposed to be my big adventure. Single girl in a big city, experiencing life for the first time without my father staring over my shoulder. I'd fought like hell to even have the chance to go to school in Dallas, had come up with an argument to present to my parents that would've impressed a trial lawyer. In the end, the fact that my older brother was here had saved me. And to his credit, Andre had mostly stayed out of my business.

It'd been the first true stand for independence that I'd won.

And what had I done with the opportunity after all the struggle to get out here to Dallas? Not a damn thing. I'd been the obedient daughter and studious student like I'd always been. I'd even gone to Sunday mass every now and again. I'd said no to all the parties. I'd gone on a few dates, but never with anyone I was truly interested in. Hell, I'd been in Dallas for four years and the shot of tequila warming my belly was my very first.

With a rush of frustration, I poured another shot and tipped it back—the sting no softer than the first time, but the heat fueling the call of rebellion within me.

Enough of this bull. Drinking alone in an empty apartment and pining over my neighbors was freaking pathetic. I deserved a real graduation celebration. I only had a few weeks left here to get a taste of all that I'd never experienced. It was now or never. If I screwed up royally or embarrassed myself, I'd be gone soon anyway. My friends and family back home would be none the wiser.

With renewed resolve and a little liquid courage, I capped the tequila and grabbed a notepad off the refrigerator to write down a list I never thought I'd be putting into print. Just seeing the words glide from the pen had my throat constricting. The first two attempts didn't work. I scratched out and reworded a few things, my hand shaking with adrenaline and nerves. But then it was too messy. And I didn't do messy. I balled up the first few sheets and tossed them in the trash, then got it right on the third time. Nice little block letters forming statements I didn't even have the guts to say aloud. Done.

I stared at the list and took a deep breath, the neat plan of my life getting tucked away into the back of my brain for now. I folded the page in half, making a crease, and tore off the bottom half. I slipped that portion in my kitchen drawer, but kept the other half in my hand.

"One, two, three, don't look down," I muttered, repeating an old mantra from my childhood diving classes, as I slid off the stool. Hopefully, I wouldn't drown.

Before blind panic could take me over, I grabbed the liquor bottle, toed on my flip-flops, and headed out the door.

It was only four steps to apartment 3G, but it seemed my blood pressure had reached near-stroke rate by the time I lifted my hand to knock on the door. Even then, I almost spun on my heel and scampered back to the safety of my quiet apartment where everything was normal and predictable.

And boring.

And lonely.

I knocked.

For a few moments I didn't hear anything, and I wondered if they weren't going to come to the door. Maybe it was a sign from the universe that I had no business being here, that I'd truly lost my mind. Because really, I probably had. But then there were voices and the shift of the lock, and my muscles seemed to turn to stone. The door swung open, Pike and the scent of pizza greeting me. He leaned against the doorjamb, looking edible in his tight black tee and worn jeans. His mouth curved upward, and I forgot to breathe for a second. Oh crap, how was I going to go through with this?

He glanced down at my outfit and the tequila tucked under my arm. "Well, hi again, doc. Changed your mind?"

"I, uh . . ."

"Cela?" Foster appeared a few steps behind Pike, his hair wet and his chest bare. *Oh, blessed, blessed Lord.* My eyes automatically shifted downward, drinking in the real view of what I'd only imagined the many nights I'd listened to him through the wall—broad shoulders, honed pecs, and an abdomen so lickable that the sight of it made my tongue press to the back of my teeth. I knew I should look up, say something, but my gaze snagged lower, following the trail of dark hair that disappeared into the waistband of his low-slung track pants.

God help me. He was even prettier than my imagination had conjured—and my imagination had been aiming for the outfield already. Every feminine molecule in my body seemed to lurch toward him, my fingers aching to trace the lines of muscles he'd been hiding beneath his suits, to lick off the water droplets that had fallen from his hair onto his shoulders. My body went into full, rolling boil.

I clenched the bottle of liquor like it was a life raft. "Hi. Um. Yeah.

So I decided I really was hungry, and I'll never drink this much alcohol myself, and I know y'all are probably settled in for the night now and don't want company, and I don't know if y'all really wanted me over or if you were just being nice . . ." *Shut up, shut up, shut up.* "But if you weren't just being nice and wanted to share me—"

Pike's eyebrows lifted.

My face flamed. Oh God, had I just said that? "I mean, share *the tequila* with me, then well, here it is and if not then that's fi—"

Pike pressed two fingers to my mouth, the touch shocking me into silence. "Take a breath, doc. We still have pizza, we will always accept free liquor, and we will never turn down good company."

My shoulders sagged, mortification bleeding through me. Way to be smooth. If they really had been flirting with me earlier, they were probably regretting that decision now. *Warning: Awkward girl, straight ahead.* I wet my lips when Pike lowered his hand, inadvertently tasting the salt his touch had left behind. "I'm sorry. I just don't want to intrude or anything."

"Is she intruding, Foster?" Pike asked, still looking at me.

I peered past Pike's shoulder. Foster's gaze was unwavering, making it near impossible to hold the eye contact. Maybe he didn't want me there after all. I glanced at my feet, but then heard the low notes of his voice. "Of course not. I don't extend invitations I don't mean."

Hot goose bumps chased over my skin, something in his firm tone making me shiver.

Pike's smile was pure warmth. He leaned over and took the tequila from me. "Come on in, doc. Foster decided to jump in the shower before eating, so there's still lots of pizza left."

"Thanks." I stepped inside and when Pike shut the door behind me, I had the distinct feeling of the safety net of my existence ripping to shreds beneath me.

"I'm going to get us a few glasses," Pike said, veering toward the kitchen.

Foster glanced to the left toward the open bedroom door, then back to me, his expression unreadable. "Make yourself at home, Cela, and help yourself to pizza. I'll be right back."

I moved around the breakfast bar and down the short hall toward the living area. The apartment was similar to mine, but the kitchen and living space weren't open to each other. Plus, this was the bigger two-bedroom version and had a decidedly more masculine decor. The couches were leather, the furniture sleek and modern, and the artwork on the walls black-and-white photography. The stuff looked refined and expensive, like it should be in some high-rise loft downtown instead of in my modest apartment complex.

I took a seat along the side of the ginormous wall-mounted TV, and a spaceship flew across the screen, the surround sound vibrating in her ears. *Uh-oh.* Panic flitted through me when I remembered Pike's words from downstairs. Had he not been kidding about the *Star Wars* porn?

Pike sauntered into the living room, setting the liquor, a few beers, and a couple of glasses on the coffee table, his triceps flexing beneath his gorgeous tattoos as he arranged everything. He glanced up at me, frowned. "You okay?"

I ventured a peek at the television, saw Harrison Ford, and let out a breath. No *Star Wars* porn. Just straight-up *Star Wars.* "Yep, I'm fine."

"Liar," he teased, handing me a paper plate with a slice of pizza. "You're so tense, you're almost vibrating. And that's after"—he eyed the tequila—"at least a couple of shots of liquor."

I sighed, forcing my neck from side to side, trying to slough off my anxious state. "I'm sorry. It's been a really long day. And I think graduation affected me more than I expected."

"Is that right?" Foster asked, coming back into the living room wearing a soft gray T-shirt that covered his skin but not the peaks and valleys of the man beneath. He slipped between the couch and my chair, his fresh soap scent drifting over me, and took the spot on the love seat across from me. "How so?"

I took a bite of pizza, taking a moment to gather myself so I wouldn't start rambling again. They were just two guys. Yes, they were beautiful and sexy and had starred in too many of my fantasies, but I was a woman who had just graduated at the top of her very competitive class. I was capable of coherent speech. Mostly.

I swallowed my bite and attempted a shrug that said *yep, I'm carefree and totally at ease, fellas.* "Well, it's something I've been working at for seven years."

"Seven?" Foster interrupted.

"I got into vet school a year early."

"Of course." He made some face akin to a scowl, but covered it so fast I couldn't be sure.

"And so I've had my eye on this one prize, this one goal. And now it's done."

"But that's good, right?" Pike asked, peeling off a pepperoni and popping it into his mouth. "Wasn't that the point? God knows I was happy to finally scrape through my four years."

"Sure. It's great," I said, mustering up some semblance of a smile. "But I realized I've done little else besides work on that goal. These were supposed to be the fun times before I went back home to south Texas to settle down and work in my father's practice. But I've lived here for four years and have spent ninety-five percent of it either in class, studying, or sleeping."

"Now that," Pike said, pointing at me with his pizza, "is a goddamned tragedy." He looked to Foster. "It's a good thing we invited her over, dude, because we were like three days away from her going all *The Shining* on us."

I laughed. "I'm not quite that bad off."

"No, I'm serious. I can see the ax in the door now. All work and no play can only lead to homicide."

Pike's grin was infectious, and some of the tightness in my chest eased a bit. "So really having me over is a self-defense move on your part, then?"

"Completely selfish," Foster agreed, his own smile finally peeking through at the corners of those stark blue eyes.

Pike leaned forward and tossed his grease-stained paper plate onto the coffee table, then rubbed his hands together. "So, now we've got a big responsibility on our hands. We have to make sure your first night away from school is a killer one—and not in an ax-swinging kind of way. Pizza and *Star Wars* aren't going to cut it."

"No, really. This is fine," I said, waving him off.

"Nah, come on. I'm not letting you off that easy. We were supposed to play Never Have I Ever. Anything you've never done that you're dying to do?"

The list I'd written seemed to warm in my pocket. I shrugged, my tongue glued to the roof of my mouth.

Foster glanced at the clock on the cable box. "It's still early. We could take you out to celebrate in style. Pike can get into any club within a hundred-mile radius once he tells them he's the drummer in Darkfall."

Pike sniffed. "And Foster can bribe us into the swankier ones that want to keep me out for the same reason."

I glanced down at my outfit. "I'm not dressed for that. And I know y'all didn't have plans to go out tonight."

"Plans can change," Pike said.

I pressed my lips together, my logical side telling me to call it a night, stop while I was ahead. But the thought of going out with these two, possibly dancing with them, had my pulse climbing. "I'll need more alcohol before either of you can convince me to dance in public."

Pike laughed. "That can be arranged. You up for it, Foster?"

Foster looked at me, his blue-eyed gaze seeming to penetrate right through all my attempts at a calm façade. "You sure you want to spend your big night with the two of us, Cela?"

The question and his tone seemed to hold more layers than the simple words he'd said. And for a second I wondered if he knew what I'd been thinking, knew why I'd talked myself into coming over here in the first place, knew about that list tucked against my hip. But of course, there was no way he could know all that.

I met his stare head on, my bravery building like a staircase beneath my feet, one tentative step after the other until I could see the door to the unknown rising before me, beckoning me to open it. My chest rose and fell with a steadying breath. "I couldn't think of two better guys to spend the night with."

His jaw twitched and something feral flashed through his eyes as he stood. "All right, Cela. Then go back to your apartment, put on something for dancing, and meet us downstairs in fifteen minutes."

The authority in his voice scattered my thoughts like dry leaves on a windy day. I scrambled to gather them back together. "Fifteen minutes? But I'll need to redo my makeup and do something with my hair."

"No." He walked toward me, frowning in a way that cut off my words. "You don't need any of that. You look great already."

"Agreed," Pike chimed in.

I rose to my feet, feeling vulnerable and quivery with Foster looming over me. "Thanks, but—"

He reached out, his hand going to the back of my head, and my words got logjammed in my throat. He tugged at the clip I'd twisted my hair into, and released it, letting my hair tumble down my back.

"And wear your hair down," he said, pressing the clip into my hand as he bent forward. His lips brushed the shell of my ear. "I want to be able to run my fingers through it when we're dancing."

All air evaporated from my lungs.

He backed away and smiled casually, as if he'd simply informed me of the weather forecast. "See you in fifteen, neighbor."

I clutched the clip to my stomach, not trusting myself to respond, and turned toward the door. I had to be having a dream. I'd dozed off on my couch and was spinning erotic fantasies in my sleep.

But when I got back to my apartment and pinched my arm, everything was still the same.

Everything except me.

FOUR

Foster paced the apartment lobby, stalking the small space and trying to quell the hum of anticipation running through him. He checked his watch—five minutes past when he'd told Cela to be here. If she were his sub, every one of those late minutes would be earning her a fun punishment for later.

But of course, she wasn't his. He doubted Cela had ever even heard of sexual submission. She screamed innocence with every unintentional dip of her lashes, every unsure smile. He'd had to fight a hard-on sitting across from her in his apartment, despite the fact that minutes before, he'd jerked off in the shower to thoughts of her.

Pike leaned against the wall of mailboxes and crossed his arms, the picture of placidity. "What did you whisper to her before she left?"

"Doesn't matter." Foster had said the first thing that had sprung to his lips, had been unable to resist seeing those sable locks fall over her shoulders and telling her how much he wanted to run his fingers through them. It'd been stupid. He'd felt her startled panic electrify the scant column of air between them. Maybe all the innuendo he'd been playing with tonight had gone over her head. Maybe she had simply wanted to go out and dance—as friends, neighbors.

"Maybe she's not coming," Foster said, forcing himself to stand still. Pacing was going to do no good, and perhaps it was better if she didn't show up. She'd been as jumpy as a bird on the highway as she'd stood in their doorway. She was too sweet for what he and Pike brought to the table. They could break her. Or at the very least, freak her the fuck out.

Unfortunately, her sweetness was the very thing that had Foster's dominant side busting through the seams and hijacking his best intentions to stay away from Cela.

"There's our girl," Pike said, coming up behind Foster as red high heels appeared on the top step, drawing Foster's rapt attention. Red. Shoes that said she wasn't going to spend the night at the library. Cela's bare calves came next—smooth, touchable skin that sent Foster's heart rate speeding up. Then a snug black dress came into view, one that hugged her above the knee and molded over flared hips and a narrow waist.

A bolt shot straight downward to Foster's cock.

Pike's hands landed on Foster's shoulders from behind. "And holy fuck does she look hot."

Pike had stolen the thoughts right out of Foster's head. Ms. Lives in Scrubs looked like a goddamned pin-up girl sashaying down those stairs. The only thing that didn't match the come-hither outfit and fuck-me shoes was the hesitant expression on her face.

When she hit the bottom step, she offered them both a tentative smile. "Sorry I'm a few minutes late. I couldn't find my shoes. I haven't worn them in a while."

Pike stepped around Foster and took both of Cela's hands in his, holding her arms outward so he could get a good look. "Damn, doc. I changed my mind. Let's send Foster out to dance, and you can just come back upstairs with me."

A laugh broke through the nervous compression of her lips, proving she wasn't immune to Pike's natural gift of putting women at ease.

Pike guided her into a little twirl, giving Foster a delicious view of how the material clung to the curve of her ass. "You look smoking."

"Thanks." She sent a shy glance Foster's way, hope for his approval in her eyes.

The move reached into Foster's gut, wrenched something sideways. He took her hand and kissed it. "You look stunning, Cela. And if you make one move to go back upstairs with Pike, I'm tackling his ass."

Her pleased look had him tightening his hold on her fingers, not wanting to let her go. Her eyes dipped down, taking in his blue button-up shirt and dark jeans. "I don't think I've ever seen you in jeans."

His mouth curved. So she'd been surreptitiously observing him in their hallway passings, too. "I work a lot. Suits are part of the deal."

"You pull off both well," she said, her voice still dancing a bit with nerves, the Latina accent peeking through.

"Thank you." He took her hand and tucked it in his elbow, taking control, hoping it would help ease some of her anxiety. "Let's get going. There's a stiff drink and a dance floor with our names on it."

"Now we're talking," Pike said. "The cab's waiting outside."

Foster watched Cela's throat work as she sipped her margarita. The club was in full swing, but Pike had used his connections to get them a table on the balcony so that they could all have a drink and talk without the music drowning them out.

This kind of club wasn't usually Foster's speed. Too loud. Too crowded. If he was going to go out, he usually drove to The Ranch where true privacy could be had if needed. But when Pike had suggested dancing, Foster couldn't resist the thought of having Cela's body pressed against his, the scent of her swirling around him.

But unless Cela relaxed, they were going to be cemented to these chairs all night. Her salt-rimmed drink sloshed precariously in her unsteady hand as she sent the tables nearby a darting glance and sipped. If he said "boo," she'd probably leap off her seat.

Way to go, genius, he chided himself. It was his and Pike's job to make sure Cela had fun tonight, and they were reaching epic-fail status quickly.

Pike was at least trying to put her at ease. "So how long do you have before you move back home?"

"I'm going to help out in the clinic at the vet school for a few more weeks. I've been interning there this year, and I wanted to make sure they had a replacement for me before I left. So before the end of June."

"Wow, that soon, huh?" Pike asked.

She looked at her drink and seemed to sink into her thoughts. "Yeah."

Damn, they needed to turn this night around quickly. Cela seemed to be getting more morose instead of relaxed. Enough sitting around. He didn't have Pike's talent for settling women with humor and the occasional off-color comment. If he said half the stuff Pike did, his face would be permanently marked from angry slaps. But he did have one potent tool in his arsenal—one that only worked on a special type of woman. And all his God-given instincts were telling him Cela was exactly that kind of girl, *his* kind of girl. Even if she didn't know it yet. Time to do what he'd been wanting to do since he'd first met his shy neighbor.

He reached out and plucked the glass from her hands. "Stand up, Cela."

She turned toward him and blinked as if to clear her vision of some afterimage. "What?"

He stood. "Up. Now."

She glanced at Pike with a what's-going-on look but rose to her feet anyhow.

"Thank you." He stepped around the small cocktail table to stand in front of her, using his height advantage to the fullest. "Look at me."

Her head tilted upward without hesitation—like he'd tugged a string attached to her chin.

Good girl, his mind whispered. But he shoved the instinctual response to the back of his brain. "We brought you here to have a good time tonight."

Her lips rolled inward, nervously smoothing her lip gloss, and she took a breath. "I know. I want that, too."

"Good." He glanced at Pike, who was watching the exchange with deceptively casual interest. Pike gave a barely perceptible nod, somehow always in tune with Foster's thoughts, and climbed out of his chair. He moved behind Cela with easy confidence and slid his hands along her waist.

She jolted a bit at the touch, a flush creeping over the skin exposed by her V-cut neckline, but she held Foster's eye contact.

"You're shutting down on us." Foster reached out and cupped her face, running a finger along her cheekbone. "I need you to let go of the nerves. You have no reason to be anxious around us."

She scoffed, then bit her lip when she realized the sound had escaped.

Pike smiled over her shoulder and moved in closer, pulling her gently against his chest, swaying a bit to the music. Foster knew this would be the make or break moment. She'd either jump in with both feet or shrink back into her shell like a hermit crab. But he was done trying to resist his urges with her.

So far, she was responding just as he'd hoped, the submissive undercurrent almost a taste on his tongue. The desire to take control, to take her over, surged inside him like lifeblood. His dominance could calm her. "You're safe with us. Neither of us would ever make you do something you don't want to do. Understand?"

Her gaze shifted, and he could see her body going rigid. Her fight-or-flight was kicking in—which only served to activate his chase-and-conquer gene. But right as he thought she may wiggle out of Pike's arms and run, she blurted out, "But I don't know how to do this!"

The honest response made him want to smile, to kiss her, to soothe that insecurity. "Do what?" he asked calmly, letting his hand drift to her throat, feeling her pulse quicken against his palm. "Tell me what you fear."

She closed her eyes as if gathering her strength around her—finding that steel core he sensed resided under all that cottony soft innocence. "I'm . . . not used to this. Being out with guys. I don't know how to act, what to do."

"Ah, sweetheart," Pike said, pressing a kiss to her bare shoulder. "You're doing just fine."

Foster breathed slowly, willing his own heartbeat to slow, his protective instinct flooding him. Oh, how he'd like to show her exactly what he wanted her to do when she was with him, how to act, how to submit. But she was so young, so untouched. He'd fear crushing her under the weight of all he desired.

Despite his body screaming for a different outcome and knowing that he and Pike could seduce her into their bed tonight, he forced the right words to come out of his mouth. "Listen to me, Cela. Tonight, we're just going to dance. All you need to do is relax and have a good time. We don't have any expectations beyond that."

What if I want you to? The question sat full on my lips, my body already in overdrive from Pike's warm chest pressed against my back and Foster's commanding gaze holding me captive. But I couldn't deny the unwinding ball of tension in my stomach at Foster's statement. They weren't expecting anything from me. All I needed to do was get the stick out of my backside and have fun. Give myself over to the night.

Give myself over to them.

They would take care of me. I didn't know them well, but on some primal level, I knew that much. They wouldn't hurt me or take advantage of me.

"I don't know where to start," I confessed. "I've never been good at letting loose."

Foster's dark smile was devastating in the changing lights of the club. "Good, let's start our Never Have I Ever with that one. Letting loose. Your instruction is to simply act, don't think. If you want to do something, do it. No one knows you here. And even if you fell on your ass in the middle of the dance floor, who gives a shit?"

I smiled. "That's a distinct possibility."

Pike nuzzled the back of my ear, inspiring a line of goose bumps down my back. "Don't worry. If you fall, we'll be there to pick you up, doc."

"We won't let you fall in the first place," Foster said. "Not with four hands on you."

Four hands. My skin tingled at the image—or maybe the alcohol was finally doing its job. My quaking nerves dipped to a manageable level, my confidence rallying. These two guys weren't there to embarrass me or laugh at my lack of experience. I'd had that happen once before and would rather become a nun than face that humiliation again. But both of these guys obviously knew I wasn't Ms. Experienced. If they'd wanted some smooth-talking seductress, they could've come here alone and picked up any woman in the place. They were here to have a good time, and they wanted to have it with me. Wasting that opportunity would be like throwing away dessert—a travesty.

I laced one of my hands with Pike's and reached out for Foster's, channeling the version of myself that I played in my private fantasies. "I'm ready. *Never have I ever* . . . danced with the two best-looking guys in the place."

"That's my girl," Foster said, grabbing my offered hand and tugging me toward him, sandwiching me between the two of them. "Let's go show these bastards how it's done."

We made our way down to the dance floor and the pulsing mass of humanity. Foster pressed a palm to the small of my back, and Pike kept his grip on my hand as they guided me into the throng. Having the two men flank me gave me the sense of being protected by some invisible bubble. Hands and limbs snaked around us, bodies brushed me, but somehow instead of feeling claustrophobic like I'd expected, it awakened my senses, made me feel alive. We slowed as we neared the center of the dance floor, and Foster turned me into Pike's arms.

"Hey, gorgeous." Pike's smile glowed in the black lights as he dragged me against him and looped an arm around my neck.

I grinned back, relaxing into him. Despite the full-sleeve tattoos and hardened edge of Pike's bad-boy rocker look, his presence was boyishly charming. I could imagine days with him being full of open laughter and sexy teasing.

I started to move and tried to focus on not stepping on his feet. But before I could get in time with Pike's movements, Foster's hands were spanning my waist from behind, sending sensual awareness sparking through me like static electricity. His lips tickled my ear. "Just take a breath and let us lead, Cela. I can feel you thinking."

Thinking. *Always* thinking. He was right. I nodded and softened my spine, letting the sounds and sensations flow over me, trying to give over the control. I held Pike's gaze and moved with the two of them— the bass pounding through my ribs like some tribal anthem and the smooth elixir of tequila flowing through my veins. Yes. This. This was what I needed tonight . . . freedom.

The song ended and changed into one with a weighty, sensual beat and no lyrics. *Thump. Thump. Thump.* The guys didn't say a word as our movements slowed, but it was as if the air shifted around us, grew heavier, warmer. Foster's pelvis brushed against my backside, and Pike pressed his forehead to mine as we swayed in time to the music. Both men's colognes filled my nose—Pike's clean, like salty ocean air and summer nights, Foster's laced with dark spice. And underneath all that—sweat and desire. Mine. Theirs. *Ours.*

I closed my eyes, letting myself fall into the moment, the men's presence and touch waking up places that had never stirred. My feet moved, my body rocked, hips swayed. But none of it was from my focused effort anymore. The throbbing beat of the song seemed to enter my bloodstream and sync with my heartbeat, lifting me up on the wave of movement around us.

"That's right, baby," Foster soothed, his voice like melting wax. "Let it all go."

I allowed my head to fall back, landing against Foster's shoulder, surrendering. One song turned into another and then another until I lost track when one would end and another began. Heat and alcohol and their touch coalesced, making all the normally awkward edges inside me blur. Time seemed to slow and stretch, until there was just this one continuous rhythm. Just the three of us dancing without regard to the world existing around us.

Foster's hold on my waist roamed, exploring my belly, the curve of my rib cage. His knuckles grazed the underside of my breasts, and sharp need tightened my nipples, dampened my panties. *Mercy.* My eyelids fluttered open and met Pike's riveted gaze. Gone was the affable smile. A ripple of delectable apprehension glittered along my nerve endings. Pike may be a good-time guy, but unapologetic desire had surfaced in those hazel eyes. I wasn't used to guys looking at *me* that way. The power of it almost knocked me down.

Pike's palm slid beneath the curtain of my hair and cupped the back of my neck, a firm grip. Foster's breath danced against my opposite ear. "He's going to kiss you, baby. Stop him if you don't want that."

Kiss? Pike wanted to kiss me. I didn't know why this came as such a shock.

But the earth would've had to quit moving for me to say anything to stop him. I was spellbound. Things like this didn't happen in my life. I didn't allow them to. My world was safely constructed and populated with people who didn't push my boundaries. But right now, I couldn't think of anything I wanted more than these two men doing whatever they wanted to me. Old me had apparently left my body and stayed upstairs to babysit my drink.

Pike paused long enough to give me a window to say no, hovering inches from my mouth, his soft puffs of breath touching my cheeks. But

I didn't turn away. Instead, I slid my fingers along his chest, gathering the soft fabric of his T-shirt in my fists, afraid that if I didn't hold on to something, I'd disintegrate into a heap of ash between the two of them. His lips met mine in a slow, coaxing dance, matching the beat of the music—teasing me, tasting me, licking along the seam, and then finally when I thought I'd go mad, sliding his tongue into my mouth.

I moaned into the kiss, the power of it like a thunderclap to my system. The taste of mint and alcohol mixed in with the potent flavor of unrepentant desire.

Foster groaned, as if watching another man kiss me both pained and pleased him. His hands slid down to the tops my thighs, precariously close to where I ached the most. And for the first time all night I didn't feel like a girl among men. I felt womanly and sexy and . . . brave. No longer filtering my actions through my brain, I acted on pure instinct and arched my hips back toward Foster, seeking.

He met my silent request without hesitation, fitting my backside against him. The hard length of his arousal pressed against the curve of my ass.

I gasped into Pike's kiss.

"I'm trying to be good with you, Cela," Foster said, his voice a low growl. "But keep doing things like that and my moral compass may malfunction."

My body shuddered at the threat, my pelvis tilting backward, dragging myself along Foster's erection. I couldn't help it. I was fascinated by the fact that he was so turned on. That I'd done that to him.

"Fuck."

Pike released me from the kiss, leaving me panting for breath, and Foster spun me around, the ice blue of his eyes going black as he took in the view of me. I'm sure I looked like some crazed version of my former self—swollen lips, stained cheeks, begging eyes. He didn't hesitate. Where Pike had left off, Foster picked up, cupping my face and coming down for a crushing kiss. My eyelids drifted shut, everything seeming to spin around me as Foster's mouth consumed mine. Unlike Pike's slow and sensual approach, Foster was demanding, overpowering. My legs went boneless beneath me.

But Pike had me, his hands planted on my waist, his mouth laying soft, sucking kisses to the back of my neck, my shoulders.

Holy shit. Every erogenous zone in my body flared with desperate want, and heat slicked my panties. I gripped Foster's damp hair, holding on with everything I had, and whimpered into his kiss—a plea. For what exactly, I wasn't sure. I didn't know what to do with all this . . . wanting.

"Ah, God." He said, breaking from the kiss, but threading his hand in my hair and insinuating his knee between my thighs, putting pressure where I needed it most. "You're killing me."

The contact was like tossing my brain into the deep fryer, my better judgment evaporating in a cloud of wanton desperation. The music continued pounding around us, and my hips rocked shamelessly as he ground the hard muscle of his thigh against me, sliding my panties against tender, needy flesh. I bowed back, leaning on Pike for support, no longer noticing the crowd undulating around us. The quest for release, for Foster's touch, kidnapped all of my senses. I had lost myself and all sense of appropriate behavior.

"Please," I whispered. "I need . . . I need more."

"Jesus." Foster's thigh lowered, removing the stimulation, and my eyelids slid open to find Foster raking a hand though his hair, a frantic edge to his movements. "Let's take a break. I can't—I need a breather or I'm going to drag you into a dark corner and give you exactly what you're pleading for."

My tongue swept at my bottom lip, the suggestion only making the throbbing between my thighs more pronounced. "Maybe I don't need a break."

Had I said that out loud? Once again I questioned where Cela had gone. I couldn't actually be considering taking him up on that offer. I needed a taste of reckless abandon tonight, but I wasn't qualified for the dark-corners-in-clubs kind. Did people actually do that?

"Doc," Pike said wrapping an arm around my waist, already turning me to guide me off the dance floor. "We promised you we'd just dance. You've been drinking. We're all a little . . . overheated. I think a break is a good idea."

I clamped my lips together, stopping myself from the urge to protest. My body was ruling my head right now. This is what my parents used to warn me against, right? You let a guy go too far and you make mistakes—like my sister did. I needed to get some air, some perspective. The guys were trying to do the right thing. I should let them.

I allowed Pike to lead me away from the dance floor back upstairs. Foster trailed behind, a tight expression on his face. When we made it back to our corner, Pike joined me on a cushioned, curved bench, draping his arm across my shoulders, and Foster took the seat catty-corner to us. He adjusted his pants before sitting, and I felt the blush rise to my cheeks. Guess I wasn't the only one left half-cocked.

Pike, who was clearly handling what had transpired on the dance floor better than Foster or I, ordered another round of drinks—beers and empty shot glasses. I sent him a curious look. "Interesting choice."

He smirked. "No more hard liquor for any of us tonight. But I thought we could take a breather, cool down, and finish Never Have I Ever the proper way."

"I think we should take Cela home," Foster said, his tone as stiff as his posture.

I frowned over at him. Is that really what he wanted?

"Screw that. The night is young," Pike said, that mischievous edge back in his voice. "And your blue balls will ease up soon enough."

Foster smirked and sent Pike a one-finger salute.

My gaze dipped down to the fly of Foster's pants, the urge to ease that discomfort for him palpable. What would he be like when he dropped all that calm, refined control? Just the glimpse I'd seen on the dance floor had made my blood race. Part of me wished I had seduction skills already in my arsenal, like those women in the dirty books I used to borrow from my dorm mate in undergrad. I imagined crawling over to Foster, situating myself between his open thighs, and taking him in my mouth, tasting him until he made that sexy groaning sound again.

My teeth dragged along my bottom lip as I raised my lashes.

Foster's eyes locked with mine, the fierceness of his stare stealing my breath. "Tell me what you're thinking, Cela."

Never have I ever . . .

Given a guy head.

Almost climaxed in public.

. . . Wanted someone so much.

"I'm thinking I need a drink."

FIVE

Foster counted to a hundred backward in his head, trying to calm down his racing heart and his determined libido. It had taken every ounce of his willpower not to drag Cela somewhere private so he could ruck up her dress, wrap her legs around his waist, and fuck her hard against a wall.

He'd known dancing with her would be a lesson in restraint, but he had no idea how goddamned responsive she'd be. She'd been on the verge of coming from the simple pressure of his leg rubbing against her—her pupils dilated, her body tightening, her sexy scent drifting to his nose and scrambling his brain. If he'd been at The Ranch, he would've torn her panties off her right there in the middle of the dance floor, tucked his fingers inside her, and made her scream while Pike held her up.

Fuck. His cock pushed against his zipper, and he adjusted his position again. He needed to stop letting his mind travel down those roads or he was never going to be able to sit here comfortably.

Pike poured one of the beers the waitress had brought over into three shot glasses and smiled over at Cela. "Alright, doc. The way this works is one person says 'never have I ever,' then lists something they've never done. If the other two have done it, they have to drink. If they haven't done it, they don't. Got it?"

She peeked over at Foster then back to Pike. "I have a feeling y'all are going to end up drinking a lot more than I am."

Pike laid a hand on her knee and squeezed, sending a tweak of jealousy through Foster. "No worries, doc. It's all in good fun. Why don't you go first?"

"Okay." She fidgeted with the cocktail napkin in her lap, folding it into thirds, thinking. "Hmm, well, never have I ever . . . watched *Star Wars* porn."

Her sly smile pulled a laugh from Foster despite his plummeting mood. "Low blow, doctor."

Pike glanced at him, shrugged, and both of them tipped back their shot glasses and swallowed.

"Oh my God," she said, laughing. "So you guys were only half-kidding when you mentioned it."

"It was college," Pike said in mock protest.

"I couldn't look away," Foster said at the same time.

"Pervs," she declared, but her eyes were crinkled around the corners. "Okay, your turn."

Foster refilled the shot glasses and sighed. He needed to come up with something neutral. Safe. "Alright, never have I ever . . . owned a pet."

Cela's jaw dropped as if he'd just admitted he liked to dress up in women's clothes and sing Broadway tunes. "Like ever?"

"Nope."

"Not even like a fish or something?" She drank her shot.

He watched her throat work as she swallowed, imagining things he shouldn't. "My parents traveled a lot. They didn't trust me to take care of a pet."

She frowned. "Kids usually do a better job than most adults."

"Yeah, well, my track record on taking care of things wasn't so great," he said, failing to keep the tinge of bitterness out of his voice— the old, always-present guilt surfacing.

"I'm sorry." The stark sympathy that swept her features had something knotting in his chest. God, why had he admitted something so personal? He could've just said no and left it at that.

Pike drank his shot, and Foster sent him a curious look. When he'd met Pike, the kid had barely owned enough clothes to get him through a week. He and what passed for his family wouldn't have been in a place to fund a pet.

Pike shrugged. "A stray cat used to live under our house when I was a kid. I named him Jagger and fed him, so I think that counts. I wanted him to be mine."

Cela looked between the two of them. "I'm dragging both of y'all to the vet school shelter. Clearly, you need a pet."

Pike laughed. "Doc, we can barely be trusted to care for ourselves. Let's not inflict a poor animal with owners like us."

Owners. Foster could think of one thing he'd like to own right now—at least for a little while. He dragged his focus away from Cela and nodded at Pike. "Your turn, drummer boy."

Pike narrowed his eyes, that nickname always serving to annoy him, which is why Foster loved using it so much.

"Fine. Let's see if I can come up with something less depressing than yours." Pike sat back on the couch, his eyebrow arching in challenge. "Never have I ever . . ."

The pause was long. Too long. Pike smiled and leveled a gaze at Foster.

Oh shit. Foster knew that look. *Don't do it, Pike.*

"Gotten off while eavesdropping on my neighbor," Pike finished.

You fucker.

Cela's expelled breath was audible even over the music. Well, shit. Now he was going to look like a creepy asshole. Foster ventured a glance her way, his gaze colliding with hers. Her panicked-rabbit expression made him wish time could be rewound and deleted.

"Dammit, Pike," Foster said, gearing up for damage control. "Cela, look, Pike's just messing around. He likes to—"

But before he could finish, Cela reached out, lifted her shot off the table, and downed it. When she finished, she wouldn't look up. She stared down at her hands and the empty glass, her knee bumping up and down—as if she were contemplating running.

The silent admission and ensuing bashfulness were like strokes to Foster's cock, oil on a fire he was trying to tame. This girl may be inexperienced, but she was brave—bold in a way that had him getting surprised at every turn. And it'd been a helluva long time since anyone had surprised him. He leaned forward in his seat. Like a predator scenting blood in the water, the dominance rose in him, locked her in its sights.

"Cela."

She put her hand over her face, shaking her head. "Let's just go to the next turn. Please."

"Look at me, Cela," he commanded, his tone harsh.

Her attention snapped his way, as if she couldn't stop herself from obeying.

He held her eye contact and slowly drained his own shot.

Poured another, drank again.

Then another, drank again. "I could keep going."

In Foster's peripheral vision, Pike gave a slow, satisfied grin. "Honesty. I like it."

Cela's throat worked as she swallowed hard, her lips parted, closed, opened again as if she had words to say but couldn't pick which ones.

"Tell me what's going on in that head of yours," Foster said, keeping his voice even. "You don't need to be afraid to say what you're thinking."

She licked her lips, the pulse at her throat visibly jumping. "First, I need to know what this is—tonight."

Pike angled toward her on the couch. "We told you, doc. It's your night to have a good time, whatever that may be."

She looked to Pike, then back to Foster and lifted her hand to the neckline of her dress. Her fingers dipped underneath the material and moved along her sweat-dampened skin, riveting Foster's gaze. She pulled a small square of paper out.

"What's that?" Pike asked.

"In less than a month, I'll be back in the small town I grew up in. Everything there is planned out for me in a nice, neat path. The job I've always known I'd have, the guy I'm supposed to date, the place I'm going to live."

She hesitated and stared down at the paper, her thumb rubbing across the smooth white surface over and over again. Pike put a palm to her back, a gentle grounding touch that seemed to replenish Cela's resolve. She gave them both a wavering half smile before continuing.

"I've lived my whole life working toward exactly that goal. It's what I've wanted for so long. But I realized tonight that I've missed out on a lot of experiences that weren't bullet points in the plan. I don't want to go back home with a Never Have I Ever list a mile long." She set the square of paper on the table, let her fingers linger on top of it for a moment, and then pushed it toward the center. "And I was hoping you two might help me scratch some things off the list."

Foster's attention zeroed in on the note, his heartbeat climbing up a notch.

"Whoa," Pike said, her declaration apparently stunning the nothing-shocks-me musician.

Before Pike could take the liberty, Foster reached out and laid his palm over the small square, the paper slightly damp from being against Cela's bare skin. He resisted the urge to bring it to his nose and inhale.

"That is," she rushed on, her eyes darting toward Foster's grip on her note. "If y'all are, you know, really interested in me or whatever but if not . . ."

"Shh . . ." Pike said, pressing his fingers against her lips. "Doc, if what's on that sheet has anything to do with getting to touch you again, I have no doubt we'll be all for it."

Foster lifted the paper, unfolded it carefully, and stared down at the neat, bulleted list Cela had written on half a notebook page.

Never Have I Ever . . .
Broken the rules.
Had a one-night stand.
Lived out a fantasy.
Slept with the hot neighbors I've been crushing on for a year.
Lost control.
But I want to . . .

The paper crinkled beneath Foster's fingertips as all sights and sounds around him seemed to fade, the words on the page nearly glowing at him. *But I want to . . .* He looked up at Cela, the vulnerable expression on her face reminding him of her youth, her innocence. But his stampeding libido trampled over those concerns, his cock hardening past the point of maybe. Yes, she was sweet. Inexperienced.

But the woman who wrote this list knew what she wanted, what she craved.

And he'd be damned if he was going to let someone else give it to her.

If Cela wanted to lose control with someone, he knew the guys for the task.

He stood, tucking the note in his pocket, and holding out a hand. "I think we're done dancing."

My heart was pounding hard enough to make my chest hurt, and a fine sheen of sweat had gathered on my neck, but I managed to get to my feet and take Foster's offered hand. This is what I had wanted when I'd knocked on their door tonight. Wanton abandon. A departure from all that my predictable life normally was.

But now that I was standing with my toes peeking over the edge of the precipice, preparing to leap, the ingrained voice of my father was firing in my head like a machine gun. *What are you doing? You don't know these men. You're not this kind of girl. What would people say?*

And the ever popular, *Don't shame the family.*

My father had used that one ad nauseam throughout my childhood. My older sister, Luz, had fallen into the wrong crowd in high school, had a boyfriend who'd stolen from people in town, and had gotten pregnant at sixteen. The taint of that had hung over us for years, even after my father had sent Luz away, disowning her after she terminated the pregnancy. So with my oldest brother away in the military and Luz gone, it had been left to me and Andre to prove that "those Medina kids" weren't all bad.

Be a good girl or you won't be part of this family anymore. My father had never stated it that way, but the sentiment had hung in the household like a stench you couldn't air out. And now here I was putting myself into the hands of two men, giving them a laundry list of sins I'd like to commit.

Foster's fingers laced with mine, and he pulled me closer to him, dragging me from my swirling thoughts. He brushed my hair away from my face and graced me with a smile that sent warmth bleeding through me. "You're panicking already, angel. Don't. There's no need."

The endearment and soft tone were like soothing strokes to my climbing anxiety. He probably called girls angel all the time. I wasn't under the delusion that I was any different than the women I'd heard in their apartment over the last two years. But something about the way he said it, the reverence in it, made me want to curl into him, to block out the harsh voice in my head.

"Is it okay that I'm a little scared?" I asked, offering my own attempt at a smile.

He cradled my face, his blue eyes seeming to read me as if every emotion were printed in permanent marker on my forehead. "It's all right to be scared of the unknown, to be nervous about exploring things you've only thought about in private moments. But you don't have to be scared of us."

Pike stepped up behind Foster. "He's right, doc."

"But I have no idea what I'm doing. I want this, but I know I'm in over my head," I said, the men's stark gazes pulling blatant honesty out of me.

Foster chuckled. "Lucky for you, there isn't anything I like more than being in charge and giving directions."

Pike smirked. "No truer words have ever been spoken."

"Come on." Foster's grip tightened on my fingers, and Pike came around to flank my opposite side, grabbing my other hand. "Your only instruction for tonight is going to be an easy one to follow."

One instruction? My mind flipped through possible scenarios like a day calendar in a wind gust as Foster and Pike led me down the stairs and through the crowd on the bottom floor. What would they expect from me? What if they asked me to do something I couldn't handle or didn't know how to do? What if they laughed at me like the frat guy had my sophomore year?

Pike retrieved my purse from the coat check stand, and by the time the three of us finally pushed through the doors and the night air hit us, my nerves were gnawing at me, chewing through my resolve. I glanced back and forth between the two guys, but neither was giving anything away.

The valet hailed a cab and Pike climbed in. I peeked over at Foster, gathering courage. "Can I ask what my one instruction is going to be?"

He grinned and pressed his lips against my ear as he guided me toward the cab. "To show us exactly how much pleasure you can take before you beg us to stop."

"Oh," I whispered, my insides liquefying.

He slid into the cab next to me, pressing me against Pike. Pike draped his arm around me, and Foster laid a hand along my exposed thigh.

"The Hotel St. Mark, please," Foster said to the driver.

"Hotel?" I asked.

He traced a small, sensuous circle along my inner thigh, making me think of gentle tongues and nips of teeth moving higher. My sex clenched.

"Wouldn't want to wake the neighbors."

PART II

Not Until You Risk

SIX

I was in a cab on the way to a *hotel* with Foster and Pike. *Foster* and *Pike*. I kept blinking, staring out at the road in front of me, wondering if the whole scene was going to fade before my eyes. Maybe I'd passed out drunk in my apartment and was hallucinating. Could you hallucinate from alcohol? Because surely this couldn't be me—Cela, the high school valedictorian, the no-I-can't-go-out-tonight-because-I-have-to-study good girl. Nice girls like that didn't get in a car with two sexy, older guys for a one-night stand—a one-night *threesome*. Shit. This was crazy.

Cuh-razy.

I'd never been so simultaneously excited and nervous in my entire life. But despite all the implications about what kind of girl this made me, I found myself desperately hoping that this wasn't some dream, that it truly was real.

"You okay?" Foster asked me after giving the driver instructions.

I nodded, though the move felt stiff and jerky. "You bet."

He chuckled quietly and settled in, his hand resting casually on my knee. His mouth dipped close to my ear. "Breathe, Cela."

"Trying," I whispered, my heart stuttering at the warm feel of his skin on mine. Pike stretched his arm over the back of the seat and sent me a reassuring smile.

I closed my eyes and inhaled a long, deep breath before opening them again. Surprisingly, it seemed to help a bit. Well, that and the fact that the guys seemed to refuse to let me be anxious for long. I expected the cab ride to be tense, the question—*Am I really going to do this?*—on thunderous repeat in my head. But with Foster's hand caressing my thigh and Pike's fingers teasing the hair at my nape, I was losing myself in the rising tide of hormones. The nerves were siphoning off with each gentle touch, each caress. And the question of *Am I going to do this?* transformed into *if not now, why not?* It wasn't like I could find guys I was more attracted to. And they weren't going to pressure me. If I didn't like something or changed my mind, they would stop. I knew that in my gut. This was my chance to have a fantasy night, and I'd be stupid not to take advantage of it.

Internal pep talk complete, I relaxed against the seat, Foster's and Pike's body heat bookending me, their combined scents like bottled sex and man. *Mmm.*

Foster smiled down at me. "Feeling better?"

"Getting there," I said as I closed my eyes, my voice taking on a dreamlike quality even to my own ears. No longer was I thinking of the past, my lack of experience, or what kind of girl this supposedly made me. All I was thinking about was twisted hotel sheets, naked skin, and feeling these two guys against me, on top of me . . . inside me. Even thinking those last two words gave me a hard shiver, a heady cocktail of desire and fear filtering through my blood.

Foster's hand drifted higher, the strokes against my thigh deceptively light. If the cabbie turned and peeked back, Foster's touch would look like an afterthought, casual. But the soft, circular glides were a silent, relentless assault on my starved libido. I ached for more, for the intensity I sensed lurking in this man. Foster's touch moved even higher, and as if acting on their own volition, my knees parted a bit further than was appropriate.

I opened my eyes, surprised by my own involuntary response, and caught the hint of Foster's smile in my peripheral vision. He kept his eyes forward as he asked the cab driver a question, but his pinky snuck beneath my dress and grazed my satin panties.

Oh, Lord. A hot ripple of heat sizzled up and outward. I bit my lip to keep from gasping. This was *not* happening. Couldn't be.

Pike joined in the conversation with the driver—something about the basketball finals maybe—but I couldn't be sure. My brain was in reboot.

Foster's hand disappeared beneath my dress again, this time more boldly. If the driver really looked back now, he'd know something was up. I set my purse on my knees, blocking the view. Foster's fingertip dragged across the damp satin, finding my hot button through the thin fabric and circling around it.

My muscles tensed like I'd been Tasered, and my fingernails curled into the leather of my purse. Pike's hand cupped my neck and squeezed, letting me know that even if he was carrying on a mundane conversation, he knew exactly what Foster was doing to me and how my body was responding.

Foster stroked me through the fabric once, twice—knowing exactly where to touch. I tried not to squirm in the seat. My body was near detonation already after what had happened on the dance floor. I hadn't been touched like this by anyone other than myself in years. And, God, how many times had I fantasized about this very guy being the one to do it? I wasn't going to be able to hold it together.

And apparently he didn't want me to, because before I could even catch another breath, he was moving aside the fabric. The pad of his finger brushed embarrassingly slippery skin and dipped lower, finding my entrance. He slipped one long finger inside. I did gasp this time, unable to hold it back, but Pike conveniently coughed over the sound.

Foster moved his finger back to my clitoris, gliding over me with the exact amount of pressure that offered pleasure but not release. I had to fight hard not to make a sound, while Foster continued his calm conversation. "Can you take a left? It's the longer way, but I don't want to get caught in that overnight construction."

"No problem," the cabbie said.

"And do you mind turning up this song?" Pike asked. "I love this band."

The music filled the cab, and Foster's teasing touches turned purposeful. I curled my lips inward, a moan building in my throat. Oh, God. If he didn't stop, I was going to climax right here in the cab. Loudly, if my lungs had anything to do with it.

He leaned close to me, his words barely audible against my ear. "Come for me, Cela. Let's scratch something off that Never Have I Ever list of yours."

His finger dipped inside me again, his thumb strumming my clit, and everything went white behind my eyes. *Oh, God, oh, God.* I turned my head, my lips parting, as the orgasm crashed over me. I wasn't going to be able to stay quiet. But before a sound could slip past, a hot mouth was on me, my cry swallowed by Pike's kiss.

My mind went blank, and inhibition dropped from me like a snapped anchor. I tumbled into the moment, the touch, the kiss. My body fluttered around Foster's fingers, begging for more, for the real thing. And I poured that need into the kiss with Pike.

"Hotel's right around the corner," the cabbie said, clearing his throat and yanking me from my slow drift back down to earth. "Do you need to go through the lobby entrance or are you heading to their wine bar?"

"The lobby," Foster said, tracing his fingers along my inner thigh again. Pike eased away from our kiss, his gaze hooded. "The next one's mine."

My brain and body were buzzing in some lust-laced haze when I turned to face forward, and everything was hot, flush. Foster's hand was back in his lap, but the bulge in his jeans was prominent. After a few breaths to return my breathing to normal, I demurely straightened my dress, then reached out and squeezed Foster's knee in silent thanks— almost afraid to look at him because I knew I'd lose my stoic façade.

He lowered his head next to mine as the car rounded a corner and nuzzled the shell of my ear, sending a hot ripple down my left side. "That was beautiful, angel. I love feeling your fear slip from you as you let your desire take over. There's nothing sexier than a woman who knows what she wants and has the guts to ask for it."

I closed my eyes, letting the warm honey of his voice slide over me.

"The Hotel St. Mark," the driver announced.

"We're going to make this very good for you, Cela," Foster promised, and then Pike was taking my hand, helping me out of the cab, and leading me into the vast unknown.

Pike steered me with a hand on my back into the lavish lobby of the St. Mark. Unlike the modern lines of the club we'd just left or the sleek hotels that filled this part of downtown Dallas, this building had the look of lovingly cared-for historical opulence—inlaid marble tile, rich dark wood furniture, and a grand staircase that would make a bride-to-be weep.

"Wow, this is beautiful," I whispered, feeling as if I needed to keep my voice down, lest the building realize I was far too small town to be staying in a place so elegant.

Foster smiled down at me as we made our way over to the front desk. "Glad you approve. I book all of my out-of-town clients here."

Clients? The statement was like a one-two punch of reality. My step stuttered.

Both guys paused, as if totally in tune with my every movement. "Everything okay?" Pike asked.

I glanced between the two of them. "Yes. Fine. I just . . ."

"Go ahead," Foster said, giving a nod of encouragement.

"Well, I just realized two things. One, there's no way I could afford to pay for even half a room here. And, two, I have no idea what you do for a living, Foster."

Foster leveled a gaze at me. "First, you won't pay for anything, ever. So let's get that out of the way."

"But—"

He put a finger to my lips, my scent still on him. "That part is non-negotiable. Secondly, I own a tech company called 4N Solutions."

My eyebrows lifted. He *owned* a company? And he shared an apartment in my complex? Either he was very bad at his job, very frugal, or something else was going on there. Maybe he had a lot of college debt or a greedy ex-wife or child support to pay. The last couple of thoughts had my lungs constricting.

"You're panicking again, doc," Pike said softly.

Foster lowered his hand. "Cela, if you need to ask more questions, need to know us better before we do this, just say the word. We can go to the bar and talk . . . or even go home if you want."

I swallowed past the knot in my throat. What did it matter if he had an ex or even if he had kids? This was not the start of a relationship. This was not a compatibility test. This was sex. A fun, hot diversion before I moved home. I knew I was safe with them, and God knows I was attracted to them. Those were the only must-haves for this type of thing.

I nodded. "I'm okay. Maybe y'all can help me shut off my overanalytical brain."

Pike grinned. "Challenge accepted."

He slipped an arm around my waist and gave my hip a squeeze, instantly easing that last coup of my old self.

Foster stopped at the front desk and gave the pretty blonde behind the desk his name. "We'll need a suite for the night."

"Absolutely, Mr. Foster," the woman said in that elegant, library-quiet voice that luxury hotel employees must practice. She tapped on her keyboard with long fingernails, then looked up, taking in the three people standing in front of her. "Two queens?"

"Just a king," Foster said smoothly.

"Of course." The woman's lips pressed together, and her gaze slid over to mine.

I braced for the impact, but where I expected judgment, I found envy in the other woman's eyes. Huh.

Three key cards appeared on the granite countertop. "You'll be on the top floor to the right. Is there anything else I can help you with? I'm about to go on break, I could show you to your room if you'd like."

I heard an extra dose of suggestion in the seemingly innocuous statement, but Foster's response was swift, his smile painstakingly polite. "No thank you . . ." He glanced at her nametag. "Tabitha. We have everything we need."

Foster grabbed my hand and gathered me to his side. "Come on, angel. I have a feeling the view upstairs is going to be fantastic."

Oh, I had no doubt. The thought of seeing these two naked had crossed my mind so many times, I could paint a detailed portrait of what I imagined was beneath their clothes. But as the elevator loomed in front of us, my conscience niggled at me, urging me to tell the guys the whole truth about my Never Have I Ever list. I hadn't put anything on that list that wasn't true. But like any former Catholic school girl knew, lies of omission were just as bad as blatant ones.

The gold doors of the elevator dinged, and Pike took a quick step forward to hold the door open for me and Foster. We slipped into the elevator, and Pike followed, along with an older couple who were deeply involved in their discussion of the symphony they'd seen earlier. As the gray-haired lady tried to convince her husband that the tickets had been worth the price, I pressed my back against the side of the elevator, holding the rail behind me and listening to the warring factions in my head.

Pike glanced down at my tight grip on the rail, then nudged me with his shoulder. "Got a fear of elevators, doc?"

I made a weird sound—some hybrid of a nervous laugh and a snort. Totally attractive no doubt. "Not quite."

Our ascent slowed, and the doors opened to the other couple's floor. The lady offered a cursory good-night to everyone, then stepped out with her husband, leaving me alone with the two guys and my thoughts.

Pike stayed where he was, but Foster crossed over to the other side and turned to face me. "Cela, look at me."

With a sigh, I dragged my gaze upward.

"Tell me what you need from us. I'm not stepping out of this elevator if I think you're going to be white-knuckling your way through this. I want you to enjoy tonight."

I held his stare, willing myself to say something, anything. The last thing I wanted to do was go home. But I also couldn't bring myself to tell him what was knotting me up. *Speak,* my brain shouted. The loud ding of the elevator was like a clap of thunder in the silence. The doors slid open with a smooth whir.

Foster reached out and pressed the Door Open button but made no other move. Pike glanced at me, questions in his eyes. Neither of them were going to step out until I said something.

I wet my lips, and my throat seemed to narrow. Panic was edging in now that the moment was here. *No, no, no. Don't back out now.* I thought back to the cab, the way I'd felt when Foster had touched me, and how he'd taken what he wanted without asking. The shock of that had shut down my brain, had pulled me deep into those minutes and scared off any errant thoughts. It'd just been a taste, but I wanted more of that, more of that free fall.

I forced my fingers off of the bar behind me. If I was going to jump, I couldn't keep ahold of anything. My eyes stayed focused on Foster, on the commanding set of his jaw. "I had a bad experience the last time I was . . . with a guy. I fumbled a bit, things were awkward, and he made fun of me. Not in a playful way."

Anger flared in Foster's eyes. "What an asshole."

"And an idiot," Pike offered.

I gave a little smile. "Definitely. But even knowing it was him who was in the wrong, it's left me a little gun-shy."

The door tried to shut, but Foster pressed the button again. "You have to know that we would never disrespect you that way, and I kind of wish I had the address of the jerkoff who did that to you, because I'd like to pay him a visit and teach him some manners. But beyond that assurance, is there anything else you need to feel more comfortable? We can take things as slow as you want."

I looked up at him again, the rest of the story hovering on my lips. I knew I should spill it. It was the right thing to do. But if I told him the whole truth, it would ruin everything. It wasn't worth the risk. He said he liked a girl who wasn't afraid to ask for what she wanted. I could do that. I knew what I hoped for tonight, had heard all I needed to know listening to Foster through my thin wall. Now I just had to say it aloud. I flexed my fingers, trying to shed the nerves. "I don't want to make any decisions tonight. I need you two to take over. Tell me what to do. I don't want to be asked each step of the way."

Foster's shift in expression was like dark falling over snow-covered fields, icy calm and inescapable. His nostrils flared as he inhaled a slow breath. "Cela, are you sure you know what you're asking?"

"Yes," I whispered.

His eyes stayed locked on mine, unblinking, intense. "Do you know what a safe word is?"

I couldn't even shake my head, it was as if his gaze was holding me in some suspended state. "No."

"If either of us does something that you want to stop immediately, you call this word and we'll stop, no questions asked," he said, his voice disconcertingly calm. "That's the only power I require you to keep. Everything else, Pike and I will gladly take tonight."

A heavy shiver worked its way through me, the thought of really surrendering everything to these two guys was a dark fantasy I'd barely had the nerve to admit to myself. "Okay."

He stepped to the right, putting his back against the straining elevator doors and held out his hand. "Your safe word is *tequila*."

"Tequila," I repeated. I looked down at his open palm. This was going to be my last decision of the night. And it was one that felt more right than anything had in as long as I could remember. I took Foster's hand, then reached back for Pike's with my other. Pike smiled and laced his fingers with mine.

I left my free will in the elevator and watched as the doors closed, whisking it away.

Now I was theirs.

SEVEN

Foster backed his way through the hotel room's doorway, tugging me and Pike with him. Before the door even clicked shut, Foster's mouth was on mine, his hand cupping the back of my neck, his tongue exploring and stroking. The kiss was more fervent than the one in the club, more purposeful—controlled violence. I could almost feel restraint vibrating off of him, as if one popped button and all the passion I suspected lurked behind that calm façade would rush out like a levee break.

I looped my arms around Foster's neck, holding on and losing myself to the moment. Pike's hands pressed against my hips as he trailed kisses along my shoulder. The two men's scents swirled around me, and my body's engine kicked into gear, warming me in all the right places.

"Take off her dress, Pike," Foster directed as he pulled away from the kiss, his eyes like blue fire. "I wanted to take my time with you, angel. But that'll have to be later. I've spent too many nights listening through the wall to those soft sounds you make when you come, imagining what you look like when you climax. I'm not willing to wait another moment to see all of you."

The proclamation was like being doused with hot water, sending need cascading over me. Pike's fingers tugged my zipper down in the back, his lips following the track of skin exposed. After planting a kiss on the dip at my tailbone, he straightened and eased the dress down and off me. The material fell to my feet, leaving me standing between them in only my lacy panties and bra. Near naked that fast. No backing out now. *Oh, God, oh, God, oh, God.*

The hotel room's air-conditioning was blasting, but the cool air did nothing to ease my burning skin as Foster's gaze trailed over me. "It's a crying shame that you've been hiding under scrubs all this time." He cupped the side of my face, running a thumb over my cheek and meeting my eyes. "You're stunning, Cela."

I looked down, my hair falling forward. I'd been told I was pretty before. But never before had those words sounded so genuine, so stripped down. It was almost as if Foster hadn't wanted the compliment to escape, but couldn't help himself.

Pike stepped around from behind me and smiled a smile that unwound the last tangle of tension inside me. Foster's intensity had always drawn me, had laced my fantasies, but Pike's sexy boldness brought out my confidence. Shame had no place here with these two. They weren't here to judge me on my sexual prowess or experience. And they'd never laugh at me. They *wanted* me. And I wanted them. That was all that mattered tonight.

I'd figure out the rest as I went along.

"Tell us what's on your mind, gorgeous," Pike said. "What's making you bite your lip?"

I paused, not even realizing what I'd been doing and released my lip from beneath my teeth. "I'm not sure what to do next."

The curve of Foster's mouth filled with illicit promise. "Close your eyes, angel."

I let my eyelids fall shut and clasped my hands in front of me. Vulnerability rippled through me, but I focused on my breath, counting the inhales and exhales. I could sense Pike and Foster standing there, watching me. Then there was the faint rasp of cloth, movement around me. Smooth palms touched my shoulders and squeezed. "Walk forward, Cela. I won't let you run into anything."

Foster guided me with gentle nudges, his big body pressing against my back, until my knees brushed against something—some piece of furniture. He spun me, staying behind me, and then his fingers were touching the hook of my bra. I sucked in a breath as the front clasp gave way, exposing my nipples to the bite of cool air. My hands moved upward, an automatic shielding reaction. But Foster's hands were around my wrists in a flash, pulling my arms down to my sides.

"Gorgeous," Pike said from somewhere in front of me, the reverent tone making my insides go liquid. "Take off the rest. It's my turn to make you moan like you did in the cab."

My pulse jumped, the suggestion almost enough to send me halfway there already. Foster released my wrists and the couch springs squeaked faintly as he took a seat behind me. I hooked my thumbs into the waistband of my panties, thankful for the alcohol I'd had tonight. I wasn't drunk, but there was definitely some liquid courage still pumping in my veins. After one fortifying breath, I slid my panties down my thighs.

When I reached my heels, I had to balance carefully to slip the underwear off, leaving me bent and exposed to Foster. A rumbled groan sounded behind me, and then Foster's hands were spanning my hips. "Stay just like that."

I halted in place, one hand on the floor to keep my balance—not that I ever felt balanced around these two. Foster's thumbs traced along the cleft of my backside, making me momentarily tense, and then ventured lower, finding the lips of my sex and spreading me. I bit the inside of my cheek, fighting hard to be still and not let my knees buckle. Then the hot, wet flat of his tongue was on me, tasting my heat and launching a bottle rocket of sensation through every one of my nerve endings.

"Oh, God," I said on a sharp breath. My hips tilted upward, putting me teetering on my toes, but there was no way I was going to let myself fall and miss a second of the blissful sensation that was radiating outward from the caress of Foster's skillful mouth.

The tip of Foster's tongue teased my clit and then ran along my crease, his thumbs keeping me exposed to him. My eyelids squeezed even tighter. Only one other guy had ever attempted to go down on me, and clearly he'd been a novice because it'd felt nothing like this. And though I'd become quite proficient in taking care of my own needs, feeling Foster's tongue against me wasn't even on the same continent as that sensation. This was just . . . *guh*.

His breath was hot against me, his stubble rasping along my tender skin. "So sweet, angel. I could spend all night tasting you, feeling you come against my mouth."

My back bowed, my body aching for him to do just that. But instead of continuing, he shifted away, caressing the outsides of my thighs.

"But I'm being selfish," he said, a dark smile hiding in his tone. "Stand up."

After taking a second to make sure I'd heard correctly, I pushed myself to stand. A head rush and the pulsing need between my legs sent me swaying on my feet. "Whoa."

Foster's hands kept me steady. "Sit back on me, angel. I think it's time we reward Pike's patience, don't you?"

I gulped at the thought, anticipation spinning in me, but managed a nod. "Yes."

A quick pinch at my waist made me gasp, then Foster's smooth, commanding voice: "If you want me to be in charge, I expect you to call me by my name or sir. Do you understand?"

The command made my thoughts stutter, trip over each other. *Sir?* The idea should've been laughable, but for some reason it made something snake low and hot in my belly. I swallowed past my parched vocal cords. "Yes . . . sir."

He kissed the spot he'd pinched. "Good girl. Now sit back and let us enjoy you."

Good girl. Those were the most ironic words of the night. It was who I'd been all my life, but right now I was as far removed from that label as I'd ever been—uncharted waters. I kept my eyes closed and let Foster guide me in between his spread thighs.

He looped my arms above me, securing them around his neck, and then hooked his ankles with mine, parting my legs and opening me to Pike. I may have ceased breathing.

"You can open your eyes now, doc," Pike said, his voice devoid of the playfulness that usually colored it.

I felt like a butterfly pinned to a board, totally exposed and vulnerable. But something about being held in place, Foster's hard body beneath me, had everything in me pulsing and my body aching. This is what I'd asked for—the absence of choice. Knowing that they were deciding the moves took away some of the awkwardness that would've swamped me otherwise.

I lifted my lashes, colliding head on with Pike's heated stare. He'd stripped off his shirt, gifting me with the sight of all that tawny muscle and tattooed skin. I wanted to touch him, to explore, to taste, but as if invisible bonds had wrapped around my wrists, I kept my hands locked above me, clasping Foster's neck.

Pike took a step closer, and my gaze drifted downward, tracing the hard line of the erection pressing against the front of his jeans. My sex clenched, my body aching to know what he'd feel like inside. I knew it would hurt tonight, was prepared for that. But the fear was quickly fading to a distant beat in the back of my brain. Need trumped that anxiety the moment Foster had put his mouth on me.

Pike rubbed his palm over the bulge. "That's what you do to me, doc. What you do to us." He reached out and caressed my knee. "I could get off just seeing you like this." He knelt down in front of me. "But I'd rather do more than look."

Foster adjusted his legs and pulled my thighs further apart, spreading me for Pike. I glanced down my body, seeing the hard points of my nipples, the glistening pink of my sex. Pike blew a gentle breath over my damp skin, sensitizing everything and making me shiver. "So wet and pretty already."

Then he lowered his head and put his mouth on me—hot, wet, and maddeningly gentle. I arched against Foster, and his sexy grunt pressed against my ear. "Don't let go yet, angel. Let Pike tease you."

"But," I gasped as Pike circled his tongue around my swollen nub, licking and laving. Everything inside me already felt ready to blow to bits. This was so much more than my own fingers or even my vibrator. "God, I've never . . ."

"Have patience," Foster murmured. "It'll make it better. I promise you're going to get to come. Many times."

I watched Pike's pale blond head rock between my thighs, the sight one of the most erotic I'd ever experienced. He lifted his gaze, as if sensing my stare, and glided the flat of his tongue along my folds while holding the eye contact. I shuddered hard, the link almost too intense.

Then he lowered his head again, and two fingers slid inside my soaked channel. The fit was deliciously snug. I whimpered and undulated against his hand and the intensifying pressure of his tongue. A surge of need built behind the dam inside me, pressing against the resistance I was trying to hold strong. My lids fell closed, and my hips began a rhythmic, involuntary rocking.

"Ah, angel, that's right. Fuck his mouth. Take what you need. God, you're beautiful when you let go."

Foster's dirty whispered words were a soundtrack from my most private fantasies. All I could do was moan in response, the canting of my hips picking up pace. Then Foster's hands were cupping my breasts, holding me in place.

"You want to go over, baby?" he asked, his voice raspy with grit.

"Yes. Please . . ."

"Beg Pike. Tell him what you need," Foster commanded. He pinched my nipples, a swift erotic pain that made me cry out and go desperate for release.

I squeezed my eyes shut, beyond embarrassment or shame. "Please, Pike. I need to come. *Please.*"

Pike groaned and then his fingers were curling inside me, hitting a spot I'd heard of but had never been able to find myself. The world splintered behind my eyelids. I bowed off Foster, and my thighs clamped around Pike's head as orgasm enveloped me. My cries sounded unfamiliar to my own ears—the abandon as foreign as the emotions coursing through me.

I rode the wave of sensation until I was panting and writhing, edgy with both satisfaction and the need for more. Need for them. Pike eased back once I'd loosened my headlock on him, then he was climbing up the length of me. His mouth met mine in a lust-filled haze. My arms released Foster's neck as the taste of Pike and my own arousal filled our kiss. Foster continued to tease my breasts, his hands trapped between my and Pike's bodies, and he kissed my shoulder, my neck. Hungry. Wanting.

Foster's erection pressed against my bottom as he shifted forward. I wriggled against him even as I continued to kiss Pike. The swirl of sensations overtook me. I lost track of whose hand was where, whose scent filled my nose. It was both of them, all of them, coalescing into one heady moment.

Pike pulled away, gasping for breath. "Fuck slow. Bedroom. Now."

"Agreed," Foster growled.

Pike pushed away from the couch, and Foster turned me into his arms, standing up and lifting me with him. I linked my arms around his neck again and caught his gaze. The stark need that filled those sea glass eyes seemed to reach inside me and twist everything into something new and different. Unrecognizable. I knew then that whatever happened next, I'd never be the same. Even if it was just this one night. This man would change me.

Maybe already had.

He carried me toward the bedroom, Pike ahead of us. And I tore my gaze away from Foster's, the connection almost too powerful to bear. For the first time since walking in, I noticed the elegant creams and golds of the suite, the refined decor, the fresh flowers. Every detail had been finely attended to. It was romantic. And expensive. Fit for a honeymoon.

Or a girl losing her virginity.

"I've been imagining this for a long time," Foster confessed as he stepped into the large bedroom.

I smiled, warmth spreading through me, the feeling of rightness settling in my gut. "So have I, Foster."

So have I.

EIGHT

Foster set me on my feet in the bedroom and didn't let go until he made sure I was steady. He brushed my hair away from my face, his expression unreadable in the combination of soft lamplight and shadows. "Undress me."

It was a simple request, but hell if it didn't make a ripple of *Oh, my God, yes* go through me. I lifted my hands, my fingers almost forgetting how to work as I reached for the buttons on his shirt. How many times had I pictured his naked body in my fantasies? When I'd hear Foster come in late, I'd lie there in bed, holding my breath and listening to the sounds he made. The TV turning on, the plunk of shoes coming off and hitting the floor. I'd imagine his clothes sliding off of him, the hard muscle and planes of his body coming into view. My eyes would shut and without pausing to think, I'd trace my hand down my belly, below the band of my panties, and pretend it was his touch instead of mine.

As I reached the bottom button, Foster put a finger beneath my chin, tilting my face toward him. "What are you thinking about, angel?"

In the corner of my eye, I saw Pike sit on the edge of the bed, his attention fixed on the two of us. Nerves crept in, making my skin go hot then clammy.

I tried to look away from Foster, but he tapped my chin. "No you don't. Look at me and tell me without filtering."

I forced my focus upward and tried to swallow past my parched throat. My cheeks burned hot—guilt and shame, my old Catholic friends, pumping through me. But I was not going to chicken out now. If I wanted people to stop treating me like I was a naive little girl, I needed to stop acting like one. "I was thinking about how many times

I've touched myself while listening to you get undressed in your room, how many times I've imagined you naked."

His grip on my chin tightened, and his jaw flexed, the pleased look in his eye its own reward. "I think we've both imagined things long enough, don't you?"

"Yes, sir," I said, the words quivery in the quiet room. *This is going to happen. This is really going to happen.*

I pushed his shirt off his shoulders, letting my fingers travel over the ripples and dips of his pecs and shoulders. Hard muscle and hot skin. The shirt hit the floor, and I went to the button on his jeans, knowing that if I stopped moving, I'd start questioning myself. So without examining the urge, I lowered myself to my knees and pulled down the zipper. The thick outline of his erection pressed against the denim—intimidating and enticing all at once. I grabbed the waist of his pants and lowered them along with his boxer briefs. His cock slipped free, hard and heavy with arousal. I bit my lip so the gasp wouldn't escape.

I'd seen a naked man a time or two before, had fooled around with a few guys. And I had definitely looked at more than my share of illicit photos on the Internet. But I'd never been this close, this intimate. It'd always been hands fumbling around in the dark while making out. And he was definitely bigger than any guy I'd been with before. Just the sight of him had everything inside me stirring and aching. I couldn't remember ever being so desperate to touch and taste a man. I wanted to explore every inch of him, wanted to feel the dark thatch of hair beneath my fingers, wanted to feel the soft skin against my cheek, in my mouth.

Foster ran a hand over my hair. "Hope reality lives up to the fantasy."

I looked up to finding him with a teasing smile. I shrugged, though it took everything inside me to appear casual. "This'll do."

He laughed. "Smartass."

"No, smart girl." Pike stood, coming to my side. He'd undone the button on his own jeans, giving me a peek beneath. No underwear, just smooth, hard belly behind the zipper. "He doesn't need any help with his ego."

Foster sniffed.

Pike stepped behind me, sifting his fingers through my hair. "Do you want to taste him?"

I curled my fingers against my thighs, nerves pushing through again. What if I screwed it all up now? One wrong move and I'd expose exactly what I was most trying to hide. "I want to, but I'm not very experienced at this."

Or experienced at all.

Pike reached around and cupped my jaw with a gentle hold. "Don't worry, beautiful. I'll guide you. Take him in your mouth. Believe me, you can't do anything wrong, except teeth."

I lifted my gaze to Foster, to find the smile had left his face, replaced by hard-edged desire. "Keep your eyes on me while you do it, angel."

I licked my lips, my fingernails cutting into my palms. I wanted to get this right, wanted to bring him as much pleasure as the two of them had given me already. But with my complete lack of experience, I feared I'd be a disappointment. How could I compare to all those pretty girls I'd seen come and go from their apartment over the last two years?

But before my anxiety could steal away with my nerve, Pike eased my head forward, guiding me over Foster's cock and taking away my choice—just like I'd asked. My lips parted, and I took Foster into my mouth, holding his eye contact as he slid inside. The salt and musk of his skin painted my tongue and filled my senses, his flavor and scent like potent aphrodisiacs dumped into my bloodstream. God, I hadn't known what to expect, but liking the taste surprised me. My friend Bailey had always made blow jobs sound like a chore. But having Foster pushing along my tongue felt like anything but. It felt like a privilege.

A new rush of desire pulsed between my legs, making me moan around Foster as I brought him as far to the back of my throat as I could manage.

"Ah, God," he said, his voice like soft, warm strokes to my skin. "That's it, angel. Perfect. Touch me while you do it."

Emboldened by the feedback, I lifted my hands and tracked up and down his thighs, feeling the hard muscles there, the tension. He ran every morning and it showed. The thought had a spark of self-consciousness blooming through me. Had he expected me to be this built? I was soft everywhere he was hard, my curvy figure something I'd never been able to change even when I did get on a regular exercise plan.

"She's thinking again, Pike," Foster said with a *tsk*ing tone. "Fix it."

Pike's grip on my hair tightened. "Eyes open, doc. And touch him like you really want to. I know all those nights in your room you weren't thinking about touching his legs."

The command snapped me out of my tanking thoughts. I opened my eyes and found Foster's gaze again, the heat there like an anchor keeping me from drifting too far from shore. There's no way he could look at me like that if he didn't like what he saw. I bobbed my head, taking him deep again, and refocused my efforts. Also, knowing Pike was one hundred percent right, I let my hands find their way to the area I really wanted to explore. I cupped his sac, caressing the delicate skin there, loving the weight of him in my palm. My mouth and tongue slid over the length of him again, Pike's grip on my head determining my pace now. I'd asked to not have to make any decisions and they were keeping their promise. I was there to be used how they wished.

The idea should've rankled me. Being used. I *wanted* it to bother me. But instead it only served to dial up the intensity of this experience more and to deflect my near-constant sexual insecurities from overtaking me. I wanted to please Foster, wanted to do well. Like my innate inclination to be the best daughter, the best student, the best everything, this need seemed to stem from some place I couldn't define. Whether I liked it or not, his level of pleasure was directly tied to mine. If I thought too hard about it, I'd lead myself to no place good.

"Eyes on me, angel," Foster reminded me, dragging me back again.

I brought my attention back upward, finding Foster's eyes filled with naked lust and a dangerous edge—like it was taking every stitch of his control not to completely overtake me. The sheer power of that look had my mind emptying, my worrisome thoughts winking out of existence like stars at dawn. I moved forward and ran my tongue along the vein at the base of his cock, then tried to relax my throat, working to keep my teeth clear of him at the same time. I wanted all of him inside me. I gagged a bit when he hit the far back of my throat, but managed to breathe through it without letting go.

Now Foster was the one to break the eye contact, his head tilting back and a low groan slipping from him. "Not sure what you're doing, huh? You're about to bring me to my knees."

The praise rained over me like a summer storm. I closed my eyes and hollowed my cheeks, sucking him with the level of need rising in my own body.

"Jesus." Another hand was suddenly in my hair, pulling me away. Foster stepped back, his grip gentling after a second. "Not yet, angel. I've waited this long. When I come, I want to be face-to-face, deep inside you."

Hot goose bumps trailed over my skin, the glimpse of his slipping control giving me a rush of feminine confidence. Not only had I not messed up, I'd almost made him come. I couldn't stop the smile from lifting my lips.

Foster chuckled. "Well, don't you look pleased with yourself."

"She should be," Pike said, letting her go. "She didn't even touch me, and my head's about to explode."

I turned toward Pike, staying on my knees, the praise making me brave. "I could help."

Pike smiled. "It's okay, baby. I can be patient. Tonight's about you."

I sent him a raised eyebrow and boldly tugged at his zipper. What the hell was I doing? I didn't recognize this version of myself but liked it. My hand dipped inside his fly, pulling his thick cock free of its denim prison. A bead of moisture glistened at the top and without giving myself time to think, I leaned forward and swiped it with my tongue.

"Well, don't fucking listen to me," he said, laughing. "Clearly you have better ideas."

"Sit on the bed, Pike," Foster directed from my left. "And Cela, on your hands and knees."

Pike helped me to my feet, obviously used to Foster taking charge, then led me to the bed. He climbed onto the mattress, pulling me onto it with him, and settled back on the puffy pillows, his tattoos like gorgeous art against all those white linens. He cradled my face, bringing me in for a soft kiss first, then guided me down his torso to lower my mouth down on him.

I took Pike's length between my lips and tucked my knees beneath me, inadvertently exposing my backside to Foster's view. The bed dipped as Foster joined us. A hand caressed the curve of my ass, and I had another brief moment of panic about my body. But when his fingers dipped between my legs, finding that wet and aching spot, all thoughts dissipated. I whimpered around Pike's cock, unable to stop the desperate sound from escaping.

"Mmm, I love to hear how badly you want this." Foster moved his fingers, teasing my clitoris without directly touching it. "You're so beautiful when you give in to it. So sexy. I'm finding it hard to play nice."

Pike's hand was threading through my hair, his pelvis rocking toward me, but Foster's words landed heavy on me. I wanted to respond to him, to answer, but I also didn't want to break the moment. And I wasn't even sure what I'd say. All I knew was that whatever he wanted to do, I was game for it, especially if he kept touching me like that. I widened my knees, showing Foster in the only way I knew how that I trusted him. I had put himself in their hands and meant it.

Foster made a sound of approval. His hand tracked over the curve of my backside. "I like to play a little rough, angel. And even though I know you're not ready for most of that right now, I'm not sure I can resist this pretty ass."

My pace stuttered a bit, unsure of what he was suggesting—the possibilities both scaring and exciting me.

Pike's fingers went gentle against my scalp, and he eased me upward until I was looking up at him. His hazel eyes had gone black, yearning. "He wants to spank you, baby. If you're not cool with that, say so."

Foster wanted to . . . *oh*. Rough. He wanted to *hit* me.

I peeked over my shoulder, finding Foster, seeking reassurance. His hand was still against me, but his focus was solely on my eyes. There was power in his gaze, steely control, but underneath there was a vulnerability that reached right into my chest and tugged. Asking for this was costing him something. He hadn't planned to show me this side of himself.

"I trust you," I said, my voice as even as I'd ever heard it. I couldn't say the same for my heartbeat. I knew there was some line we were about to cross, some highly uncharted territory for me. But I couldn't find the word *no* in my vocabulary, not when he was giving me that look. I may have walked across glass in that moment to peek past that door he'd just cracked open.

At my words, the wrinkle in Foster's brow softened, his features shifting from concern to resolve. "Finish what you started with Pike. And touch yourself while you do it, angel. It will make this all the better."

Touch myself? In front of them? Instinctive shame bubbled up in me again—the damn emotion always running right below the surface ready to burst through. But just as quickly I shoved the thought from my brain. I was naked, ass in the air between two men. I'd already jumped that shark.

"Yes, sir," I said then turned back to Pike. He was stroking himself, filling in where I'd left off. For a few seconds, I was held in suspension, fascinated by the slide of that strong male hand, by the total lack of self-consciousness as he took his pleasure.

But then a sharp smack hit my backside and snapped me out of the spell. I yelped, more from surprise than anything else, and a stinging heat traced over skin. *Ow.*

Pike's mouth hitched up at the corner as he gently guided me downward again. "Close your eyes and give yourself over to it, doc. It'll be worth it."

Despite my burning rear, I listened to Pike and closed my eyes as my mouth enveloped him again. He tasted of salt and man and illicit fantasy—a combination that had my brain teetering on the edge of some place I hadn't been before. I didn't know what the spanking was supposed to accomplish, but I wanted to try to do what they asked. To let go and see where they took me. Foster delivered another slap to my opposite cheek, and the stinging burned just as much. I barely bit back the urge to tell him to stop. Then another lighter one came, popping me right along my exposed folds. This time the flash of pain was followed by a hot, rolling warmth that started low and surged all the way out to my fingers and toes. I moaned, pressing my lips harder around Pike's shaft and earning a shudder from him.

Holy mother of God. Was that supposed to feel so good?

My nerve endings tingled as Foster continued with a quick volley of slaps—the backs of my thighs, my ass, my sex again. *Smack, smack, smack.* The sharp sounds filled my ears, and I started to lose count. Chasing the burning sting was a rush of desperate, clawing need that was emptying my brain. It was as if I hadn't just orgasmed minutes before. No longer caring how it may look, I braced myself against Pike and reached down with my free hand to relieve some of the pressure building behind my clit.

Even the slight touch had my body tensing, begging for release. I slid my fingers along the folds as Foster continued to spank me, the sharp bite of the hits only driving my desperation higher. My sex was slick with arousal, swollen with need. I tucked two fingers inside the way I did when alone, and my inner muscles clenched around the invasion. *Ah, God.*

"You're not allowed to come," Foster said, his words like an iron blockade to my climbing need. "Not until I tell you to."

The force of his tone sent me reeling. My hand moved back to the bed as if on autopilot, and my mind spun into the yawning abyss of the moment, my whole body riding the edge of release. I couldn't cling to anything except the sound of Foster's voice and the feel and touch of the two men. The state was disorienting, like being submerged in dark, ocean water and only holding on to a piece of driftwood. But no fear entered my system. Instead, I worked harder at bringing Pike pleasure, at taking all of him. The desire to please beat through me like a chant.

"Fucking hell," Pike groaned. "Yes, like that . . . so good."

Pike's belly rose and dipped above me, his breath going rapid, his muscles coiling tight. A swell of feminine power went through me. I was doing this to him. Foster's hands smoothed over my backside, soothing the stinging skin. "Make him come, angel. Let me see you send him over the brink."

I swirled my tongue around the tip of Pike's cock, my confidence building with every stroke, and Pike's fingers pressed hard against my scalp as his hips lifted off the bed. A strangled moan wretched from him, and at the same moment, Foster slid his fingers along my clit.

"Go over with him," Foster commanded, his fingers delivering a quick pinch, a devastating blow.

I cried out as orgasm, sharp and instant, roped me and dragged me under.

"Ah, fuck," Pike groaned. His cock swelled against my tongue, and then he was spilling his pleasure inside my mouth, gripping me like he'd die if I stopped.

Pleasure rolled through me like sparking electricity, waking up every sensory system, and making me want to writhe. But I worked

Pike until I'd swallowed every salty drop of what he had to offer, loving his taste and abandon, loving the wanton feeling of being between him and Foster.

After both of us drifted down from the high, Pike eased away from me with gentle movements. I lifted my head, feeling drunk on lust—satisfied but not quite sated. My body still ached for one more thing. The thing I'd never had before.

And I only wanted one man to give it to me.

Pike helped me off my knees and rolled me onto the pillows next to him. Leaning over me, he gave me a smile that could break every heart in its path. He pressed a soft kiss to my lips. "That was amazing, doc. Thank you."

My lips curved, my brain still buzzing, words not forming.

Pike glanced at Foster, then back to me, brushing my hair off my forehead. "I'm going to give you two some time alone. I don't think Foster's quite done with you yet."

My gaze slid over to Foster, who had moved to stand at the foot of the bed. The quirk of his lips was wry, but the hot blue of his eyes was pure animal—like a wolf quietly sizing up its dinner. "You ready for me, angel?"

My tongue darted out, wetting my lips. Ready? God, I'd never felt more ready for anything in my life than this man and this moment. Even seeing him standing there, all hard muscle and proud arousal, had my skin tingling anew. "Yes, sir."

Pike gave me one more quick kiss on the forehead then climbed off the bed. As Pike passed by Foster, Foster put a hand on his shoulder, halting him. He whispered something, and Pike nodded with a brief, knowing smile.

I couldn't hear the exchange, but my thoughts were too languid to even care. All I knew was that whatever came next, I wouldn't regret it. I'd waited my whole adult life for this moment, and regardless of how things may feel tomorrow, how the light of day would change this, right now nothing felt more right.

NINE

Foster waited until Pike had closed the door behind himself before daring to look at Cela again. She looked so perfect there laid out on the soft down comforter, like a naked angel perched on a cloud. Her dark hair was fanned out behind her, a few strands sticking to her damp forehead. He wanted to kiss every bare spot of skin, draw out every kind of sound she was capable of.

He hadn't planned to use any D/s play with her, definitely hadn't intended to spank her. He knew better. Bringing in kink with vanilla girls wasn't his style, especially with someone as sweetly innocent as Cela. But something in her had tugged at his dominance, had called it forth like a sorceress's spell. And then he'd seen her sink.

Subspace had claimed her like it'd been simply waiting for her to knock on the door. Her muscles had gone lax, her voice thready. Even her pupils had gone large. And it'd been the sexiest fucking thing he'd ever seen.

He'd brought women to subspace many times in his life, but never had it stirred up the intense possessiveness Cela had inspired. The second he'd seen her go under, he'd had the distinct urge to drag her away from Pike, to kick his friend out of the room altogether. He'd wanted her all to himself.

To own her.

It'd been a dangerous thought.

But when Pike had offered the opportunity for alone time— something he'd never done in a threesome before—Foster hadn't been able to stop himself from thanking the heavens for the unexpected gift. And when he'd told Pike to not come back until he gave the all clear, his friend had only smiled. Like he'd known exactly the nature of Foster's possessive thoughts.

Now Cela was all his. At least for a little while.

He walked next to the bed, trailing his fingers along the edge of the duvet and letting his gaze track hot over Cela's bare skin. When he reached her side, he traced a finger around a dusky nipple, bringing it to a hard point. "I love how responsive you are."

"Thank you, sir," she whispered, her eyes closing when he gave the little nub a soft tug.

His already stiff cock twitched. The word *sir* rolled off her lush lips like they'd been made to say it. There was no force there, no this-is-just-a-game smugness. He drew a finger along the bow of her lips, remembering how they'd felt around him—the heaven that was Cela's hot, eager mouth.

"Hold on to the slats of the headboard, angel. And don't let go until I tell you."

Her dark eyes flared with heat and her lips parted, but she followed his directive without an ounce of hesitation. She was sliding deeper, he could see it in the softness of her expression, the looseness of her muscles. If the simple act of holding the headboard sent her to that lovely place, he could only imagine how she would respond to true restraints, to real roughness. His blood hummed at the thought.

Maybe another time.

But he knew there would probably not be another time.

This was her wild ride before she went home to her real life. He'd made the mistake of reading too much into a woman before, and he wouldn't do it again. He'd barely survived the first time.

He needed to accept his role for what it was—the kinky neighbor she was working out a few fantasies with. But that didn't mean they both couldn't have a fantastic time tonight.

Once he was sure she had a good grip on the headboard, he climbed onto the bed, straddling her. The soft curls of her mound brushed against his cock, and he had to suppress the urge to bury himself inside her that instant. But he didn't want this to end too quickly. If he only had tonight, he wanted to savor every part of her like fine wine. He braced his arms on the side of her and laid soft, wet kisses along her neck, pulling the delicate skin into his mouth and tasting the brininess of her exertion. There were few flavors he enjoyed more than the salty taste of a woman's sweat or tears. He liked to bring both forth when a woman was under his command.

Cela whimpered softly, her back curving, as he made his way down to her collarbone, nibbling. Her body brushed against his, petal soft and burning hot, begging. Every move, every sigh she made tested his own resolve to go slowly. But as he found his way to her breasts, he knew rushing would be a crime. Her nipples were hard and dark in the lamplight of the room, inspiring worship. He lowered his head, drawing his tongue around the point, bringing goose bumps to the surface, then gave the treatment to the other side.

She squirmed beneath him in quiet desperation. Her knuckles went white along the headboard. He smiled and traced her sternum with a featherlight touch. "What do you need, angel?"

Her teeth pressed into her lip, her eyes closed. "I need more. Please. Sir."

"Mmm, good girl," he said, cupping her breast, loving the weight of it in his hand. He adored how curvy she was. He'd only imagined what she looked like under those scrubs she always wore, but the reality was so much better. A body strong enough to withstand a rough hand but built for sin. Lush indulgence. "You have no idea what your sweet begging does to me."

He plumped her breast with his hand and drew the nipple into his mouth, teasing and then sucking with enough force to make it count.

"Oh," she gasped, lifting into his touch.

Her knees parted, and the aroma of female arousal drifted up to his nose, wrapping around his cock like a hot fist. Fuck, even her scent was mouthwatering, every bit of her edible. He gave her nipple a gentle bite, and the grinding noise that escaped from the back of her throat nearly made the top of his head blow off.

If he waited too much longer, he was going to go off like some inexperienced teenager. And even though the thought of her smooth, honeyed skin being painted with his seed spoke to his deep, primal desire to mark her, he wasn't going to settle for anything less than being inside her tonight.

He kissed his way down her belly, then licked along the creases where leg met pelvis. Her thighs fell open further, the ultimate invitation, exposing the smooth lips of her pussy. He loved that she'd only left a triangle of hair on her mound. Everything else was blessedly pink and glistening with arousal. He used the tip of his tongue to tease the swollen button at her center, and her breath went choppy.

He pulled back with a smile. "Not yet, angel. Not until I have these legs of yours around me."

"God, yes," she said, her belly quivering as she tried to reel herself in, then she stilled as if just realizing something. "Did you bring—I didn't . . ."

"Shh, I've got it." He reached for the condom he'd pulled from his wallet earlier and set on the side table to sheathe himself. "You can let go of the bed now."

Her arms melted into the mattress, releasing the headboard, and she raised her eyelids as he settled himself over her. The look was one of pure trust, untainted surrender. He didn't deserve it, but he wasn't going to question it right now.

"You ready, angel?"

"You have no idea."

He laughed and positioned himself at her entrance. She was so wet, so hot, as he pushed forward. It should have been a smooth glide of an entry. But as soon as he got a little ways in, her body seemed to fight him, the clasp of her heat squeezing him hard. "Fuck, baby. You're tight."

He nudged a little, and he caught the wince she tried to cover.

"Am I hurting you?" he asked, an arrow of worry shooting through him.

She circled her arms around him, her hold on him deathly tight, like she was afraid he was going to get up and walk away. "No. It's just been a long time. And you're . . . big. Please, don't stop. Just go for it."

"I don't want to h—"

"I have a safe word," she said, a pleading look in her eyes. "Please, I need this. I need *you*."

A niggling concern pressed at the back of his brain, but the way she felt around him clouded any coherent thoughts he was trying to have. He needed to have her, wanted to feel her around him. He rocked his hips forward, gently at first, then with a bit more force, pushing past the resistance and burying himself deep.

She cried out, her head titling back and her back arching. He couldn't tell if it was pain or pleasure. Her nails dug into his shoulders, and she seemed to not breathe for a long moment. He held still, afraid he was doing more harm than good. "Tell me you're okay, Cela."

She took a breath finally, panting. "Yes. Please. Keep going."

He slid back and plunged inside her again, this time meeting no resistance—just the pure ecstasy of being surrounded by her heat.

"Oh, God," she moaned, her grip on him easing and a softness smoothing her tense features. "Yes . . . this."

And that was all he needed. He moved inside her again, the feel of her like hot cashmere around his cock. God, she was so snug, so maddeningly sexy. He didn't know if he'd ever experienced such an intense feeling. Sweet agony bled through his veins as he pumped into her with a cadence that belied the urgent need building in him. He would not rush this.

He didn't want it to end, didn't want to lose the beautiful sight of her beneath him, the pained bliss that was coloring her features. "You're so beautiful, Cela. So fucking perfect."

She lifted her lashes and reached up to touch his face, to brush her fingers along his stubble. The tender intimacy of the move almost undid him. "And you're better than the fantasy, Foster."

He dropped onto his forearms, unable to bear another second without kissing her. His mouth met hers in a hungry rush, tongues and lips clashing. She laced her fingers in his hair and pulled tight. Out of his conscious control at this point, his hips begin to thrust into her with more force. She whimpered into his mouth, and the bed squeaked beneath them as sweat glazed his skin.

He didn't break the kiss, but reached a hand in between them to find her clit. The moment he touched it, her pussy gripped him, contracted.

"Come with me, angel," he said, lifting up only far enough to watch her face and then picking up speed.

He angled his hips to brush his cock over her where he knew she needed, and strummed her clit. A long, gritty moan passed her lips, and he felt the precise moment she shattered. It was all he needed. His balls drew tight and the all-encompassing explosion of pleasure shot through him like a bullet train.

The sweet, erotic sounds of her orgasm danced around him, driving him higher as he emptied every bit of him inside her, his body throbbing and pulsing, all with need for her. Just her.

And the realization didn't hit him then.

It didn't even hit him as he lifted off her, kissed her face all over, and eventually tucked her into a robe.

But then he went into the bathroom to toss the condom.

And saw red.

And he knew, knew what had been haunting her eyes in the elevator.

Never have I ever . . .

He leaned against the bathroom wall, his heart sinking.

Fuck.

TEN

I rolled to the left, bumping into tattooed, sleep-warmed skin. The obstruction spun my hazy brain into confusion for a moment. Where was I? Was I dreaming? I blinked in the predawn darkness, finding Pike snoring softly, his bare back to me. My mind stumbled, then rewound, the memories of the night dropping back into place.

A long breath pushed past my lips as I lay back on the pillows and rubbed my eyes. No, this had been no dream. My achy, tender body punctuated that conclusion. I'd actually done it—shoved past all my worry and inhibitions and gotten naked with not just one of the neighbors I'd been fantasizing about, but both of them. And I'd had sex with Foster. Sex. I was a virgin no longer. I waited for the shame to hit me. The morning-after regret I'd heard about from friends, but none came.

The only thing clawing at me was the memory of the way I'd felt when Foster had held me and kissed me, the way he'd felt filling my body. The physical discomfort of it had been expected, the initial wave of it breath stealing. But that pain had faded to a soft hum in the background when my eyes had locked with his. Something far deeper than the sensations my body was experiencing had passed through me. An intense oneness with him.

It'd probably been the simple fact that he was my first. Girls were wired to get romantic notions about that, right? But later when Pike had joined the two of us in bed again, I hadn't felt the same thing kissing and cuddling him. Being with Pike was fun—he was sex personified and he made me laugh—but I didn't get that tight feeling in my stomach when he looked at me.

I turned to my right, seeking the man who was stirring up the turmoil in me, but that side of the bed was empty. I reached out and touched the rumpled sheets. Cold.

I frowned and squinted at the clock—a little past five A.M. Careful not to disturb Pike, I scooted across the bed and climbed to my feet, grabbing the robe I'd thrown over the high-backed chair in the corner. My body protested at the movement, soreness fully setting in now. But in a way, I welcomed the discomfort, the proof that the night had really happened and wasn't some fantasy. After a quick trip to the bathroom, I padded across the plush carpet and slipped out of the bedroom.

The living room was still in twilight, but the silhouette of a man standing in front of the large windows drew me. Foster stared out at the coming dawn, the lights of downtown Dallas starting to blink off, preparing for the sun's appearance. He held a mug in his hands, blowing across the top of it.

I hung in the shadow of the far side of the room, simply enjoying watching him. The muscles in his back shifted and caught the light as he lifted his coffee to his lips and sipped. There was an elegance to his economy of movement, to his stillness. His brows were drawn low, his profile a sculpture of deep thought.

I almost turned back toward the bedroom, afraid to interrupt the sanctity of his quiet morning, but when I stepped backward, my robe brushed a nearby lampshade, sending the lamp chain clinking against the metal base.

Foster tipped his head in my direction, a slight turn, but didn't take his eyes off the view. "You're up early."

I wrapped my arms around myself. "Said the rooster to the chicken."

He looked at me then, a quirk of a smile. "I'm not so good at the sleeping-in thing. Hope I didn't wake you."

"You didn't." I stepped out of the dark and headed to the oversized chair near the window. When I sat, my body reminded me again of all I'd been through in the last few hours. But even the tenderness of my backside had a flash of lust zipping through me. God, I was a glutton for punishment. Since when was pain a good thing? I tucked my legs beneath me and resisted the urge to go over to Foster and kiss him good morning. "I'm not sure what woke me up. Maybe Pike's snoring."

Foster chuckled. "Don't tell him he snores. It will devastate his Mr. Suave self-image."

"Never." I pantomimed zipping my mouth shut.

Foster's smirk remained in place, but I sensed this lighthearted conversation was simply pretty decoration on top of a pile of crap that wasn't been said. The lines around his mouth, the way he gripped his coffee, even the set of his shoulders had my nerves rising, my fingers fiddling with the tie of my terrycloth robe. He knew.

He released a long sigh and moved away from the window to perch on the arm of the couch across from me. "Why didn't you tell me?"

I stared down at fidgeting hands. "Tell you what?"

"Cela," he said in that commanding tone he'd used in the bedroom. "Look at me."

A hot quiver rippled through me, but I raised my gaze to him.

Sharp disapproval edged his features. "You left something pretty important off that list of yours."

My cheeks heated. "I know. I'm sorry. I didn't want to say anything."

"Didn't want to say anything?" he said, his exasperation loud in the dead quiet of the hotel room. "Cela, we could've hurt you. If you had told me, I would've been gentler, more tender. I hit you for Christ's sake." He dragged a hand through his already disheveled mop of hair. "Your first time's supposed to be sweet and romantic and I . . ."

"Stop," I said, sitting up taller in the chair. "You didn't hurt me. And this is exactly why I didn't want to tell either of you. The guy I told you about, the one who made fun of me? I had gone on a few dates with him and when things started to heat up, I let him know before anything happened. He laughed and asked if I was some religious fanatic. Then he left because taking a girl's virginity was 'too heavy' for a hookup."

"Well, thank God for that. That idiot definitely didn't deserve to touch you. But you know I wouldn't have done that."

"I know you wouldn't have teased me, but you would've backed out the instant you found out."

"No, I wouldn't've."

"Liar," I said, frustration building in me. "You just said it. Everybody has all these notions about what a first time is supposed to be like, and it freaks people out. Dudes are afraid the girl is going to cling to them like some let's-be-together-forever teenager, and girls are afraid that if the heavens don't open up and the angels don't sing that it's a losing-your-virginity failure. I didn't want any of that."

He shook his head. "What did you want?"

You, my mind whispered, *exactly what happened*. And angels *had* sung. Or maybe those were devils . . . I kicked the thought aside. "I wanted a good time. I wanted to get that big branded *V* off my resume before I have to go back home and start my real life."

Something flickered through his blue eyes, like a biting wind in a winter storm. "A good time. Right. Well, that's our specialty."

He stood and walked back toward the window, dismissing me.

The iciness in his voice and stance cut though my thick robe, chilling my skin. The shift in his mood had my defenses rising, anger welling. "Isn't it? Or are all those girls I've heard visit your apartment your '*twu wuv*.'"

His wince was almost imperceptible, but I caught it.

I rose to my feet, arms crossed. "Be honest, Foster. If I had told you last night that I was a virgin, would you have slept with me?"

He stared out the window, his jaw twitching, and I thought he may ignore me. But then after a few long seconds, he spun on his heel, set his coffee down, and stalked into my space.

His nearness had my thoughts scattering, my emotions splintering. Words wouldn't come.

He cupped my shoulders, a grip that vibrated with restrained power. "I don't know. But if I had, I would've made it different. I would've made it special for you, would've taken my time, gone slow. And I certainly wouldn't have invited Pike or used any kink."

I swallowed hard, his earnest speech curling around me, making me ache for him all over again. "It *was* special, Foster. And yes, I'm new at all this, but what you did . . . how you acted . . ."

"Was irresponsible."

"Was hot."

His eyebrows lifted.

"I asked you to take control. I didn't realize you would take it where you did, but . . . I liked it. I felt lost and safe all at the same time. I never expected sex to feel like that. I had an idea what it would feel like physically. I know my way around a vibrator. But this was . . ." I paused, not sure if the right words even existed. "Transcendent."

His thumbs caressed the curve of my shoulders as he stared down at me, his head tilted ever so slightly, like he was working out some riddle in his head.

A door squeaked behind me.

"Why the hell are you guys up so fucking early?" Pike groaned. "And why am I alone in a cold bed?"

Foster's hands dropped from my shoulders, and he stepped back, the moment broken. "Sorry, we couldn't sleep."

"Great, two insomniacs," Pike muttered and made his way over to us.

I couldn't help but smile at him, his spiked hair flat on one side and his eyelids heavy. He looked like an overgrown teenager shuffling in for breakfast. Before saying anything else, he grabbed Foster's cooling coffee off the side table and swigged. Grimaced.

"Cream is an option, you know," he said to Foster.

"So is getting your own damned coffee."

I laughed. "Y'all have lived together too long."

"No fucking doubt," Pike said, setting the cup down and then reaching for the belt of my robe. He pulled me to him like I was a fish on a line and wrapped his arms around my waist. "And how are you this morning, gorgeous?"

The embrace was warm, affectionate, but suddenly being this close to Pike felt strange. Even though I'd happily pleasured him last night, had even curled up with him when I'd fallen asleep between the two of them, something had changed in those early morning moments. The attraction was still there, but the dynamic was askew. My gaze flicked to Foster, who stood like a sentry behind Pike—stiff and stoic.

Some vulnerable part inside me wanted him to intervene, to pull me into his arms instead of letting Pike embrace me. But then I realized how ridiculous I was being. Just because Foster was the one I'd had actual sex with, didn't mean we had something different between us than Pike and I did. All of this was exactly what I had described it as—a good time. Naughty fun.

No big deal.

Right.

I brought my focus back to the man in front of me. "I'm exhausted, but in the best way possible."

"Mmm," Pike murmured. "I know what you mean, doc. Last night was fantastic." He peeked over his shoulder. "Even though Foster hogged you at the end."

"Oink, oink," Foster said, his voice too tight to deliver the intended humor.

"Well," Pike said, pulling the tie on my robe and slipping the halves open, his hands along my waist. "Why don't we rectify that? I think there's a big ol' hot shower with our names on it."

Despite feeling a bit off balance, Pike's soft touch against my skin had interest stirring in me. And if my heart was getting all mixed up because it was pulling the virgin-getting-attached card, maybe a morning wake-up call with Pike was just what I needed.

I closed my eyes, trying to block out Foster, and leaned my forehead against Pike's. "That sounds like a great idea."

"That's our girl," Pike said, his tone dipping into that low, sexual place that was impossible for my body not to react to despite the tug-of-war in my mind. "Come on, doc."

He guided me toward the bedroom, all sleepiness gone from his face.

Before we crossed the threshold, he called back to Foster. "Shower fits three, my brother. Door's open."

But when I sent one last glance Foster's way, he hadn't moved an inch.

PART III

Not Until You Crave

ELEVEN

The trip home from the hotel was painfully quiet. I sat in between Foster and Pike in the back of the cab. Pike was leaning against the window, eyes closed, half dozing, and Foster was like an automaton version of himself—only speaking when absolutely necessary.

I had no idea what had changed in the span of the last few hours, but my wild night out had morphed into something decidedly more somber. I tugged on the short tennis skirt Foster had bought from the hotel shop to save me the walk of shame in my wrinkled dress. The gesture had been thoughtful, sweet even. But he'd shirked off my thank-you like he hadn't even heard me.

Anxiety bubbled in my stomach at the thought of the good-bye this morning. Why in God's name had I chosen my neighbors? Last night, the crush-driven idea had seemed ingenious. Now I realized how stupid I'd been. Morning-after awkwardness was bad enough, but there was no way I was going to be able to avoid facing them regularly during these last few weeks I was living here.

The cab rolled to a stop at the curb in front of our building, and Foster paid the driver. He slid out of the car and held his hand out to me, the consummate gentleman, even in his cool state. Once I was on my feet and had grabbed my plastic bag of discarded clothes, I moved to let go of Foster's hand. But instead of allowing me to escape, he gathered me to his side, planting a hand at the small of my back.

I sent him a curious look but let him guide me toward the door. Pike jogged in front of us and grabbed the door to hold it open for the two of us.

"You're a hard man to read," I said, half under my breath.

"Am I?" Foster asked, continuing to look forward as we climbed the stairs. "I would think I'm painfully transparent at the moment."

"You're angry," I said, speaking what I already knew.

He sighed, his fingers pressing into my back. "Not at you, angel. Not at you."

"We need to—" I began, but my words lodged like popcorn in my throat when I reached the top of the stairs and saw the imposing figure leaning against my doorway. "Oh, shit."

Foster tensed like a Rottweiler spotting a pit bull in his path. "What the hell?"

Andre turned around and spotted me, my brother's dark eyes filling with relief. "Marcela. Jesus, you're all right, thank God," he said, coming toward me.

But when his gaze jumped to the man beside me, Andre reared up, stiffened, and took on that badass cop pose I knew so well.

I instantly moved away from Foster's touch. "Andre, what are you doing here?"

He stared down at me, his eyes jumping to the Hotel St. Mark insignia on my polo shirt, then back to my face. I could almost hear his teeth gnash together. "I stopped by to take my baby sister out for brunch to celebrate her graduation."

"You could've called."

He raised his hand, cell phone facing out. "I did. Four times. *And* your house phone. You know how scary it is to have your sister tell you she's in for the night and then she's nowhere to be found the next morning? I was picturing you dead on the road somewhere, Cela."

I winced. "Sorry. I decided to go out."

"And not come home until the next morning, wearing hotel clothes?"

"I really don't think that's any of your business," Foster said, his tone almost bored.

Of course, Pike, who'd stayed behind to grab the mail, chose that moment to step up behind us. "Hey, doc, you forgot your purse in the cab."

I closed my eyes, wishing my brother would just poof into thin air and that this was some waking nightmare.

But when I opened my eyes again, Andre's face had gone red—a feat, considering his skin tone. "Tell me you didn't."

"Andre," Foster said, obviously nonplussed by the imposing force that was my brother. "I suggest you take a breath and stop talking to your sister like she's a child, especially considering the glass house you're about the throw a rock through."

That caught Andre's attention—and mine. I looked between the two of them. Andre's eyes narrowed as he studied Foster. "I know you from somewhere."

Foster smirked. "Yeah, you do." He leaned over and kissed my cheek. "Let's talk later."

I nodded numbly, not sure exactly how these two could possibly know each other or what Foster's comment to Andre had meant. "Sure."

Pike sent me an apologetic smile, handed my purse to me, and then both men disappeared into their apartment, leaving me there with Andre.

The minute the door shut, my fists curled around the plastic bag I was holding. "I cannot believe you just embarrassed me like that. What the hell is wrong with you?"

I shoved past him and stabbed my key into the lock. Andre was right behind me, following me into the apartment like a dark cloud flooding the room. "You had me fucking worried, Marcela. I've been in a near panic trying to find you. And then you walk in, dressed in clothes that aren't yours with not just one but two strange dudes."

"Foster and Pike aren't strangers."

"Foster and . . ." He paused, a light switch seeming to flip on in his brain, and grimaced. "Ah, fuck me."

"What?"

"Nothing. What are you thinking hanging out with guys like that?"

I tossed my keys, purse, and bag onto the kitchen counter. "This is not your business."

"They're grown men, and you're, you're . . ."

"A grown woman, Dre," I said, exasperated. "Despite what you and Papá seem to think. They even let me vote and pay taxes. Can you imagine?"

"Don't be a smartass. You had me ready to call hospitals."

I sighed, the lack of sleep settling on me, and lowered myself onto one of my barstools. My body was still tender, and I tried to cover the inevitable flinch.

Andre's lips went white from pressing them together so hard. "Did those jerks hurt you? Because if they did, I swear—"

"Oh my God," I said, pressing the heel of my hand to my brow bone. "Stop. Of course they didn't. And I am so not discussing this with you."

The last thing I wanted to do was talk about my sex life with my big brother. It was awkward enough growing up, watching girls completely throw themselves at him. And I'd walked in on him in compromising positions more than once not realizing he had a girl over. My parents had willingly let Andre have dates over, and he could use the rec room with the door closed. But when I wanted to even have a guy friend over, it was living room only, parents on guard.

"Look, I'm sorry that you were worried. My phone died, and I didn't have my charger. I didn't think it was a big deal because I wasn't expecting anyone to call this early. But what I do with my personal time is no one's business but mine. How would you feel if I barged into your place demanding details about your love life? Why don't you tell me who slept in *your* bed last night?"

Andre looked away, some strange flicker crossing his features—guilt? But finally he ran a hand over the back of his hair, a telltale sign his anger was deflating. "Fine. You're right. That wasn't fair."

I tipped up my chin. "Thank you. Now can we start over and pretend the last five minutes didn't happen?"

"I'll try." He pulled his phone from the pocket of his jeans and checked the time. "But I think we've missed brunch. I told Evan and Jace to go on without me when I couldn't find you."

"Bummer. I haven't seen those two in a while. Are they engaged yet?"

Andre frowned, a dark curtain falling over his face. "Not officially."

Andre lived with his best friend, Jace. And Evan, Jace's girlfriend, had moved in a few months ago. "You know when they make it official, you're going to have to find a new place. I know you like living with your BFF and all, but you've got to feel like a third wheel now."

He shoved his phone in his pocket, shifting like his clothes had suddenly gotten too tight for his body. "It's complicated."

"Ah, don't do that to yourself, Dre." I slid off the stool and patted his shoulder on my way to the fridge.

"Do what?"

I grabbed two bottles of water and tossed one to him. "I know you've got a crush on Evan. I've seen how you look at her when you don't think anyone's watching."

He unscrewed the cap, his gaze shuttered, and sipped the water. "It's not like that."

I sighed. "I know we just agreed to not meddle in each other's personal lives. But you got one free shot at me, so now I'm taking mine. Don't mess things up with Jace for a girl, all right? Your friendship is more important that that."

"Duly noted." He swigged another sip of the water, then set it on the counter. "Tell you what. How about I let you catch up on sleep and we plan to hang out another time? Things are a little crazy at work right now, so I'm tied up for a while. But we're throwing a little birthday party for Jace's brother, Wyatt, the Friday before you leave. Evan's cooking and everything. You in?"

I bumped the refrigerator door closed with my hip and thanked the heavens that I was going to be able to go crawl in bed instead of socializing on three hours' sleep. "Sounds like a plan."

He smiled and stepped forward, cupping the back of my head and planting a kiss on the crown. "And I guess if you want to bring . . . a friend, you can."

I could tell the offer cost him something. I managed a smirk and ignored the longing ache the suggestion stirred. After this morning, I didn't know if I'd even speak to Foster again. "Thanks. But uh, it's not like that."

Andre closed his eyes briefly and shook his head. "Oh, I wish there was a machine to help you go back in time and un-know things."

I shoved his shoulder. "Grow up, bro. I have."

With a God-give-me-strength sigh, he turned and headed for the door. "Try to stay out of trouble, Marcela."

I gave him my best choir girl smile. "Always."

Foster stretched out on the couch, his head booming and frustration wrapping around him like itchy rope. It was probably a good thing that Pike had gone to sleep in his room, because Foster was spoiling for a fight—an unjustified one—but at this point he didn't really care about details like that. When Pike had put his arms around Cela this morning, Foster had wanted to slug him. He'd also wanted Cela to push Pike away, to come to him.

But instead of any of that happening, Foster had just stood there like an asshole and let it all happen. Cela had gone off to the shower to do devil knows what with his best friend, and he'd stayed there frozen to the spot. For a breath of a moment, Foster had found himself imagining more with Cela. The way she'd described her experience submitting to him had lit something inside him, had awakened the desire to have her under his hand for longer than a night, to show her what that kind of power exchange could really be like, to bring her submission fully to the surface.

But if he'd had any illusions about her even considering something like that, they'd been annihilated the minute she'd left the room with Pike. Last night had been exactly what she'd said—a good time, a way to lose her virginity, a one-off wild night. The whole reason she'd chosen them was because they were low risk. No feelings. No attachment. She was leaving in a few weeks, and he and Pike had made an offer that fit those requirements perfectly.

And now he was going to have to leave it at that. No way was he messing with that rattlesnake of a situation again. He'd tried once before to woo a girl who wanted a vanilla life. Darcy had been submissive, he'd seen it plain as day when they'd played. But she'd only wanted to explore kink for fun—for kicks. She'd had a preacher's daughter upbringing and had wanted to rebel.

Of course, Foster hadn't realized that while he was tumbling into the love abyss like an idiot. Pike had warned him, but he hadn't wanted to hear it. He and Darcy had dated for a year, and he'd been sure she was the one for him, meant to be his. Finally, someone who would stay in his life. He'd thought the only hurdle would be convincing her that she could have everything she wanted even if she fully embraced the submissive role with him. But it'd all been an illusion created by that lonely, hopeful kid that lurked inside him.

On their one-year anniversary he'd offered Darcy a ring and a collar. She'd offered him a good-bye.

Lesson learned.

Foster pressed his thumbs to his forehead, trying to exorcise both the headache and the bad memories, but a loud banging interrupted the effort. "Fuck. Not right now."

But the sharp knocking came again, and Foster pushed himself up and off the couch. He rubbed his hands over his face as he made his way to the door, too mentally drained to face what he knew was going to be on the other side.

He swung the door open and stepped aside, letting the imposing force of Andre Medina stride inside. Foster didn't know Andre personally, had never spoken with him. But he knew *of* him, knew he was in the tight inner circle of Grant Waters—owner of The Ranch, the BDSM resort Foster belonged to. And Foster had watched Andre scene.

"Sure, come on in," Foster said dryly.

Andre spun around, arms crossed, pissed-off cop face in place. "Believe me, this won't take long."

Foster scrubbed a hand over his stubble. "Guess you figured out where we know each other from."

The muscle in Andre's jaw twitched. "The different name threw me, but yes. Ian."

"Outside of those walls, everyone calls me by my last name."

Andre didn't even seem to hear him. "So what's your game?"

Foster walked around the breakfast bar, heading toward the coffee-pot. He didn't have the energy for this conversation without more caffeine. "I don't know what you're asking."

"Your kink, Foster. Is it going after vanilla girls? Because that's about the only reason I could see why you're messing with my baby sister," he said, anger rippling like a deadly undertow below his calm tone.

Foster scooped coffee into the filter and poured the water in, refusing to snap at the bait Andre was waving. Sparring with Cela's overprotective brother wasn't going to get anyone anywhere. And with the foul mood Foster was already in, a fistfight was a distinct possibility if Andre got in his face. Last thing he needed to do was take a swing at a cop.

Foster hit the On button to start the coffee then turned around to face his uninvited house guest.

"I'm a dom. But I'm sure you already figured that out. And no, going after vanilla girls isn't a hobby of mine. Last night wasn't planned. And what happened should, frankly, be none of your goddamned concern."

Andre put his hands on the breakfast bar, palms flat, and leaned forward. "Maybe not, but I'm asking you, man-to-man, to stay away from Marcela. She's leaving soon and doesn't need any complications in her life. She's worked hard and has a nice life waiting for her back home. I know how guys like you—like us—can affect a woman who's innocent to our world. It can be overwhelming and exciting, can make them question what they want. Don't do that to Cela. Have a fling with someone else."

Being told what to do by anyone raised Foster's hackles, but he couldn't deny the truth in Andre's words. Even if Cela had wanted something more than last night, which she obviously didn't, it'd be irresponsible for him to open up that submission, expose it, with only a few weeks together. Discovering that side of yourself brought up a lot of shit, even for a dominant. Coming to terms with those feelings and urges often took time and a support system, someone to guide a person through the pitfalls.

The idea teased at him like the scent of forbidden fruit. He'd love to be the one to lead Cela through that, uncover the layers of submission if last night hadn't been a fluke and that need was truly there. He gripped the counter behind him, trying to get a hold on his quickly derailing thoughts. "You have nothing to worry about. Cela is a great girl, but I'm looking for a long-term sub. I steer clear of vanilla girls. Usually. Like I said, last night wasn't planned."

Andre straightened and nodded. "Good. I'm glad we're on the same page then."

Foster smirked. "So I guess Cela doesn't know anything about your . . . proclivities."

For a brief moment, the hardened-cop act flickered, and Andre's shoulders dipped as if heavy hands were pushing down on them. "No, she doesn't know any of it. She wouldn't understand. *My family* wouldn't understand. And I'd appreciate it if you don't say anything to her."

The coffeepot beeped, but Foster kept his attention on Andre. Foster knew what it was like to have to hide part of yourself. And from what he knew of Andre's situation, the guy was having to hide a helluva lot. "I wouldn't, but Cela may be more understanding than you think."

Frown lines etched his face. "See you around, Foster."

And with that, he was out the door.

The second Medina to walk away from him in a day.

TWELVE

"You okay, boss?"

"Hmm . . ." Foster turned away from the computer screen.

Lindy, his assistant, nodded toward his computer. "You're on the same newspaper article you were on when I stopped in here half an hour ago."

"Oh, right." He rubbed a hand over the back of his neck. "Guess I'm having trouble focusing today."

"Rough weekend?" she asked, setting the take-out lunch he'd ordered on the corner of his desk.

"You could say that." Rough. Amazing. Frustrating.

Lindy lifted a file folder in her other hand and waggled it in the air. "This should cheer you up. They found that little girl in Ohio last night. Scared to death and hungry but totally unharmed. She'd wandered off and gotten lost in the woods outside of her neighborhood. The Home Safe bracelet led them right to her."

"Thank God." A wash of relief went through him. No matter how many times he got that kind of news, each successful outcome was a triumph to be celebrated. And he had to hang on to those because he knew how many similar stories didn't wrap up with that kind of happy ending. "That absolutely does cheer me up."

"The father called in a few minutes ago. He wanted to know what he could do to thank you or help get the word out about our products. He's already mentioned us in their local newspaper."

Foster took the file from Lindy and opened it. The big smile of five-year-old Madison Dore greeted him. He touched the photo, the memory of another little girl always hovering at the edge of his mind. One who hadn't been found. He closed the file quickly. "Tell him there's no need to thank us. But if he really wants to help, he can make a donation of bracelets to a local school or he can do a testimonial for the website."

"Awesome. I'll tell him. And I'll add her picture to the board. That's fifteen this year. And the tenth for the bracelets alone." She did a little fist pump. "Go team!"

He laughed. His assistant's enthusiasm was one of the main reasons he'd hired her. There were often dark days at 4N. The situations they made products for weren't happy ones. So the office needed all the positivity it could get. "Been hitting the coffee hard today?"

Lindy gave a sheepish smile. "Diet Mountain Dew, but yeah, probably need to lay off a bit."

"Go eat something, absorb some of that caffeine." He grabbed the bag of takeout. "I've got an article to read."

"The key is to read left . . . to . . . right," she said, talking slowly like he didn't understand English.

He tossed a ball of paper at her. "Out, minion."

Lindy shut his office door, and he pulled out the roast beef sandwich she'd brought in. But right as he was about to take his first bite, his cell phone rang with a familiar thrashing drumbeat. He sighed and pressed the speaker button on the phone. "Hey."

"Whoa, you actually picked up," Pike said, the sound of car noise in the background. "I tried to catch you before you left this morning, then tried to call."

"I had a lot waiting for me here, had to leave a little early and then got caught up in something." He took a bite of his sandwich, not wanting to have this conversation.

"Uh-huh. You're pissed at me. I get it."

"Hmm?" he asked, the noise muffled by his half-full mouth.

"Don't be a dick. You've been avoiding me since Saturday," Pike said, no ire in his voice. "Look, man, if you didn't want me to touch her again, you should've said something. I would've backed off. You just had to say the word."

Foster set his sandwich down, the bite he'd taken turning to sawdust in his mouth. "That wasn't my place. I don't have any say over her. You touched her, she didn't tell you no. That's that."

"Right. So if I go home today and head over to her place for a little afternoon delight, you're totally cool with that."

His fist clenched around his soda, nearly busting the disposable cup. "Do it and I'll fucking castrate you."

Pike's loud laugh echoed from the speaker. "Man, I love it when I'm right."

Foster grunted. "That's because it's so rare, it's worthy of cele-bration."

"Touché. So have you called her?"

"I checked in with her yesterday just to make sure she was okay."

He sniffed. "Checked on her? What the fuck? Because sex with you is so earth-shattering she needed a follow-up?"

Foster grabbed the phone to take it off speaker and leaned back in his chair with a sigh. "No. Because Cela was a virgin."

"*What*? A . . ." Pike's words trailed off like the term *virgin* was so foreign, he couldn't even speak it aloud. "Holy shit."

"Yeah. I didn't realize it until it was too late."

"Jesus." Foster could picture Pike shaking his head in disbelief. "That chick's fucking brave. Losing your virginity in a three-way? That's a rock-star move right there."

Foster tilted his head back and stared at the ceiling, trying not to think of Cela walking into that bathroom with Pike. He couldn't get the image out of his head. He'd stood there and done nothing even when she'd looked back at him with question marks in her eyes. What an ass-hole. Instead of stepping up and telling her he didn't want her to go, he'd let his ego win. He'd wanted her to turn down Pike, to come to him on her own volition.

"So are you going to take her out again?"

He wanted to. God, did he want to. If nothing else than to give her the night she should've had for her first time. "There's no point. You know I don't date vanilla girls."

"She didn't seem all that vanilla this weekend," Pike lobbed back.

"And she's leaving in a few weeks."

"Yeah, the leaving part kind of sucks," he said, his tone resigned. "But are you just going to ignore what happened? I mean, you took the

NOT UNTIL YOU ‖ 97

chick's virginity, man. Shouldn't there be some sort of something after that? A debriefing or whatever."

Foster snorted. "A debriefing?"

"What? I don't know the fucking term for it. But walking away and pretending it didn't happen is a dick move. Even I know that much." A car door slammed in the background and the connection got fuzzy with the wind. "If you're not going to say something to her . . ."

"I'll take care of it," Foster said, cutting him off, irritated that Pike was pointing out everything that had been driving Foster crazy over the past two days. Like he didn't know it was a shit move that he'd barely managed a few sentences when he'd called to check on Cela the next day, or that he'd changed the time of his run this morning so he wouldn't bump into her.

There was a swift rap on his door. Lindy stuck her head inside. "Sorry to interrupt but there's an Agent Long from the FBI on the line for you."

Foster's grip on his phone tightened, that familiar sick feeling at the mention of a call from the FBI eclipsing his ruminating. Foster only talked to Agent Long about once a year and usually it was to get a no-news update. But Foster had just talked to him a month ago, and the man never called him. "Pike, I've gotta go. Important call."

He hit the Off button and nodded at Lindy. "Put him through."

A few seconds later, Foster picked up his office phone. "Agent Long, what's happened?"

Long didn't waste time with greetings or niceties. "We may have a lead."

The breath gusted from Foster's chest. How long had it been since he'd heard those words? The case had been cold for so long he'd doubted he'd ever hear them again. "What kind of lead?"

"It's not much. But a guard overheard some jailhouse talk this weekend, a name was dropped, a nickname, and some details that seemed to fit the case. The years would work out." He cleared his throat, and there was the sound of shuffling papers. "We're going to go in and question the guy, see if we can get him to give us more. But I wanted to give you a heads-up."

Foster's stomach twisted, the desire to have the knowledge about as strong as the desire to want to cover his ears and never know. "Thanks for calling."

"Do you want me to notify your parents?"

"No," he said quickly. "Until you have something solid, let them be."

"I understand. I'll get in touch when I know more."

"Thank you, Agent Long."

Foster hung up the phone and tossed his sandwich in the trash, his appetite gone and a restless need to do something productive burning through him. Work. That's what he could control. He couldn't control whether or not Agent Long could find what they needed. He couldn't control that his parents probably wouldn't take his call even if he tried to contact them. And he couldn't control how things had gone down with Cela Friday night. But this office, the people in it, the services they provided—that he had ultimate authority over.

He pressed a button on his phone. "Lindy, let the R & D department know that I want a briefing in an hour on where we're at with the smart-phone app."

"An hour? But, sir, they said they're not quite ready to . . ."

"Tell them to figure it out." He hung up the phone, feeling a shred better.

Taking the reins always moved things back into place inside himself, whether it be at work or behind closed doors. He didn't like variables and unknowns. Didn't like surprises. And after all the surprises he'd experienced with Cela Friday night, he was desperate to do something that would put his world back into the right boxes.

He didn't need a temptation like Cela shuffling everything around in his brain.

He'd talk to her. That was the right thing to do.

But it'd only be to say good-bye.

I sat on the top of the picnic bench in the grassy area next to my building, enjoying the sunshine and the very un-Texas-like seventy-degree day, and threw the rubber ball Gerald had handed me. Gerald's Maltese mix, Sammi, took off like she'd been launched from a cannon to chase down the ball, her tail wagging so hard it was only a blur. I grinned. "I love that it never gets old for dogs. Same game over and over and they're happy."

Gerald smiled as he watched Sammi tumble in the grass when she pounced on the ball. "Yeah, she loves running. I feel bad that she's cooped up most of the day. I'm hoping to be able to rent a house with a yard one day soon."

"You could always look for a dog walker or a sitter for her while you're at work. A lot of college students do it for cheap."

"Do it for cheap, huh?" He turned to me, his blond hair falling into his eyes and the corner of his mouth curling. "You volunteering?"

For some reason, the question made the back of my neck prickle. I shook off the odd feeling. "Nah, I'm leaving in a few weeks, so I'm not a good candidate. But I can give you a few names of my classmates if you'd like. My friend, Bailey, has done it for a few families."

"Leaving?" Gerald's smile dropped. "Well, damn, I didn't know that. I'm going to have to take you to dinner before you head out. Thank you for all the advice you've given me about Sammi."

"Uh, I—"

"She can't do that," a firm male voice said.

I startled at the sudden interruption, then spun around to find its source.

Gerald turned with me, scowling. "Excuse me?"

Foster stood behind the picnic table, arms crossed, laptop bag slung over his shoulder, and a fierce expression on his face. "You asked her out. I said she can't go."

I stared at him, dumbfounded.

"And who the hell are you?" Gerald asked, an edge creeping into my neighbor's normally affable demeanor.

"Not your concern." His gaze slid to me. "Come on, Cela."

I reared up at his bossy tone. All these days with barely a phone call and now he was going to order me around? Screw that. "I'm playing with Gerald's dog."

Foster's mouth thinned. "I think he wants you to play with more than that."

My jaw fell open, and Gerald jumped to his feet. "The fuck's your problem, asshole?"

Gerald stalked toward Foster, but Foster didn't move. He simply stared the coldest stare I'd ever seen a person give another. Even my blood chilled, and the look wasn't directed at me.

"Yes, please," Foster said smoothly as Gerald neared. "Give me a reason to hit you. I'd so enjoy that."

Gerald halted, clearly disconcerted. "Look, man. I don't know what your problem is, but don't fucking threaten me. You don't know who you're dealing with."

"I know exactly who I'm dealing with." He pinned me with his gaze. "But there will be no problem as long as Cela comes with me and you don't ever talk to her again."

"She doesn't have to go—"

"Hold up." This was going downhill fast. Sammi was barking at my feet, and Foster looked as if he could truly kill Gerald. I hopped off the table, my hands out in front of me. "Both of y'all just calm down. I'll go." I looked to Foster. "I'll go, all right?"

Gerald straightened. "If this guy—"

"It's fine. He's a friend." I stepped next to Foster, and he immediately grasped my elbow, as if afraid I'd change my mind. I had no idea what was going on with him, but the last thing I wanted was a brawl outside the apartment complex. "I'll see you later. Bye, Sammi."

The dog did a little spin and yapped happily in reply.

"Let's go." Foster turned me with him without another word and led me toward the building.

But I wasn't letting him get away without an explanation. As soon as we cleared the lobby doors, I turned toward him, shaking his grip. "What the hell was that? Have you lost your mind?"

"You don't need to talk to that scum," he said, the disgust clear on his face before he turned to climb the stairs.

I followed behind him, seeing red. "Excuse me? Did I miss the part where you have the right to tell me who I can talk to?"

He spun around, two steps higher than me, expression grim. "Gerald Mondale is a registered sex offender. He used to be a high school teacher until a freshman girl came forward with molestation charges. He got early parole on a technicality."

My stomach dipped. "Oh my God."

Foster climbed up the rest of the stairs, and I trailed behind in stunned silence. Gerald? The neighbor I'd chatted with almost weekly about his sweet little dog? When we both reached the hallway, Foster turned back to face me. "I know I don't have the right to tell you who to talk to. But when I saw you with him, heard him make a pass at you, I wanted to choke the words right out of him. Promise me you'll stay away from him."

My throat was knotted and dry, the post-danger rush of adrenaline filling my veins. But I managed to nod. "Sure, yeah, I promise."

He gave a swift, matching nod. "Good. Thank you."

I stared at him for a few long moments, the from-a-distance crush I'd had for him before Friday night now morphing into a desperate longing inside my chest. I wanted to step forward, press against him, loosen that tie from around his neck and wipe that tense expression off his face. But everything about him said I wasn't invited. I tore my gaze away to glance toward my apartment door. "Well, I better get going."

"Cela . . ." he said, his gentle tone tearing into me.

God, why did that make me want to cry? What the hell was wrong with me? I'd seen Pike in the hallway earlier when I was heading out, and it hadn't been like this at all. I forced my gaze back to his. "So is this where we have the awkward 'let's still be friends' conversation?"

He frowned. "It's not like that."

"Right. So if I asked you over for dinner . . ."

He glanced away, his guilt like a fog invading the small hallway.

I shook my head, more disgusted with myself for asking the question than his response. "See you around, Foster."

Before he could respond, if he had even planned to respond, I unlocked my door and shut him out.

The stupid tears came then.

So much for not getting my feelings involved.

Epic, one-night-stand fail.

THIRTEEN

Foster lay in his bed in the dark, staring holes into the ceiling. The fan was on high, the chain *clink-clink-clinking* against the base, but he was still too hot and restless to sleep. He'd heard Cela come into her room about an hour earlier. The TV had gone on for a while, then off again. So he was all too aware that she was right there, beneath the sheets, barely a foot behind his head.

It'd been two days since he'd done everything wrong in the hallway. Now he was convinced she was avoiding him as much as he was avoiding her. It was juvenile of him. He'd never avoided a woman he'd slept with. Not even Darcy after she'd ripped his goddamned guts out. He'd had awkward before, but never had he experienced the brutal assault on his restraint that Cela caused. Being anywhere near her flipped all his fucking switches. When he'd seen her with that scumbag, Gerald, he'd been ready to kill the guy for even daring to breathe on Cela. He hadn't even had time to form full thoughts—all he'd seen was red. It'd taken all he had to give Cela a chance to come willingly instead of simply picking her up and hauling her over his shoulder so he could get her safe as soon as possible.

Then in the hallway, she'd gone pale, shaken by the news of Gerald's background. Everything about her had called to Foster. He'd pictured himself crowding her space, kissing away that fear, and dragging her into his apartment to make her forget about it all. But he'd stayed glued to the spot and had turned down her invite to come over. His knuckles had ached from clenching his fists so hard to hold himself back. After she'd gone into her apartment, he'd stood in the hallway for a full five minutes, staring at her fucking door.

Pathetic.

He rolled onto his side, yanking the sheet off his legs and closing his eyes, trying to will himself to sleep. But the loud *ding* of his phone had him lifting his head. "What the hell?"

He grabbed for his phone, pawing around in the dark, and flipped it over. A text message. He sat up on his elbow.

> For the love of God please turn off whatever is making that annoying sound.

He blinked, once, twice, shocked at the name of the sender. He peeked at the wall behind him, then tapped a message back.

> Sorry. Crappy fan. Will turn off.

He climbed out of bed and hit the switch. His phone dinged again.

> Thx. Hope I didn't wake you.

He sank back onto his pillows, hearing the words as if they were said in that spice-laced voice of hers. He typed back.

> No. Can't sleep.

He held the phone in his hands, wondering if she was going to respond, half hoping she would, but knowing this was merely a neighborly transaction—the modern equivalent to banging on someone's wall and telling them to keep the racket down.

When nothing appeared on the screen, he reached over to set the phone back on the bedside table. But as soon as he put it down, the perky noise filled the silence again.

> Count sheep?

He chuckled and tapped back a message.

> Those bastards fell asleep hours ago. Got tired of all that jumping.

There was a soft sound from her side of the wall. Had he made her laugh? The thought warmed him. His phone dinged again.

I could sing you to sleep.

He stared at the words, not registering them for a moment. It was so out of the blue that he didn't know how to react. He typed back:

U sing?

Former choir girl. :)

Of course you are.

Watch the virgin jokes, smartass.

He laughed out loud, knowing she could probably hear it on her side of the wall. Somehow being in the dark, having that thin barrier of drywall and wood between them made it all easier, lifted some of the weight from the last time they'd seen each other.

I'd love to hear u sing.

There was a long pause before her reply, but when it came, it was a simple one.

OK.

He could almost sense her taking a deep breath, building up her nerve. Then, as if putting a needle to a record, the slightly muted sound of her voice leaked through the walls. A low, haunting melody filled his ears, and he involuntarily closed his eyes so that he wouldn't miss any of it. He couldn't pick out the words, but it was vaguely familiar, something he'd heard before. And it was beautiful, her voice strong and unbroken, a sound befitting the nickname he'd given her—angel.

And he knew this was supposed to be putting him to sleep, soothing him. But instead, he felt his body prickling with each note, awareness brewing in his nerve endings as her voice strummed through him, stroking his senses. He could picture her there, sitting up in bed, wearing probably next to nothing because it had to be hot in her room as well, and belting out that song. A song that, though he couldn't hear the lyrics, spoke of longing and need. Loneliness.

Those feelings bled through him, mirroring his own, and tightness built in his chest—like rope being wrapped around him and cinched. His body went unbearably hot. Too much more and she was going to drive him to middle-of-the-night madness. The sexy, throaty sound of her last notes drifted through the barrier between them, and he reached up to press his palm against the wall, feeling the faint vibration of her words.

When all had gone silent again, he opened his eyes and took a breath before lifting his phone again.

That was beautiful, Cela. *in awe*

Thx. Did it make u sleepy?

It made me hard. But of course he wasn't going to type that.

Yes.

Liar.

He ran his thumb along the side of the phone, knowing he shouldn't, but unable to stop himself.

Ur right. It made me want you.

Full minutes passed as he stared at the screen. She wasn't going to respond. He'd given her the cold shoulder two days ago and now was making a pass at her. He *was* a fucking dick. He was about to type back an apology when his phone dinged.

I've heard that's good for sleep too.

He rubbed a hand over his face and climbed out of bed with a groan—paced. But his good sense and self-control had left the building fifteen minutes ago. Hell, who was he kidding? Those two things hadn't been around since the moment he'd invited Cela over to their apartment. The girl undid him.

There was a soft tap from her side. He stopped at the spot on the wall where it'd come from and leaned his head against it, imagining her mirroring him on the other side, staring back at him with as much longing as he knew resided in his eyes right now. He lifted his phone.

Invite me over, Cela.

Another long stretch of a pause, then:

Isn't that against one-night-stand rules?

I'm good at making rules not following them.

His phone sat silent. He rolled to the side until his bare back was against the wall. His heart was thumping hard against his ribs, everything in him willing her to respond. He had no idea what had gotten into him. It was like being a fucking teenager all over again, waiting for the girl he liked to call him back. This wasn't his style. But all he knew was that one time with Cela hadn't been enough. This was a bad idea. A selfish one.

What the hell was he planning to do with her anyway? He wasn't even sure he remembered how to have vanilla sex.

His phone dinged.

I don't want to follow them either.

He tossed the phone on the bed.

This was stupid. I was stupid. Stupid. Stupid. Stupid.

What in the hell had made me think texting Foster tonight was a good idea? I'd lain in bed for over an hour, listening to that incessant fan noise through the wall, unable to sleep because I couldn't stop replaying Friday night. The way Foster had talked to me, how he'd felt against me, the sensations he'd coaxed out my body. I'd lived my whole damn life without having sex, and now I'd had it once and couldn't stop thinking about it. About *him*.

And freaking hell—if I wasn't mistaken, I'd just made a midnight booty text. I flipped my phone in my hand over and over again as I walked the perimeter of my apartment. It'd been at least ten minutes since I'd sent the last text. I'd managed to brush my teeth and pull on a pair of boxer shorts to pair with my SPCA charity walk T-shirt, but that was about as much prep as I could manage. Some seductress I'd make.

And this was a terrible idea on so many levels. First, I was sending the message to Foster that I was the kind of girl who'd make late-night hookup calls. And second, I'd already been struggling with my feelings about Friday night. Touching him again was only going to make it worse. But I couldn't walk away yet. Even when he'd been hauling me away from Gerald, acting like an overbearing tyrant, I'd wanted to freaking melt at his feet.

God, how fucking lame. Who was this person? I didn't act like this. I'd never lost my shit over a guy.

Maybe this was just how sex affected people. Maybe that's why my friends got so insane when they were pursuing someone new. But somehow I couldn't bring myself to believe it. Even though I'd been a virgin, I'd dated a few guys here and there. And the things I'd done with them had felt absolutely nothing like being with Foster. Everything seemed to be amplified with him—bathed in neon and pulsing color. I couldn't turn off the desire.

I freaking *craved* him.

The sharp rap on my door made me yelp. I slapped my hand over my mouth, hoping to God he hadn't heard that, and made my way to the door. After one, two, three breaths, I swung it open. All the oxygen I'd sucked in whooshed out of me. Foster stood there as disheveled as I'd ever seen him—black hair sticking up in a few places and falling over his forehead, a five-o'clock shadow turned full stubble, and his T-shirt wrinkled.

I'd never, ever wanted to touch someone so damn much.

"You should never open your door without the chain on, especially at night," he said in a serious tone.

I blinked at the random comment, still breathless from the fact that he was really here. "I knew it was you."

He stepped forward, filling up the doorway, and put his hands on my shoulders. "Always double-check."

"Right," I said, still a little foggy brained.

"Promise me."

"I promise." At that moment, I would've pretty much promised him anything—money, sex, my firstborn child—anything as long as his hands stayed on me and he kept looking at me like that.

He nodded and without another word, backed me up into the apartment, kicking the door shut behind him. His eyes devoured me in one long, sweeping glance.

Self-consciousness swamped me. "Sorry, I didn't get a chance to change. I don't really have anything that . . ." *Is sexy. Worthy. Grown-up.* "Isn't this."

"Hush, Cela," he said, his voice like a warm gust in bitter winter. "Never apologize for how you look. I've spent two hours lying in bed, unable to sleep or cool off because I was imagining you on the other side of the wall looking just like this."

"Sloppy?"

"Fuckable."

"Oh." My body went hot all over, his crudeness pressing some unknown button inside me.

He closed his eyes and took a deep breath before opening them again. I got the sense he was reeling himself back in. "Sorry."

"For what?" I whispered, my brain still humming from the previous comment.

"Never mind."

Then I realized what he was saying. "Please. Don't censor yourself because of me. I'm inexperienced but not innocent."

He stepped closer and cupped the back of my neck, the firm touch sending branching bolts of awareness through me. "You *are* innocent, angel. More than you even realize because you don't even know what you don't know. But God help me if that doesn't make me want to do really, really bad things to you."

I swallowed hard, every nerve in my body standing at attention, begging him. "Show me."

Something flashed in those blue eyes, predatory, but he hid it quickly and brushed a soft kiss over my lips. "Not tonight, angel. Tonight I want to show you what a first time should be like."

FOURTEEN

Foster swept my legs right out from under me before I had a chance to process what he'd said. One second his lips were on mine, the next I was cradled against his chest, and he was moving toward my bedroom. His heartbeat was a hard, steady thump against my side—utterly calm—whereas mine was trying to crack a rib and tear through my chest.

He turned both of us in the hallway and pushed my bedroom door open with his foot. I'd left a lamp on and had hastily made the bed, but I still cringed, knowing there was a pile of dirty laundry in the corner and boxes waiting to be packed stacked against the wall. It definitely wasn't an opulent setting like the room at the Hotel St. Mark. "I'm sorry I didn't get a chance to clean up."

Foster's gaze dipped down to me, amused. "First rule of first times—they usually occur in less-than-romantic surroundings. It's part of the deal. But I love this room. Red. I never would've guessed you'd pick such a bold color."

I smiled. "Maybe I'm more daring than you give me credit for."

He set me down on the bed and cocked an eyebrow. "Angel, you went to a hotel room with two older, obviously demanding guys to lose your virginity in a threesome. I haven't met a girl with more guts than that."

I leaned back on my elbows to enjoy the glorious view as he tugged off his T-shirt. Foster was in my room, getting naked. My brain could hardly process that. "I'm not that brave. I didn't sleep with Pike."

Foster paused, his head out of the shirt but his arms still wrapped in it. "Hold up. You *didn't*?"

I attempted a casual shrug even though absolutely no part of me felt casual or relaxed right now. "We just ended up chatting in the bathroom while we took turns showering."

Foster didn't smile, didn't comment, but his eyes glinted with something that made my stomach flip. He finished tugging off his shirt and tossed it aside, then he was crawling onto the bed, an imposing figure looming over me—one I'd lain in this very bed and pictured above me more times than I'd ever admit to.

The cool material of his athletic pants brushed my bare legs as he insinuated a knee between my tightly clenched thighs. His dark hair fell across his forehead as his eyes crinkled around the corners and the hard length of his erection brushed against my hip. "Relax, angel. I'm not going to make demands on you this time or hurt you."

"You didn't hurt me," I said, my words hardly a whisper. I was breathing too hard, heady with the smell of his skin, to manage much else. "Not on purpose."

He lowered his head, finding the curve of my neck and kissing me there. The soft press of his mouth made my nipples go hard against my T-shirt. "I hit you, Cela. Hard enough to raise welts. And believe me, it was very much on purpose."

I shivered as he nipped at my collarbone. "I don't remember the pain."

Just the pleasure. The grind-my-brain-into-useless-bits pleasure.

He lifted up, his elbows braced alongside me, and gave me a searching look before the veil slid over his expression again. "Are you still sore from the other night?"

I knew he wasn't asking about the spanking this time. I reached up and looped my arms around his neck, relishing the freedom to not just look but touch him. "Totally recovered."

His smile was slow, wicked. "Good. In that case, you have far too many clothes on."

He lifted me up a bit and eased my T-shirt over my head, then let me fall back to the bed. His pupils went black in the lamplight as he gazed down at me and drew the tip of his finger around one of my nipples. I moaned at the featherlight touch.

"I love how sensitive you are," he said, offering the same gentle touch to the other side. "The slightest touch makes you shiver and flush. It's beautiful to watch."

I almost admitted that even a look from him made me shiver, but I knew revealing how much he affected me would only make me look like some girl with a mad crush. Hell, I *was* a girl with a mad crush. "You're good at the touching."

He laughed softly before leaning down to take my mouth in a long, languid kiss. His bare chest pressed against mine, the light dusting of hair teasing my sensitive skin, and his lips took command of mine. Unlike the urgent hunger of our first few kisses together, this one was like a lazy summer night, making everything go slow and warm inside me. He tasted of toothpaste, and I smiled against his mouth at the thought of us both rushing into the bathroom after the text message to erase all signs of midnight breath. Somehow I found the humanness of that comforting. Here in my bedroom he wasn't the untouchable sophisticated businessman, just Foster—a guy who was maybe trying to impress me as much as I was him.

But I couldn't hold on to the thought for long because Foster's hands were cupping and kneading my breasts, and his tongue was sliding along mine in a way that had moisture gathering fast between my thighs. I lifted my hips against his, and his erection pressed hard against me. He groaned into the kiss, biting my bottom lip. His fingers dug into my ribs, hard enough to make me gasp.

His grip instantly released, and he broke away from the kiss, breathless. "Sorry."

"It's okay." I slid my hands into his hair. Every part of him that pressed against me was tense, as if he was the only thing standing between me and some avalanche. "Please, don't stop."

He turned his head into my palm and kissed it. "Not a chance."

He grasped my wrist and trailed kisses down my inner arm until he reached my shoulder and gave it a gentle bite. I closed my eyes and worried I might simply sink into the sheets and never get out of bed. As long as he kept doing what he was doing, I couldn't imagine anything worth getting dressed for again. I wanted to stay here, beneath him, feeling his mouth on mine, his body molded against me.

Foster's mouth worked down over my sternum, touching and tasting and teasing. Then his lips were closing over a nipple, sucking firmly enough to make sharp bolts of pleasure shoot downward and make my clit throb—as if the erogenous zones were connected by some invisible wire. I shifted restlessly beneath him, and he clamped a hand over my thigh. His tongue flicked my nipple again. "Stay still, angel. Let me enjoy you."

"I'm trying," I said, desperation lacing my voice. "Maybe you should've tied me down or something."

His head lifted, his gaze dark when it met mine. "Don't tempt me."

My vocal cords seemed to twist and knot, that dangerous look of his not unlike the scary one he'd given Gerald. Only instead of this one chilling me, it made me burn. "Yes, sir."

His eyebrow lifted. "I didn't ask you to call me that tonight."

"What?" My mind scrambled for a moment. Then I realized what had rolled off my tongue—some weird automatic response. *Sir.* "Oh, right, sorry."

His jaw twitched and so did his cock, right against my thigh. "Lie back and relax. One rule I'm breaking about first times tonight is that you get to come. Often."

Before the *oh* even slipped past my lips, he dragged my boxers down my legs, leaving me in my white cotton bikini underwear. I remembered too late that I probably should've switched those for something sexier—not that I had anything really impressive. But before I had time to stress about it, I saw the heat flare in Foster's eyes. He dragged a knuckle along the front of my underwear, the material clinging to my wet skin. "You're so fucking sexy, Cela. Even more so because you have no idea."

He probably said that to all the girls—an experienced guy who knew how to say the right thing. But somehow I couldn't find it in myself to care. With the way he was looking at me, I *felt* fucking sexy. Powerful. "You're not so bad yourself. Though I have a feeling you know exactly how crazy you drive women."

He grinned, unrepentant. "Women? Or you?"

I licked my lips. "Me."

He hooked two fingers in the waistband of my panties and slid them down, leaving me completely bare while he still wore a low-slung pair of black track pants. "Believe me. The feeling's mutual. All those nights you made those sexy sounds on this side of the wall . . . I can't even tell you what that did to me."

The corner of my mouth lifted. "I probably have some idea. Remember, I've listened to you, too. Though, your noises weren't always solo like mine."

His eyes lifted to mine and darkened, as he ran gentle hands along my thighs. "Did that bother you?"

I wanted to look away but couldn't. I also wanted to say no and brush off the question, but I couldn't do that either. That stare of his was like feeding me truth serum, making it impossible to lie. "Part of me was jealous, though I had no right to be."

"Hmm," he said, his touch tracking lower, closer to where I most needed to be touched. "And the other part of you?"

Heat spread up my neck. "The other part of me was turned on, picturing it all. Picturing you."

"Want to know a secret?" Two long fingers slid inside me, making me gasp with pleasure. "I knew you could hear us."

My eyelids fluttered shut, his stroking fingers making it impossible to concentrate. "You didn't care."

The bed dipped as he situated himself between my thighs, all while continuing to touch deep inside me. "Oh, angel, I cared. I liked knowing you were listening—probably a little too much."

His tongue slid along my folds, making me arch against his mouth. God, how was I supposed to form sentences when he was doing that? "You liked to torture me?"

He chuckled against my skin, his soft puffs of breath making my damp skin tingle and tighten. "Torture's a favorite pastime of mine."

He was torturing me right now, that talented mouth of his hovering right above my needy flesh. I tried to lift my hips upward, and he held me firm against the bed with his free hand. But before I could let loose a whimper of protest, he lowered his head, and his tongue was back on me, his fingers pumping inside me in time with the hot assault of his mouth.

"Oh, God," I whispered, the tide rising inside me like a flash flood. I grabbed fistfuls of his hair and canted my hips against him, riding the growing waves of sensation. How could he bring me to the brink so fast? Everything inside me felt ready to crack open already. I squeezed my eyes shut, trying to breathe through it, but when he curled his fingers inward and sucked my clit between his lips, light flashed behind my eyelids and a sharp cry burst from me. He held on to me with his free hand, keeping my orgasm going until I thought I'd die from the intensity of sensation. Then he was easing away and letting me sink back into the bed.

I lifted my heavy lids. He was there between my knees, smiling like a wicked god—beautiful and dangerous. He brought his glistening fingers to his mouth and sucked them clean. The move made my still throbbing sex, clench. "You're good at the torture and the rewards."

He slid his wet finger along my bottom lip. "Both can be fun. And maybe I would've felt a little guilty about you having to listen to me had I not heard you getting off whenever I was done with someone else. You're a dirty little voyeur, Cela Medina."

The words fell over me, chilling some of the bloom of warmth from the orgasm. *Dirty.* That inevitable stab of humiliation washed over me. He was right. What was wrong with me? The guy I liked had been screwing other women on the other side of the wall, and even through the jealousy, I hadn't been able to stop my body's reaction. Listening would make my skin flush, my panties wet, and I wouldn't be able to sleep until I touched myself. "God, you must've thought I was pathetic."

His grip on my hip tightened, displeasure marking his features. "Cela..."

I put my hands over my face, unable to handle that judgmental stare right now. The glow of orgasm was fading fast, and the reckless abandon of being too turned on to care shut down. Suddenly, the truth of the situation was there, swooping in. And as if it'd been lying in wait to claim me after all of the crazy crap I'd done since graduation night, shame enveloped me. Once again, I was fourteen and in the rec room at my parents' house, my mother having a conniption because she'd caught me looking at a naughty site on the Internet. The words *depraved, perverted,* and *sinful* being thrown my way. I'd been dragged to the confession booth at church before the sun had set that day, my mother's words ringing in my ears. *What were you thinking, Marcela? Imagine if your father had seen.*

And I'd felt wrong, so very wrong, for not just looking but also liking what I saw, feeling my body stir and heat at the scenes portrayed. It'd been the first time I'd felt separate from that nice, obedient girl I'd been raised to be—different and other. Bad.

I tried to roll from beneath Foster, but he slapped my thigh with a sharp pop. I gasped, the pain snapping me out of my memory and freezing me in place. But still, I couldn't face him.

"Look at me, Cela," Foster commanded.

I shook my head, my hands staying over my face.

He grabbed my wrists and pried my hands away, pinning them alongside my head. His face was inches from mine when I forced my eyes open. "Don't you dare be embarrassed."

"Foster, please, I can't." I focused over his right shoulder, unwilling to meet his eyes.

He released one of my wrists and cupped my jaw—none too gently—guiding my gaze back to his. The firm grip both shocked and focused me all at once. "Listen to me. You will *not* lie here and feel ashamed. That's unacceptable, angel."

I blinked, stunned—both at the ferocity of his tone and the instant *oh yes* melting reaction of my body under his. God, what the hell was wrong with me? He was pissed and pinning me down, and I was getting hotter?

"Of course I never thought you were pathetic. I thought—think—you're the sexiest damn woman I've ever seen. *I'm* a voyeur, an exhibitionist, and a laundry list of other things that would probably make most people want to lock me up in a padded room. *I* should be the one worrying that I'm going to freak you out with the things that get me going. So don't you dare apologize for what turns you on. Ever." His thumb grazed my parted lips, a glimmer of gentleness despite his firm hold. "You understand?"

I closed my eyes, trying to find my breath and my voice. "Yes."

He let out a breath and released my jaw. "Open your eyes, Cela."

I complied, finding his dark blue stare warm and determined in the lamplight.

He took the wrist he'd pinned down and brought my arm down in between us. He pressed my palm along the heat of his erection through the soft material of his pants. Instinctively, I closed my fingers around its hard length, need firing in me anew. "This is what you do to me. Feel how much I want you. You're not pathetic, you're maddening."

The words wrapped around me, soothing the vulnerable places that had cracked open and stoking the embers of my desire for him. Somehow Foster knew exactly what to say and do to bring me back from the brink of panicking and reminding me that the only one judging me was me. I stroked along his erection, the heat of his skin searing me even through the fabric of his pants, and felt the shudder go through him— the quiet rumble of his own desire radiating outward and making the muscles of his arms and chest flex and ripple above me.

"What gets you going, Foster?" I asked softly, desperate to know what he was holding back, what he thought would freak me out. "What's on your list?"

His smile was rueful as he lifted up, shucked his pants, and pulled a condom out of the pocket before tossing them to the side. "Right now, number one is to fuck you until you make those noises I love to hear so much."

"Good plan," I said, a little breathless as I watched him tear open the condom packet and roll the latex over his length with deft fingers. I didn't know if I'd ever get over seeing him naked. No man should be allowed to be that gorgeous. It was unfair, really, an embarrassment of riches that he was smart and successful on top of that. But despite the mouthwatering view, I didn't miss his deflection of my question. "But you're not going to tell me the rest of your list, are you?"

He braced on his elbows over me, his gaze gentle. "I'm just your one-night stand, angel. There's no reason to go there."

"Is it that bad?"

But instead of answering, he was kissing me again—a deep and passionate takeover of my sensory system, blotting out my thoughts and questions and replacing them with only awareness of skin on skin and my need for him. In every stroke of his tongue, every caress, I could feel that this was it, the last time we'd touch this way. I wrapped my arms around his back, holding on with everything I had, and opened my body to him.

With sure movements, he grasped the underside of my knee, lifting it and positioning himself at my entrance. Before I could take in a breath or prepare for the pain, he was pushing inside me. But instead of the sharp agonizing seconds of our first time, the stretch of my body around him, that sense of fullness, sent intense pleasure snaking up my spine. I groaned, my nails digging into his back.

"I second that," he said, releasing my earlobe from between his teeth. "You okay?"

"Yes," I said, arching up to take more of him inside me. "I'm so very, very okay."

He laughed softly against the curve of my neck and rocked his hips back to thrust with a little more strength this time. I gasped in pleasure. "Things only get better after that whole virginity thing is out of the way."

"So I've heard," I said on panted breaths.

But as he moved inside me, murmuring both sweet and dirty things against my skin and touching me in ways that made every part of me light on fire, I knew one thing for sure. I'd better enjoy the moment because the words were a lie.

Nothing was going to be better than this.

Or him.

And hours later, when I stirred from the exhausted sleep I'd fallen into after Foster had dragged out every last ounce of pleasure I was capable of, I could barely make myself roll over to see the inevitable. The other side of my bed—empty.

In the center of the wrinkled sheets where he'd lain was a small square of torn-edged paper. I reached out to flip it over. Familiar handwriting stared back at me.

Never Have I Ever.

It was my list with all the items scratched off.

Foster had given me my fantasies. Now we were done.

FIFTEEN

I balanced on my tiptoes on the ladder, trying to cut in the paint near the ceiling. Why I had ever thought I *needed* to have this room maroon in the first place was a wonder. When I'd moved into the apartment, the white walls had seemed as stark as the labs I spent my days in at school. I couldn't handle all that bright white and had tackled my first DIY project to make my bedroom cozier. But the apartment manager had told me that whatever painting I did, I'd have to undo when I moved out or be charged an extra two months' rent to fix it. And of course, the guy at the paint store hadn't told me that when it came time to cover up red, it would take an act of God and a truckload of primer and paint.

So the tail end of the week had been spent busting my ass at the clinic during the day and then coming home to work in a fume-filled room, watching my walls go from maroon to red to Pepto-Bismol pink. Now it was Saturday, and I hoped after one more coat, it'd start to resemble white again. My shoulders and arms ached, but I almost welcomed the physical distraction. Since the last night with Foster, I'd been able to think of little else than the way he'd looked at me when he'd kissed me good night—the good-bye eyes.

He'd called me once since then to apologize for leaving before I'd woken up that morning. He'd explained that he had to be at the office early that day and didn't want to wake me since we'd stayed up so late. The phone call had been light and casual on the surface. But awkward as shit in the undercurrent. There'd been no mention of the note he'd left and no offer to get together for any reason in the future. The message had been clear. We weren't anything more than two people who'd had a good time together.

And I refused to let myself turn it into anything more. The reason why he'd probably freaked over the virginity thing in the first place was because he feared I'd get all clingy and needy afterward. No way was I even showing a hint of that. No sirree. I was a strong, sexually liberated woman who could have a good time and walk away unscathed.

Right.

A door slammed on the other side of my bedroom wall, startling me. My hand flinched and a blotch of paint hit the ceiling. "Dammit."

I grabbed a rag that I'd hung on the ladder and stretched to blot the paint. The ceiling had been white at one time, but the aged gray it'd become was definitely not a match with the new paint. *Sonofabitch.* Now I was going to have to paint that, too.

Music cranked up on the other side of the wall as Foster moved around the room. I tossed the rag down to the drop cloth below in frustration. Great, just what I needed—the torture of picturing Foster coming home from work and stripping off one of those tailored suits of his. Tie unknotting, buttons flicking open, zipper lowering . . . that beautiful naked body striding across the room.

My insides clenched, and I had to grab on to the top of the ladder to keep myself steady. Another door sounded and heavy footsteps. Usually I couldn't hear all of this so well, but I sensed Foster stomping around a bit, maybe mad. Did he have a bad day at work?

I shook my head. Not my concern. *Focus.* I dipped my brush in the paint can and rose up on my toes again, doing my best to reach the last corner and block out thoughts of the guy on the other side of the wall. But as I stretched one last inch, the ladder teetered beneath me.

"Shit!" I grasped for the wall, something, but it was a lost cause. My weight had pitched too far to the left, and I was going down. My shoulder crashed against the sticky wall, followed by the clanging ladder and the half-full can of paint. I landed half on my bed, then slid to the floor, pulling the drop cloth with me. All of my air left me with an *oof,* and paint spread along the floor like a creeping white oil spill.

I closed my eyes, trying to catch my breath and not cry. I'd gotten lucky on the fall, but the mess all around me was like ripping the last shred of fabric in my I'm-totally-together sham. The move. Graduation.

New job. New guy. Losing my virginity. All of it piled on me, threatening to smother me with the weight of it all.

But I wasn't allowed to wallow long. A loud rapping sound came from the other side of the apartment, yanking me from my spiral of doom.

"Cela!"

The booming voice was all-too familiar, and I almost couldn't bring myself to go face it. But girl-who's-okay-with-it-all wouldn't be afraid to answer the door. That girl would be all cool and "Hey, what's up?"

So with only a thread of dignity intact, I wiped off my hands and pushed up from the floor. I stepped around the mess and made my way to the front door, where Foster was banging again, calling for me.

I pulled the door open, realizing too late how I must look, and found a frantic-eyed Foster. He stepped inside and put his hands on my shoulders, his gaze scanning me as if searching for blood. "Good God, what the hell was that? Are you okay?"

I shoved my hair out of my face, trying to stay nonchalant even though the simple act of him touching me had my heart flipping over. "I'm okay. Just klutzy. I uh . . . fell off a ladder."

He touched the side of my hair. "Christ, did you hit your head? Hurt anything? From my side of the wall, it sounded like the whole room collapsed."

I should say yes, that I did hit my head. Then I could explain away the ridiculous urge to kiss him, to tuck myself into his embrace. "No, luckily my ass took most of the impact," I said, attempting a joke. "Good thing for the extra cushion."

A little flicker of something lit the center of those blue irises of his, and I couldn't hold the eye contact any longer. He let his touch drop away, and for the first time since I'd opened the door, I noticed he was wearing leather pants. *Leather? In June?*

But as my gaze drifted down, and I took in the way the pants hugged him just right, outlining what I knew lay beneath them, thoughts of weather evaporated from my mind. I wet my lips, tasted paint. Terrific.

He chuckled and wiped a smudge of white from my cheek. "You do realize that you're supposed to get paint on the *walls*, right?"

I looked up at him again, arms crossed. "Are you seriously going to kick a girl when she's down?"

The corner of that sensuous mouth curled. "No, I'm not quite that mean."

That statement had a layer to it I didn't want to peel back, but my mind couldn't help but wander there. I shook off the illicit images that flickered through my mind like a movie reel. Foster being a little rough with me that last night together, Foster demanding things of me the night in the hotel.

I cleared my throat. "Well, I'm fine. My floor not so much. But thanks for checking on me. Didn't mean to interrupt . . ." I gave him an up and down look. "Whatever it is that calls for leather pants in ninety-degree heat."

He shifted, dark brows falling to brooding level. "Cela."

"What does one wear leather pants for anyway?" I asked, knowing I didn't want to hear the answer, but unable to stop myself. "You don't own a motorcycle, do you?"

"No," he answered, the simple word holding warning.

"So what then?" I knew what I sounded like, could hear that hint of challenge and jealousy trickle into my voice. It was completely uncalled for and totally out of my control. *Irrational girl, aisle one.*

"I think it's best we don't have this conversation," he said, all still waters and calm authority.

"Right," I said, the word sharp as a jab. "Of course. You jumped on my case for keeping secrets that first night, but you get to hold on to your own. That's fair."

He pressed a finger to the space between his brows, closing his eyes and rubbing. "Cela, I'm not trying to be an asshole. But you don't want to hear this, don't need to."

"No, I think I do," I said, hurt already grinding my insides. Pulp. That's what I became around him.

He sighed and clicked the door shut behind him. "Fine. Let's just get it out there, then. I'm dressed in leathers because I'm going to The Ranch, a BDSM resort I belong to."

I blinked. The words and letters filtered through my brain but didn't line up to make any sense.

"BDSM?" I said, more to myself, only having a vague recollection of hearing the term before.

"Yes. Some still call it S&M."

"Oh." *Oh.* Pictures flashed through my mind. Scary ones. "So like . . ."

"I'm a sexual dominant," he said, watching me, gauging my reaction. When I apparently still looked unsure, he added, "I like to restrain women, cause pain for pleasure, be in total control."

A cold fist seemed to lock around my throat. *Total control.* Another "oh" was all I could manage. I'd known he was kinky but had never really let myself think through what that could entail beyond the threesomes.

He took a step toward me, his presence seeming to swallow up the entryway. "Which is why I haven't called and asked you out again, why I've forced myself not to knock on your door the last few days, and why I've been playing music nonstop so that I don't hear you in your room."

I swallowed, trying to get my vocal cords to loosen. "I don't understand."

The edge of the kitchen counter hit my tailbone, and I realized I'd been backing up as he inched toward me, an instinctive response to his predatory movements.

His smile was grim, almost wistful. He stopped in front of me, the sliver of space between us sparking with something I couldn't even identify. The scent of leather and soap hit my senses, making me want to close my eyes and hold on to the air.

"I know you don't, angel. And that's why nothing else can happen between us."

I straightened at the finality of his tone, my hands clenching at my sides. "What? Because you think I'm some innocent young twit playing big-girl games?"

His eyes flashed with displeasure, and the strong urge to grab back my words went through me—anything to get that look off his face.

"Cela, I suggest you don't try to pick a fight with me. You know I don't think you're a twit or a little girl. But you *are* inexperienced and young. And what you saw of my dominance that first night was barely a peek, and I fought hard to keep it at that level." His hands slid onto the counter, caging me in, his nearness stealing my functioning brain cells. "I don't trust myself with you. Even when I was trying to be gentle with you the other night, I pinned you down, corrected you, was rougher than I intended. I can't help myself. The dark part of me sees that innocence in you, that sweet yielding, and foams at the mouth—makes me wants to capture it for myself, to own it."

With each word, each breath against my skin, my heartbeat climbed higher up my throat until it seemed like my whole head was pulsing. My lips moved, but nothing came out. I closed my eyes.

"Am I scaring you yet, Cela?"

Yes. My body seemed to be vibrating with it—like being caught in a panther's line of sight and not being able to move. But something entirely different was bleeding into the fear, mixing with it and making my thoughts blur and my skin warm, making me want to stay right there.

I raised my gaze to him and homed in on his face, my eyes tracing over every contour, every angle, the fierce beauty there. Then I saw it— in a brief second where the hard shield slipped—a mirror reflecting the desperate ache pinging inside my own chest.

I was affecting him as much as he was me.

"You never asked me why I didn't sleep with Pike," I blurted.

He blinked as if someone had snapped a camera in his face. "What?"

"I know you assumed it was because I was still recovering from the night before, but that had nothing to do with it . . ." I paused, the right words proving elusive. "I didn't have sex with him because I felt like the privilege should only belong to you."

He closed his eyes, his nostrils flaring with a deep breath. "You're not making this easy, angel. Not when you say things like that."

On a surge of bravery, I reached up and slid my hands along his neck, pulling his forehead down to mine. His skin was fever hot against me. My voice was a soft rasp, nerves still constricting my throat. "Can you show me, Foster? Show me what you like?"

"Cela," he groaned, his voice laced with gravel, taut. "Don't."

But I was rolling down a hill too fast to stop now. "Did you know I've been bitten by a mastiff or that I've groomed the meanest Shih Tzu the vet's school ever seen and ended up with stitches? Or that I grew up with a brother who made me spar with him so that I could defend myself? I could totally kidney punch you right now."

He lifted his head, the blue of his eyes like a January storm.

I took a deep breath. "I'm not that fragile. And I'm tired of other people sheltering me from things. I *liked* what happened the nights we were together. I know I don't really know anything about your . . . lifestyle. But I do know that you taking control in bed made me feel comfortable, took away any worries of doing something wrong. Chased off the shame."

"Did it now?" he asked, a shade of surprise coloring his voice.

"Honestly, I haven't thought about much else since." I looked down at my paint-splattered feet. "In fact, I think it's all your fault I fell off the ladder—you having the nerve to walk around all naked in your room."

He laughed then, a bark of a thing that seemed to surprise him. "How dare I change clothes in my own room."

"Sadistic bastard."

He sniffed and cupped my shoulders. "You have no idea."

"So show me," I said, my voice calmer than I felt inside. "Teach me how this works. I'm a no-risk investment, Mr. Businessman. I'm leaving soon, so you don't even have to worry about me getting all where-is-this-all-going, relationship obsessed on you."

His hands coasted up and down my arms, a war raging in his eyes, then he leaned down and put his mouth to mine. I gasped at the contact, the simple softness reaching down inside me and bending everything out of alignment. His lips moved over mine, his tongue easing inside, caressing and invading my senses like a drug. He tasted of cinnamon gum and want—the need pouring out of him and making me desperate to press my body against his.

But his hands stilled on my shoulders and kept me in place, fastening me to the edge of the counter at my back. I wanted to touch him, to deepen the kiss, to strip down and have him take me right there in my little kitchen. But before I knew it, he was lifting his mouth away from me, sadness etched into his face.

"What's wrong?" I asked, breathless.

He cupped my chin and laid one last brief touch to my lips. "I don't want you to be my fling, angel."

The words slashed right through me, opening up a gaping hurt. I bit the inside of my cheek, fighting off the stupid burn of tears that climbed up my throat. "You don't think I can handle it."

He took a step back and shook his head. "Whether you can or can't is not the point. *I* can't, Cela. I'm tired of one-night stands and living my life like I'm some frat boy. Being with you the other night, feeling that connection, that pure moment, it made me realize what I want and need. And what I need is something real. Not a week or two getting a taste of what could be, then letting it go. I don't want a woman to play submissive to me every now and then. I want to find the woman meant to be mine, want to own her submission . . ."

My jaw went slack, my mind snagging on part of that last sentence. "You want to *own* a woman?"

He gave a ghost of a smile as he reached out and swiped a thumb over my lips. "The kind of relationship I desire is intense and unpalatable to most. I'm not an easy man to be with. And even if there could be something between us, you're not ready to make that kind of decision—not without some experience behind you. Go be young and live your life. Figure out what you like and don't. I'm not on a path you need to follow right now."

"Foster," I whispered, so many emotions whirling through me, I couldn't pin one down.

"Thank you for letting me be your first, angel. I didn't deserve that privilege. But I'll never be sorry for it."

I closed my eyes, wanting to protest, to say a hundred things back to him, but words were sticking like hot marshmallows in my throat, expanding and blocking my air.

This wasn't supposed to feel this way. A fun night with the neighbor wasn't supposed to tear at me like this when it was done, was it?

"Good-bye, Cela," he said softly. Then his touch was gone, and his footsteps were hitting the tile. The door closed before I had the energy to open my eyes.

PART IV

Not Until You Trust

SIXTEEN

My penmanship was appalling as I scrawled down information on the paper in front of me. Since Foster had walked out of my apartment last weekend, I couldn't seem to do anything without a flourish of frustration. I dotted an *i* with pointed vigor and slashed through a *t*.

"Well, aren't you all sweetness and roses today," Bailey said, turning from her computer to eyeball me. "What did that intake form do to you?"

"It required me to fill it out. All those tiny little boxes."

She lifted a brow. "Who are you and what have you done with my Cela, the paperwork Nazi?"

I sighed and set down my pen. "Sorry, long week."

Bailey frowned. "You should go home and open that tequila I bought you."

Heh. The tequila. Bailey had no idea that her gift had actually been the match that set my previously predictable life on fire. "I don't have any left."

"Wait, what?" Bailey swiveled in her chair, her streaked blond hair whipping behind her as she whirled to face me. "Dude, there's no way you drank all of that already."

"I didn't. I shared it."

Bailey huffed. "So you finally decide to let loose, and you didn't invite me to the party? Lame."

I leaned back in my chair and rubbed a hand over my forehead, Bailey's accusatory tone blending with the sound of barking dogs in the kennels in the back. "It wasn't a party. Just a . . . date."

"Shut. The. Eff. Up." Bailey's chair squeaked, and without looking I knew she'd pitched forward—on the prowl. "You had a date and didn't tell me? Oh my God, that's why you've been so all over the place for the last couple of weeks. You met a guy!"

I could hear the squee in her voice and had no doubt she was about to morph into some cheerleader version of herself. If I didn't head it off at the pass, it was going to quickly disintegrate into hand grabbing and bouncing with glee as she begged for details. Bailey was only two years younger than me and was the closest thing to a best friend I'd found since moving here, but sometimes her enthusiasm made me want to duck and cover. I held my hands out. "Calm it down, chica. *Met* is the operative word here. Past tense."

Her bright smile instantly dimmed. "Oh, no. What ha—"

But before Bailey could play Oprah to my Gayle, Dr. Pelham strode in from the back, already rambling off information she needed Bailey to pull up on the computer. Bailey spun around, instantly tapping away at the keyboard, her game face on. I smiled a greeting at our boss as she stepped behind us to the wall of file cabinets, and went back to finishing the intake form I was supposed to be doing.

"I have a surgery scheduled first thing tomorrow morning for that Yorkie that came in on Monday," Dr. Pelham said in my direction as she flipped through the folders in the file cabinet nearest me. "Poor thing's got a pretty aggressive tumor, but I think we may have caught it early enough. I'm going to use the new laser. You should assist."

I looked up from my mess of an intake form, my heart doing a little leap and spin. "Really? That'd be great. I haven't seen this new equipment in action yet."

Dr. Pelham smiled, pushing her reading glasses onto her head, making her salt-and-pepper bangs stick up every which way. "Yes, *Doctor* Medina. I'm hoping if I tempt you with our fancy new gadgets, you won't leave us at the end of the month. Have you given my offer any more thought?"

I pressed my lips together, the offer tempting me to no end every time she brought it up. The clinic couldn't pay as much as I'd make in my dad's practice, but since it was funded by the university it meant the vets had access to the latest technology and experimental treatments. And Dr. Pelham knew more about veterinary oncology than anyone in the state. Working under her would give me experience I couldn't get anywhere else. But I didn't *need* to specialize in oncology. When I'd mentioned it to my father, he'd dismissed it with a sniff.

You don't need to waste time specializing, Marcela, he'd said with that exasperated tone. *I need a Jill-of-all-trades for the clinic. You'll learn what you need to know down here.*

I tried not to let my face belie how torn I was. I knew I couldn't accept the position. My father was counting on my picking up the slack in his practice. But anytime Dr. Pelham brought up the job, I couldn't bring myself to give a firm no. "I'm giving everything a lot of thought."

Her smile climbed up to her eyes. "Fantastic. I'm interviewing a few candidates next week, though, so think quickly."

"I will, thank you. I promise I'll let you know by then," I said, misery making my stomach burn. Why was everything that seemed so simple a few weeks ago starting to feel like a maze filled with ticking grenades and no right decisions?

I waited until Dr. Pelham disappeared back into the clinic before I groaned and lowered my head to tap it against the desk. "I'm having a midlife crisis."

"I think it's called a quarter-life crisis," Bailey offered brightly, still tapping away at her computer.

"Yes. That. Maybe I *do* need more tequila."

"Be careful what you wish for, doc."

My head snapped up so fast I almost flipped backward in the well-oiled office chair. I grabbed for the edge of the desk with a curse.

Amused green-gold eyes stared down at me. "Sorry, didn't mean to startle you."

I put my hand to my chest, his sudden appearance sending my heartbeat into staccato mode. "Pike? What are you doing here?"

"Well, the sign does say open to the public," he said with a good-natured smirk.

"Right." Seeing Pike standing in the waiting area of my job had my worlds banging together—the crazy mixing with the mundane. It seemed a dangerous mix, like coming face-to-face with yourself in time travel. That shit never ended well.

In my peripheral vision, I could see Bailey turning forward to see our new guest. Pike seemed to notice her for the first time and sent her a tip of an imaginary hat before turning back to me. "So, I'm here because I'm thinking you were right."

"I was right?" I shook my head, trying to clear it. "About . . ."

He grinned. "That I should get a dog."

The gears in my head ground to a halt. "Wait, you're here for a dog?"

"Um, excuse me," Bailey interrupted as she rolled her chair closer to me. I turned to find her staring up at Pike with stars in her eyes. "You said your name is Pike?"

He glanced her way. "It is."

Bailey's hands gripped the arms of her chair. "Are you, like, *the* Pike? From Darkfall?"

Pike leaned his forearms on the counter and graced Bailey with a smile so panty melting it should be outlawed. "I am."

Bailey's gasp was audible. She sent me a look with a capital *L*, apparently registering that Pike and I already knew each other. Then her mouth dropped open. Her eyes said *Him? He's the guy?!*

I cleared my throat and stood before my dear friend had an aneurism. "That's great, Pike. We've definitely got a lot of dogs looking for homes here. Why don't we go in the back, and I can walk you through the kennels so we can get an idea what you're looking for?"

"Sounds good, doc." His gaze slid away from Bailey and alighted on me—all good humor and mischief. No doubt he was fully enjoying Bailey's bedazzled reaction. Like a vampire who fed on blood, he fed on making girls go giddy and tongue-tied. "Lead the way."

"Come on." I left a gaping Bailey behind us and stepped around the front counter to lead Pike toward a door opposite from the one Dr. Pelham had gone through. As soon I pushed through, the cacophonous chorus and the telltale scent of doggy-ness greeted us, instantly soothing me. This was my territory and Pike was a friend, no need to freak out just because we'd seen each other naked. "So you know Bailey is now texting everyone she's ever met telling her she just met you, right? And probably that she's going to marry you and have your rockstar babies."

Pike laughed. "Yeah, I got that."

We walked down the hallway toward the main adoption area. "Just another day at the office for ya, huh? Girls falling at your feet."

He lifted an eyebrow and tucked his hands into the back pockets of his jeans. "You know, doc, I'd make a cat sound right now and poke at you about being jealous. But you've been at my feet, and I know you aren't all that interested in returning there."

I choked on my gasp and peered over my shoulder at the empty hallway. "*Pike.*"

"Don't worry, doc. No one's in here with us. I was just trying to get the potential awkwardness out of the way."

We reached the end of the corridor, and I pressed my back to the door we were about to go through to face him. "I'm sorry, I just don't know how to do this. I've never been in this kind of situation before."

He smiled, good-natured as always. "Not that complicated. We fooled around. We both enjoyed it. Thoroughly, I might add. But you've got the hots for my best friend."

"I—"

"Plus, if I even thought about making another move on you, Foster would stab me with one of my own drumsticks."

I blinked, the words not computing for a moment, then I turned back toward the door to yank it open. "Yeah, well, Foster told me good-bye."

Pike sighed and laid an arm across my shoulders as we both stepped into the adoption area together. "He had to, gorgeous. Doesn't mean he wanted to."

I couldn't even respond to that. At the mention of Foster, everything crappy about my day came rushing back, and my mood plummeted. I slipped out from beneath Pike's arm as soon as we got to the first row of kennels. The smell of his cologne was only reminding me of that first night with the two of them. Something I definitely did *not* need to think about right now. I switched into professional mode, my spiel robotic. "These first two rows have your smaller dogs—terriers, toy breeds, et cetera. Over in the back to the right are the bigger dogs. There are a number of purebreds, but the majority of what you'll see are mixed breeds. If you prefer a puppy, we have a litter of Lab/shepherd mix that will be ready to adopt out in about a week."

Pike crossed his arms over his chest and frowned. "No puppies. Those are the easiest to adopt out, aren't they?"

I shrugged. "Families can't resist them. Cute. Clean slate with no previous trauma to worry about."

"And which ones are hardest to adopt?"

I cocked my head toward the back-left corner. "Row five. Those are the dogs that have been here longer than any others or have been returned after an unsuccessful adoption."

He headed that way without another word. I had to hurry to catch up and keep pace with his purposeful stride. I heard myself warning him that these dogs were great but had issues and maybe were better for experienced dog owners, but I don't think Pike even heard me. After only a few minutes of scanning the kennels and coaxing the occupants within, he zeroed in on Monty, a brown-and-black dachshund/schnauzer mix that had been cussed at by more staff than any other pet in there. Pike leaned forward to slip his finger inside the gated front, but Monty backed into the corner, barking like he was on fire. "What's this guy's story?"

"Monty's been returned twice. Once for snapping at a little girl and another for being resistant to any kind of training." I sidled up next to Pike and frowned down at the deceptively cute occupant. Monty had the body of a dachshund, but longer legs, and the face and wiry hair of a schnauzer. But his cuteness had been his downfall. All the young families were drawn to him, but he was easily overwhelmed by the chaos of children. "He was a rescue dog. We suspect the original owner dealt with Monty's feistiness by abusing him or outright neglecting him. He came in with a broken rib, internal bleeding, and barely any meat on his bones."

"Fuck," Pike said, moving his hand away but keeping his focus on Monty. "And been brought back twice. No wonder he's snarling at me. I'd have trust issues, too."

"He's a bit of a project," I agreed.

"I want him," Pike declared, turning to me.

"Pike, I don't know, this isn't exactly a job for an inexperienced owner. Maybe you . . ."

"Doc, this dog has issues with authority, is still feisty even after being treated like shit early in his life, and has spiky hair. Monty is made for me."

The corner of my mouth lifted. "Made for you?"

He shrugged. "Let's just say I can relate to what he's been through."

My heart squeezed, his quiet tone saying more than he probably realized. I found myself wondering what was behind those seemingly carefree smiles, who Pike was beneath the I'm-a-sexy-badass-drummer persona. "Don't you want to go into one of the private rooms and visit with him to make sure this is the one you want? I'd hate to see him get brought back again."

"No chance that will happen, doc. I won't give up on him."

The resolute look on his face was about as serious as I'd ever seen him. I nodded and turned back toward the door. "Okay, then. Let's go fill out some paperwork. And you'll need a list of supplies. You'll have to buy some things today and . . ."

"What time do you get off?"

I stopped and looked back at him. "About half an hour."

The Pike grin returned. "Good. Because you're coming with me. I don't know what the fuck I'm doing or what I need to buy. I need professional guidance."

"Pike, I—"

"I'll order Chinese. My treat. I already know you like lo mein, and Foster's out of town tonight so no worries there. We can just hang out while you help me get Monty settled in."

I blew out a breath, the offer tempting. The thought of spending another lonely night in my apartment, painting, held about as much appeal as rolling around in poison ivy. And if Foster wasn't going to be there, it shouldn't be an issue. I trusted that Pike was only making a friendly offer, not a flirty one. And he did sound a little scared at the prospect of going home alone with Monty. I shook my head. "You know, the shelter doesn't offer a house visit from a vet complete with purchase."

He made a praying motion with his hands and batted those sooty lashes at me. "Pleeease. Have mercy on me, doc."

I put a fist on my hip, amused. "You know? Maybe you and Monty really are soul mates because those puppy dog eyes you're giving me should come with a warning label."

He grinned and threw his arm around me again. "You're the best."

"Somehow I can't even feel angry at you despite knowing you just blatantly manipulated me."

He gave me a squeeze. "Don't feel bad. That's my way. You'll get used to it."

I laughed and leaned into him, all the weirdness from earlier dissipating. Yes, Pike and I had hooked up. Yes, I thought he was one of the hottest men I'd ever laid my eyes on. But at the core, we were meant to be friends only. I felt it that first night, and I felt it now.

And after the emotional roller coaster I'd been on with Foster the last couple of weeks, being with someone who didn't make everything in me turn inside out was probably just what I needed tonight.

Even if it wasn't what I craved.

SEVENTEEN

"The fucker wouldn't talk," Foster said, staring out at the dark road in front of him.

"Shit." A full sigh came through the speakerphone. "I thought—"

"Yeah, so did I. He said he'd only talk if I was there, but then he backed out at the last second. He told Agent Long that he didn't have anything to say now. Someone either got to him in the prison, or he was just spinning stories in the first place."

"I'm sorry, Foster."

He leaned his head against the headrest, feeling beat down. "The FBI isn't going to dig much further now that there's no new information. They're spread too thin to be wasting time on a cold case. I need you to take over with what little the guard overheard from this guy in the first place. He threw out a few nicknames, maybe start with that."

"Will do, boss," Bret said without hesitation. "I'll see what I can find."

"Thanks." Foster turned into the parking lot. He'd been working with Bret for years now and knew the relentless private investigator would turn over every new rock even if they continued to find nothing under them. "Keep me posted."

"Of course. And Foster?"

"Yeah."

"Let me handle it and take a break. You sound like shit."

"It's midnight. Of course I sound like shit." He swung the car into his normal parking spot.

"Don't be a smartass. You know what I mean. Go get drunk or laid or something. You've been in a crap mood every time I talk to you lately."

"Good night, Bret."

He hit the Off button without waiting for a response. No way was he going to tell Bret that his perpetual foul mood had nothing to do with the investigation. The case had been part of his life for as long as he could remember—dead ends were part of his existence. Frustrating and disheartening but nothing new. No, he knew exactly what—or who, rather—had turned him into some Mr. Hyde version of himself.

Foster glanced up at the darkened window on the third floor of the building in front of him. He'd done the right thing with Cela. Taking her up on her offer for a fling would've been selfish. He'd seen how wide her brown eyes had gone when she'd realized he didn't just want to dish out a little spank and tickle—that he wanted to own a woman. She'd been shocked at the prospect . . . and appalled. Not that he'd been surprised. Most people wouldn't respond positively to what he truly desired. He'd learn to accept that a long time ago. And he couldn't change it, even if he wanted to.

And, boy, were there times he wanted to and tried to. But he'd learned that even if he could quell that side of himself, it was only a temporary fix. He'd tried to adjust his needs with Darcy, had been easy on her when he wanted to be rough, had watered down the experience so as not to scare her away. But it'd been the worst way to go about it. He'd created a farce of a relationship where neither of them was getting what they wanted, but no one was talking about it.

Foster knew he could've given Cela the pied piper song and dance, could've softened the extent of what he was seeking, made it more palatable. He could've spent a few more days in her bed, constantly reeling himself in. But he was done with painting pretty pictures that only showed the surface of something. He was walking away from her to protect her from something she wasn't ready for and to protect himself from attaching hope to a hopeless situation. She was too young and inexperienced. And she was leaving. End of story.

Of course, his dick hadn't gotten the memo. Even staring up at her window like some pathetic stalker had his cock growing hard. "Fuck."

He yanked the keys out of the ignition and pushed open his door. This day needed to be done. And he had to schedule some time to go back out to The Ranch. The last time had been a bust. He hadn't been able to muster up interest in anyone after his talk with Cela. All his thoughts had stayed there with her in her apartment—those dark eyes and her paint-smudged cheeks. But he couldn't be walking around this wound up anymore. He didn't just need sex; he needed to beat someone—to tie a sub up and channel all his frustration into those exquisite moments where all ceased to exist except his dominance and a woman's utter surrender.

He slammed his car door behind him and headed into the building. For now, he was going to have to settle for a hot shower and a cold bed. He trudged up the stairs, unbuttoning the top two buttons of his dress shirt before he even hit his door. Hopefully, Pike was already asleep because the last thing he felt like doing was answering questions about the failed trip out to the prison. And he'd need to be quiet because he'd originally planned to spend the night in the small town where the prison was located, so Pike wasn't expecting him.

Foster turned his key in the lock and quietly opened the door, blinking in the darkness of the entryway. He could see the blue flicker of the television still on in the living room. He sighed. Pike was forever falling asleep on the couch with the TV still on. It was like the guy had an aversion to his own bed. Foster stepped into the kitchen, setting down his keys and his wallet, and toeing off his shoes. He was about to head down the hallway to turn off the TV when he heard Pike's hushed voice and a soft answering laugh. A feminine one.

So Pike had a girl over. That actually could work out in Foster's favor because then Pike wouldn't be inclined to shoot the shit with him. He'd have to pass by the living room to get to his bedroom, so he continued walking. But when the female voice responded to something Pike said, Foster froze in his spot.

Cela?

"So it's all about dominance?" Pike asked.

"Mmm-hmm," Cela replied. "If you're not in charge, it won't work."

Foster went icy cold, everything inside him crystallizing and cracking. Pike had Cela over on a night he thought Foster was out of town. Cela was laughing and talking about Pike being in charge. The day from hell had just turned into a waking nightmare.

"I can be dominant."

Foster couldn't handle another word. He rounded the corner and found the two of them sprawled on the floor, propped up on pillows like they were at a fucking slumber party.

"Just make sure you project calmness. He'll sense if you're not and act up," Cela said, her back to Foster.

"Will he—shit." Pike noticed Foster standing there.

Foster crossed his arms over his chest, trying not to let any emotion peek through his expression. "Sorry to interrupt."

Cela's head moved like it was on a swivel, her eyes going big in the flickering TV light. "Foster."

Pike pushed into a sitting position. "I thought you were—"

"Yeah, well, plans changed," he said, unable to keep the bite out of his voice. "And seriously, Pike, sneaking around behind my back? At least have the balls to tell me you want to fuck her."

"Foster!" Cela gasped and scrambled upward.

"Whatever. I don't fucking need this tonight. I'm going to bed. Try to keep it down." He turned around and strode toward his bedroom ready to charge right through the solid wood of his door just to take the edge off his anger.

"Dude, calm the hell down," Pike said from behind him. "It's not—"

He slammed his door, blocking out the rest of Pike's sentence. Asshole. All the girls in the world Pike could have, and he was going to mess with the only one that Foster couldn't bear to imagine with anyone else.

There was a hard knock on his door. "Come on, man. Let me in."

But Foster just ignored him as he unbuttoned the rest of his shirt, one of the buttons popping off completely in his haste to get in the shower and block out everything outside. But right as he tossed his shirt on the bed, there was another knock on the door, this one not as heavy but just as urgent.

"Foster, open this door right *now*," Cela demanded.

He turned toward the door, surprised at the ire in her voice. He'd heard her nervous, he'd heard her confused, and he knew exactly what she sounded like when he drew his tongue along the shell of her ear or up her thigh—but never had he heard her angry. Despite knowing it was a bad idea, he stalked to the door and swung it open. There she stood in her wrinkled pink scrub pants and a T-shirt, cheeks stained with color, and hair a little wild—looking as enticing as he'd ever seen her.

"We don't need to do this, ang—Cela." He caught himself right before he called her angel.

"The hell we don't!" She pushed past him and into his room without invitation. "You can't just walk in and throw out accusations when you don't even know what's going on."

"Well, it's not that hard a puzzle to put together."

She gave him a disbelieving look, then put her hands to her temples and let out a diatribe in Spanish—his shy neighbor switching into some fiery Latina mode he didn't know she was capable of. "You're so—ugh. I can't even believe you're acting like this. Pike got a freaking *dog*, okay? I've been here all night trying to help him get everything set up for Monty, to teach him how to train him."

"He did what?"

"If you had taken the time to ask the question or see the kennel in the corner, maybe you could've saved yourself from lighting into Pike and insulting me."

"Insulting you?"

She held her hands out to her side, exasperated. "Foster, you just accused me of being the kind of girl who would sleep with you and then sneak around with your best friend. Why not just call me a slut and call it a day?"

He cringed. "I didn't—"

"Speaking of which," she continued, apparently not in the mood to listen to an apology. "What right do you have to come stomping through here like you have some right to me anyway? *You* walked away. You said good-bye. Who I hang out with is not your business."

He raked a hand through his hair. "You know why I walked away."

"Right. Yes. You're the Big Bad Wolf, and I'm innocent Little Red Riding Hood. Got it. Let me go find my freaking picnic basket."

She moved to walk past him, hair whipping behind her, but he grabbed her wrist, halting her. "You know it's more than that. Don't act like it's a small thing."

Those chocolate eyes held challenge as she met his gaze. "Isn't it, though? So you're a little kinky. Whatever. Big deal."

"*Whatever?*"

She gave a petulant little shrug, and he wanted to turn her over his knee right there.

"Okay, fine." He kicked the door shut behind him and tugged her in front of him. "You want to play this game, angel, and know what I'm really like? Want to see what you think is such a *little* issue? Because I've had a real bad day, and there's nothing I'd like more right now than to fuck that notion right out of you."

That got her attention. Her eyes darted to his tight grip on her wrist, and he could feel her pulse hopping against his thumb. "Foster."

"Am I scaring you yet, Cela?"

She glared at him, but he could see the flicker of trepidation there, the bravado faltering. "You're trying to."

"You're right," he said, leaning in and pressing his lips to her ear, the part of him he'd held back from her rising to the surface and taking hold. "Because I like that, angel. This kind of fear gets me hard."

The soft intake of breath was barely audible, but he felt her body stiffening, every muscle going taut and still. She closed her eyes and swallowed hard. "I'm not scared of you."

He huffed a dark laugh, the quiver in her voice giving away her lie. True to form, he was hard as hell behind the fly of his jeans.

"Sure you're not." He pressed a palm to the side of her face and kissed her temple. "Go home, Cela. Sorry I jumped to conclusions tonight. It won't happen again."

He stepped around her and walked toward his dresser to pull a drawer open and find a pair of boxers to sleep in. He didn't want to look back, didn't want to watch her walk out. He'd had a hard enough time with the first good-bye. But when he lifted his head, Cela hadn't left the room, she'd simply turned his way and was staring at him in the mirror.

He frowned at her reflection. "What's wrong?"

"I don't want to leave."

He turned around to face her. "Cela—"

"Why don't I want to leave?" She closed her eyes and shook her head.

Her words caught him off guard, the desperation in her voice—the *want*. He let his gaze drift down her body, taking in the quick rise and fall of her chest, the shadow of her nipples pressing against her top, the restless shifting of her body. The sight wrung the breath right out of his lungs.

The fear hadn't run her off. It had triggered something else entirely—something that had glued her feet to the floor. Cela was completely and utterly turned on.

Every impulse in Foster's body rushed past his better judgment, and good intentions died a quick death. This he couldn't walk away from.

Oh-so quietly, he let the words pass his lips. "Tell me your safe word, angel."

She stood there for the longest time, eyes closed, fist balled; but then as if it were being spoken by some force outside herself, she said, "Tequila."

And the soft-spoken word was like a gunshot ringing in his ears, signaling the starting gates opening. Everything that had been building in him over the days since he'd been with her, every frustration, every long night, poured into his veins, fueling him. Tonight would either scare her away from men like him forever or it would prove him wrong about what she was and wasn't ready for. Either way, the time for debate was done.

Tonight, she'd be his.

EIGHTEEN

I couldn't open my eyes. Couldn't move, really. Everything in me was in full-fledged panic mode—red lights flashing, sirens sounding.

But I was locked in place. Dying.

Dying for Foster to touch me. Dying to see this secret part of him. And dying to know why, when every part of my good sense said to run, my body had decided to wave the white flag.

"Eyes on me, Cela," Foster said, his firm voice breaking through the quiet of the room and the sound of my own harsh breathing.

I swallowed past the dryness in my throat and forced my eyes open, finding a shirtless Foster leaning against his dresser, his arms braced on each side of him. The muscles in his shoulders rippled and flexed, as if his hold on the piece of furniture was the only thing restraining him from charging me.

"You have five seconds to walk out if you don't want to be here. One . . ."

My heart was beating so fast, my chest hurt—like actually *hurt*.

Foster pushed off the dresser and took a step forward. "Two."

Never had I felt like this. Not even when Dalton Roarke, the hottest guy in my high school, had kissed me with tongue during a skit in drama class. I thought I'd pass out back then, but that light-headedness was nothing compared to being under Foster's purposeful gaze.

"Three."

I wasn't going anywhere. I knew it. *He* knew it. I shook my head.

"Two."

He was arm's length away now, and I could see a glimmer of his own trepidation behind the intensity. If I wasn't scared before, that put me right over the top. On some instinctual level, both of us knew he was opening a door that couldn't be closed again. This would be the *before* moment in our relationship—if you could even call it a relationship. Once he took that last step, we'd be entering the *after*. But I was mired in the quicksand already. For good or bad, I was a willing victim in whatever tonight brought.

Instead of saying *one*, he moved into my space and cupped my shoulders. The energy humming through him seemed to seep through my skin and make everything inside me crackle with tension. "Cela."

"I'm still here," I said, my voice a tremble of a thing.

"So you are."

But I couldn't tell if he was at all happy about that fact. I glanced at his neatly made bed—dark blue striped comforter, pristine white sheets and pillows—the bed he'd fucked other women on. Women I'd heard whimper and mewl from my side of the wall. The thought made my stomach twist, and not in a good way. I closed my eyes and took in a long pull of air. What was wrong with me? Any guy I slept with would've screwed other girls in his bed. That's how beds worked.

Except mine. He'd been the only one in *my* bed, the only one to leave the faint scent of his cologne on my sheets.

When I opened my eyes, I saw that he'd followed my line of sight to the bed. He looked back to me, and I expected him to lead me there. Instead, his lips curled at the corner. "You wear your thoughts on your face, angel."

"I—"

He pressed his hand over my mouth. "Enough talking. I think your mouth has gotten you in enough trouble tonight."

I stared up at him, my words clogging in my throat and my thoughts splintering.

When he was apparently convinced I wasn't going to say anything else, he dropped his hand from my mouth and tugged at my T-shirt, yanking it over my head. I didn't have anything sexy beneath. I'd thrown on comfortable things after getting out of the shower and coming back to help Pike with Monty. But it didn't matter, because Foster clearly wasn't there to linger over lingerie. He unsnapped my bra and tossed it to the side, leaving me naked from the waist up. He cupped my breast greedily and with his other hand, grabbed my hip to drag me against him. His erection was a hard promise, the straining denim of his jeans brushing my belly.

"It's not even fair how fucking tempting you are," he said, his thumb teasing my nipple and making everything in me arch toward him. "Tempting and too damned brave for your own good."

He gave my nipple a firm pinch, and I gasped. "I'm sorry?"

He smiled but there was a darkness behind it. "Yeah, you may well be when all is said and done."

His hand slid up from my breast over my collarbone, then curled around my throat, briefly applying pressure there before moving up to grip my jaw. He held me there, his cool blue eyes tracking over my face, the slope of my nose, the curve of my mouth—like he was evaluating an item before purchasing. I didn't dare move. Then he lowered his head and dragged the tip of his tongue along the seam of my lips. I shuddered at the sensual jolt the simple move sent through my nerve endings. Automatically, I opened to him, and he nipped along my bottom lip, pulling it between his teeth and sucking gently. Every move was methodical, deliberate—like he had all the time in the world.

But I didn't. My body was screaming already, needing something that only he could give me. I'd gone wet and achy the moment he'd grabbed me and stopped me from leaving the room the first time. Patience was not an option. I pushed up on my toes, trying to go in for a full kiss, but he immediately pulled back and hauled me against his bedroom door. The door rattled against my back, and my breath rushed out from the unexpected move.

"No, angel, that's now how this works. You're here for my pleasure tonight. If I want to go slow, we go slow. If I want to tie you to my bed and lick every part of you but not let you come, I'll do that. Your only decision is whether or not you use your safe word." He crowded me against the door, his breath hot against my ear. "You understand?"

Every errant thought in my mind seemed to fall away, everything zooming in and focusing on the man in front of me—the rumble of his voice, the night-air scent of his skin, and his firm words falling against my ear. My response came out as a whisper. "Yes, sir."

"Very good," he breathed, the heat of his chest brushing against my already sensitive nipples. "Though, hard and fast has its merits, too. Turn around and put your palms against the door."

"But—"

He grabbed my shoulders and spun me toward the door. "Wrong answer. Hands on the door, Cela."

My palms landed against the wood with a smack, and Foster yanked my scrub pants and panties down and off, leaving me like some criminal preparing for a pat down. My brain was spinning, my anxiety like electrical pulses hopping along my spine. What was he going to do to me with my back turned? My imagination went on a wild ride down way too many paths. I peeked over my shoulder, needing to see what was happening, but a sharp slap to my thigh had me yelping.

"Eyes forward," Foster said, no emotion in his voice.

I snapped my focus back to the door, fighting my knee-jerk instinct to tell him to go to hell, to grab my clothes and walk right through the door I was braced against. He'd warned me. He was trying to scare me. Or piss me off. Break me and my demand to see him this way.

Footsteps sounded on his hardwood floor. His closet door squeaked open. It took every bit of my self-control to not look back at him. A minute or two passed and then his body heat was radiating on my back, his scent filling my nose. "Raise your hands above your head."

I did as I was told, and he grabbed one of my wrists. I glanced upward to watch him wrap smooth black leather around it. A cuff. He slipped a finger between the leather and my skin, checking how tight it was, then strung a chain into the metal loop on the outside of the cuff. Blood rushed through my ears, the white noise sound pulsing with my frantic heartbeat. Sweat dampened my neck. Foster strung the length of chain through something above the door—a black eyebolt that I hadn't noticed before. Once he had it threaded, he hooked a matching leather cuff to my other wrist.

When he released my hand, my arms lowered a fraction, the cuffs holding me in place with only a bit of slack. I jerked at them, the metal links rattling, but there was no slipping through the cuffs. I was now chained to the goddamned wall in the bedroom of a guy I thought I knew—but maybe didn't know at all. The feel and the sight should've scared me shitless. But instead of the pure fear of danger, it was like the anxiety of getting on a roller coaster for the first time—adrenaline coalescing with anticipation . . . and trust. Trust that no matter how terrifying the ride, the cart wouldn't fly off the tracks.

But when Foster squatted down behind me and locked cuffs around my ankles—cuffs that were attached to each other with a metal bar— my this-is-just-a-thrill-ride mentality faltered. Words tumbled out of me. "You don't have to lock me down. I promise I won't run."

"Not now you won't," he said, a wicked smile crossing his face as he looked up at me. "And this is the *B* in BDSM, angel. You don't know what it does to me to see you like this—all bound and helpless."

He rose from his crouch, gliding his hand up from my ankle over my calf and thigh, sending hot shivers twining through me. I pressed my forehead to the door as his touch moved higher.

"I like knowing that I can do this to you." His fingers slid along my folds, revealing just how embarrassingly wet I was, before tucking inside me. I whimpered and, instinctively, I tried to clamp my thighs together—the stimulation after so much waiting almost overwhelming me. But the bar between my ankles didn't allow me to close them even a little. "And you can't do a damn thing about it except stay open to me and accept it."

"Foster," I whispered, not sure what I was asking him for.

His fingers slipped out of me, and then the length of his body was pressed up against my back. He was still half-dressed, the cool touch of the metal button on his jeans like an ice cube to my overheated skin. His left hand collared my neck, and his right hovered in front of my face, his index and middle fingers shiny with my arousal. "Taste, Cela. Taste how goddamned sexy you are."

I closed my eyes and shook my head, almost frantically. He wanted me to . . . I couldn't. Not with him right there, watching.

He kissed the shell of my ear. "Aww, don't be shy now, angel. You're telling me in all those nights you've touched yourself, you haven't taken a taste?"

My cheeks went fever hot. Of course I had. And I'd tasted myself on his lips after he'd gone down on me that first night. But somehow, admitting this pressed that shame button inside me, giving me that sick feeling in my stomach.

And that pissed me the hell off. Why? Why couldn't I push past that part of myself that wanted to label everything *dirty* and *wrong* and *sinful*? Fighting past that instinctual response, I bent my head and sucked his fingers into my mouth, even as the flush of embarrassment burned its way over my chest, and cleaned every bit of them.

He groaned against my ear and pressed his hips harder against my backside, his erection like steel against my softness. He pulled his fingers from my mouth with a *pop*. "Good girl. Now I won't have to flog you as hard."

My eyes snapped open at that. "Flog?"

He ran a hand along my hair in a deceptively gentle gesture. "Yes, angel. Still want to see this part of me?"

I bit my lip. Did I? My body was giving a big *Hell, yes!* But anxiety was clawing at me. Would it hurt? Would I hate it? God, what if I *liked* it? That possibility seemed even more disturbing. But I'd fallen too far down the rabbit hole to back off now. "Why do you have to hit me?"

He ran a finger along the notches of my spine, slowly, reverently. "Because it turns me on."

No other explanation. In this world of his, that was enough. I swallowed hard.

He pinched my hip and I gasped. "And maybe it'll turn you on, too. Or not. Only one way to find out."

Before I could even process the dart of pain from the pinch, I heard him walk away again. So this was it. He was going to flog me—whatever that meant. I wasn't even sure. God, why hadn't I googled this stuff before goading him into showing me?

Because you were too afraid to look, my mind whispered.

Something soft and a little ticklish brushed over my shoulders. I glanced to the side just in time to see the strips of leather slide over my skin. Goose bumps followed in its wake. "What is that?"

Foster trailed the tails along my shoulder blades, the touch oh-so soft. "It's a flogger, angel. Strips of elk hide. Worried?"

"Yes."

He chuckled. "Good, that will make it better."

Before I could ask another question, delay him further, I heard the swoosh of the flogger cut through the air. The tails of it striped right across my back on the diagonal. I reared up and cried out in surprise, the chains of my cuffs clinking. But instead of the sharp stinging sensation I'd been bracing for, the blow hit like a heavy thud against my back—impactful and breath stealing, but not painful.

I sucked in air, gasping for it, but another hit came down in the opposite direction. The tails wrapped around my hip a bit, leaving little stings where the end of the leather strips landed. And my back went warm and tingly. Foster paused. "Still with me?"

My fists flexed, and I swayed a bit in the cuffs, but the tingling sensation was oddly pleasant—almost calming. "Yes, sir."

"Beautiful," he said, his pleased tone doing more to me than it should. "You should see how pretty your skin is as it heats."

I squirmed a bit, trying to lift my feet, a restlessness growing in me, but the bar restricted my movement too much. I needed . . . I don't know, something.

"Easy, angel," he said softly. "I'll give you more, but if you keep trying to move, you're going to hurt yourself."

More? He thought I was asking for *more*? But even as I thought the question, some part of me knew he was right. My body was humming for more contact, for that rush of tingling that seemed to spread from my back along all my nerve endings.

And I didn't have to wait long for it. Foster landed blows along my ass this time and on the backs of my thighs. And there was no pause this time. As if he were making figure eights in the air, he rained the leather down on me in a very precise but increasingly intense pattern. The soft thudding from the first few blows morphed into something edgier and more intense. Pain . . . but pain mixed with this electric feeling that had my legs quivering, and my moans turning into some sound I didn't recognize—desperate, wanton need.

Sweat dripped down my neck, sliding down between my breasts. I was acutely aware of every sensation. The smack of the flogger, the sound of my ragged breathing, the scent of arousal, and Foster's presence behind me. Even without seeing him, I could feel him there—his intensity a palpable thing. He was in some other zone, and I was quickly tumbling into with him. Another hit, and my thoughts went hazy. I pressed my damp forehead against the door. "Please, please, please . . ."

I didn't know if I spoke the words aloud or not, but no other hit came. The flogger clattered against the wood floor. Vaguely, I was aware of the sound of a zipper, rushed movements. Then my ankles were slipping free of the restraints.

Foster adjusted something above me, and then he was turning me, my hands still cuffed but the chains going with me. When I'd made the one-eighty, I managed to open my eyes. Foster's blue-eyed gaze collided with mine—the ferocity making my stomach flip.

I opened my mouth to say something, though I wasn't sure what, but he cut me off instantly with a kiss—his tongue and lips clashing with mine as he wrapped a hand behind each knee and lifted me off my feet. My back hit the door, and he pushed deep inside me, opening me wide and wrapping my legs around his hips. I gasped into the kiss, the feel of him inside me mixing in with the snap of pain from my sensitive back hitting the wood. My head spun, and my sex clenched around him. Everything inside me hummed like live wire, waiting for one more spark of pleasure to burn me to ashes.

Foster's fingers dug into the backs of my thighs, and he thrust into me harder than he'd ever done before. The door rattled behind me, and my fingers clawed for him, but my hands were still captured above me. The rock of his hips pushed him along my clit with every forward motion, driving me higher and higher until I was writhing against the door like some inhuman thing. I broke from the kiss for air. "Foster."

His jaw was clenched, his pale eyes wild, and his dark hair clung to his temples, but he didn't stop fucking me. "Come for me, Cela."

He wrapped an arm around my waist, holding me in place, then moved his other hand between us. He rubbed my clit, the rough pads of his fingers firm over slippery flesh, and everything went white behind my eyes. I tilted my head back against the door and cried out as my orgasm rocketed through me. My back was banging against the door, the power of Foster's thrust almost knocking me right through it, and I rode the tide of pleasure as he groaned long and loud and spilled inside me.

When we were both back on Earth, I sagged in the bindings and let my head lower to his shoulder. He whispered soft, soothing words in my ear as he held on to me and uncuffed my wrists with his free hand. My arms circled around his neck, half-numb and near useless. He carried me to the bed and lowered me to it, sliding out of me in the process. My eyes cracked open for a moment as he pulled off the condom and disposed of it. Then he was back at my side again. He brushed my damp hair off my cheek, a reverent expression on his face. "Lie down, angel. I'll get you some water."

He didn't have to tell me twice. I curled around one of his pillows on top of his comforter, no longer giving a shit who he'd slept with in this bed. It was a bed, and I was exhausted. I wasn't awake long enough for him to return with the water.

NINETEEN

I rolled over in bed—groggy, achy, and filled with the desperate need to pee. My body bumped into warmth, and it took me a second to remember that I was in Foster's bed—naked. He mumbled something in his sleep but didn't wake up. Trying not to jostle the bed too much, I shifted to the other side and slipped from beneath the covers. The air chilled my bare skin, but it was still pitch-dark in the room, so I had no shot at finding my discarded clothes. It was going to be challenging enough finding my way to the bathroom.

I put a tentative foot in front of the other, trying to make sure not to trip over anything or run into any furniture. His room was the mirror opposite of mine, so I knew where the door to the bathroom should be at least. With a little bit of hands-out-in-front-of-me groping, I eventually found my way there and shut the door behind me. I took care of the necessities, then went to the sink to wash my hands, rinse my face, and swish some mouthwash. No need to have Foster be greeted with the full heinous version of my morning self.

After double-checking to make sure the door was still shut, I turned around and peeked over my shoulder to get a view of my backside in the mirror. Despite the tenderness that still lingered, I didn't see any obvious marks left from Foster's flogger—though, if I was going to bruise, that'd probably take a little longer to show up. I frowned at the reflection, unsure whether I was happy or disappointed to see no evidence. I sighed. My brain was like a steaming pile of scrambled eggs over this whole thing.

After flipping off the light and letting my eyes adjust for a moment, I opened the door and headed back toward the general direction of the bed. But apparently I misjudged the distance, because before I knew it, my shin smacked the edge of the wood-framed bed. A harsh curse passed my lips as I grabbed for my throbbing leg. Foster rolled over.

"Cela?"

"Yeah. Sorry," I said as I braced a hand on the bed and rubbed my shin with the other.

"You okay?" he asked, his voice all slow and sleep-heavy. And sexy. Of course. The man could probably sneeze and I'd find something hot about it. What was wrong with me?

"I'm fine, just clumsy. I was trying not to wake you."

"Mmm," he said, pushing up on his elbow and reaching a hand out to me. "Get back in bed, angel. It's safer in here."

I took the offered hand and let him pull me back under the covers. "I'm not so sure about that."

He pulled me against him, my back to his front, and chuckled softly against my neck. "I promise to be good."

His body curled around mine, chasing off the chill I'd caught on the way back from the bathroom. I closed my eyes, absorbing just how good it felt to simply lie with him. "Sorry about waking you up."

"No worries. I don't sleep that soundly anyway. Doesn't take much to wake me up." He pulled the blanket a little higher over us. "Go back to sleep, angel. We still have some time before morning."

I nestled my head deeper into the pillow and closed my eyes, but after a few minutes, I realized that the knock to my shin had woken me up fully, and I wasn't going to drift off easily. I shifted a bit in his hold and could tell that he hadn't fallen back asleep yet either.

"Is this position irritating your back?" he asked.

"No, it's fine. Just awake."

"I would offer to sing you asleep like you did for me, but I'm not that sadistic. No one should be subjected to my singing voice."

I smiled. "That bad?"

"It's only suitable for the shower and when I'm riding in the car alone."

We both went quiet for a while, and I thought he was going back to sleep, but then his low voice broke then silence.

"I'm sorry that I got angry with you tonight, when I saw you with Pike. That really was uncalled for."

I rubbed the corner of the pillowcase between my thumb and forefinger, staring into the darkness. "You said you'd had a bad day. What happened?"

He sighed and his hold on me loosened a bit. "I thought I was going to get some answers about a situation I've had questions about for a long time, and I hit another dead end."

I chewed my lip, debating whether or not to push for more details. It really was none of my business. Just because we were curled up naked together didn't mean I had some right to know about all his personal business, but I couldn't help myself. "I'm sorry. What kind of situation?"

"A family one." He was silent for a long time after that, and I figured he'd decided that was enough of an answer—even though it was no answer at all. But then he laced his fingers with mine and let out a breath. "I'm searching for my sister, Neve."

I turned in his hold to face him, confused. "What do you mean—'searching'? Did she run off?"

I couldn't see him well in the dark, but I felt the tension in his muscles. "No, angel, she was taken—a very long time ago. Has been missing since I was ten."

"Oh my God." The weight of the words landed solidly on my chest, pressing down. "I'm so sorry."

He brushed his knuckles over my cheek. "It's okay. I've lived with that knowledge for a very long time. I just got my hopes up tonight that we'd have a breakthrough in the case, and the informant backed out. I should've known it'd be a dead end. They always are."

"Oh, Foster," I said, my heart breaking at the hopelessness underlining his tone.

"Shh," he said, pressing a kiss to my forehead. "I'm just sorry that I took my frustration out on you. You didn't deserve that."

"It's okay, I—"

He put his fingertips over my lips. "No, it's not. But let's not get into it now. It's late, and you need to get some rest."

I let my head sink back into the pillow, and he turned me to spoon again.

His embrace was comforting, the bed warm. But it was a long time before I was able to fall asleep.

I could handle mysterious, sexy neighbor Foster.

And funny, texting Foster.

Even intimidating, kinky Foster.

Those are guys I could write off as fun fling candidates.

But I had no idea how to handle this man. This man with vulnerabilities and wounds and history. A man who hadn't given up on finding a sister who'd been gone for more than twenty years. I didn't need to know these things about him. The more I learned, the more this mattered. The more *he* mattered. And the harder it was going to be when I left.

Maybe Foster had been right all along.

We had to end this.

Because as I lay there, listening to him breathing, I found myself wanting it to be real, wanting to be his.

"What the hell are you doing, man?"

Foster glanced over his shoulder at Pike, who'd plunked down at the breakfast bar, the new dog sniffing at his feet. Foster couldn't even tackle *that* turn of events yet. Pike taking on the responsibility of a dog. The mind boggled. "I'm making pancakes. What does it look like I'm doing?"

"And what the fuck was that last night?"

Foster sighed, keeping his back to Pike as he waited for bubbles to appear in the batter he'd ladled onto the griddle pan. Bette, the housekeeper who'd taken care of him for much of his life, had told him never to flip a pancake until there were bubbles. "Sorry I jumped your shit. Yesterday . . . sucked, and well, I was already in a bad place when I came home."

"Dude, I'm over that. You're a possessive asshole. Not breaking news. But I'm talking about what you did with her. What happened to leaving the vanilla girl who's moving away alone? Now you're making her pancakes? You don't cook breakfast for anybody."

Foster flipped the pancake with a little more vigor than necessary. "Last night wasn't planned. I gave her the chance to leave. She didn't."

"Ah hell, don't do this to yourself."

Foster turned to give Pike a narrow look. "Do what? Sleep with her? It's not like it hadn't happened before."

Pike took a sip of his coffee. "Don't give me that shit. You didn't just fuck her, and you know it. You're getting attached. It's written all over you. You're making fucking pancakes, for God's sake."

"It's just a pancake," he said a little too loudly, holding the spatula out to the side. Batter dripped to the floor, and the dog scrambled to take care of it. "I'm well aware she's leaving. I'm *not* attached."

The lie rolled off his tongue with ease.

Truth was, he was a fucking mess after last night. He hadn't slept after their middle-of-the-night talk. He'd just lain there, watching her sleep, trying to come up with a scenario where she didn't pack up and move away in a week. He turned back to ladle more batter onto the griddle, avoiding Pike's pointed stare.

"She can't stay, Foster." Pike said quietly. "She won't. Last night, she was telling me about what's waiting for her back home. She's spent her whole life preparing to take over half of her father's practice. And she loves her family and the career she's chosen. Her life is there."

"I wasn't going to ask her to stay," he replied under his breath. Though, he was more than tempted to. But what could he possibly offer her in exchange for veering off the life plan she'd set up for herself? Sure, they were great together in bed. And yeah, he had enough money to give her anything she could want or need while she was here. But they hardly knew each other. Even if she liked last night—which he hadn't even had a chance to confirm yet—there was no way she could be ready for the type of relationship he craved.

The smell of smoke snapped him out of his ruminating. He turned down the heat as the pancake started to burn around the edges. The sound of a door opening somewhere behind him had him turning around again, though. The dog scampered that way with a bark. Cela appeared in the kitchen a few moments later, wearing her wrinkled clothes and a haphazard ponytail. She had her arms wrapped around herself as if she were cold. And when she bent down to scratch the dog under the chin, she moved so gingerly, he cringed.

Shit.

"Hey there, Monty," she said softly.

"Morning, doc," Pike said, as casual as could be. Like Cela was here every morning. "Coffee?"

She rose and gave him a small smile, her eyes darting briefly toward Foster. "Actually, I really need to get back to my place. I'm due at work in an hour."

Foster frowned and set down the spatula. "You should at least eat some breakfast before you go."

"He made pancakes," Pike said, a wry tilt to his mouth.

Foster shot him a shut-the-fuck-up glare.

She curled her lips inward and glanced toward the door, clearly ready for escape. But he could tell manners were so deeply ingrained in her that she couldn't do it. She gave a quick little nod. "Yeah, okay, I can stay for a minute. You didn't need to go through so much trouble."

Foster breathed a brief sigh of relief that she wasn't leaving yet and turned to pile a few pancakes on a plate. "No trouble."

Pike sniffed.

Foster put the burnt pancake on Pike's plate.

When he turned around with both plates in his hand, Cela was sliding into the chair next to Pike, the strained press of her lips the only indication that she was feeling the effects of last night. God, he was an asshole.

Yes, she'd pushed him last night, had asked to be with him, but he'd taken it too far. Not that he'd never left a girl with marks or bruises the next day—it was part of the deal. But up until now, he'd only done it to women he knew were totally into it, who thrived on submission and pain play. But with Cela, he had no idea what her pain tolerance was or if she had limits he'd crossed. It'd been completely irresponsible on his part to scene with her. The girl didn't even know what a scene *was,* and he'd chained her to his fucking door. Then later, he'd laid his shit about his sister right on her. Like she needed to know about his family's tragedies on top of everything else. No wonder she was ready to bolt.

He set the plates in front of them and grabbed the bottle of syrup off the counter. "You okay?"

"I'm fine," she said, though there wasn't much conviction behind it, and took the syrup from him. "Thanks."

Pike grabbed his plate and stood. "I think I'm going to eat this in the living room. Hit me with a little syrup, doc."

"Pike, you don't have to—" Cela started.

"Nah, doc, it's okay. My morning show's on. Gotta get my daily dose of Lara Spencer."

Cela frowned but poured syrup over his pancakes and said nothing else.

"Come on, Monty, let's see how you like Foster's cooking." Pike gave Foster a quick glance, then sauntered off toward the living room, Monty fast on his heels.

Cela put a bite of food in her mouth, looking down at her plate like it held all the answers. He had no doubt everything was setting in now. Last night when she'd woken up, it'd all still been comfortable in the darkness—safe. But now in the light of day, her body was probably aching, her skin sensitized, leaving no path for her mind to deny what she'd participated in last night. And knowing Cela, that probably meant a heaping dose of shame and guilt.

Foster blew out a breath and served up his own breakfast, then grabbed a bottle out of the cabinet. He tapped out two pills and set them next to Cela's plate, then poured her a glass of water. "Take those. It'll help."

She eyed the pills. "What are they?"

"Ibuprofen."

"Thanks." She picked them up and swallowed them down, her gaze staying on him. "So will I have, like, bruises and stuff? I kind of feel like I got tackled by an NFL lineman."

He leaned against the counter, arms crossed, leaving his food untouched next to him. "You shouldn't. That particular flogger is pretty harmless in that regard. Though you may get tiny speckle bruises where the tips wrapped around your hip."

"Oh."

"Does that bother you?"

She pushed a syrup-soaked bite around her plate with her fork. Great, she couldn't even look at him. "I don't know."

He carded a hand through his hair and sighed heavily. "I knew I shouldn't have gone there with you."

She looked up sharply.

"I'm sorry. Last night . . . it never should've happened."

"Right." She shook her head, smirking, and shoved her plate away. "Look, thanks for breakfast, but I've got to go."

"Cela," he said, pushing up from the counter. "Wait. Don't leave yet. We need to talk about last night. If I freaked you out . . ."

She grabbed her keys off the edge of the counter and looked at him. "You didn't freak me out, Foster. I freaked myself out. A few weeks ago, I was virgin. Now I'm waking up in some guy's bed feeling like I've been rolled over by a truck and can't even find my panties."

Some guy. The words punctured his chest like rusty nails.

"This has become too . . . intense. And I'm starting to like this, *you*, too much. You told me you want to own a woman. And as I was lying in your bed this morning, can you believe I actually found myself wondering what that would be like?" She looked heavenward. "How fucking insane is that?"

His heart leapt at the mere mention of her even entertaining that notion, but reality quickly kicked it right back down. Clearly, she wasn't happy about that thought. And she was leaving. *Leaving.* He had to get that through his head. "Cela . . ."

She continued like he hadn't even spoken. "Being with you has been—well, I can't even describe it. But Foster,"—she met his eyes and put her hand to her chest—"I don't even know who this person *is*. I'm not sure I want to know."

Tears brimmed in her eyes, and he couldn't stop himself from walking over to her and pulling her against him. She let him fold her into his embrace. He set his chin on the top of her head. "It's going to be all right, angel. You've just been through a lot of big life changes these last few weeks. You're still the same person you always were. I'm sorry I added shit to that mix that made you even more confused."

She sniffed against his T-shirt. "You didn't make me do anything. I brought this on myself."

"Shh, you're just going through life trying to figure stuff out like all of us are. In a week, you're going to go back home to your family and the job you've worked so hard for, and things will get easier. Everything will fall into place." The words hurt coming out, but what else could he say? *Hey, I just met you, and this is crazy . . .*

Shit. Now he was quoting ridiculous pop songs. This girl was making him lose his mind.

Cela pulled back and looked up at him, gaze somber. "I can't keep doing this. It's starting to hurt."

He wiped a tear off her cheek. "I know, angel." *Me, too.*

She nodded, resigned. "Maybe if I didn't have to leave, but . . ."

He pressed his fingers against her mouth, unable to bear the conjecture. "No *what-ifs* in life, just *what is,* right? Let's not go there."

She grabbed his wrist to move his hand then pushed up on her toes to brush his lips with a soft kiss. "Thanks for giving a small-town girl a walk on the wild side."

He forced a smile, even though the words were way too reminiscent of how things had ended with Darcy. Maybe he'd always be relegated to that role in his life—the kinky guy to have fun with for a while before a woman went looking for something real. Something normal. "Hey, the pleasure was all mine."

She smirked. "*That* is definitely not true."

He laughed despite himself.

"I'll make sure and stop by before I head out of town. And tell Pike if he has any more questions about Monty to call me."

"Will do. Do you have everything you need for the move?" he asked, moving into safe conversation, topics that wouldn't remind him that he would never touch her again.

"I still have a lot of painting to do, but I'll get it done in time." She was heading toward the door now.

"Let us know if you need help."

"Thanks." She peeked back at him and smiled, but he knew she'd never call for that help.

This was the end. And they both knew it.

He stood there staring at the door long after she'd shut it behind her.

TWENTY

I turned up the radio as I pulled onto the highway on the way to my brother's place, trying to chase away the depressing thoughts that were infiltrating my brain. I'd come home last night after going to a movie with Bailey to find my apartment fully painted, every corner cut, every baseboard glossed. An invoice from a local painting company had been on my kitchen counter, the charge paid for by one Ian Foster.

The gesture had both touched and frustrated me. I'd spent the last week trying to forget the way Foster had looked at me, the way he'd made me feel that night in his room, the crazy things he'd made me want. I'd almost walked next door a hundred times to try to talk to him about it—to try to figure out why I was feeling so . . . undone. But I knew the minute I saw him, it would just tear the bandage right off the wound again. No matter how electric the connection had been between us, I needed to stay away from him. I was leaving in just a few days. And he was looking for something bigger than what I could offer anyway.

That last night with him *had* scared me. Everything had been so intense, so out there. And I'd responded to it, given in like some slave girl. The more he'd pushed me, the more turned on I'd gotten. I'd wanted to please him, and probably would've allowed him to take me even further than he did. Plus, I got the sense he'd only shown me a glimpse anyway. I couldn't imagine what other things lurked in that closet of his.

And the next morning, instead of being appalled at how achy and sore I was, I'd gone into the bathroom to look at my back in the mirror. When no marks were there, I'd actually felt *disappointment*. Which proved I was losing it. I was a doctor, goddammit. My whole career was focused on healing, and here I was letting some guy hurt me. And not just letting him, but enjoying it.

Yes, I needed to stay away.

Even if I couldn't stop thinking about him.

Even if part of me was desperate to know why he made me feel this way.

My life waited for me somewhere else. My family was counting on me. I was moving. And even thinking of changing that for some guy I'd slept with a few times was ludicrous. It had to be that whole weird evolutionary chemical thing that made me want to fall for the man I'd lost my virginity to. My body was under some misguided impression that it was going to mate for life. Logically, I *knew* this.

But when Foster did things like paying for my whole apartment to get painted, he made it harder for me to keep my scientific brain in charge. So, despite knowing it was a bad idea, I'd stopped by his apartment on the way out to thank him and to tell him I was going to pay him back. I didn't want guilt-laden gifts. He didn't owe me anything. But only Pike had been home.

"Sorry, doc. He's out," Pike had told me as he leaned against the doorframe. No smile. No invitation inside. The completely un-Pike-like behavior had made my stomach drop to my toes.

"Out?"

He gave a little nod.

"Like leather-pants out?" I'd asked, trying to keep my tone nonchalant even though my throat had gone Mojave dry.

His gaze had slid away, his shoulders sagging. "I'm not sure."

"Got it," I'd said, the words clipped. "Thanks a lot."

I'd turned to leave. "Hey, doc."

I'd spun back around, arms crossed in what probably looked to be anger but felt more like a desperate attempt to hold myself together.

"I know you feel something for him. I get it. But if you're not sticking around, just let him go," he said quietly. "People think I had it rough with what I went through as a kid, but despite his family having money, Foster had it worse. He was alone *all the time*. The people who were supposed to love him bailed when he needed them the most. He doesn't want to be left again."

My fingers dug into my biceps, the sadness in Pike's voice, the picture he was painting, making me want to reach out to Foster even more. "Is that why he wants to . . . own a woman?"

The words were hard to even get across my tongue—the concept so foreign.

Pike brushed a hand over his head, the spikes springing back as soon as he swiped over them. "Maybe? There's no doubt he's a dominant. He's always been a bossy fucker—at least as long as I've known him. But I think him wanting something so clearly defined is a way to try to control who leaves him. But of course, it's a false sense of security. A woman can walk away at any time—vanilla relationship, slave, submissive, or anything in between. One day he's going to have to accept that caring for someone is always going to be a risk, no matter what."

I digested his words. "Which is why you steer clear of relationships?"

"Nah, doc, I'm just too fucked up to inflict myself on someone long term. I'm best in small doses." He smirked, but there wasn't much enthusiasm behind it. "And I'm not trying to scare you off Foster. I can tell something is different when he's with you. I've never seen him get so . . . possessive. But I love the guy and don't want to see him get his heart handed back to him again."

I frowned, an unshakeable melancholy falling over me, but nodded at Pike. "You're a good friend to him."

He shrugged. "I'd be in a cemetery if not for him. And blood or not, he's my family."

I leaned over and kissed his cheek, a good-bye. "Thanks, Pike. He's lucky to have you in his life."

He pushed away from the doorjamb, his expression resigned. "Want me to tell him you stopped by?"

Though part of me had wanted to say yes, I'd shaken my head no and walked away. If I wasn't going to stay, then it wasn't fair for me to keep dragging this along. For Foster or myself. Even if I figured out some way not to leave, how could I begin to be what Foster wanted? I was intrigued by the glimpses of his dominant side I'd seen, enjoyed fantasies that went down that path. But the idea of giving that much control to anyone made my skin go clammy. I'd barely escaped from beneath my father's thumb. How could I consider being under someone else's?

So if Foster was at that resort place, looking for some other woman to be in that type of relationship with him, then I shouldn't begrudge him that. He deserved to be happy, even if I wasn't the one making him that way.

Well, at least that's what I'd been trying to tell myself during the car ride.

But when visions of another woman touching him came to mind, completely unfounded territorial feelings rose to the surface, darkening my mood. For someone who was supposedly looking for something real, Foster certainly was going about it an interesting way. I didn't know a lot about his lifestyle, but looking for Mrs. Right at a sex resort didn't sound so romantic. And if he'd really felt anything toward me like he'd implied the other night, he'd gotten over it mighty fast.

I merged into traffic, gripping the steering wheel a bit too hard and cursing the ballad that was playing on the radio. *Stupid frigging song.* But before my thoughts could careen further down the destructive path they were on, the notes of my phone's ringtone filtered through the music. I lowered my radio and hit the Speaker button on the phone. "Hello?"

"Marcela," my dad said, his heavy accent making my name sound so much more exotic. "I finally caught you. I've been trying to call."

"Hey, Papá," I said, trying to muster up an apologetic tone through my clenched teeth. "Sorry, I've been busy getting ready for the move." *And having threesomes. And getting chained to doors. And maybe falling for some guy who likes to torture women for kicks.*

"You make me worry, Cela. I had to call your brother to make sure he'd heard from you."

I sighed. "I'm sorry, but you shouldn't worry so much. I'm not nine. I can survive a few days without being checked on."

"Don't be smart," he said, using that father tone that used to make me want to hide in my room. "But never mind, it won't matter soon. You'll be home. We have the house all ready for you. I'll be able to see your car from across the street and will sleep easy knowing you're safe."

"Wait, what?" My stomach did a nauseous roll as I tried not to look down at my phone in horror.

"Your *tía* was only renting that house from me. I told you that. She wanted to move closer into town, so we're going to let you stay there. Think of all the money you'll save. You'll only have to cover the utilities. You can start your retirement fund early."

"You want me to live across the street?" I asked, unable to keep the *what the hell?* out of my tone. "I've already put a deposit down on an apartment."

"Now, Marcela, don't be ungrateful. And it's just a deposit. Let them have it. You're going to be working at the clinic with me, so you might as well be close by. We can even save gas and ride together. And believe me, I can't wait to have your help. I've had to hire an extra tech just to handle the patient load. And your mamá is buzzing around like she's got a bee up her dress. She'll be so happy to have you back."

Cars whizzed by me on each side as the world seemed to slow inside my car. My father continued to ramble on, and a movie of my life started to play in my head. I'd known I was going back and would be around my family again, but the picture my father was painting was like a thick, itchy blanket covering me. Smothering.

"Papá, I don't think living so close is a good idea. I need my space."

"Space? You'll have a whole house to yourself," he said, then muttered something in Spanish, which meant he was getting annoyed. "You know how many children would love to have their family pay for their mortgage? We want to take care of you, Cela."

I breathed in through my nose, trying to stay focused on the road and not letting myself completely lose my shit in the car. I loved my father, but the urge to scream, shout, and curse at him was pounding through me. I'd thought with the last few years of my being gone, my parents would've loosened their grip a little bit. But it sounded like they'd only been lying in wait until I came home to resume their control over my life.

I pulled at my necklace, the jewelry suddenly too snug.

"I have to go. We can talk about this later," I said in a rush, my instincts going into cornered-rabbit mode. "I'm visiting Andre tonight and I don't want to be late."

My father grunted. "Fine. But we're not done with this conversation.

And tell your brother to call me. I want him to ride down with you when you come home. It's been far too long since he's visited his family."

I wanted to ask him if I should invite Luz, too. My older sister only lived a town over from my parents. But I knew what my dad's answer would be. Forgiveness was one gift my father never granted. Being cut out of the family was a permanent condition. My sister's name wasn't even spoken anymore.

And as I pulled in front of Andre's building, I wondered what my father would do if he knew what I'd done with Foster and Pike . . . or if I refused to live in the house he'd offered me, changed the blueprint of my life.

Would I be discarded, too?

With a deep sigh, I grabbed the small gift I'd bought for Jace's brother, Wyatt, and climbed out of the car. By the time I made my way to the loft on the third floor, I was praying this party had alcohol, because I had a feeling a nervous breakdown was waiting in the wings for me otherwise. One more crappy thing tonight, and I was going to lose it.

I knocked on the door, and it swung open a minute later, the space filling with the imposing force that was Jace Austin. Andre's roommate grinned wide, his green eyes lit with the kind of jovial ease I longed for. "Well, if it isn't the prettier Medina."

The man was downright contagious. I couldn't help but smile back as he swallowed me with a bear hug. "Hey, Jace. Depressed as usual I see."

He laughed and stepped back. "You know it."

I walked in and set the gift on the entryway table while Jace closed the door behind me. The loft space was already echoing with conversation, Andre sitting on one of the couches and chatting with Wyatt. I had only met Wyatt once before, but I remembered him being the exact opposite of what I'd expected him to be.

I'd anticipated an older version of Jace, but he couldn't have been more different. Where Jace was laid-back and quick with a joke, Wyatt had seemed quiet and intense—intimidating. I'd heard Jace call him genius, and I suspected that was more than a playful nickname. It was no secret that he was second in command at his father's financial company and was freaking loaded. But it was obvious his knowledge extended beyond his field. When he'd gotten into a discussion with me about animal testing, his opinions and astute observations had made me wonder if he'd gotten a medical degree on the side. But when I'd joked about as much, he'd shrugged and said he liked to read medical journals in his free time.

"Hey there, little sis," Andre said, raising his beer in acknowledgement. "Welcome."

Wyatt turned and greeted me as well, his smile restrained but genuine.

"Drinks are in the kitchen," Andre offered.

"You read my mind."

I headed toward the kitchen and found Jace's girlfriend, Evan, berating something in the oven. "Twenty minutes, my ass."

I grinned. "I don't think insulting the food makes it cook faster."

Evan turned toward me, the frustration melting from her pretty face. "Hey, you. Long time, no see."

She came over and gave me a quick hug, leaving flour marks on my black blouse.

"Oh, hell," she said, trying to brush it off for me. "I shouldn't be trusted with baking. I can cook a meal, but let me near anything having to do with cake, and I'm as skilled as a five-year-old with an Easy-Bake Oven."

I waved her off, the flour coming off easily. "Everything smells great. So that counts for something, right? Anything I can do to help?"

Evan pushed her dark bangs up her forehead, looking like some fifties throwback with her frilly polka-dot apron. "Grab a beer and relax. I got this. Mostly."

"All right, but yell if you need me. I have no baking skills either, but I know how to put out a fire."

She laughed. "Duly noted."

I made my way back to the living area, but all the guys had moved out to the balcony. I snaked through the arrangement of couches and chairs toward the large sliding glass door that led outside and pushed it open. The sound of conversation abruptly halted with my entrance. The men looked up liked they'd been caught looking at girlie magazines. I

NOT UNTIL YOU ‖ 169

hesitated. "Uh, sorry. Am I interrupting some secret boys-only meeting?"

Wyatt was holding an envelope and a piece of paper in his hand. He glanced back down at it, some weird expression morphing his dark features. He rubbed his thumb over the red wax seal he'd broken on the envelope.

Jace leaned back in his chair and propped his ankles on the lower bar of the balcony's railing. "Nope, just giving Wy his birthday gift."

"Oh," I said, taking a tentative step onto the balcony. "What is it?"

"J." Andre shot Jace a quelling look.

"No big deal. Just a complimentary visit to a . . . spa called The Ranch," Jace said, ignoring my brother's warning.

I lowered myself into one of the chairs, an oh-that's-nice response jumping to my lips. But then the name settled on me, kicked my memory bank. My gaze snapped back upward and over to Wyatt. He was carefully sliding the note back into the envelope.

"Uh, you really shouldn't have," Wyatt said, his voice and posture stiff. "I'm not really a *spa* person anymore."

Jace's mouth lifted at the corner, obviously having way too much fun seeing his brother's discomfort. "Oh, no, it's been way too long since you've relaxed. I think it's exactly what you need. I'm sure they'll have treatments there that will whip that stress right out of you."

Andre choked on his beer, coughing loudly and leaning forward, his gaze darting to me. Jace gave him a friendly thump on the back, and I stared at my brother, snippets of conversation colliding in my head, mashing together.

The Ranch. Andre recognizing Foster. Every cell in my body seemed to cringe. *Oh, sweet Jesus.* Things I didn't want to think about flooded my mind. I wanted to put my hands over my eyes but of course that wouldn't help block the mental pictures.

Andre stood in a quick rush, setting his beer on the table. "I need some water. Anyone else want anything?"

They all declined and Andre disappeared inside without another word. Jace smiled as if nothing had happened. "So, Cela, are you all ready to head back to south Texas? Dre told me you're leaving soon."

It took me a second to form a response, my mind still reeling from the knowledge that my brother and his friends were familiar with a BDSM resort, *Foster's* resort. I took a long pull off my beer, trying to beat back my racing thoughts. "I guess I'm ready."

Wyatt smoothed invisible wrinkles from his slacks. "You don't sound too enthusiastic."

I shrugged. "I'm ready to be a vet. Just maybe not so ready to go back home. Living here has kind of grown on me."

Jace grabbed a handful of chips from the bowl in the center of the table. "So stay. There've gotta be animal practices here that'd be happy to have you."

I sighed and reached for a few chips as well. "There are. I got offered a great position at the place I'm working at now. But it's not that easy. My dad's been grooming me to take over his practice since I was old enough to spell *dog*. He's held the spot for me and is counting on me being there."

Wyatt frowned, his dark blue eyes evaluating me. "I know what that's like. I never followed any other path than my father's footsteps. I think he may have had a CEO-in-training plaque attached to my crib."

"So you understand why I have to go," I said, shoving a chip in my mouth in an attempt to choke down the morose feelings that were trying to well up.

Jace sniffed, but kept his opinion to himself.

Wyatt leaned back in his chair and set the envelope in his lap, his thumb still playing over the wax seal. "I know that I enjoy what I do and that I'm better at it than anyone else in my family's company. But I also haven't done much else in my life besides work. I've spent a lot of time doing what's been expected of me and have passed by many unbeaten paths that maybe I should've tried."

I looked down at my beer, the words landing solidly on me.

Wyatt glanced at Jace. "Sometimes forging your own path is the way to find what you're really looking for. Look at this guy. I thought for sure he'd end up in prison or worse—on reality TV. But turns out he's found his way to a pretty happy life."

Jace smirked. "You've still got a shit ton more money than I do, though."

Wyatt laughed. "Well, there is that."

I smiled, the response automatic, polite, but my head was already chasing a thought I couldn't quite tear myself away from. I hauled myself up from the chair. "I'm going to see if Evan needs any help."

But when I walked back into the air-conditioning, I was on the hunt for someone else. My brother's muffled laughter drifted from down the hallway. I turned on my heel and headed that way, mission in mind.

But when I reached the end of the hallway and caught a glimpse through the partially open door to one of the bedrooms, I froze in place. Andre's arm was wrapped around Evan's waist, and his face was buried against her neck, kissing it. Evan's eyes were closed, her head tilted back with an openmouthed smile.

"Stop," she chided. "I didn't get any icing over there."

His other hand drifted beneath her skirt. "What about here? Should I take a taste and find out?"

My beer dropped to the floor, making a racket but not breaking. Andre reared up, looking toward the door as lager fizzed across the floorboards. I wanted to yell, to turn around and escape, but I was locked to the spot, outrage boiling up and over.

"Marcela." Andre strode forward.

Evan stayed back, biting her lip, worry in her eyes.

Andre pushed the door wide and reached out to me, but the touch snapped me out of my stunned state. I shrugged off his hand. "What *the fuck* are you doing?"

I never cursed like that, especially around my family, but nothing else fit the situation or the blind anger racing through me. My brother, the one who made his living on making sure people did the right thing, was screwing his best friend's girl?

"Cela, listen," Andre said, raising his hands like I was a dog that could bite.

"He's your best friend, Andre! Your *best friend*. How could you do this?" I asked, wanting to shake him, to throw things that would injure.

He closed his eyes, took a breath. "Evan, give us a minute, okay?"

Evan nodded and hurried past the two of us, giving me wide berth.

"I don't need a minute," I said, watching Evan walk away. "Nothing you can say makes this okay."

I tried to turn so I could leave, but Andre did grab for me this time, capturing my wrist and tugging me into the bedroom. "Hold up. Sit. We need to talk."

I crossed my arms, refusing to sit. "Talk, then."

He sighed and rubbed a hand over the back of his neck, suddenly looking like the teenaged version of himself, the one who wasn't so self-assured. "Look, I know this seems bad, but you have to trust me. I have good reason to kiss Evan."

"Sure you do. You're a pig."

"Cela . . ." He stared back at me like he was searching for the right words. As if any response could explain away what I'd seen. I had to hold myself back from screaming at him some more.

When no response came, I shook my head, and took a step toward the door. "I'm leaving."

"I'm with her, too," he said finally.

I barely resisted rolling my eyes but did halt my exit to look at him. "Well, obviously."

"No, I mean . . . Jace knows."

My lips parted, my jaw going slack. "He what?"

"He knows that I'm with her."

Before I could blurt out my disbelief, he raised a palm, cutting off my response.

"I promise you he's fine with it. I know it's a lot to understand because it's not the norm. That's why I didn't want to tell you. But it works for the three of us. We all love each other and are happy being together."

I blinked, the way he'd said the last part giving me pause. "All?"

He wiped a hand down his face, closing his eyes like it was too hard to look at me and answer at the same time. "I'm with Jace, too."

"With," I repeated, almost more to myself. "Like *with*?"

He gave a slight nod of admission.

"Holy shit," I murmured and sat on the edge of the bed, the truth breaking through the neat structure of my reality. My brother was in a relationship with two people. And bisexual? My brain hurt. "And did you ever plan on telling me this?"

He looked away, confirming my suspicion that no, he wouldn't have. "I wanted to protect you. It wouldn't be fair to ask you to keep such a big secret from the family."

My parents. Oh, God. If my father even had a suspicion that Andre was interested in guys, it'd be Armageddon all over again. I suspected this may even be a higher offense to him than my sister's teen pregnancy and abortion. He'd have the priest over for an exorcism.

"And I didn't know what you would think," Andre said, his voice quiet.

I peered up at him then, catching the rare vulnerability in his dark eyes. God, how could he even have worried about what I'd think? I loved him. That didn't come with conditions. "What I think is that I want you to be happy. If they make you happy, then that's all I need to know. I'm just hurt that you didn't feel like you could share that with me. That you'd think I'd judge you."

He sighed and sat down next to me on the bed. "I guess part of me still feels like you're my baby sister and too young to know that kind of thing about me."

"I'm twenty-three, Dre. I'm not a toddler."

His lips curved. "I know."

Then another thought hit me, and I punched him hard in the arm. "Oh my God, and you totally jumped my case for being with two guys. Meanwhile, you're doing the same damn thing!"

He grabbed his arm, rubbing the spot I'd hit. "Hey, do as I say not as I do."

"That's bullshit," I declared. "And you're so going to make that up to me."

He lifted an eyebrow. "Oh, really. And how am I going to do that?"

I pressed my lips together, thinking of the earlier talk with my father and then with Wyatt, the plan that had come to mind when I'd seen that wax-sealed envelope. And I knew exactly how Andre could pay me back. "You, dear brother, are going to take your little sister to The Ranch."

He shot off the bed like a roman candle had been shoved up his ass.

"The hell I am. That's not even kind of an option. You don't know what type of place, what kind of stuff, what happens . . ."

"I do. And you will. I have someone I need to talk to who's there and it can't wait." I stood up and straightened my skirt. "After cake, we're going on a road trip."

"Cela," he warned.

"If you don't, I'll get the address from Jace and go myself."

Lines appeared around his mouth. "They won't let you in. It's members and their guests only."

"Young, innocent woman wanting to try out some new things. I'm guessing I could convince someone to help me out and get me in."

He groaned. "Dirty fighting, Marcela."

I smiled and grabbed his hand. "I learned from the best. Now, come on. Cake!"

He gripped my hand, halting me from my exit, and I turned back. His eyes were searching. "Why are you doing this, Cela? What purpose could it serve? You're leaving in a few days."

I wet my lips, nervous to say the words aloud even though they'd been floating through my brain for longer than I'd care to admit. "Maybe I won't."

"Oh, Cela," he said on a weary sigh, his hand releasing mine. "Don't do this. Not for a guy."

I looked away, unable to deal with that big-brother stare and that disappointed edge in his voice. "Maybe I'm doing it for me."

"Sure you are." He stepped over to me and pressed a kiss to the crown of my head. "But I'm not going to be Papá. Your life, your decision. I'll drive you out there if that's what you really want."

I wrapped my arms around his waist and hugged him. "Thanks, Dre."

Tonight would probably turn out to be a huge mistake. Clearly, Andre thought it was. But it was my mistake to make.

I couldn't walk away.

Not yet.

PART V

Not Until You Beg

TWENTY-ONE

"There it is," Andre said as we cruised down the deserted highway at a speed only a cop could get away with.

"Wow," I murmured.

The large stone and cedar building cut an impressive silhouette against the star-flecked dome of sky, the behemoth seeming to grow straight out of the sprawling land around it. Warm lights glowed from some of the windows and the front entrance, but everything else about The Ranch screamed, *Exclusive! Private!*

Andre slowed down as we drove by a sign for Water's Edge Vineyards. He cruised past the entrance for that building and turned left onto an unmarked drive a quarter mile farther down. A wide, low gate stretched across the road, and he pulled to a stop.

"This place is at a vineyard?" I asked, squinting to see if I could make out any of the grounds in the dark.

Andre rolled down his window and pressed his thumb to a touch pad that was mostly covered by creeping vines. The machine scanned Andre's fingerprint, the little green light piercing the blanket of night around them. The smell of wildflowers drifted into the car. "The owner, Grant Waters, owns both. He tells anyone who asks that the big building is his private residence."

The touch pad beeped and the large wooden gate, which looked far from electronic to the naked eye, swung open smoothly. Andre pulled forward, gravel crunching beneath the tires.

"How do people even find out about this place?"

He gave me a sideways glance, his expression unreadable in the near darkness. "The local BDSM community is pretty tight. You know the right people, have the right amount of money, and you'll hear about this place."

I gnawed on that for a moment. "So this is your thing, too?"

"I'll take 'Things I Don't Want to Discuss with My Sister' for five hundred, Alex."

I huffed. "Stop being such a prude. After what you told me tonight about you, Jace, and Evan, I don't think much else could shock me." Then another thought hit me. "Wait a second, if this place is so elite and expensive, how did you get in? No offense, but I can't imagine a detective's salary qualifies."

He sighed, drumming his fingers against the steering wheel. "No, it doesn't. Just the application fee for a dom is ten grand, then there are annual fees."

"Holy shit," I said, unable to stop myself. Had Foster spent that much to come here? That'd pay for rent on his apartment for almost a year.

"But I came in as Jace's guest and got to know the owner. He waived the fee. Plus, I think he likes having a cop on the premises if needed."

Andre pulled into the parking area and found a spot. I glanced around at all the luxury vehicles lined up in the crude country lot, amazed by the number. There were this many people out at some sex resort on a Friday night? I scanned the lot to see if I could catch sight of Foster's SUV, but I didn't know cars well enough to distinguish between one or the other in the scant moonlight.

Andre cut the engine, then held on to the steering wheel, staring forward, not moving.

"What's wrong?"

The seat groaned beneath him as he adjusted himself to turn toward me. "I'm trying to stop myself from driving you back home or at least putting my hands over your eyes when we walk in. I'm not ashamed of this lifestyle, but I can't help wanting to shelter you from it all. Things here can be intense. Can't you wait until Foster's back home, and you can talk to him then?"

I shook my head. I'd considered that. But knowing Foster was here had urgency building in me. I knew I had told him good-bye, that I had no right to be jealous if he was with some other woman tonight. But even the thought of him touching another had me ready to storm the castle and take him hostage. "I need to see him tonight. Here. In his element."

Her brother still didn't look convinced. "Cela, you're . . ."

"Going to be fine," I finished for him. "Dre, I think it's sweet that you still want to protect me, I do. But I'm tired of always doing what I'm 'supposed' to just to make sure you, Papá, and Mamá can feel like I'm safe in my little bubble." My gaze swept over the building. "There's a guy in there who made me feel really, truly alive for the first time in maybe forever. I'm not pretending to understand all of this or even my reaction to it. And he may run me out of there. But if I don't get answers to some questions, I'm always going to wonder."

Andre stared at me for a long few seconds and then the corner of his mouth lifted like a white flag, signaling my victory. He reached out and touched the tip of my nose. "When you'd get so grown up?"

I snorted and reached for the door handle. "Apparently, during the time you were falling in love with your harem."

"Touché." He laughed and climbed out of the car. "And, for the record, Jace would be totally offended that you called it my harem instead of his."

"Would he now?" I got out and peered at my brother from over the top of the car, a question hovering on the back of my tongue. I shouldn't ask, but I couldn't help myself. Curiosity and I were too old of friends. "So is Jace the one, you know, in charge of things within the relationship?"

I couldn't imagine anyone bossing my brother around, but there was something about Jace that screamed confident authority—a presence about him.

Andre leaned his forearms along the top of the car, his eyes wary again. "Is it important for you to know?"

I fiddled with the strap of my purse, trying to look nonchalant. "I just, well, I'm new to all this, and I was wondering if the whole submissive thing means a person is weak or screwed up or something."

"Oh, baby girl," my brother said, his tone going soft. "Of course not."

But I couldn't stop now that the fear was spilling out. "I mean, Papá has always wanted to rule my life and I hate that—God, do I hate that. So why would I like it if some guy took control? Why would I want that?"

"Hey," he said gently as he walked around the front of the car. "Look at me. Do you think I'm weak or screwed up? Do you think Evan is?"

"No. Well, you're a little screwed up, but not in any padded-room kind of way," I glanced up with a small smile. "You and Evan are both submissive?"

"Evan is, yes. I'm a switch, so I can enjoy both sides. What you like in this arena doesn't necessarily translate to who you are outside of it. And it takes just as much personal strength to submit, maybe more, as it does to be the dominant one."

I nodded, his words giving me more reassurance than I expected. If someone as tough, bossy, and hardheaded as my brother could be submissive even some of the time, then it sure as hell couldn't be a sign of weakness. "Thanks, Dre."

He smiled but then pointed a firm finger toward me. "But that doesn't mean you should jump into this without examining everything closely. It can take a while to figure out if this kind of thing is really for you. And while you're exploring, you need to make sure you're with someone who is well-trained and trustworthy, a guy who isn't going to take advantage of your inexperience."

"You couldn't resist one more warning, could you?" I asked, poking his shoulder. "And don't worry. I have just the guy in mind."

He grunted, obviously still not sold on this whole idea, but kept his comments about Foster to himself.

I hitched my purse higher on my shoulder. "All right, big brother, I'm ready. Time to get your baby sister into the den of iniquity."

"*Ay, dios mío.*" He tilted his face to the heavens as he threw an arm over my shoulders. "I'm so going straight to hell."

Foster paced along the deadly quiet hallway, the dark red walls seeming to pulse around him in time with his thumping heartbeat. He turned up the volume on his earbuds, trying to drown out the oppressive silence with the indie rock playlist Pike had put together on the iPod. The sconces along the walls had been dimmed low, but even the subtle light seemed too much for Foster's edgy senses. He closed his eyes and tried to focus on the grinding beat of the music, on getting into the headspace he needed to be in for his role.

Last time he'd come to The Ranch he'd totally blown it. A submissive he'd played with before had requested to scene with him, and he'd agreed, hoping to chase away the vision of Cela in her paint-spattered clothes, wearing hurt in her eyes. But as soon as he'd gotten the girl restrained, he'd lost all desire to continue. He'd bailed and had to call over another dom he knew she'd played with before to give her the whipping he had planned.

But tonight he was determined to move forward, to stop hanging on to something that couldn't be. Cela would be gone soon. He'd steered clear of her since she'd left his apartment. Hanging out with her would only lead to him trying to talk her into staying, asking her to change a future she'd worked hard for to be with him—something that would've been entirely self-serving.

No, things had to end the way they did. He knew the difference between a sexual, we're-good-together-in-bed connection and one that had the potential to ignite that all-encompassing, be-mine dominant side of himself. Cela wasn't the kind a girl to play with, she was the kind he wanted to own—a submissive to train, cherish, and spoil. He'd felt the beginning of the fall the second he'd kissed her on that dance floor, knew that the plunge wouldn't have been far behind.

He groaned and rubbed his hand over his jaw as he leaned against the wall. *Focus, Foster. Stop thinking about her.* Grant, The Ranch's owner, had come to him half an hour earlier, asking him if he was up for scening with a submissive who had a stranger fantasy. Foster usually liked a good role-play, and Grant knew he could be trusted with an inexperienced sub. But the excitement that usually came with such an idea hadn't materialized. Even so, Foster had downed the rest of his club soda and agreed. Something needed to snap him out of this ruminating.

So here he stood, trying to psych himself up as he waited for one of the dungeon monitors to help the sub get set up on the other side of the door. Grant had told him that the woman didn't want to know his identity. She'd be blindfolded and bound and was open to him being a little rough. Fine by him. He could stand to get some frustration out. If he could get his brain in order and stay in role that is.

Colby, one of The Ranch's trainers, stepped out of the room, shutting the door behind him, and Foster pulled the earbuds out. Colby nodded at Foster. "She's ready for you and has been informed of the safe words."

"Thanks," he said, rolling his shoulders, trying to push the unease from his system.

"Gotcha a pretty one in there, Foster," Colby said, his Houston twang filling up the quiet hallway. "But nervous."

Foster tucked his iPod into the outside pocket of his toy bag. "Nervous good or nervous freaked out?"

"A little of both," he said, giving a pleased smile that only a fellow dominant could appreciate.

"Beautiful. Thanks, man."

Colby headed back down the hallway, leaving Foster standing in front of the thick soundproof door. There were discreet cameras inside that would allow the staff to monitor things for safety, but he knew that the sub in there would feel totally isolated and alone nonetheless. He took a deep breath, channeling his dominance, bringing everything into focus. A submissive deserved nothing less than his full attention. She didn't deserve a dominant who was thinking of someone else.

After one more cleansing breath, he turned the knob and opened the door. It was warmer inside than in the hallway, candles throwing flickering light around the lush space. He'd chosen the playroom that most resembled a high-end hotel suite over one of the dungeons or themed rooms. Most women who wanted the stranger fantasy usually liked the idea of meeting said stranger in a real-life type of setting.

He shut the door behind him slowly, giving his eyes time to adjust to the change in lighting, and enjoyed the sharp little breath he heard from across the room when the door clicked shut. Yes, she was nervous all right. He could almost smell her anticipation mixing with the soft vanilla scent of the candles. Vanilla. He always thought it amusing that Grant only stocked The Ranch with that particular scent. The guy had a sense of humor. Foster blinked, waiting for his vision to sharpen, and then drew in his own sharp breath.

At the base of a large, four-poster bed was the outline of a woman on her knees, back exposed. Her arms were stretched up and out, cuffed to the bed's posts, and her dark hair was loose down her back, the ends brushing the top of a gorgeous, heart-shaped ass. A hard, trembling ache went through him. Of all the women he could've played with tonight, the universe was going to torture him with one who looked like the very one he couldn't have. He set his toy bag on nearby table, his hand shaking more than he liked.

"I'm here," he said, the words harsh in the thick silence.

Her arms sagged in the chains, her head dipping forward—in relief or surrender, he wasn't sure. "Thank you, I wasn't sure you'd come."

The softness of her voice, the way her consonants rolled over each other, went straight to his cock and nudged at something in his brain. He wet his lips, a weird electric feeling crackling over his skin. He stepped closer, letting her hear his heavy footsteps, feel his presence. "Tell me why you're here."

Her fingers twisted around the chains, her body rocking with that edge of nerves. "Because I don't want to be anywhere else."

The response hit him like a swift blow to his sternum, her voice morphing in his ears into Cela's. He rubbed his forehead, a sick feeling knotting his insides. Now he was going to turn every woman into a version of her?

He let out a long, frustrated breath. "Stand up and turn around."

Her body went still for a moment, obviously surprised by the command. But after the beat of hesitation, she rose to her feet and turned, crossing her hands above her head to accommodate the bindings. She kept her head down, her hair curtaining her blindfolded face.

Her breasts sat high in her lacy black bra, and the warm glow of her golden skin could inspire prayers of worship, but Foster couldn't bring himself to take advantage. He could play the jerk when needed, but he couldn't use a sub while thinking of another woman.

"I'm sorry, sweetheart. I can't do this." He reached out to lift her chin and pull her blindfold off. But when the swath of black silk fell away, everything inside him seemed to short circuit.

Cela's dark eyes blinked back at him, her teeth tugging at her bottom lip. "Hi."

He stared back at her, wondering for a moment if he really had lost his mind and was having visions. The two worlds he lived in smashed into each other like cars going the wrong direction on the highway. The sight of Cela here, in this place, was almost too much for his brain to compute. "What the fuck are you doing here?"

She winced, and he immediately regretted the coarse words. But his filter had shut down along with everything else.

"I forced my brother to get me in," she said, a tiny tremor weaving through her voice.

"You what? Why?" Blood rushed through his ears in a deafening roar. Even with the confusion, his body was reacting to her presence, seeing her like this in front of him. His cock pressed against his leathers, and he had to fist his hands at his sides so he wouldn't touch her— or demand she touch him.

"I wanted to see you. Needed to see you . . ." Her gaze traveled down the length of him, her cheeks darkening in a way that made his skin feel too hot.

He raked a hand through his hair, his libido and good sense waging a battle inside him. "Cela, angel, you're killing me. We agreed to no more."

"You don't want me here?"

"Want you?" He scoffed. The universe really did want to fuck with him tonight. "That's an understatement. You standing here like this is like waving the most tempting of fantasies in front of me. But you know why we can't."

"Because I'm leaving."

"Yes," he said, frustration building, making his back teeth clamp together. Why did she have to come here and make it worse—extend the torture? Maybe *she* was the sadist.

"So ask me to stay," she said, her voice as unsteady as the candlelight flickering wildly in his peripheral vision.

Her words took a moment to translate in his twisted-up mind. Then it hit him—what she was really suggesting. "*What?*"

She smoothed her lip gloss, her nerves palpable. "I haven't been able to stop thinking about the other night. Or any of the nights with you, really. I don't—I don't understand this. And I'm scared. I'm not going to pretend I'm not. I don't know if I can even be . . . submissive. But ever since I graduated, anytime I think of moving home, I can't even picture it—leaving my place, leaving a chance at a job I know I would love, and now, leaving you."

He closed his eyes, the words everything he wanted to hear but nothing he could accept. "Angel, I can't ask you to stay. You have a whole life waiting for you. What if you walk away from all of that and this doesn't work out? You've only seen a sliver of who I am. You may hate being submissive. It may make you hate *me*."

The thought terrified him down to his marrow—the idea of her submitting to him, then realizing she wanted something else, someone else, and walking away after he was already half in love with her.

She smiled. "This isn't a marriage proposal, Foster. I understand that this could blow up in my face at any moment. But what if I leave and realize this was real, that this feeling I only get with you is more than initial attraction? I wouldn't be staying for you. I'd be staying for me. I'm tired of following some script someone else wrote for me. I want to live in a place I choose. I want a job that excites and challenges me." She looked directly at him, her eyes fierce. "I want to try this—with you."

"Cela . . ." Desire wrestled with the cold fear curling around his gut. He knew what she was saying. This wasn't *I want to be your submissive.* This was *I'm curious and want you to show me why this excites me.* What they'd done together had stirred up things inside her that she didn't understand. Home for her meant the status quo, the life she'd always had. He represented the unknown, the wild, the rebellion. And right now, with all the outside pressures on her, she wanted to rebel.

She held his gaze, her eyes shiny in the ambient light. "I can't promise you that everything is going to work out. This is a gamble. For both of us. I'm asking you to take it with me."

He reached out, fingering a lock of her hair, her bold bravery wrenching something inside him. Even realizing this was probably a passing whim for her, he couldn't help but recognize that she was laying way more on the line than he could ever have asked her to. Putting her job back home and plans on hold. Not to mention being willing to try a lifestyle she had no experience with.

Like everything else with her, he found it hard to say no to that kind of leap of faith. "What will happen if you tell your dad you're not coming home to help him?"

Her gaze shifted away. "It won't be good."

He frowned. "Angel, I don't want you to mess up things with—"

"You were supposed to help me finish my list, right?" she said, cutting him off. "So here's the rest: Never have I ever . . . been in a real relationship. I know we're not there yet. And it scares the crap out of me to even say that word out loud. But I feel something different with you. And I know I don't have a lot of experience, but I've never felt that before. I don't want to walk away without knowing if this is real." She glanced up at her chained hands, then back to him. "So, if you'll have me, I want to be with you, Ian Foster. I want to feel what it's like to submit to you, *sir*."

He was supposed to respond, to say something romantic and brilliant, but her words had knocked him right on his ass. She wanted to stay. She wanted to see what it was like to be *his*. And she was throwing serious words out there like *real* and *relationship*. His heart thumped against his ribs. The risk of starting something with someone who could affect him this quickly, this thoroughly, was downright dangerous. He'd fallen in love—or thought he had—once before and had been blindsided when she'd ended it. But standing there, watching Cela, breathing her in, hearing her take hold of what she wanted, had temptation trampling over all the warning signs that were popping up in his path.

Cela was willing to take a risk on him. Shouldn't he be brave enough to do the same? If he didn't have the balls to try something with her, then what kind of coward was he?

He brushed his knuckles along the butter-soft skin of her cheek, allowing himself for the first time to believe that this could work, that maybe the bottom wouldn't always fall out from under him. It was a scary thing to even consider that hope.

"What do you say?" she questioned, her words holding caution.

He ran his thumb over her plump bottom lip. "You're so green to all of this, angel. It won't be easy. If you really want to do this, I would need to train you on how to submit. Would need to show you what this truly entails."

She tilted her chin upward. "I'm a quick study."

He smiled, warmth spreading through his body like a fast-growing vine as the notion took hold. "Then I can't imagine anything I could want more than having you stay."

Her lashes fell against her cheeks, everything in her stature giving way—natural breathtaking submissiveness. "I'm all yours, sir."

The statement struck him on an elemental level, echoed something he desperately craved. But he wasn't going to let himself believe it yet. The idea of submission was quite different from the reality. He would need to train her without kid gloves. Not show her just the pleasant parts like he'd done with Darcy. If she could survive that without running away, then maybe . . . just maybe, he could start to hope.

"Thank you, angel." He kissed her forehead, breathing in her scent.

Then he unhooked her cuffs and lifted her onto the bed.

Lessons could start later.

Right now he just needed to be inside her.

TWENTY-TWO

Mmm. I shifted beneath the covers, my legs sliding languidly through the luxurious linens as my mind drifted in that haze between sleeping and wakefulness. Pitch-black darkness pressed against my eyelids, and I felt as if I were floating in a sun-heated ocean, the waves rocking me gently. My skin had gone warm all over, and some sound was drifting from my lips, but I couldn't quite grab on to what I was trying to say.

"Time to wake up, angel." The statement was quiet, as if coming from a place just out of my reach.

Wake up . . . wake up . . . But before my mind could grab on to the words or their meaning, something warm and wet moved between my thighs, stroking me. That vaulted me right to the surface of consciousness. My eyelids flew open in the darkness, and I automatically tried to reach out, but my arms jerked backward—bound to something behind me.

Teeth nibbled.

"Oh, God."

Foster laughed softly, his puffs of breath coasting over my already damp skin. "There you are. I was starting to wonder if you were going to come in your sleep."

He licked me again right along my cleft, and I tried to push my knees together. But, of course, my legs didn't cooperate. "I can't move."

"Kind of the point." His tongue circled my clit, teasing and tasting like he was exploring me for the first time even though he'd been deep inside me only a few hours ago. A languid rush of *oh yes* went through my nerve endings, my body responding as if I'd never come before, everything stirring to life and aching already.

I moaned and he tucked fingers inside me while laving at my sensitized skin. My back curved upward off the bed, and my gaze rolled toward the ceiling. Everything was so black, the windowless room providing no relief—an abyss of pleasure and feeling without the distraction of sight. But before my eyes shut again, a small red dot in the far corner of the room snagged my attention.

"Foster," I whispered.

"Hmm" he said, obviously distracted with his strategic destruction of every bit of my self-control. Because even as anxiety was welling, my muscles were tightening and my hips were rocking toward him, urging him on.

"What's that red light for?"

There was the sound of sheets rustling and then little sparks—the dark so absolute that I could see the static electricity firing. He kissed the inside of my knee, and I could sense he was looking at me now, his gaze holding weight even in the void. "It's a camera, angel. A lot of the rooms here are monitored."

My heart jumped in my throat and lodged there. "People are *watching* us."

"Shh," he said, kissing down my thigh again. "It's not for public viewing—we could open the window by the door if we wanted that. It's only dungeon monitors who keep an eye on things for safety reasons."

"Can they see us in the dark?" I asked, my voice sounding tiny in the cavernous room.

"I imagine so. Grant doesn't spare expense on equipment." His hand gripped my thigh with gentle pressure. "But relax, Cela. You're safe here with me. Your privacy is protected."

"How can I know that for sure?" I suddenly felt beyond vulnerable— naked and tied down in the dark.

"Because you trust me," he said simply. "That's your only job with me—to trust. I would never put you at risk. And I promise you, that if you're going to be mine, you're going to need to get used to being exposed at times. Remember that laundry list of mine I told you about?"

"Yes." His fingers were working inside me again, and I was having trouble holding on to my fear, the rhythmic, mind-melting motion drawing all of my energy toward the need for release.

"Being watched kind of turns me on, angel."

I writhed as he curled his fingers to rub on that spot that made everything want to break open inside me. "Oh . . ."

"And I suspect, if you really let yourself think about it—let yourself imagine someone on the other side of that camera getting hot because you're so fucking sexy spread out like this for me, you might kinda like it, too."

I whimpered.

"And even if you don't, you'll do it because it pleases me."

His mouth settled over me again, and white light leaked into the dark behind my eyelids. I bowed up and the images drifted from my mind. All that was left was Foster, in the dark, his tongue and fingers bringing me past the point of shame. A stadium could've been watching at the moment, and I probably wouldn't have cared.

He sucked on my clit and moved a third finger inside me. My control splintered, and I cried out, bucking against the bindings and rocketing into the arc of release. He held on to me, his mouth working me with expert precision as I turned into some mindless, begging thing.

Then, as if attuned to my body in a way even I wasn't, he slowly backed off, easing me down from the orgasm with soft touches and words until I stopped writhing. Then he was unhooking an ankle and a wrist and rolling me onto my side. The sound of a foil wrapper being torn open registered in my buzzing brain. Hot naked skin pressed against my back, the coarse hair on his chest brushing me, and a hand gripped me below the knee. "Open for me, Cela. I need you."

Foster guided my knee toward my chest. The arm and leg of the side I was lying on were still tethered, so I could do nothing but let him put me in position. Then he was sliding deep, his thick heat pushing over tender, needy tissues. I moaned again, not sure I could handle more stimulation. But as he banded an arm around me and stroked me with gentler fingers than before, I knew there was no fighting it. This man knew exactly how to wring every drop of pleasure out of me, whether I was exhausted or not. My body wanted to give it to him.

He was in no hurry, no sprint to his own finish line. Instead, he seemed to be savoring and drinking in the sensation with every long, lazy stroke. A dream lover sneaking into my dreams and slaying me with murmured words and sure hands.

And I knew it was because we were both tired.

And it was late.

And dark.

But it felt different. Special. Like making love instead of just sex. Or what I imagined making love would feel like.

And even though I knew it was too soon, I wanted it to be so. Those feelings.

Without being able to hold it back, another orgasm rushed toward me—languid and lush. Hitched breaths passed my lips, and his arm tightened around me. Then Foster was groaning and thrusting to the hilt, filling me with his own release and holding me against him like he was afraid I'd vaporize and disappear.

Minutes later, he remained buried in me. He kissed my shoulder, my neck—the scent of his shampoo, sweat, and my own arousal drifting over me. His stubble scraped across my cheek as he laid his head against mine. "I should probably move."

"Mmm," I mumbled, not ready for him to go anywhere. "Moving is so overrated."

He murmured an agreement but slid out of me anyway and rolled away briefly, probably taking care of the condom. But before I could even catch the chill of the room, his heat was back against me, cocooning me. He unhooked my arm from the cuff and rubbed my wrist gently. "We'll have to leave once it's morning. The room isn't ours to keep."

"Boo."

He tucked me closer to him and pulled the covers fully over us now that our heated skin was cooling. "I know. You make me not want to return to the real world."

"It won't be so bad," I said sleepily, feeling as content and calm as I could ever remember.

"I hope you're right, angel," he said, his words featherlight touches against my ear. "I really do."

But the grimness etching his tone spoke loudly in the quiet night. He didn't think this was real. He didn't expect it to work.

I was only temporary. I laced my fingers with his and closed my eyes, wondering, not for the first time, if I didn't believe the exact same thing.

He shifted behind me with a silent sigh. "Get some rest. Dawn will be here soon."

"Where are we going?" I asked Foster as I stepped out of the bathroom, freshly showered and wrapped in a robe that guy Colby had given me the night before.

Foster was gathering the rest of our things from the armoire on the far side of the room. "Breakfast and then we need to pay someone a visit before we head out."

I had no idea who we could possibly have to visit, but I kept that opinion to myself. "Did you see my phone? I need to let Andre know I'm okay. I promised him I'd text him this morning. He said he was going to stay the night in case I needed a ride back home."

Foster walked over to the bedside table, the soft leather of his pants molding over his backside with every step. Hmm, I was beginning to see the appeal of leather. He grabbed my phone and walked it back over to me. "Tell Andre that I'll make sure you get home safely. Then get dressed. Normally, if we're here together, you won't be wearing much. But even I'm not sadistic enough to take the chance of you running into your brother wearing lingerie."

I grimaced at the thought and grabbed my things from him. After tapping out a text message to my brother, I pulled on my skirt and blouse from the night before and slipped into my strappy sandals. My phone dinged and I picked it up. "Andre said he's heading out."

Foster wrapped his arms around my waist from behind and peered over my shoulder at my phone. "And that if I hurt you, he'll kill me. Nice."

I dropped my phone into my bag and turned around in his embrace. "Yeah, you should know he's entirely serious. The guy does carry a Taser and a gun."

"I don't doubt it. He stopped by my apartment that morning we ran into him coming back from the hotel to give me the stay-away message."

NOT UNTIL YOU ‖ 193

I gaped. "He did what?"

"Don't worry about it. I respect that." Foster cupped my chin and pressed a quick kiss to my lips before stepping back and letting me go. "A brother *should* be overprotective of his sister. It's his job."

Something in his tone made me frown. It was like one moment there was comfortable intimacy between us and the next there was this instant distance, like he'd vaulted onto the other side of some wall. But before I could ask him what was wrong, he was heading toward the door.

"Come on, angel," he said, holding out his hand. "Don't want to be late for what I have planned this morning."

My throat tightened at the thought. I hadn't seen much of what lay outside these doors. Andre had introduced me to his friend, Master Colby, and had set up the plan, but then Colby had led me straight here through a bunch of hallways. Now that I'd raced here to try this with Foster, my nerves at the unknown were catching up. Here, between four walls, just me and Foster was comfortable. But I knew there was a whole other world outside—a world I knew nothing about, really. "What exactly do you have planned?"

Foster's brows lowered as his hand closed around mine. "First lesson. When we're here or in this mode at home, you don't get to question every move I make. You have to learn to trust me. If something truly frightens you or goes to a place you don't want, you use your safe word. But other than that, I'm in charge. Do you understand?"

I bit my lip at his gentle admonishment. "Yes . . . sir. Wait, am I supposed to call you master?"

Somehow the word didn't sound right in my mouth. It made it seem like a game, and that's not what this felt like.

He considered me a moment, his blue eyes evaluating. "Everyone here calls me Master Ian."

"Oh, right," I said, looking down at our linked hands. "The other women here."

The last part was out before I realized I'd spoken the thought. And I hated that it came out sounding so petulant. *Grow up, Cela.*

He sighed. "No, not just the women. It's how doms are addressed here. But I also can't stand here and say that I've never been with other submissives here."

My stomach felt like it was made of knotted rubber bands, snapping and popping. "I know."

"Look at me," he said. Reluctantly, I did. "While we're together, you have my absolute word that I won't touch another woman. And I expect the same faithfulness from you. But I can't pretend that I don't have a past. I'm not a kid, Cela."

"Right," I said, irritation welling in me. "Like me, you mean."

Displeasure shadowed his features. "Don't put words in my mouth. All I'm saying is getting jealous over people I was with before I knew you is a waste of energy. If they were that spectacular, I'd be with them now, right?"

Logically, I knew that. But it didn't stop the ugly emotion from brewing in me like some poison. I tried to tamp it down. "So why Ian and not Foster?"

"Because it gives me some sense of privacy. No one in my everyday life calls me Ian. But I don't want you calling me what other submissives have. You *are* going to be part of my life outside of here. So call me what you've always called me. Foster."

Something relaxed in me at that. I *was* different than those other women. I needed to hear that, needed to believe it. "So no 'master'?"

He smirked. "You hate that idea, don't you?"

I tried to fight my smile—to no avail. "Honestly, I think I'd have trouble keeping a straight face. It makes me think of a hunchbacked Igor. *Yessss, Massssster.*"

He shook his head, but I could tell he was amused. "Well, we can't have that. Though after you're exposed to the lifestyle for a while, it may begin to take on a different connotation for you. But like I said, call me by name. And if *sir* feels natural to you, use it. If it doesn't, then don't. I'm not that concerned about semantics."

Sir did come surprisingly easy to me, even that first night. I blew out a breath. "Thank you."

His eyebrow lifted. "You seem surprised."

I pushed an escaped lock of hair behind my ear. "I guess I'm not sure what to expect yet, how much say I have in . . . this kind of thing."

"Which is exactly why you need to come with me," he said, opening the door. "If we're going to do this. Let's get those eyes wide open."

Oh, boy.

TWENTY-THREE

After a long morning at The Ranch, Foster and I were standing inside my doorway. He handed me the thick binder he'd gotten from Colby. Foster had made me sit in on a new members class but had warned me that the introductory session had only scratched the surface. My mind was still whirling with all the information on pre-scene negotiations, contracts, and hard limits—all mixing in with my epic lack of sleep last night, it made for a foggy brain. I hugged the binder to my chest.

Foster crossed his arms and looked down at me, the professor to the student. "Here's what you're going to do. I have some things to take care of tomorrow, and Monday I'm out of town. If I'd realized this was going to happen, I wouldn't have scheduled all of that, but now it's too late to get out of it. So you have the next two days to study the binder and call me or email me with any questions that come up. Anything you're not sure about, ask. When we get together next time, I want you to have a working knowledge of the basics."

My jaw went slack. "You want me to learn all of this in two days?"

He smirked. "Cela, all you've done these last few years is study and cram; you're a pro. And, of course, you won't learn everything in two days. This will give you a foundation. We'll work on the rest together through direct instruction. That's the fun part."

I wet my lips, the image of exactly how he would instruct me making warmth stir low and fast. "Yes, sir."

"What's your schedule like this week?"

"I'm off. I was supposed to be going home, so they'd scheduled someone else in my place. And I can't tell Dr. Pelham that I'm accepting the new position until next week. She's on a cruise."

He reached out and shut my front door, not allowing the empty hall-way to eavesdrop on us. "Perfect. That will give you time to focus on this. And until I see you again on Tuesday, you aren't allowed to get off—by any means."

My cheeks went hot. "I think I can restrain myself for two days."

"That confident, huh?" His lips curled as he slowly backed me up against the wall, the binder trapped between us. "Reading about all those illicit things, imagining me doing them to you, is going to get you hot, angel." His hand slid down my hip and cupped my ass, pulling me tight against his erection. "You're going to get flushed like you are right now. And wet. And suddenly it's going to be very tempting to relieve all that tension."

I swallowed hard, the words making everything go needy and des-perate inside me. Even after our night and morning at The Ranch, I couldn't seem to get enough of his touch. He was creating some sort of weird, addictive response in me. I thought of all those animal experi-ments I'd had to learn about in school—mice hitting levers for pellets. Maybe he was right. At the moment, I was ready to smack that lever again and was finding it hard to imagine not having an orgasm in the next five minutes, much less the next few days. "I'll manage."

He kissed the spot behind my ear, sending goose bumps down my shoulder and along my back. "Is that right? Well, I was going to give you a little something to get you through the next few days. But if you can manage . . ."

He tried to step back, and I grabbed fistfuls of his shirt. The binder thumped on the floor between us. "Wait, please."

His low laugh sent a ripple of anticipation through me. "Stay against the wall and take off your panties. Now."

Guh. I shivered. What *was* that? Why did my body go tingly and hot the minute he got bossy? Even after finding out about this whole sub-mission thing, I still couldn't wrap my head around the thought that I really fit that label. But I wasn't going to question my responses right now. Not when he was looking at me like that. I pressed my back against the wall and let him go this time when he extracted himself from my grip. I quickly slid my underwear off and tossed them to the side, ready for whatever he was about to do as long as it meant him relieving this throbbing need inside me.

He walked over to the black bag he'd carried back with him from The Ranch and dug through an outside pocket. His back was to me and blocked the view of whatever he was getting. But when he turned around, he had some kind of dark purple silicone toy in his hand. My gaze darted from it to him then back to the toy. My knees went a little weak.

He stepped in front of me and shoved my skirt up to my hips, exposing everything. Cool air kissed my damp skin. "Spread your legs."

"Yes, sir." Pressing my palms to the wall behind me, I followed his instructions, my high heels wobbling a bit beneath me as I widened my stance.

He braced a hand next to my head against the wall and leaned into my space, his breath hot against my cheek. Then he was rubbing the cool silicone against my cleft. A little moan escaped. I was so wound up already, even such gentle stroking had my body tightening. "You're so very wet, angel. The challenge for you is going to be to keep this in place. Because this is the only way you'll get what you want."

Before I could respond, the tip of the toy was pushing inside me, stretching me and sliding deep. I closed my eyes to breathe through the sensation, but then Foster settled the other curved part of the device against my clit and turned it on. Everything began to hum. "Oh, God."

He sucked on the lobe of my ear before whispering. "Don't you dare come before I do or there will be consequences. Now, on your knees, Cela."

My eyelids snapped open, but his gaze was dead serious. He guided my legs back together to make sure I held on to the vibrator, then he was pressing down on my shoulder to push me to my knees. I landed on the little flowered rug I had bought at a thrift store. Never had I imagined it'd be used for this purpose. But where I'd gotten my decor soon fled from my mind as Foster's belt buckle filled my vision. His erection was outlined by the leather, and I'm not sure I'd ever seen a more erotic sight. I wanted to lick him through it.

"I expect you know what to do, Cela," Foster said, his gaze heavy on me.

The vibrator was making my thoughts knock into each other, but as if my body caught up before my mind did, I lifted my hands and unfastened his buckle and pants. There was nothing beneath but skin—flat belly, a smattering of hair, and unrepentant arousal. God, he was beautiful. Every part of him so potent and masculine. My inner muscles clenched around the toy, and I had to take a long breath to pull myself back from the edge.

"Good girl," Foster said, sliding his fingers into my hair and taking his cock in his other hand to stroke it. "You'll learn to channel your focus. Your pleasure will be dependent on mine, and your own release will not be your end goal—pleasing me will be. That will be where you'll find your satisfaction."

In the light of day, that statement might've sounded ludicrous, sexist, and misogynistic. But in that moment, as he slid his cock into my mouth, his taste gliding over my tongue and my body riding the vibrator, I wanted nothing more than to do exactly that—please the everloving shit out of him.

I relaxed my throat and moved forward, bringing him as far back as I could, then swirled my tongue around him as I pulled backward again. I laved around the head. He groaned with appreciation, and I felt it all the way to my bone marrow. "You're better at this than you realize."

I smiled inwardly. The A-plus, perfectionistic student in me had actually researched technique on the Internet the other night, but no amount of torture would make me admit that information out loud. So instead I went to work on demonstrating what I'd learned and driving him into oblivion. Nothing was hotter than hearing the gruff sounds he made, tasting him on my tongue, and inhaling his scent—clean sweat and leather and something uniquely his. Falling into that moment almost took my mind away from the relentless, coaxing stimulation between my thighs—the climbing urge to come.

"That's right, angel," Foster said, his voice going a little hoarse as he begin to rock into me faster. "Show me how bad you want me to fuck that pretty mouth of yours. You have no idea how hard it's been not to take you like this at The Ranch this afternoon—to show everyone what a sexy little sub I have, to stake my claim of you in public."

I moaned around his cock, the hot images and his rough tone nearly pushing me over the cliff. My nails dug into his thighs as I held on to the last threads of my self-control.

"Ah, you like that idea," he said, his grip on my hair tightening. "My sweet, innocent girl, I can't wait to uncover all those secret sides of you."

I whimpered, the coil of pressure building in me too much to hold back. I lifted my eyes to his, pleading.

His gaze branded me with its intensity. "Not yet, Cela. I'm not fucking done with you."

I breathed deeply through my nose, fighting the need, and focused on him. I didn't want to come before him. I didn't want to leave him unsatisfied. I needed to feel him lose his own control. That alone helped me push back the oncoming tide. I pulled away for a moment and dipped lower, gliding my tongue along his sac and taking one of the globes in my mouth to suck gently.

"Fuck . . ." Foster's groan rattled through him, and he pressed the back of my head against the wall, securing me in place. "Open."

I did and he was back pushing between my lips with a ferocity that had my will obliterating. I couldn't move my head. All I could do was take him and work my tongue around him as he ruthlessly ravaged my mouth. Everything began to blur, my body revving. Then his cock jerked against my tongue and lovely, hot fluid hit the back of my throat, Foster's loud groan sending off trails of sparkling desire inside me.

And that was the final switch. My body clenched hard around the vibrator and I tilted my hips forward, riding the soft, humming nub pressed against my clit until everything burst open inside me. A muffled cry ripped past my throat as Foster continued to pump inside me.

I bucked against the force of my own orgasm, the power rocking me, and held on to him like he was the life raft keeping me from drowning. He pulled out of my mouth and grabbed my wrists, then slid to his knees in front of me. I pitched forward automatically and pressed my face into his shoulder. He wrapped his arms around my convulsing body, holding on to me.

"I can't—please, take it out," I panted, the intensity of sensation getting past the sanity point, but he held on tight, not allowing me to remove the vibrator.

"Shh, angel. You can. Come for me, again. You're not done."

I squeezed my eyes shut, water leaking from the corners. "Foster, *please.*"

But even as the begging word passed my lips, my body charged up another hill, and this time the orgasm was so intense, so breath stealing, that only silence emerged when I opened my mouth to cry out. I swayed in his arms as he whispered sexy, coaxing things against my ear.

Finally, when every ounce of strength seemed to exit my system, Foster gently slid the toy from me. Not even caring where I was, I moved my legs from under me and lay down on the floor, my head against his thigh and my body curled up on the rug in the fetal position. My blouse clung to my sweat-slicked skin. I was done. Not sleeping for much of last night, all the emotional upheaval of the previous day, and two orgasms had pushed me past any sense of decency.

Foster combed my hair with his fingers, caressing my scalp with long, luxurious strokes. A soft sigh escaped me. Somehow, lying there on the floor half-naked, my knees rug burned, and my jaw aching from the rough use, I'd never felt more comfortable or cherished. I could've slept there and been happy about it.

Foster traced my eyebrow with his finger. "You want me to run you a bath, or do you want to worry about that after you get some rest?"

"Rest," I murmured.

"Good choice." He extricated himself from under me and then turned me to lift me into his arms.

I didn't fight it. If he wanted to lift me, so be it. He carried me into my bedroom and laid me on my unmade bed. I reached for my blouse, but he gently pushed my hands away.

"Let me." He unbuttoned my blouse and took off my bra, brushing soft fingers against my still-beaded nipples. Then, he guided me down to my pillows and pulled the sheet and blanket over me.

"Are you staying?" I asked sleepily.

He rubbed a thumb over my cheekbone. "No, angel. I can't. But come Tuesday, we'll be spending a lot of time together. Take the next few days to enjoy the solitude . . . and the freedom."

"If this is what captivity feels like, I think I'm becoming a fan."

He chuckled softly, a warm, masculine sound that made me want to crawl back into his lap. "We'll see what you think when you're not high on post-orgasm, subspace bliss."

"Mmm," I murmured, fighting to keep my lids open.

He kissed my forehead. "Get some rest, angel."

Then he was gone.

And so was I.

TWENTY-FOUR

"Marcela, this better be a joke," my father warned. "If it is, it's a particularly unfunny one."

The acid in my stomach churned, and I shot Bailey an *I'm dying here* look. She gave me a weak double thumbs-up for me to keep at it. "Papá, the clinic needs me right now. It would be bad to leave them in a lurch."

Lie. Lie. Lie. But somehow, even though I'd had the best of intentions when I dialed his number, I couldn't bring myself to tell him the truth yet.

"I know of another clinic in a lurch," my father said through what sounded like clenched teeth. "Mine. *Tu familia*."

I pinched the bridge of my nose, and Bailey poured me a second glass of wine in sympathy. "I know. But you've managed this long without me, surely—"

"How long do they need you for?" he asked, his tone clipped.

Indefinitely. "Uh, I'm not sure. They're looking for a replacement. A couple more weeks?"

He muttered a slew of something I couldn't understand. "You've put me in a bad spot, Marcela. The house is ready and sitting there, and I've been setting things up at the clinic, too. You better be here for your birthday. Your mamá has been planning a big family dinner, and I will not see her disappointed. *Comprendes?*"

"Yes, Papá," I said, shrinking under that tone of his. "I promise I'll be there for my birthday."

Even if it wasn't to stay. I pressed my face into the throw pillow I had in my lap. I was lying to my father. And leaving my family in a tough spot—for what? To have some crazy, kinky relationship with a boy? I was going to hell.

Worst. Daughter. Ever.

"Good night, Marcela," my father said coolly.

"Good night. Tell Mamá I miss her."

"Tell her yourself. Or are you too busy to call your own mother now?"

I swallowed past the dryness in my throat. "Of course not. I'll call her tomorrow."

The phone went dead.

I tossed the phone onto the love seat and groaned as I ran my hands over my face.

"That bad, huh?" Bailey asked from her cross-legged position on the floor. She twirled a forkful of spaghetti in the bowl she was holding. She looked so comfortable there hanging out in my apartment. I'd rarely invited her over because if I was home, I was studying. And usually she had to drag me to go out so I'd see something besides my four walls. But it was nice having her here now.

"I lied through my goddamn teeth," I said, reaching for the glass of wine. "I don't know how I'm going have this conversation. I thought I could, but how am I supposed to tell him I'm going to deviate from the path I've been planning all my life? He'll hate me, Bay. *Hate* me."

She frowned. "Your dad may get mad, but he won't hate you. You're just trying to live your own life."

"No, you don't know him. Forgiveness is not his strong suit."

"What do you mean?"

"Well, my sister, Luz, got pregnant at seventeen and . . . didn't go through with the pregnancy. My dad cut her out of our family like she didn't exist. She was just a kid who made a bad decision with her boyfriend, but there were no second chances. That was it. Done. He gave her money to get an apartment and then told her not to come home again."

"Wow, that's . . . harsh."

"I know," I said, between gulps of wine. "Now you know why I'm terrified to tell him. Luz has struggled every day since then—alone with no support around her. If Andre, my oldest brother, or I want to talk to her or see her, we have to do it on the sly without my parents knowing. She puts on a brave face and is too proud to accept money from any of us, but I can't imagine what that must be like. My family is everything to me. Going through life without them being there, I don't even want to think about it."

Bailey set her bowl in her lap, sympathy crossing her features. "Your brothers wouldn't disown you."

I sighed. "No, they wouldn't. But how could I walk away from my mom?"

"It's not like you're breaking the law or anything. You don't think your mom would forgive you?"

"Not if my dad told her not to. She does everything he says without question. It nearly killed her when he kicked Luz out, but she didn't stop him. Honor thy husband and all that crap. She just went to church and prayed for days on end, lighting candles and saying her rosary novena. I remember crying for my sister at night because I had no idea why they wouldn't let her come home. I was too young at the time for them to tell me the real reason, so all I knew was that she did a 'very bad thing.' After that, I thought anytime I broke a rule, the same thing would happen to me."

"Geez, talk about pressure. No wonder you're such a straight arrow," she said, shaking her head.

"Ha. Right. A straight arrow," I scoffed. "Not so sure that label applies anymore."

She cocked an eyebrow at me. "Seriously? You're going to take a kickass job instead of going back home. It's not like you've gone all Britney and shaved your head during a drug bender or something."

I kicked back the last of my wine, letting the warmth of it burn through my chest before meeting Bailey's gaze again. "I'm not exactly staying for the job alone."

Her fork hovered halfway to her mouth, then after a beat, my comment apparently registered. She set the bowl and fork on the glass coffee table with a clank.

"Oh. My. God. There's a guy, isn't there? I knew it! You've been acting so weird lately." She pushed up from the floor and plopped on the other side of the couch from me, her dinner forgotten and her eyes wide. "Is it *Pike*? Please God, tell me it is. Because, seriously, if you've seen him naked, I'm going to need detailed descriptions. And possibly drawings. How comfortable are you with hidden video? Because I'd be willing to pay you for that, too."

I snorted. "Fangirl much?"

She grabbed a pillow and swung it at me. "Yes. Talk, bitch!"

I dodged the blow with an elbow and set down my empty glass. "Calm down. Lord, wine makes you mean, you know that?"

Bailey narrowed her eyes.

"Fine. No, it's not Pike. We're just friends. Though,"—I gave her a conspiratorial look—"I have seen him naked, and believe me, a drawing could not possibly do him justice."

Bailey's mouth formed a perfect *O*, making her look like one of those dolls that you squeeze to make sing, only no sound came out.

"But I'm kind of in a thing with his roommate, Foster," I finished.

She closed her eyes and held up a finger in the I-need-a-moment gesture. When she opened her eyes again, she had the expression of a girl on a mission. "Let's put a pin in that whole, I have a 'thing' with some guy you've never mentioned to me before. And rewind back to the part where you've seen Pike—the drummer of frigging Darkfall—*naked*."

I curled my lips inward, debating on how much I should tell her. I'd never really had a friend I talked about sex things with. Well, mostly, because I had no sex things to actually share. And my closest friends back home were raised even more conservatively than I was—nice girls don't talk about those things aloud. But Bailey had sure done her fair share of telling me about her escapades. She didn't have much of a filter.

And though she'd prodded me about my reasons for not dating anyone, I'd never admitted to her that I'd been a virgin. Mainly because she would've staged her own version of *The Bachelorette: Virgin Edition* to get me laid. However, tonight the need to talk to someone about all that was going on in my life was filling me like helium, leaving me ready to burst. Maybe it was time to trust Bailey as a real friend instead of holding her at arm's length like I'd been doing with everyone since I started school.

Plus, I had been studying the binder Foster had given me. It *did* say a good safety net to have in place was to make a friend you could trust aware of what you were doing so you could check in with that person when you were out with someone new. Foster wasn't exactly new, but I figured the rule could still apply.

"So, okay," I said, gathering my courage and pretending to study a chip in my nail polish so I didn't have to look at her. "I sort of went out with both Pike and Foster the night of graduation. Your tequila was involved. And, you know, I didn't come home until morning."

A soft gasp. "Ho. Lee. Shit, Cela. *Both* of them?"

Blood rushed to my face as I braced for the judgment. "I didn't sleep with Pike. We just fooled around but—"

"You are my fucking hero."

My gaze snapped upward. "What?"

"Are you kidding me? I would lose my shit being within three feet of Pike. I could barely string a sentence together when he walked in the other day. And you, Ms. All Study and No Play, managed to snag not just him but his roommate, too? And I bet the roommate's just as hot, right? The hot ones tend to group together."

"*So* hot," I said, sagging into the couch, relieved to get the confession out. "Like I can barely look at him without wanting to jump and squeal like a twelve-year-old with Bieber fever. It's ridiculous."

Bailey sighed wistfully. "Just rub it in, Medina."

I rolled my eyes. "Like you don't have dudes lining up."

"Dudes, Cela, frat guys who want to show me how proficient they are at keg stands. Not smoking-hot rock stars."

"Foster isn't a rockstar. He's a business guy, owns a company."

"He owns a company." She blinked then reached for a garlic breadstick, shoving a bite of it in her mouth and chewing a little furiously. "I love you, but I'm totally kind of hating you right now. So a sexy CEO, which means he has money and is smart. Oh, how you suffer. And now you have a 'thing' with him? What kind of thing? Obviously enough to keep you here."

I looked at the closed binder sitting on the bottom shelf of the coffee table. I nodded at the wine bottle. "You better pour us both another glass. This may take a while."

Her eyebrows disappeared beneath her bangs, but she filled up the glasses again.

I had a feeling it was going to sound even crazier out loud than it did in my head, but there was no turning back now. She'd either grill me for every last juicy detail or drag me to the campus psychologist for an eval. *Here goes nothing.*

Foster looked up from his laptop at the sound of ferocious growling. On the far side of the living room, Monty had his head sticking out from under the blanket in his dog bed, teeth bared, and Pike was standing over him in a bouncer stance, an odd expression on his face.

"What are you doing?"

"Projecting calm, dominant energy," Pike said, his voice even as he looked forward and not at Monty or Foster.

"I don't think Monty has the mental capacity to enter a Safe, Sane, and Consensual agreement with you. And to be honest, I think he may be a top."

Pike turned then, his face contorting as he tried not to laugh. "Stop. I'm trying to send a message here."

"Not sure he's getting it."

Monty snarled and snapped at Pike's boot, and Pike bent over and touched Monty's side with his fingers in a quick, snake-strike motion. *"Tsch!"*

Monty ducked his head and backed off.

"Ha!" Pike said, grinning at Foster. "Look at that. Shit actually works."

Foster laughed. "And what shit would that be exactly?"

"Cela told me about how training dogs is all about teaching them to be calm and submissive so you can be the pack leader. And so I downloaded all these episodes of *The Dog Whisperer*. That dude could make Cujo turn into Benji. But I think it's starting to work. That's the first time Monty hasn't gone into full attack mode when I corrected him. Your girlfriend's a genius."

"Cela's not my gir—" Foster started, but then his lips clamped shut. He'd been about to correct Pike on the erroneous term. Foster didn't have girlfriends. Not since the Darcy debacle. But wasn't that exactly what Cela was going to be? He could dress it up with the D/s terms. She was his submissive. But this was so much more than a play partner at The Ranch. He was inviting her into his life. His throat narrowed a bit, making it hard to breathe for a moment.

"Uh-oh," Pike said, stepping away from Monty's bed. "I know that look. Don't get all freaked out now. You brought this on yourself."

"Brought it on myself?" He scowled. "You make it sound like I've come down with an illness."

Pike plopped down in a chair and propped his heels on the coffee table. "Look, I'm not judging. I think Cela's great and hot and smart and *hot*."

"I got it," Foster said irritably.

He smirked. "But just be careful. She's young and doesn't know what she wants right now."

"She knows. That's why she's staying here," Foster said, the conviction in his tone faltering only slightly.

"For now," Pike said with a frown. "You've dazzled a virgin with your worldly ways. Bravo, boy wonder. Big feat."

Foster pushed his laptop closed with a loud snap, Pike's sarcasm digging right under his skin. "Now wait a second—"

Pike held up a hand. "Hear me out. You remember me telling you about, Ms. Briarstone, my junior year math teacher?"

Foster leaned forward and slid his computer onto the table, annoyance pumping through him. "Yeah, you never shut up about her back then. You said she wore skirts that inspired even *you* to learn quadratic equations."

Pike gave a wistful sigh and got a far-off look in his eye. "Ah, those pencil skirts. When she'd lean over her desk to grab her notes, you couldn't see any panty line. Not one. I lost days of my life wondering what was beneath—something sexy or nothing at all?"

"What does this have to do with anything?"

He brought his gaze back to Foster. "Because the night of my junior prom, I didn't fuck the girl I'd taken to the dance. I lost my virginity to Ms. Briarstone at a shitty little motel she drove me to outside of town."

Foster's brows dipped. "You told me you did it with Laurel Woods freshman year."

"Yeah, well, I lied. Laurel was my first blow job." He pulled his feet off the table and braced his forearms against his thighs. "But my point is that I lost my virginity and fell in fucking love, dude. I thought that was it. No one could ever be as hot or perfect as her. I mean, she wore thongs and garters and shit. No girl in high school was going to top that."

Foster sniffed, having trouble picturing Pike with hearts in his eyes.

"But of course all that rush of feeling wasn't real. It was just me being young and stupid and horny as shit. We fooled around a few more times, but the novelty eventually wore off and we moved on."

"Man, that's kind of fucked up. She was a grown woman, and no offense, but you were a pretty screwed-up kid back then. She shouldn't have messed with you."

He shrugged. "Fucking a beautiful older woman was the least of my potentially psychologically damaging experiences back then. And hell, if I was with her, at least I didn't have to go home to sleep."

Foster sighed and leaned back against the couch, Pike's warning echoing his own worries. "For the record, you're not telling me something I'm not already worried about. I know I'm a novelty to Cela right now, and that on some level, I represent all the bad in her good-girl world. But it *feels* like more, Pike. When we're together, there's this sense of . . . rightness. Like she's supposed to be mine. And she chose to stay here. But, don't worry, I'm keeping myself in check about it."

"Sure you are." Pike shook his head, but there was a smile there. "You're so fucked, my friend."

Monty barked, as if seconding that remark.

"No, I'm serious. I'm not letting myself get too deep yet. I'm just seeing how it goes."

"Uh-huh," Pike said, obviously unconvinced. "Just be careful."

There was a loud knock at the door and a shout of, "Delivery!"

Pike glanced toward the sound as Monty scrambled toward it in full guard-dog mode. "What's that about?"

Foster pushed off the couch. "You don't want to know."

But Pike was already hopping up from his chair and beating Foster to the door. He swung it open. The guy on the other side handed Pike a clipboard. "Delivery for Ian Foster. We wanted to make sure you were home before we brought it up."

Pike looked down at the paperwork, obviously scanning it to see what was being delivered. He turned to Foster with his jaw slack. "Tell me you didn't."

"Shut up." He grabbed the clipboard from him and signed.

Pike laughed and put a hand on his shoulder. "So. Fucked."

TWENTY-FIVE

I walked up the stairs to my apartment Tuesday afternoon with butterflies the size of mutant bats in my belly. Foster had emailed me informing me that we'd be going out tonight, and that he'd left instructions for me in an envelope he'd slipped under my door.

When I unlocked my door and saw the innocuous white rectangle lying atop the rug I'd knelt on the last time I'd seen him, a frizzle of anxiety went through me. I picked it up and brought it into the kitchen to set down the rest of my stuff. But that was about all I could manage before tearing it open. Inside were a note and a key.

I unfolded the letter.

Cela,

Thank you for emailing me your hard and soft limits. Tonight you will accompany me to dinner to further work out the details of our arrangement. I've selected what I'd like you to wear. It's hanging in the entryway closet in my apartment. Use this key to retrieve it. Only wear what I've provided. Nothing else. Wear your hair down.

Do not drink any alcohol beforehand. I need you clearheaded and totally focused tonight.

I will pick you up at seven. Be ready.

—F

My breath whooshed out of me, the curt instructions waking something inside me. And so it would begin. Deep end of the pool, here I come.

After a long shower, a detailed grooming session, and a blowout, I slipped into the strapless dark magenta dress Foster had picked out for me. The luxurious material slid over my bare skin like a soft caress, inspiring images of Foster's fingers gliding over me. Warmth gathered between my thighs. Hell, if I was already getting worked up, it was going to be a long dinner. I'd managed to obey his instructions not to get off, but reading through all the information over the weekend, and even talking about some of it with Bailey, had wound me tight enough to feel constantly on edge.

I took a calming breath and reached for the panties he'd included—a little triangle of satin that barely covered anything. I was surprised he'd even given them to me. I figured any guy, given the chance, would have a girl wear nothing at all beneath her dress. But after I slipped them on and headed to the other side of my bedroom to get the black belt and heels he'd provided, I realized exactly why he'd chosen the panties. The fabric instantly molded to my freshly shaven skin and the wetness that seemed to be ever present since I'd gotten home, making me that much more aware of my arousal. I groaned and ventured a glance toward my bedside drawer, where my handy-dandy vibrator was stored.

But Foster was going to be here in a few minutes, and I'd held out this long, what was another few hours? Right? The argument didn't do any good convincing my body. I sighed and slipped into the heels and fastened the belt around my waist. I took one final glance in the full-length mirror on my closet door.

Damn. The guy knew how to choose an outfit. There was no sign of the girl who spent most of her time wearing scrubs, a ponytail, and layer of cat hair. I looked . . . sexy. And elegant. I didn't know much about brands, but I had a feeling what I was wearing didn't come from the local mall. Once again, I found myself wondering why someone who could afford these kinds of things was living with a roommate in my complex.

I mean, my complex was nice. My dad had insisted on helping me pay for something in a good neighborhood so I didn't have to live on campus and could feel safe. But it wasn't some swanky high-rise or anything. Foster could clearly afford more.

The thought was like a burr in my foot, a constant niggling reminder that there was so much I didn't know about the man I was entrusting myself to. A knock on my door pulled me from my worried reflection.

I took a steadying breath and made my way to the door. I had a feeling when Foster said be ready, that meant not making him wait even for a minute. I swung open the door, but instead of finding Foster on the other side, Gerald filled my doorway. Automatically, I reared up. "Gerald."

"Hi, Cela," he said with an tilted smile. "Uh, wow, you look really pretty."

My stomach dipped. I'd made a point to avoid my formerly friendly neighbor since finding out about his background. After Foster had told me, I'd looked up the information for myself, and it'd made me ill to even think about all the times I'd been alone with Gerald. "What are you doing here?"

"Hey, uh, I'm sure your friend told you about my . . . past. And I'm sorry I didn't say anything. It's just—that was a much younger, much stupider version of myself. Mistakes I wish I could undo. And I liked hanging out with you—with someone who didn't just see that creep from back then."

I shifted in my heels and glanced over his shoulder at the empty hallway. "Gerald, I appreciate the apology, but I think it's best we leave things as they are."

"Is it because of your boyfriend?" he asked glumly.

I saw the out and took it. "Yes. He's very . . . protective."

"Right," he said with a frown.

"Well, I understand. I only wanted to tell you that I was sorry and that I found a dog walker for Sammi. She's doing well with her."

I managed a small smile. "That's good to hear."

"Yeah, well, I guess I'll be seeing you then." After one last look, which strangely mimicked how Sammi had looked at me when I wouldn't throw the ball again, he turned on his heel to head back toward the stairs. But before he made it all the way there, Foster's door opened. Foster stepped out, looking like a *GQ* model in a sharp dark gray suit and a tie that coordinated with my dress.

Simultaneously, relief and fear rushed through me. Relief that I wasn't alone with Gerald anymore, but also fear, because when Foster turned his head to the right to see Gerald's retreating back, every bit of him bristled. I rushed over to Foster, heels clicking on the floor, to grab his arm before he launched himself forward. "Hey, hold up."

His gaze snapped to me, eyes fierce. "What the fuck is he doing up here? Is he bothering you?"

"It's all right," I said, thankful Gerald had already disappeared around the second set of stairs, and apparently hadn't noticed Foster come out. "I took care of it."

"Took care of what?"

I could feel the anger rumbling through him, my grip on his arm quivering with it. The intensity of it scared me a little. "He came by to apologize. I opened the door, thinking it was you. But I handled it. It's fine."

He closed his door behind him with unnecessary force and walked me over to my own, guiding me back into my apartment. When he shut my door, he turned to me with accusing eyes. "What were you thinking? You just *opened* your door? No chain?"

"I forgot."

"You promised me, Cela," he said, his jaw clenched as he looked back toward my closed door. "God, do you even realize how dangerous it is for a woman to be that careless?"

I gritted my teeth at his admonishing tone and his firm grip on my shoulder. "I said it was an *accident*. I was expecting you."

"An accident?" That only seemed to heighten the furor in his eyes. "What if he had pushed his way in here, huh? He could have attacked you without anyone seeing a damn thing. Locked both of you in here together."

"Back off, okay?" I said as I slipped from beneath his hand. "It wasn't anything. I'm fine. If he wanted to attack me, he could have done it during one of the countless times I was alone with him."

Foster stared at me for a long moment, then swiped a hand through his hair, more agitated than I'd ever seen him. "You will never open your door without checking again."

"Foster."

"Swear to me, Cela. And mean it this time."

I shook my head, confused by the desperate edge in his voice. "Why are you making such a big deal out of this?"

"Because you don't even know how fucking vulnerable you make yourself sometimes," he said, his volume rising. "One second. That's all it takes. Yesterday, when I got home from my trip, I saw you running in the goddamned dark with your iPod cranked up. A guy on the corner was catcalling you and took a photo with his phone, and you didn't even notice."

"*What?*"

"That phone is no longer in working order, believe me. But it took everything I had not to haul you right off the street."

I shuddered at the thought of someone photographing me. "I'm usually more aware than that."

"No. You're not. You know how many times I've seen you walking through the parking lot at night with your phone to your ear or your earbuds in? You have no awareness of your surroundings."

I stared at him. "You've watched me in the parking lot? What the hell?"

"See, you don't even realize that for the last few months, we get home around the same time each day. I could be two steps behind you, and you wouldn't notice. I could grab you, and you wouldn't even have time to scream."

I wrapped my arms around myself, not sure how to handle this version of him. "You're freaking me out, Foster."

"Good," he said, stepping close. "I need you to be scared enough to start looking out for yourself."

"Now hold up," I said, his tone pushing all my go-to-hell buttons. "I'm not a child, so don't talk to me like I'm one. I've managed just fine without some guy telling me what to do for a long time now. You're not my dad."

He crowded into my space, energy rolling off him. "No, I'm not. But I am in charge until you tell me otherwise. And I'm ordering you to stop being so careless. Going forward, if I catch you disregarding your safety, I will make sure you never forget that rule again."

I put my hands against his chest to stop him from coming closer, unable to think straight when he was so near. "You're being a jerk."

"I'm trying to protect you."

"I don't need your protection, all right? I can watch out for myself."

"Cela," he said, his tone dangerously low.

"No. I agreed to try this with you because you taking charge with sex is exciting. I like that. But I didn't freaking agree to be talked to like I'm some dumb kid who shouldn't play outside alone."

His frown deepened, his gaze pinning me. "Then maybe I wasn't clear. I take this seriously, Cela. If you're going to be with me, that means you're my responsibility. To pleasure, to push you to your edge, sure, but also to keep you safe, to take care of you."

Tears of frustration burned in my throat, and my fists clenched against his shirt. "Goddammit, Foster, don't mess this up already. I don't need a caretaker. I've got enough people in my life trying to do that. I only want to be with you. Can't we just do that? Be together?"

He sighed, putting his hands over my fists. "I can be flexible with a lot. But not this."

"You're being unreasonable."

"Well, how about we both get one unreasonable thing each? My protectiveness can be mine."

His hands were warm around mine, and his gaze had softened. I huffed, annoyed that the one simple look could dim my ire. "I don't have anything to be unreasonable about."

His mouth lifted at the side, his head tilting. "Oh, so your jealousy of women I was with before I even knew you is totally rational?"

I sniffed. "Totally."

"Uh-huh," he said grinning fully as he released my fists and wrapped his arms around me.

My body surrendered to his embrace even though I was still stewing on the inside. "I'm not going to live my life scared."

"I'm not asking you to. I only need you to be more aware." His thumb was stroking my tailbone now, and I hated that I didn't want to move out of his hold. "I've seen a lot of ugly stories with bad outcomes in my life, angel."

"Your sister," I said quietly.

"Not just her."

I frowned. "What do you mean?"

He pulled back from the embrace and looked down at me, strain still there around the corners of his eyes and the set of his mouth. "Not tonight, okay? I don't want anything else to taint our evening. But I promise, I'll show you what I mean. Tomorrow, okay?"

"Okay," I said, nodding, not knowing what else to say. He gave me another squeeze, and we stayed like that for a few long seconds. When he released me, he seemed to have pulled himself back into the calm, unruffled man I knew. He ran a palm over my hair.

"Now, why don't we start over?" His gaze traced over me. "Beginning with how outrageously sexy you look in this dress. My God."

I should've smiled, thanked him for the compliment, but after the surprise of his intense protectiveness, all my insecurities about what I didn't know about him flooded into my system. Yes, he'd told me about his sister, but what else lurked in the depths of his past? And how far did this protective streak go? Was I going to have to report in like I used to do with my parents? The thought made my stomach tilt. Maybe I didn't really know Foster at all. I knew casual, neighbor Foster, but not dominant, boyfriend Foster.

And I was *giving* myself to him.

Doubt crawled up my spine and rooted there at the back of my brain.

Maybe my brother had been right.

Maybe this was a mistake.

Maybe I'd jumped into all of this too soon.

I turned away and grabbed my purse, a faint tremor going through my fingers. "I really appreciate the dress. You didn't have to do that."

The words sounded hollow in my ears.

"My pleasure, angel." He took my hand when I came back to his side, though his gaze was scrutinizing, like he could see the thoughts filling my head. "Ready?"

I nodded.

But for the first time since meeting him, I wasn't so sure.

TWENTY-SIX

The restaurant was buzzing, but Foster had secured one of the quieter booths in the back. Lot of good it was doing though, since Cela seemed to be in a particularly tight-lipped mood. He opened his mouth to ask her another question, trying to draw her out, but another voice interrupted.

"Well, look who it is. Glad to see you could finally make it," Kade Vandergriff said stopping by Foster and Cela's table. "Everything tasting okay?"

Foster smiled and stood to shake his friend's hand. Kade owned the restaurant and had invited him to attend his monthly invitation-only night more times than Foster could count, but he'd never been able to make it. "The meal has been excellent so far—each course outdoing the next. Thanks for the invite."

Kade glanced over at Cela with a warm expression. "And who is your lovely date?"

"This is Cela Medina. Cela, my friend Kade Vandergriff. He owns the place."

Cela smiled and lifted her hand, as if preparing for a shake, but Kade simply nodded at her, following rules Cela didn't even realize were in place. "Lovely to meet you."

"Same here," she said, placing her hands back in her lap. "And the food's been great. That avocado appetizer was one of the best things I've ever put in my mouth."

There was silence for a moment, then Kade chuckled, and Foster coughed over his own laugh.

She cringed instantly. "Sorry. That's not exactly what I meant to say."

Kade grinned. "Sorry, we look like men, but up here"—he pointed to his temple—"pure twelve-year-old."

She smirked back at the two of them, brown eyes picking up the twinkle of the candlelight on the table. It was the first spark Foster had seen in her since they'd arrived at dinner. She'd been maddeningly subdued up until then. "No worries. I've been around college boys for seven years. I don't think I'm capable of being offended anymore."

"Good to know," Kade said as Foster slid back in the booth. "Well, I'll leave you to each other. I only wanted to say hello. Enjoy the rest of your night. I'm sure I'll see you again before you leave."

They exchanged good-byes with Kade, and the waiter brought out the main course—a beautiful plate of Dungeness crab and filet mignon. Foster picked up the conversation where they had left off before Kade had stopped by, discussing some of the questions Cela had sent him when she read through the binder. But after a while, he realized she'd gone back to being pensive and quiet.

He watched her picking at her food like she had gruel in front of her instead of top-notch cuisine. He knew she wasn't one of those women who didn't eat, so obviously something was bothering her. No doubt his earlier outburst over her opening her door hadn't gone over well, but he hadn't been able to help himself. Last night, it'd taken every bit of self-control not to lose it when he'd seen her blithely running along the streets of the neighborhood in the fucking dark. That asshole who'd dared to take a photo of her should be thanking the universe that all he'd ended up with was a broken phone. And then seeing that pervert Gerald leaving her door tonight . . .

God, Foster had gotten sick to his stomach instantly, flashes of that scum putting his hands on Cela, hurting her, had raced through his mind. Cela might not see it, but he'd seen how Gerald leered at her when she wasn't looking. The guy was a sleazy predator—maybe a dormant one for now—but Foster's gut told him that it'd only take the merest slice of opportunity to push Gerald back in that mode. He'd seen too many of Gerald's kind in his life not to recognize it for what it was.

He set down his fork and took a sip of his iced tea. "So are you going to tell me what's wrong or are you going to spend the rest of the evening rearranging your plate?"

Cela looked up, a bit startled, like she'd been caught in some secretive act. "What?"

"Well, tonight got off to a rocky start, I know, but you seem to be a million miles away. Tell me what's going on."

"This meal must be costing you a fortune," she said bluntly.

Foster lifted a brow, the statement catching him off guard. "I'm not really concerned about that."

She peered toward the rest of the restaurant as if worried someone would overhear them, then sighed. "See, that's exactly the problem. One moment I feel so close to you, like we've known each other forever. Then the next, I feel like we're strangers and that I don't know you at all."

The words settled like boulders in his stomach. "What are you talking about?"

She shook her head and looked down at her plate, drawing tracks in her mashed potatoes with the tines of her fork. "We did this backward. Chemistry and sex first, dating second. There's so much I don't know about you."

He frowned, not sure what this had to do with the meal being expensive. "I'm not trying to hide anything, angel. You can know whatever you'd like."

"Really?" she asked, lifting a hopeful gaze to his.

He shrugged. "Really."

"Good. Then I have some questions."

He leaned back in the seat, willing to be open but wary at where the conversation was going. "Such as?"

"Why do you live in our apartment complex when clearly you have the means to live someplace much nicer? Do you have to save money for alimony or child support or something? Have you ever been married? Do you have kids somewhere out there?"

He stared at her, stunned by the rapid-fire interrogation and the nature of her questions. It was as if he'd uncorked a shaken bottle of champagne and everything was spilling out at once. "You're worried I have *kids*? Jesus, Cela. You don't think I would've mentioned something as big as that?"

She dropped her fork onto her plate with a clink and gave him an exasperated look. "How am I supposed to know? You're impossible to figure out sometimes. And I read all the stuff in that binder. I know how serious a decision this is—to be your"—she wet her lips and glanced toward the dining room again, lowering her voice—"submissive. I'm supposed to trust you with every part of me. How can I do that when there's so much I don't know about you?"

He nodded. "I get it. That's fair."

"So can you tell me those things?"

He sighed, understanding her desire to know everything, but not exactly looking forward to dredging up his past. "I can. No, I've never been married—though I did propose to someone once. She said no."

She blanched a bit at that but covered it quickly.

"I have no children. And yes, I could afford to live somewhere else, but I live in the apartment with Pike because I own the building, and there's no reason for me to live in some lavish house when I've got all I need there. Throwing wealth around is kind of my parents' thing, not mine. Plus, it's close to work."

"Hold up," she said, lifting her palm toward him. "You *own* the building?"

He took a sip of his water. "Yes. My grandmother used to, but she left it to me when she passed away. When I turned twenty-one that building and a number of other properties became mine. I was only five when she died so I think she was hoping I'd grow up to become a real-estate mogul or something."

Cela made some noise in the back of her throat, like she couldn't quite process that information. "So you're like . . . wealthy?"

He laughed at the distaste with which she'd uttered the last word. "You say that like it's a bad thing, angel. My business has done very well for me, and I also own a portion of my family's estate. Most women would put that in their plus column."

She shook her head, clearly a little dumbstruck by the knowledge, which surprised him. Besides living in a more modest place, he'd never hidden that fact. The furnishings in his place were high-end, his clothes tailored, and he drove a Mercedes SUV. Of course, unlike his parents, he didn't have a driver and a cook or any of that nonsense that screamed *Money!* but he lived comfortably.

"I knew you were successful," she said, almost to herself. "But wealthy is like . . . out there. Intimidating."

"Oh, angel," he said, amused. This was definitely a new reaction to his financial status. Most women, especially once they found out about his family, couldn't think of much else. "I told you I owned a company."

"But yeah, maybe it was like some little small local business. You know, mom and pop. Not 'I can vacation on my yacht in the South of France if I want.'"

He chuckled, and was about to point out that he didn't own a yacht and that he, in fact, hated boats, but quickly squashed the reaction when he realized she was panicking. He had no idea why, but there was a frantic gleam in her eyes. He tossed his napkin off his lap and got up to slide next to her, draping his arm over her shoulders and pulling her next to him. "Hey, what's this all about? What's going on in that head of yours?"

She looked over, some mixture of embarrassment and sadness reflecting back at him. "I'm thinking that I might be in over my head. That you're probably used to women who know exactly what to do and wear and be. I'm thinking that I'm just a girl who has no idea what's she's doing."

He frowned. "You're not 'just' anything, Cela."

She glanced down at her hands. "Maybe I'm a little overwhelmed by it all."

"You know what I think?" He lifted her face with a finger under her chin. "I think you're coming up with things to worry about because you're scared about what happens now. For the first time in your life, you took a huge risk and went against the grain of everything you've ever been. You followed your gut, and now your head is looking for a reason for us not to do this."

"That's not true," she mumbled, staring at his tie instead of looking at him. "I'm not looking for a reason."

"Cela," he said, his voice holding warning. "Don't. You know you can back out of this. There's always an escape hatch. But lying to me is only going to result in you getting turned over my knee, and a sore ass."

Her lips parted, apparently startled into silence at the threat.

"You have to know I see you more than just some girl," he said, his tone gentling. "So stop saying stupid things like that and talk to me. Do you need more time? Do you want out? Is it because I jumped on your case earlier tonight? Or did your family freak out over you staying? Give me the truth."

She closed her eyes and took a long breath.

"How did your family take it, by the way? I should've asked that earlier. I'm sorry. I know that had to be hard."

Her gaze met his, then darted away. "They . . . handled it okay."

The off note in her voice and shifting eye contact made his radar go on alert. "Cela . . ."

Her throat worked as she swallowed. "It's fine. I think I'm just freaking myself out. What if I can't do this? What if I'm not what you need me to be?"

His chest squeezed at the last part, and he put the previous statement aside for now. He'd handle that issue in a second. He cradled her face in his hands. "Stop putting so much pressure on yourself, angel. I want you to be exactly who you are. As for the submission thing, I'm going into this with no expectations. I know this is new to you. All I'm asking is for you to be honest with me as we go through this. Anything else can be worked out. I understand that there is a distinct possibility that I'll chase you off with all this. I know that and would never blame you if you decide you can't have this type of relationship."

Her gaze drifted downward.

"But the fact that you're still here, that you chose to stay, tells me that there's a very real possibility that at least part of you needs to explore this. And your fear tonight is normal and my fault. We've raced into this thing. It's been hard not to because when we're together, there's something so electric and addictive that all I want to do is have you with me. But I've skipped over those mundane things that are just as important, like knowing how the other person takes their coffee, or what their favorite movie is, or what they do all day at their job."

She lifted her lashes, those clear chocolate eyes searching his face.

"So let's start here, okay? I like my coffee black with just a little sugar. My favorite movie is *Shawshank Redemption*, and tomorrow I'll give you a tour of where I work."

A hint of a smile tugged at her mouth. "I like half-and-half and Sweet'N Low. My favorite movie is *Gone with the Wind*. And my job involves lots of fur and questionable fluids."

"Kinky."

Her grin spread wide now. "And I have no freaking idea how to eat this crab. The only crab I've ever had started with a *K*."

He laughed and cupped her jaw, brushing a gentle kiss over her lips. "You need to learn to tell me these things, angel. I'll take care of you. You just have to let me."

Her eyes flared a bit at that—a mixture of vulnerability and sexual heat. "I'm trying. Sir."

The softness that came over her face at saying such a simple word pleased him in a way he couldn't even describe—and made him realize something very important. When she slipped into the role, the anxiety seemed to lift from her. His being lax with her and letting her ease into everything was maybe doing more damage than good. Tonight he hadn't pushed the roles, had wanted her to feel totally comfortable so they could have an open discussion. But in doing so, it'd also caused her to overthink every last thing.

He was beginning to realize that's what his dominance could do for her—ease her mind so she could enjoy herself and let go. She had so much passion and sensuality brewing right there beneath the surface. He'd seen it for himself. But keeping it locked down was a veil of worries about what was proper and right and safe, what others would say about her, what her family would think. Hell, what God himself would think. She needed help breaking through all that. And so far, his taking charge had been the only thing that had worked, which told him exactly what he needed to do tonight.

"No more worries for you tonight, angel. I know how to take away your fear."

"How?" she whispered, her attention rapt now.

He leaned down and drew his lips along her ear. "To take away all your control."

She shivered against him, and desire surged through his blood at the subtle but clear reaction.

Yes. This. That's what he craved from her. And perhaps, it was what she needed most as well.

He turned toward her plate and cracked open her crab, pulling out a succulent piece of meat with the small fork. "Open, angel."

Her gaze stayed fixed on him, but her lips parted, and he slid the fork into her mouth. His cock swelled as he watched that lush mouth close around the bite.

"That's it," he said, rubbing the pad of his thumb over the edge of her bottom lip to catch a little bit of the butter sauce. "Just let all that other stuff go and focus on the moment. Your only job right now is to listen to me. Understand?"

"Yes, sir."

The whispered words and loosening of her posture told him everything he needed to know. If left to her own devices, Cela would think herself into a panic every time. She'd find something to fixate on—their difference in financial status or his past lovers or her guilt over what she'd been taught growing up.

He couldn't afford to be casual with his dominance. Whether she realized it or not, she was already taking advantage of how lax he'd been.

He helped her extract the rest of her crab, quietly letting her finish her meal, then declined dessert. He had bigger plans for her than chocolate mousse. Originally, he'd planned to introduce her to a few people at the after-dinner mixer, but now he realized something else was in order. Giving her the easy way out wasn't working, so it was time to make this real. For her. And for him.

After the table had been cleared and the check paid, he grabbed her hand and guided her out of the booth. "Ready?"

She reached for her purse. "Yes. Your place or mine?"

"Neither," he said, tugging at the knot in his tie, the hum of conversation in the restaurant matching the humming in his veins. "It's time for your next lesson."

Her gaze flicked to his, nerves and question marks there again. "What do you mean?"

He smiled and pulled the tie from around his neck. "Turn around, Cela, so I can blindfold you."

Full-fledged fear painted her features as her eyes darted from the tie in his hands to the diners behind him. Her whisper was harsh. "Foster."

He had information that could ease her fear, reassure her, but that would ruin this lesson. And of all the lessons, this was the most vital of them all. "Do you think I would ever do anything to truly harm or embarrass you?"

Her expression was pained—some battle waging between her instinct to please and her fear of being judged by others. "No, but Foster, we can't, what will—"

"Turn around, Cela."

She squeezed her eyes shut, her fists balled at her sides. He hated seeing her this distressed, but they had to get over this hurdle. It was put-up or shut-up time.

She stood there for a few long seconds, and his own anxiety that she'd use her safe word began to burn in his belly. But finally, by some miracle, she turned around. His breath whooshed out of him—the simple gesture a monumental display of trust. *Thank God.*

He stepped up behind her and placed the silk tie over her eyes. Her body was shaking against him, but she didn't move away from his touch. When he'd knotted it at the back of her head, he wrapped his arms around from behind. "Good girl. I don't take the gift of your trust lightly."

"Are people staring at us?" she asked miserably.

"If they are, it's only because they appreciate a pretty display of submission. These people are all like us, angel," he said, rubbing his hands along her bare arms. "Seeing a girl with a blindfold is about as shocking as seeing one with dark hair."

"*What?*"

"Kade's monthly parties are invitation-only for a very select type of people. I would never embarrass you in public, angel. You're safe with me."

Her body sagged against him. "Thank you, God."

"Don't thank Him yet," Foster said, placing a kiss on her shoulder. "I'm not done with you. You've earned a punishment tonight."

She stiffened at that. "What? Why?"

"I let you get away with breaking one promise tonight in not checking the door, but I'm not going to tolerate a second rule broken. Lying to me is unacceptable."

She turned in his arms, facing him, and even with the blindfold on, he could sense her defiant stare. "I haven't lied."

"You got upset tonight because I hadn't taken the time to be open with you about my life and my past. You wanted honesty, and I gave it to you. But you didn't give me the same courtesy."

"I don't know what you're talking about." Her tone had gone petulant, but her voice wavered—the threat of punishment, no doubt, knocking her off balance. He'd expected that. She was a perfectionist, the A student, the girl who bent over backward to do what she was "supposed to" in everyone else's eyes. Being admonished or corrected for anything would be decidedly difficult for her.

But pushing her past her comfort zone was necessary and would only make it better for them both.

"Oh, really? So when exactly were you going to tell me you hadn't told your family you're staying here?"

She made a face like he'd pinched her. "Foster, I'm sorry, it's just so—"

He pressed his fingers over her mouth, hushing her. "Don't waste any more words, angel. It's time to apologize my way."

PART VI

Not Until You Surrender

TWENTY-SEVEN

Even though the restaurant wasn't cold, I couldn't stop shaking. Foster had blindfolded me with his tie in front of all these people. Yes, apparently everyone was here for some sort of private kinky party, but that didn't make it better. This was declaring an intensely private and personal thing to a crowd. It went against everything I'd been taught growing up. You weren't supposed to do "naughty" things in the first place, but if you did, you sure as heck didn't tell anyone. Being submissive to Foster in the safety of a bedroom, exposing my desires to him, had been challenge enough. But this was far, far beyond that. I was still wearing all of my clothes. I'd never felt more naked.

Voices murmured around us as Foster guided me forward through the dining room, and I silently wished for a hatch to open up in the floor and suck me in. These people *knew* now, knew what I doing. And probably had figured out that I was in some sort of trouble. Embarrassment burned my face, and I lowered my head. God, what must they be thinking? Panic and shame coalesced inside me, swirling into a uncomfortable mix. My safe word hovered in the back of my throat, but when I opened my mouth, I couldn't bring myself to use it.

And I didn't know *why* I couldn't freaking say it. One word, and I had full confidence that Foster would end this right now. He didn't have the right to *punish* me like I was some disobedient child. I could go home and chalk this up to something that's not for me. Move on. I hadn't even told my family I wasn't coming home. I could simply revert to my original plan.

But picturing that scenario left me feeling hollow on the inside. Some strange part of me wanted to make it up to Foster for lying to him, wanted to show him that I could handle whatever he meted out. Even if

I didn't really know if I *could* handle it. If he made me do something in front of all these people . . .

My throat seemed to close up.

"Breathe, Cela," Foster said, his voice a low, warm caress over my ear as his arm tightened around me.

"I'm trying," I said in a strangled whisper.

Trust.

It was really what this lesson was about. I was at his mercy. He was making me walk on a narrow ledge with only his hand to keep my balance, and I had to put all of my faith in him in the moment—believe that he would only subject me to what he knew I could handle.

An old homily from church snuck into my brain at that last thought and I snorted—the comparison absurd considering the circumstances.

"You find something funny, angel?" Foster asked wryly.

"No, sir." I gave a swift shake of my head, my nerves making me near delirious. "I'm sorry. Just a random, bizarro thought."

"Oh, please," he said, slowing our step and, based on the swish of air that blew over my face, opening a door. "Do share with the class."

I blew out a breath and looked toward him, even though I couldn't see anything through the silk over my eyes. "I was thinking this is oddly religious—the amount of blind faith required. Our priest used to talk about trusting God to only give you what you could manage."

This time Foster's voice held amusement. "If you're comparing me to God, angel, I totally approve."

A door shut somewhere behind us.

"So you decided to play after all?" another voice interjected, giving me a start.

My mouth clamped shut, and all humor vanished from my system. I crowded against Foster's side, away from the other voice and approaching footsteps, like a mouse who'd heard a cat's hungry meow.

Foster gave my hip a squeeze. "Yes. Change of plans."

"Fantastic. Well, we have equipment set up on second level in the main space. It's not a fully outfitted dungeon since we only bring in temporary stuff for these parties, but I think you'll find it adequate. A few people have wandered up there already. We also have a few things set up in the banquet room down the hall."

I realized quickly, listening to the other man talk, that this was Kade, the restaurant owner I'd met earlier. My hold on Foster eased from death grip down to only mild panic. I'd instantly liked Kade, his manner easy and his eyes kind. Plus, knowing who was on the other side of my blindfold made me feel marginally better. He was simply the party host, telling us where we could go. I didn't let my mind process the rest of what he'd said—talk of dungeons and other people and such. Nope. Wasn't going to think about that.

Not. At. All.

Anxiety bit at me like ruthless snapping turtles.

"Thank you, Kade," Foster said, shifting me forward a bit and taking me by the elbow. "I'm not sure that's quite what I have in mind."

Thank you, thank you, thank you. My body melted in relief.

Yes, I could get totally turned on *imagining* watching others or doing things in front of them. But *actually* doing it—yeah, that might make me pass out in sheer terror. I'd barely gotten comfortable being sexual in front of Foster much less strangers.

"I understand," Kade said.

"But I was hoping," Foster continued, "you might be able to help us out in another way."

"What'd you have in mind?" Kade asked, his curiosity and interest evident in his voice. I could almost picture him there, blond head tilted, mischief sparking in those blue eyes.

Foster left my side for a moment as he spoke in low tones with Kade. I inclined my head toward the sound but couldn't make out most of the damn words. But the few I did hear made my spine go stiff. Was he *inviting* Kade to be part of my punishment? Oh, hells no.

"Foster," I said in a harsh whisper as my body started to quake with nerves again. He didn't answer. I felt like a child urgently trying to get her parent's attention, looking for a pant leg to tug on. "*Sir.*"

"Hush," he said, a bite to the simple word.

"I can definitely help you out with that," Kade said, a smile in his tone.

Oh, screw this. I stepped back, bumping into a wall, and yanked the tie off my eyes, frustration and fear surging in me like a battle cry.

Foster's frown was unmistakable in the soft light of the hallway. "Cela."

"No," I said, words spilling out of me without going through any kind of filter. I threw the tie onto the ground. "I lied, okay? So I didn't tell my family yet. Big deal. It wasn't a freaking capital crime. That doesn't mean you should get to punish me and invite your friends along for the ride."

"Invite my—" Thunderclouds crossed Foster's expression, an ominous spring storm blotting out the sunshine, and he stepped forward. Automatically, I pressed my back fully against the wall, half hoping it would just absorb me into it. To my dismay, the drywall didn't cooperate. Foster moved into my space—not touching me, not trapping me, but freezing me in place nonetheless with the hard look in his eyes. His voice was like a winter-chilled gust when he spoke again. "Not a big deal? Were you or were you not the one who wanted to stay so this could become a relationship—not just kinky fun?"

"What does that have to do with anything?" I said, my words sharp but my voice quavering and my fingers pressing into the wall for support.

"You *lied* to me. People in relationships are supposed to be honest, to talk about what they're going through."

"And it pissed you off," I said in a huff. "I get it. I'm sorry. I said I was sorry."

He scoffed. "Pissed? You think this is about me being pissed?" He bent his head toward me, his gaze boring into mine. "I'm *hurt*, Cela. If you're just using me to get some wild oats out your system, then fucking tell me that. At least I know where I stand. But don't make me care about you, and then not even trust me enough to talk to me. How would you feel if I said your punishment was that I get to tell one free lie to you when the time suits me? Would that seem like a big deal?"

I glanced away. That would, of course, be awful—wondering anytime he said something if this was the time he was going to choose to lie. *Gah.* I didn't want him to make sense. My righteous indignation felt so much better than thinking I'd actually hurt him.

"You know what it makes me feel like when you lie to me?" he asked, his voice soft now.

I pressed my lips together and shook my head, feeling a little more miserable with each passing second.

"Like your fuck buddy, Cela. Like *some* guy."

I winced at his pained tone.

So it was true. I'd hurt him.

The thought ran through my head like a storm warning on repeat. Hurt. Hurt. Hurt. Foster wasn't just angry that I'd lied to him; the lie and my lack of trust had honestly affected him. And that did something to me I couldn't even explain. Hurt meant that this was important to him. Hurt meant that his feelings were involved. Hurt meant that earlier tonight he hadn't jumped my case about the peephole because he was some overbearing asshole—he did it because he was genuinely concerned about me.

Hurt meant everything.

And even though I hadn't realized I'd needed confirmation of that, something ragged inside me smoothed. My heart wasn't the only one on the line here. We were both stripped-down and vulnerable.

And he was right. How could I demand all those answers from him over dinner only to lie to him when he'd asked about my family? I hadn't wanted to look like a coward or explain why it was so hard. But he was right. If we were going to be together, I needed to stop showing him only the parts of me I wanted him to see.

"I'm sorry," I said again, and in that moment, I realized how damn pathetic those words sounded. What did they mean anyway? Those words were supposed to make everything better? Show true remorse?

Now I understood.

Without saying another thing, I took a deep breath and slowly lowered myself to my knees. Once there, I picked up Foster's tie, and lifted it to him, staying on the floor at his feet. He stared down at me, blue eyes going tender, and took the strip of silk from my hands. "Thank you. Stand up, angel."

He took my hand in his, helping me to my feet, then lifted my hand to his mouth to brush a kiss over my knuckles. His gaze stayed on mine, conveying so much through just one look. Appreciation. Heat. And relief. He'd been afraid I was going to walk out. Finally, he turned his head and sent a curt nod toward Kade, who'd stayed in the shadows while we'd been arguing. Foster tied the blindfold over my eyes again and then placed my hand in the crook of his elbow to guide us further down the hall.

I had no idea where we were going or what awaited. But though nerves still bubbled in my belly, the rest of me had morphed into resolve. Foster cared about me. And I trusted him. If he was going to have Kade be a part of things, then I needed to have faith that he would only take it as far as he thought I could handle. And if either of them tried something I didn't like, I had my safe word. I knew down in my gut that Foster would honor that no matter what, so that gave me the courage to keep putting one foot in front of the other. Even when I felt damp night air hit my face.

"Take off your shoes, angel," Foster said, his breath gusting over my neck. "I don't want you to stumble."

"Okay." Keeping my hand on him to steady myself, I slipped out of my heels. My bare feet hit a smooth, uneven surface—like the cobblestone that paved the sidewalk into the restaurant. Surely he couldn't have me standing barefoot and blindfolded in front of the building, right? There was a parking lot out there and windows along the front of the restaurant where anyone would be able to see me. I wet my lips, worry like a heavy coat I couldn't shrug off.

"Easy," he said, lifting my hair off my shoulder and pressing a kiss to the column of my neck, sending shivers down to my painted toenails. "Just try to breathe and focus on my voice and touch. That's all you need to worry about. Not Kade or what's around you. Just me and what you're feeling."

"Yes, sir." I nodded, warmth from the simple feel of his lips against my skin gathering low. "Is Kade still here?"

"No, he's getting a few things for me. But see, you're still worrying. Focus, angel."

I sighed and closed my eyes behind the blindfold, trying to center myself and pay attention only to Foster—his gentle touches and kisses, his scent mixing with the faint scent of something earthy in the air, and the warmth of his body next to mine. Soon, I could sense my muscles starting to unwind a bit and my mind easing.

A few minutes later, footsteps sounded to my right, and I knew we were alone no longer. Foster shifted and left my side. There was a rustling sound and low-spoken words. I kept breathing. Mostly. I'd learned in the class that submitting could almost be a meditative state, like reaching some other plane, and I wanted to get there. Foster had brought me there before—the place where nothing mattered but the two of us and what we were doing, where time seemed to slow and inhibitions fell away. That was a happy, happy place.

When fingers touched my elbow again, I jumped. "It's okay, angel. I'm going to lead you a few more steps. I promise I won't let you fall or hurt yourself."

I let Foster guide me, the smooth stones cool beneath my feet, then he was turning me. On the next step, my feet pressed into something soft. I bit my lip, my mind trying to scan through where I could possibly be. Out front there was only stone and then a paved parking lot. But I didn't dare ask the question.

"Cela," Foster said from somewhere behind me. "I'm going to take off your dress."

Panic lodged in my throat, swelling. "Foster."

But his fingers were already on my zipper. "Shh, just listen to me. You are beautiful, and it pleases me to see you bared for me like this. You have nothing to fear or be ashamed of."

My fists curled but I forced myself to breathe through the panic. *Trust. Trust. Trust.* God, I'd never thought it would be this hard to put that faith in him. But my mind had me standing in front of a well-known restaurant. I'd only been semi-naked in front of four guys in my life, counting Foster and Pike. And now here I was, with God knows who looking on, being stripped down to my barely there bra and panties. My heart was making a valiant attempt to break through the prison of my rib cage and leave me behind.

Foster brought my dress down my hips, then helped me stepped out of it. The night air, though warm, instantly raised goose bumps on my skin. "Foster, I'm kind of freaking out."

His palms glided over my upper arms and his body pressed against my back. Already I could feel the stirring of his own arousal. "Take a breath, angel. Do it with me. In. Out."

I forced myself to follow his instructions, bringing oxygen into my lungs.

"I've got you, okay?" he said, his voice quiet and reassuring. "Now lift your arms for me."

Though I was still on the verge of panic, I lifted them. Hands took my wrists. Hands. *Oh, shit.* Kade was still here. And from what I could tell, he was helping Foster wrap something around my wrists—rope if I had to guess by the slightly abrasive feel of it. The heat of a full-body blush started in my cheeks and rolled downward like a crimson tide. They stretched my arms out above me at an angle and secured them on opposite sides. Before I could even process that, the same material was being wrapped around my ankles.

Foster ran a palm along my calf. I assumed it was him. I couldn't imagine Kade taking such liberties, but I couldn't be sure. "Spread your legs a little wider, angel."

It was Foster. A little sag of relief went through me, and I adjusted my stance. They secured my ankles, leaving me completely at their mercy by the end of it. I flexed my fingers, trying to maintain some sense of calm, but was failing miserably. I probably could've provided electricity to half the homes in the Metroplex with the amount of nervous energy racing through my veins.

"Comfortable, Cela?"

"Oh, yeah, totally. I hang out like this all the time." The quip was past my lips before I remembered my role here. I locked my mouth shut, prepared for a hand to land on my ass at any second, but instead I was met with chuckles from them both.

"I meant," Foster said patiently, "does anything feel too tight or uncomfortable?"

"No, sir. Sorry."

"I didn't take you for the kind who likes a brat," Kade observed, though there was humor in his tone.

A *brat*? I huffed, affronted. "Excuse me, but—"

That's when a hand smacked the back of my thigh, drawing a yelp from me. "Calm down, sweetness."

I turned my head in the direction of Foster's voice, hoping he could sense my oh-no-you-didn't glare.

"She's not a brat," Foster said to Kade. "She's just brand new. And feisty. But . . ." The volume of his voice increased as he apparently directed his words my way. "If she keeps up trying to glare at me like that, I may have to demonstrate why bratting isn't going to work out well for her. Care to add an additional punishment to your docket tonight, angel?"

I jutted my chin forward but turned my head away. I was opinionated but not stupid. Don't provoke the guy who has you tied up. That was probably a good rule to add to my arsenal. "No, sir."

"Good. Now I want you to count down from one hundred aloud. Slowly. When you get to one, I want you totally focused and ready for whatever I ask of you. Do you understand?"

"Where are you going?" I asked, stiffening at the thought of being left here.

"Do you understand?" he repeated, impatience creeping into his tone.

"Yes, sir," I said, trying to swallow down my smart remarks and questions.

"Count."

I took a deep breath. "One hundred . . . ninety-nine . . . ninety-eight . . ."

He unsnapped the hook of my strapless bra, and the bra fell away, my nipples beading from the exposure. Oh crap, oh crap, oh crap. I was naked—*outdoors*. I stumbled in my count.

The air shifted in front of me, and he gave both nipples a swift pinch. I arched my back from the shock of it, gasping

"Start your count again," he said, a quiet but foreboding demand. "Anytime you miss a number or pause too long, you'll need to begin again."

I nodded, my body going hot from the pinch and my brain trying not to short-circuit. I had a feeling it was going to be a long night. "One hundred . . ."

TWENTY-EIGHT

"Ninety-nine," I said, my voice trembling a bit as I continued counting.

Foster palmed my breasts, brushing his thumbs over the now-throbbing buds, and I moaned without wanting to. Even with the anxiety of not knowing where I was or if Kade was still there or if anyone else could see, I couldn't help but respond to Foster's touch. I tried to stay focused on saying the numbers, but that was getting harder with each caress.

Foster's fingertips coasted along the sides of my breasts, then down along my belly and hips, leaving trails of fire in their wake. When he reached the triangle of satin and lace covering my mound, every muscle in my body tightened, anticipating the feel of him. He drew a single finger along the front of the satin, sliding telltale moisture along my cleft, then pressed against my clit.

I lost count again.

"Start over," he said, gravel in his voice now. "I'm not taking you down until you get to one, angel."

"One hundred, ninety-nine." He pushed aside my panties and dipped a long finger inside me. "Oh, God."

"Mmm, so scared you're still quivering a little, but you're as wet and hot as I've ever felt you, angel." He stroked inside me with expert precision, and his stubble brushed my cheek. "If I was a betting man, I'd say a little exposure does your body good."

My eyes squeezed tight and I kept counting as he added a second finger, but hard, shuddering need went through me. I didn't know what he considered punishment. This was starting to feel like anything but. I was so wet, his fingers gliding deep and coaxing responses from me, that I knew it had to have been painfully obvious to anyone who may be near exactly how turned on and desperate I was for him. Somehow, I forgot I should be embarrassed about that. At the moment, I didn't care.

Soon, his fingers slipped out of me and he grabbed my hips, situating me against him. The hard length of his cock pressed again the wet fabric of my panties. "And knowing this gets you so turned on and slick has every man watching hot and hard for you."

My breath caught, the words sending a bolt of shock through me. "Foster."

"Start your count over, beautiful," he said as he stepped back. I could picture him standing there in front of me, that suit coat stripped off, his tie gone, and a wickedly satisfied smirk on his handsome face.

I couldn't let my mind wander to the idea that there were other people who could see me. So I just did what he'd told me to do, I focused only on him and his voice. That's all that mattered. I started my count over. His footsteps sounded off to my left, and then behind me again.

"When you get to fifty, this next part stops," he said, the words holding an ominous edge. Before I had time to digest that, a snapping sound filled my ears and a sharp, stinging sensation lit up my left thigh.

I hissed, the pain pointed and more intense than the flogger had been. Shit, that hurt.

"This is a riding crop," he explained. "Give me a color, Cela, for that level of pain."

Color? A color? My mind apparently wasn't translating English at the moment. It was too busy buzzing.

He snapped me again on the other thigh, and I cried out. "This is your test, angel. How well did you study? Stoplight colors were covered both in the binder and in class."

I shook my head, bracing for another blow, when the picture of a stoplight entered my mind. Just like when I was taking a test, I remembered where it was on the page. Green for *I'm okay*; yellow for *might be too much, check in with me*; and red for *stop, too much*. He wanted me to give him an idea of how much pain I could handle.

"Green," I said automatically, despite the angry protest my skin was giving. The level of pain wasn't a breeze, but it wasn't beyond what I could handle. In fact, after the initial sting, the warmth that chased it was kind of pleasant.

"Good girl," Foster said. "Get back to your counting."

I resumed my count, and the blows began to rain over my back and thighs in a steady rhythm. I winced for the first few, the bite of the crop hard to ignore, but by the time I got down to seventy-five, my entire backside was tingling with heat and a pleasant, heady sensation was clouding my thoughts.

As promised, he stopped when I hit the right number, and I sagged in my bindings, letting the rush of it all filter through my bloodstream. His palms ran over the welts that were, no doubt, rising on my skin. "Still with me, gorgeous?"

"Yes, sir," I said softly.

"God, you are so fucking sexy, angel." He pressed his front to my back, my skin seeming to throb in time to my heartbeat. He left a trail of kisses over my shoulder. "I've lain awake at night, imagining you like this. Tied up and trusting and enjoying being under my hand. I can't even tell you what it does to me to know you're taking this risk for me, pushing past your fear."

The words vibrated through me, creating a glowing warmth and a catch in my throat. His voice was so sincere, so reverent, that in that moment, I may have done absolutely anything he asked. It should've scared me—the depth of my willingness—but right now, I couldn't think past the blind pleasure of knowing I could make him sound so truly awed. "Thank you, sir."

He gave me one last squeeze, then stepped away again, letting the breeze soothe my burning back. "That round was for opening your door without checking. You've got one more to go for lying."

I nodded, fear getting choked out by far more potent things—like lust and need and pleasure. "I understand."

He touched the back of my head, and the blindfold slipped away. It took me a second to realize what he'd done, my eyes still closed, but soon the light registered. I lifted my lids, afraid of what I was going to find. If other people were there, I knew the panic would come back. I'd prefer to have the safety of the blindfold. But when I blinked, focusing, I saw no other soul. Instead, a beautifully lush garden spread out before me, gilded in moonlight and the glow of twinkle lights that had been strung through some of the trees.

My gaze moved downward, finding my feet nestled in the soft earth, my legs surrounded by lovely, white flowers. I lifted my head, taking in the rope holding me between two thick-trunked trees, the branches providing a canopy above me. It was like going to sleep in one place and waking up in Eden. It was . . . magical. And breathtaking.

Foster stepped around from one of the tress, riding crop rolling between his fingers and his gaze hot on me. The embodiment of temptation in the garden. "Hi there."

I shook my head, still a bit stunned. "What is this place?"

He walked forward, the low light tracing the angles of his face. "The restaurant's vegetable and herb garden."

"It's beautiful," I breathed, my eyes on him.

"Now it is." He traced the tip of the riding crop along the curve of my breast. "You look like you sprung up right out of the earth like those flowers. So naturally gorgeous."

"Thank you, sir."

I let my gaze move around the span of the garden, over the rows of bell peppers, tomatoes, and dark green bunches of rosemary and thyme. No wonder the place smelled so heavenly. "Is Kade still here?"

Foster's lips tilted. "He helped me tie you up and brought me my bag from the car. Then he left and locked the door behind him so we could be all alone."

"But I thought—"

He pressed the flat leather tip of the riding crop against my lips. "I told you every man here was turned on. And that's the truth. I am very, very turned on, angel. I needed to see that you would trust me. You did well."

Something inside me bloomed. I *had* trusted him, but doubts had lingered in my mind like mosquitos I couldn't swat away. Now I knew that he was truly worthy of that trust. He had pushed me to an edge but hadn't violated my faith in him by taking it somewhere I wasn't ready

246 | RONI LOREN

for yet. Even only knowing me a short time, he knew how far to take it, how to push yet still protect the shaky confidence that was trying to build into something more solid inside me.

I closed my eyes and kissed the crop.

An audible breath whooshed out of him, and he lowered the crop. "You humble me, angel."

My mouth curved, and I met his gaze again. "Well, if you ever get the urge to kneel at my feet, I won't stop you."

His smirk lit his eyes with humor. "Maybe I was wrong. You *are* a brat."

"Is that bad?" I asked, beginning to understand that the term must mean something significant in this world.

"It can be for some. But I have to say, I'm kind of liking your smart-ass side. Gives me more opportunity to do this in repayment." He snapped the crop against the tender underside of my breast.

I shrieked in surprise, both at the pain and the pleasure that chased right up to my nipple afterward. The ropes creaked as I shifted my weight in response to all the sensation. "Ah, God."

"Yes, now may be the time for prayer. You have one more punishment to handle." His grin was pure male promise. "Forty-nine to one, angel."

I wet my lips, eyeing the riding crop and developing an instant love-hate relationship with it. How could such an innocuous-looking thing dish out such a sting? Taking its bite on my back was one thing, but there were so many more sensitive areas on the front of me.

"I don't hear counting," he chided.

I braced myself. "Forty-nine."

The leather landed on my hip, making me press my teeth into my lip to keep from crying out. Wow, that was a different level. I breathed through it, still counting, trusting that like the welts on my back, the wallop would turn into a pleasant burn.

"Still green?" he asked.

"Yes, sir," I said, though my teeth were clenched a bit this time.

"Tough girl. I like it." He stood in front of me, his eyes raking over my form as he held the crop in his right hand. Everything about his stance and the look on his face screamed power and sex and utter confidence. I couldn't remember ever being so captivated. Having all that lust and attention zeroed in on me was headier than all the tequila shots in the world.

He lifted the crop, and holding my eye contact, snapped it right against my mound—lighter than the other hits but enough to get the attention of every cell in my body. I bowed up in the ropes, fighting hard to keep my focus and continue counting. My sex clenched, and my clit throbbed like it'd developed its own heartbeat. Jesus, that felt . . . I couldn't even describe it. Shocking. Harsh. Fantastic.

Foster didn't pause. He continued the blows on every exposed tender spot—my breasts and nipples, the tops of my thighs, my hips . . . *Snap. Snap. Snap.* My skin lit with fire and liquid heat soaked my panties. I rocked in the bindings, the twinkle lights in the trees starting to blur. Then he was back at the apex of my thighs, the hits from earlier turning into taps perfectly centered over where I needed it most. I had to start counting over again twice because my brain began to haze, all focus narrowed onto the need for release.

"Please," I whispered in between the last few numbers. "Please."

"Do not come," he warned.

I groaned and tilted my head back, fighting against the tide. Finally, I hit the number one and to my utter dismay, Foster stopped the stimulation. *No!* I balled my fists, tugging against the bindings, squirming with the need for release.

"Easy, Cela," he said, going to the ropes and untying. "Pull too hard and you'll get rope burns."

"I'm going to die," I declared. "Sir."

He chuckled—the bastard—and went to my other arm. "I promise, lack of orgasm won't kill you."

I wasn't so sure.

After he'd unfastened me from everything, I realized my legs were weak beneath me. He kept a firm hand on my elbow and helped me ease down to my knees in the flower bed. "You all right?"

My body was pulsing and hot everywhere, and my brain couldn't hold on to any thoughts for longer than a second. The chanting call for release was all I felt. "Yes, sir, but I *need* to come."

He cupped my cheek, smile grim. "Welcome to your punishment."

I blinked. "But we did that, you just—"

"And you enjoyed every minute of that flogging. That wasn't punishment. This is the part that will make you think twice before you lie to me again."

"Foster," I said, reaching for him, totally prepared to beg shamelessly at this point.

He grabbed my hands and rubbed his thumbs over the top of them. "Get dressed, angel. It's time to go home."

And though it was obvious from the erection pressing against his slacks that he was impossibly turned on, too, I could see in the hard set of his jaw that there would be no swaying him. I'd broken his rules, and now we both would pay the consequence.

Disappointment settled over me like a cold, wet blanket.

Punishment *sucked*.

TWENTY-NINE

Sitting in the car on the ride home was its own kind of torture. Foster was quiet, leaving me to my riotous thoughts. Plus, my ass
and back hurt, every bump in the road jostling my flaming skin. If I'd
hoped that the pain would distract me from being so damn turned on,
I'd been wrong. Instead, it reminded me of how it had felt being bound
and marked by Foster, how he'd looked standing there, holding the
crop—a sexy, powerful predator in that lush garden. My muscles
clenched low and tight. Goddammit. I shifted in my seat again.

He gave me a sidelong glance. "You okay over there?"

"Don't taunt me, Foster," I said, my chin tipped up, my tone exceed-
ingly polite.

He reached over and gave my knee a squeeze. "Not taunting, angel.
Only making sure you're not hurting too badly."

I sighed, sagging into the seat at first and then remembering quickly
that leaning forward was much more comfortable. I straightened my
spine. "I'm okay. I really am sorry about the lie, for what it's worth."

He pulled onto the interstate, checking his rearview mirror. Somehow even watching him drive a car was revving my internal engine
tonight. Those long fingers wrapped around the steering wheel, the
confidence with which he maneuvered his car, the long stretch of his leg
flexing when he pressed the gas. God, I was freaking hopeless.

"No need to apologize again," he said evenly. "You handled the consequence. Consider it forgiven and forgotten."

I blinked at his matter-of-fact absolution. "Seriously? Just like that.
Forgiven and forgotten?"

He glanced over at me. "Yeah, of course. Why wouldn't it be?"

I peered back out at the road, taken aback by the mere concept. "Because that is *so* not how it works in my family. Even when we completed whatever the punishment was, nothing was ever forgotten. And forgiveness—well, that's only given out for small stuff. Otherwise, forget it."

Foster's frown appeared in my peripheral vision. "Is that why you're afraid to tell them about staying here?"

I smoothed the hem of my dress with my fingers, not wanting to look over at him. "I tried to tell my dad the other day, and I froze up. He's going to freak, and I . . . well, I don't know if this could turn into one of those unforgivable offenses."

"And what happens when it's an unforgivable offense?"

I shrugged. "Could mean he doesn't talk to me for a while, could mean worse. He hasn't spoken to my sister since she was a teenager."

Foster's frown cut deeper. "What happened?"

"She got pregnant at sixteen and had an abortion. He kicked her out and basically disowned her."

"Jesus, and he hasn't talked to her since?"

"No, and he expects me, my brothers, and my mother to follow that edict, too. Andre and I don't listen, but my mother does."

Foster shook his head, sadness marring his features. "Your dad has a living, breathing daughter out there in the world and won't speak to her. It seems so shortsighted and petty even if she did make a mistake. You know what my parents would give to see my sister again?"

I reached out and grabbed his hand, the catch in his voice making my chest tight. "I'm sorry, Foster."

He laced his fingers with mine. "I'm sorry, too. I didn't realize how big of a deal it was going to be to break the news to your family. I shouldn't have been so hard on you for lying to me about it."

"No, you were right. I should've been honest with you about it. I didn't want to come across like a little girl afraid to tell her daddy something."

His gaze slid over to me as he pulled into the parking lot of our building, and his mouth lifted at the corner. "Believe me, Ms. Medina, you should have no concerns about me seeing you as a little girl."

I curled my lips inward, the unapologetic strip-me-to-my-skin look he was giving me making my neck flush with heat.

He parked the car, then released my hand and cupped my chin, tilting my face toward him. "Punishment complete, angel. I think now it's time for us both to reap the reward of surviving a very long evening."

"That sounds like the best idea you've ever had, sir."

Foster helped me out of the car, and I had to stop myself from racing up the steps in all my eagerness. Suddenly, even one second not in bed with this man seemed too long. Automatically, I headed toward my place, but he tugged me toward his instead. "This way."

"But what about Pike?" I asked, a little breathless from my overzealous sprint up the stairs.

"Not home." He dragged me against him and placed a long, lingering kiss on my lips.

"Mmm," I said, as he eased away, my fingers curling around the lapels of his suit jacket. I'd been hoping we could stay at my place. I was still having my stupid hang-up about his room. Every time I stepped in there, I couldn't help but think about the others who'd been there. But saying something would only make me look childish and petty. I needed to get over myself and move on. I smiled and threw my arms around his neck and with a dramatic flourish, said, "Then take me to bed or lose me forever."

"Show me the way home, honey," he whispered against my ear, nailing the line.

I pulled back, looking at him in surprise. "Did you just recite *Top Gun* back to me?"

His cocky grin was his answer.

"Well done, Ian Foster. Bonus points to you. And now I'm seriously tempted to rip off your clothes right here in the hallway for that."

He laughed and unlocked his door. "Control yourself, woman."

But when he pulled me inside, he did anything but control *himself*. He kicked the door shut behind us, and before I could take a step, he was lifting me off my feet and kissing me. I wrapped my legs around his waist, and he trapped me against the closed door, his lips moving over mine with hungry intent. I opened to him, and he stroked his tongue against mine, cajoling every cell inside me to stand up and swoon. Even in the simple act of a kiss, he bled dominance, commanding my body to surrender. I sighed into him and threaded my fingers in the thick, silky strands of his hair, relishing the chance to touch and explore freely.

When he finally broke away for us both to grab a breath, his wolfish grin spread wide. "I better take you to my room before I fuck you against the door again."

"That wasn't so bad," I said on a panted breath.

He laughed and swung me away from the door, keeping ahold of me. "Not tonight, angel. Right now I don't have patience for acrobats. Just need you. In my bed. Naked."

"A man of simple taste."

He shot me a dry look. "Smartass."

I continued to tease him as he carried me down the hallway toward his room, by outlining all the "simple" things he'd done to me tonight, but when he set me down on my feet in the doorway, I went stone-cold silent.

He watched me, expression a little tentative, as I took in what lay before me. When I didn't say anything, he tucked his hands in his pockets. "I was worried it wouldn't fit, but it ended up working out okay."

I turned to him, taking in his twitching jaw and the fact that he wouldn't look at me. Was he actually worried I wouldn't like it? I shook my head, awed at how this man continued to surprise me. One second I thought I had him figured out and the next, he was doing things like this. "You bought a new bed?"

"And mattress, comforter, and pillows."

For some reason, I had the ridiculous urge to cry. "Why?"

He looked at me then and shrugged. "Because it bothered you, angel."

I stepped forward and slid my hands around his waist, pressing my head to his chest. The man had completely gutted his room because I had some irrational hang-up, and I couldn't even tell him about my family earlier tonight. "I don't even know what to say. It's too much."

He kissed the top of my head. "Well, I'm into 'too much,' especially when it makes you get that look on your face."

I lifted my face to him, meeting those intense blues of his. Something deep and scary stirred in my chest. "Thank you. Truly."

"My pleasure," he said, circling his arms around me. "Now strip and go kneel on that shiny, new bed. It's time to sully its virtue."

I laughed. "Seems to be a lot of that going around."

"Have I sullied you, Ms. Medina?" he asked, his hands sliding down to cup my ass beneath my dress.

"Obviously not enough tonight."

He pinched the back of my thigh, and I yelped. "Get on the bed, woman."

"Yes, sir." I stepped back and shimmied out of my dress and underwear, then climbed onto the new four-poster bed, the fluffy white comforter sinking beneath me. I tucked my legs beneath me and put my hands in my lap, trying to emulate the proper submissive kneel I'd learned about.

Foster shrugged off his jacket and pulled off his shirt, watching me intently the whole time. Then he walked forward and braced his arms on the two posts at the foot of the bed, looking like some winged god who was about to swoop down and ravage me. "You look like some sweet, innocent thing in the middle of all that white fluff, angel. Everything except your eyes. Your eyes say that you've got a seductress inside waiting to come out to play."

I smiled, feeling shy all of a sudden at his hot perusal. "I'm not so sure about that."

"Show me, angel. Tempt me into your bed."

Cela's eyes went a little wide at his command, and Foster almost chuckled at her shock. She truly had no idea how fucking seductive she could be. But he was about to give her a chance to see it for herself.

"What do you mean?" she asked, brown eyes guarded.

"I mean," he said, keeping himself there at the foot of the bed, despite his body demanding he pounce on her right this very minute, "show me what I'm missing if I don't crawl into this bed with you."

He could see her throat work as she swallowed hard. "I'm not sure I can."

"You will," he said, a soft command. "Close your eyes if it helps."

She nodded, and though he could tell she was reluctant, she let her eyelids fall shut.

"Go ahead, beautiful. Tempt me."

Tentatively, her hands slid up from her knees, along her body, until she was cupping those full, lush breasts of hers, the nipples darkening with arousal as she ran her thumbs over them. She tilted her head back with a gentle sigh of contentment, her dark hair sweeping along the top curve of her ass.

His grip tightened on the posts as his cock pressed against the fly of his dress pants. "That's right, angel. Show me what kind of pleasure you like."

He loved how close to the surface her sensuality was becoming, how her fledgling sexual confidence was blooming and stretching toward the light. Toward him. He'd never seen anything more erotic.

Apparently buoyed by his encouragement, she parted her knees a bit, exposing that pretty pussy of hers to full effect. Sweet pink lips glistening and flush with arousal. The sight nearly had his restraint dissolving. He'd left her panties on at the restaurant, so he hadn't had the pleasure of seeing just how turned on she was until now. But he'd felt how wet she'd been and knew that she'd feel like heaven around him.

One of her hands drifted down from her breast and parted her folds, her pale painted fingernails sliding tentatively along the swollen bud he'd teased with the crop tonight. The sight was so sweetly erotic that he had to reach down and unfasten his belt and pants to free himself before he suffered permanent zipper marks on his cock. Her fingers teased at her entrance, and she hummed a moan in the quiet of the bedroom. His hand gripped his cock, giving it a long stroke as he watched her fingers disappear inside herself.

"Look at me," he said hoarsely. She hesitated for half a breath, then lifted her head and opened her eyes. Her pupils were almost full black with arousal, but her teeth bit at her lip, her insecurity returning now that she had to face him. He reached out and grabbed her chin. "You are the most beautiful creature I've ever seen. See what you do to me."

She glanced down, probably not even realizing how her natural demureness stoked his fire even further. She licked her lips as she took in the sight of his cock in his hand. *Fuck.* The last vestige of his own control snapped, and he shucked off his pants to climb onto the bed over her. "Hands and knees, angel."

She scooted backward and turned over. The faint red marks still on her back from the crop made him groan aloud. He'd been so fucking hot for her watching her take the blows in the middle of that garden. It'd taken every ounce of his strength not to back out on her punishment. But he knew the patience would be worth it. He'd earned her trust, and now she'd give herself over to him freely. Instead of wondering and worrying, they could sink into the moment and relish every bit of the reward.

He glided his hands along her hips, enjoying the way she trembled ever so slightly under his touch. He'd never taken her in this position. *No one* had ever taken her in this position. The realization gave him some perverse caveman pleasure. He'd never been one to get hung up on a woman's "virtue." In fact, he typically enjoyed women who took charge of their own pleasure and weren't afraid to seek out what they desired. But damn if he hadn't developed some primal appreciation in knowing that anything he did with Cela, he was the first one. It was like some unexpected gift. Any mark on her, any place explored, was all his.

He leaned over and kissed along her spine. "Did you consider my request about condoms, angel?"

He'd sent her his medical report this weekend, leaving things up to her. He didn't want to push her on the issue—especially now, knowing her sister had gotten pregnant as a teen. That could strike fear in the heart of any woman. But he couldn't help but ask, the thought of being inside her bare was too decadent to contemplate.

She looked over her shoulder at him. "I'm on the pill. And . . . I want to feel you. Skin to skin."

Thank God. He moved his hands along the front of her thighs, working to be gentle, knowing her skin was tender from earlier, then positioned himself at her entrance. Her heat teased at the already slick head of his cock, beckoning him. Tilting back a bit to fully enjoy the view, he pushed into her, watching his length disappear inside her cleft.

Ah, God. Now it was his turn to shudder as her warmth and wetness enveloped him whole, making him momentarily unaware of anything but the exquisite feel of their joining. His fingers dug into her hips. He'd only ever gone bare with one other woman, and he couldn't remember the sensation being this fucking fantastic.

She gasped a bit when he settled deep inside her, and he realized quickly that he was already gripping her too hard. He loosened his hold. "Sorry, angel."

"Please don't stop," she said, breathlessly.

He chuckled softly, then rocked into her again, earning another sweet sound from her. "No chance of that."

She lowered to her elbows, cheek pressed into the comforter, and he could feel her body surrender. Anything he wanted, he could have—everything from her posture to the rapt look on her face said it. The reality of that was like a heady drug dumped into his blood. She may be a smartass sometimes, may rebel against some of the rules, but god-damn if she wasn't gorgeously, perfectly submissive when she was under his touch. Pleasure, pride, and something else he didn't want to label at the moment swelled high in his chest.

She whimpered softly beneath him, and he braced himself over her back, wrapping his arm around her to reach her clit. She had taken her punishment with grace tonight, and now he was going to make damned sure he brought her to a place to make it all worthwhile. As soon as he touched the swollen button, she arched her back like a cat, pulling his cock even deeper inside her. He groaned along with her.

"You have permission to come when I do, baby," he said, increasing his tempo, no longer content to go slow and easy. He needed to hear those fuck-me screams of hers. That sound did things to him he couldn't even describe—knowing that she was out of her head, lost to it all—was like pure adrenaline for him. He continued to thrust inside while strok-ing her clit, their bodies going slick with sweat in the effort to prolong the pleasure.

Then he watched her fingers curl into the comforter, her knuckles going white. She shifted restlessly beneath him, like the buildup of

NOT UNTIL YOU ‖ 257

energy was too much to hold in her body. He knew she was past the point of return. Feeling no pain. All pleasure. All need.

"Come, my angel" he whispered.

The low, keening cry on the heels of his command was like bliss-soaked music. He gripped her hard and fucked into her like a man possessed, dying in the pleasure of her clasping, clenching heat. Her sounds. The scent of her skin and arousal. It was all too much. Right as she buried her face in the blankets to muffle another grinding moan, he came hard, spilling inside her and letting loose his own shout of release.

It was the perfect moment.

With the perfect woman.

And for just those few minutes, as they rolled over and curled into each other, he let himself imagine that it wouldn't be temporary. That'd he'd found *that* girl.

But he knew hope was a wicked bitch. One who had proven time and again that the minute you believed in something or someone, you got decimated.

And even if Cela thought she wasn't telling her parents about staying because she was afraid of how they would react, he knew the truth. She hadn't told because she still wasn't sure of her decision.

She wasn't sure of him.

And that's what had hurt him tonight.

So he knew that he had to cherish these stolen moments with her, because like everything else good in his life—there was always an expiration date.

And every instinct he had said the clock was ticking.

THIRTY

The next morning I found myself in the completely odd position of waking up in Foster's bed and getting ready to go into work with him. I'd run over to my place to shower and put on fresh clothes. But right after, I was back, hand in hand with him as we headed out for the day.

He'd offered to give me a tour of his company today, and I was looking forward to seeing it. But as he pulled up to the Starbucks drive-thru window and handed me my latte, it wasn't lost on me how very domestic this felt. How fast this was all happening. I tried to push away the anxiety that came along with that. Half of me was thrilled at how comfortable everything was, but the other half—my practical half—was warning me to slow down my assumptions.

He pulled away from Starbucks and set his coffee in the cup holder. "So have you thought any more about when you're going to tell your family?"

I sipped my drink, the too-hot liquid burning the tip of my tongue. I winced—whether it was from the coffee or the question he'd asked—I wasn't sure. "I was thinking maybe it'd be best to tell them in person."

He looked over at me, eyebrows lifted.

"I'm supposed to go home for my birthday, not this weekend but next, and I figured it'd be more respectful to talk to my dad face-to-face. Maybe I can make him understand better if he can see how excited I am about this new job."

"Sounds like a brave route to take," he said, nodding. "And a mature one."

I held my fingers around my cup, hoping the warmth could chase away the chill going through me at the thought of talking to my dad face-to-face. "I've already tried to tell him on the phone, and it was an epic fail."

"I'm sorry. If I could help make it easier for you, I would."

I leaned over and pressed a kiss to his cheek. "Thanks. I just wish I could fast-forward time and have it be done."

"I know the feeling," he said, almost to himself more than me.

Before long we were pulling in front of a shiny building with the 4N logo on it. Foster pulled into a reserved spot close to the front and helped me out of the car. "Wow, you get your own spot and everything. Fancy."

He smirked. "Watch the mocking tone, angel. I'm not opposed to locking my office door and reminding you to be respectful. My desk is the perfect height to bend you over for a spanking."

I stuck my tongue out at him and he reached up, quick as a flash, and pinched my tongue between his thumb and forefinger.

I gasped—or well, it would've been a gasp had I had a tongue in working order.

"Not very nice." He bent his head close and gave my tongue a little pinch before releasing it.

"Sorry," I whispered.

"Sure you are." He smiled and slid his hand around the back of my neck to claim my mouth in a heated kiss. His tongue massaged mine where he'd pinched, stroking against it with sensual hunger. My blood went hotter than the coffee in my hands, and I whimpered into the kiss. He broke away after another second and grabbed one of my hands, curling my fingers around the erection tenting his pants. "You're a hazard to bring to work. You're getting me hard already." He stroked my hand along his cock, then released me. "Quick, ask me something decidedly unsexy so we can actually get out of the car without me stabbing anyone."

I took a breath, trying to get my own responses back in check, and glanced at the building again. "What does 4N stand for?"

I could sense his mood shift instantly in the dip of his brow. His erection flagged almost immediately. Damn, apparently I'd chosen the most unsexy question ever. "It means 'For Neve.' Neve was my sister's name."

"Oh," I said quietly.

He blew out a breath and conjured up some version of a smile. "Okay, that totally worked. Guess it's safe to head in now."

"Right." We both climbed out of the car, the ebullient mood from before ebbing drastically.

Once we made our way to the entrance of the building, Foster pulled open the glass door and let me in. The woman at the large rounded desk at the forefront of the modern lobby stood as soon as we were both inside. "Good morning, Mr. Foster."

"Good morning, Alexis," he said, his smile polite. "Nice weekend?"

"Yes, sir. Thank you."

The redhead smiled with open curiosity at me, but Foster didn't bother to introduce us. He kept walking toward a set of elevators as I let my gaze trail over the shiny plaques that seems to line the perimeter of the lobby. "What are all these for?"

He glanced over to see what I was referring to. He shrugged. "Awards. Thank-yous."

Thank-yous to a tech company? That seemed odd.

But when we rode the elevator up to the top floor, I realized quickly that Foster's company was not your average widget builder. Along the main wall heading toward his office, there were photos of children and the occasional adult. All with their names and dates and times at the bottom. I paused at the last one—a photo of a little girl with very familiar blue eyes. I touched the letters on the frame. *Neve Juliette Foster.*

Foster stopped his stride and paused with me.

"She's beautiful," I said, my heart twisting in my chest as my fingers ran over the date. *Age 5—Missing since July 1990.*

"Yeah," he said softly. "She was."

I didn't miss the past tense he'd used, and I leaned into him. "What are the other photos for? Are they all missing, too?"

He slid a hand onto my lower back, standing next to me at the wall of photos. "No, those are our happy stories. 4N creates devices and apps to help track children, so that if they disappear, parents can have a tool to find them. We've saved a lot of kids with it, and even a few Alzheimer's patients who have wandered off. These are our successes. The people who we helped."

I looked at him then back at the substantial amount of pictures, each smiling face shining back. Alive. Home with their families now. "My God, Foster, that's amazing. I had no idea . . ."

His thumb stroked the base of my spine. "We put up the pictures to remind us why we're doing this. And to get through the tough days. Because for every happy ending, there's another child that doesn't come home at night or another woman who disappears while jogging. People are victimized every day."

I turned toward him, my heart feeling like it had doubled in weight in my chest. "Which is why you freaked out about me opening my door."

He released a breath, his shoulders dipping. "Knowing what's out there and seeing it on a daily basis makes me want to wrap you up in my arms and keep you next to me so that nothing evil ever touches you. That's why seeing you exposed to any of it, like that asshole Gerald or that guy taking a photo of you, makes me a little crazy."

I reached for his hand, saddened by what he'd been through and wanting to hug him, but knowing that probably wouldn't be good to do at his job. I was truly awed at what he did for a living. I'd known he was still actively looking for his sister but had no idea that he'd dedicated his life's work to it. No wonder he was so paranoid. If I had to face those horrible stories every day at work, I'd want to lock everyone down, too.

"I'm sorry you've seen so many ugly things," I said, squeezing his hand.

"How about you come to my office so I can stare at a beautiful one instead?" He leaned over and gave me a peck on the lips.

I smiled, enjoying how easily he showed his affection, even in a public situation like this. On the way to his office, he introduced me to a few people and explained what they did. Everyone was very friendly, but I didn't miss the curious glances, raised eyebrows, and the faint hint of whispering after we walked away. Apparently Foster didn't bring women he was dating on tours very often. Good.

When we reached his office, he made quick introductions between me and his assistant, Lindy, who burst into a grin when he called me his girlfriend. Foster gave her a quelling look and Lindy tucked her lips inward, her eyes still smiling.

Foster ushered me past her desk and opened the door to his expansive office. Before closing the door, he called back over his shoulder, "Lindy, hold my calls for a while."

"Yes, sir," she chirped. "I'm on it!"

I crossed my arms, cocking my head. "So *she* gets to call you sir, too. I see how it is."

He laughed and pulled me into his embrace. "They all do. Even Herb in accounts payable. Jealous?"

"Wildly," I said, tipping my head back and looking to the heavens.

"Well, your patients get to bite and lick you. So I have my own jealousy to deal with."

I leaned back in his hold, eyeing him. "Oh, you bite, do you?"

"On occasion." He snapped his teeth together with a growl, then chuckled when I yelped in surprise. "But I've had my shots, I promise."

"Good to know."

"Now come on, I have something I want to give you." He released me and pulled out the chair in front of his desk for me. I sat down, as he went around his desk and grabbed a small box from his drawer. He came back around to my side and perched on the edge of the desk.

"Now, Foster," I teased. "I think it's a little too early for a proposal. I mean, I know I'm spectacular in bed, but . . ."

"Hush, smartass," he said, bumping my leg with his foot.

"Yes, sir."

"So I know you heard about the symbol of a collar in your class and how serious being collared is. It's like getting married."

I nodded, my gaze darting down to the box with a small pinch of panic. He wasn't going to collar me, right?

"We're not ready for that step yet, but I wanted to give you something to mark our commitment to being together like this." He opened the box. Inside was a delicate silver bracelet with a small Celtic knot charm on it.

I reached out and touched the links. "It's beautiful."

"We make these here. It's a Home Safe anklet."

I tucked my hand back into my lap, looking up at him. "What does it do?"

"In the charm is a small transmitter. If someone goes missing, it can either be activated by the victim or remotely activated by whoever is looking for them. It will send out a signal to help find them—like a remote GPS. This is how we've saved a lot of those people on that wall out there." He lifted it from the box and handed it to me. "I would love for you to wear it. As a symbol. But also as an added safety device. I'd feel better knowing you had one."

I stared at the anklet, guarded now and growing more and more uneasy by the minute. "It tracks someone. Will *track* me."

"It's not like—"

"God," I said on a bitter laugh. "My father would've paid a fortune for this when I was a teenager. Instead of going through my cell phone records and having neighbors report in on me, he could've just sat at his computer and tracked my every move. How convenient!"

Foster frowned. "It's not meant to be used that way. It can only be activated in emergencies. If it's a false alarm, the customer has to call in and have it reset. Each only gets two resets before the person has to buy a new one."

But my mind was already chasing the line of thought like a dog racing after a mailman. A customer would have to buy a new one but not Foster. It was his product, his company. He could probably activate or reset one whenever the hell he wanted. "You really lack that much trust in me?"

"Cela," he said patiently. "This is not about me not trusting you. I care about you and want you safe. The chances of anything ever happening are slim, but I'd sleep better knowing that you had an added layer of protection."

"Oh," I said. "Well, let's make sure *you* sleep better. Doesn't matter if I have to wear some device like I'm on house arrest. What if I'm late one day or want to go somewhere and don't tell you? You could just hit a button and *poof!* know all my business? Or better yet. You could add in a feature like a dog's shock collar. If I stray to far, you can just deliver a little jolt."

"Forget it," he said, pushing up from the desk and tossing the empty box on top of it. "You're right. This is about trust. You not trusting that I'm doing this with good intentions and not to fucking stalk you. I'm not like your father."

"And I'm not your sister," I retorted.

"No, you're not," he said, full anger rolling off him now. "Because I'm actually trying to protect you. The day Neve was taken I was supposed to be watching her in the front yard. She was *my* responsibility. But she'd been annoying the hell out of me all afternoon, wanting me to play Barbies. I told her to go play her stupid baby games somewhere else. So while I was busy climbing trees with my friends, my baby sister was grabbed off the street by some monster. Because of me. *My* fault."

I stared at him, stricken.

"So fine, be pissed that I want to protect you."

"Foster—" I said, stuck tears slowing the words in my throat. "God, that's not your fault, it was the—"

"No, it was mine. Just ask my parents."

The words echoed through his big, modern office, pinging through my chest. His parents. The ones who'd left him alone, who'd bailed on him. Now I knew why. They blamed their son for something that some sick criminal did. My heart broke for him, right there in his office, little pieces falling to the floor.

He let out a long breath and sagged back onto the desk, his eyes haunted. "I need you to wear the anklet, Cela."

I wanted to stay angry, needed to fight the idea of what the anklet represented, but I couldn't bear the flat, empty look on his face. I went to him, lowering to my knees and laying my head in his lap.

He threaded his fingers through my hair, his voice grim. "I don't know how to care for someone and not worry, angel."

I wanted to reassure him, to take that pain out of his voice, but I couldn't agree to something like this just to make him feel better. I lifted my head and took his hands in mine, meeting his gaze. "I am so sorry for all that you've been through. And I wish I could take that all away for you. But this is asking a lot—too much. I've spent my whole life under someone's thumb, and I'm not sure I can ever put myself in that kind of position again."

"Angel . . ."

"I need some time, Foster," I said, the bleak truth bleeding through me, making my limbs feel heavy. "To think about all this. We've moved fast. And it's been intense and fun and wonderful, but I'm beginning to wonder if I'm capable of being what you want and need. Maybe I'm not cut out for this role."

His expression went stony and he stood, rocking me back from my kneel. "Of course."

I shoved myself to my feet, his icy tone chilling me. "Foster, I—"

He picked up the phone, his whole posture closed off to me. "Lindy, please call a cab for Ms. Medina. She's heading out. And give Bret a call, too, tell her to come by the office for a chat. Make us lunch reservations at that Italian place she likes."

I blinked, icicles spiking through my chest. "What are you doing?"

"Giving you time, space, whatever," he said, hanging up the phone and sitting down behind his desk. "I told you in the beginning, you could always pull the escape hatch. Frankly, you lasted longer than expected."

The words hit me as well as if he'd slapped a palm right across my face. "So that's how you're going to handle this?"

He glanced up, gaze cool. "What? Would you prefer I tie you to the chair and demand you be with me? I'm not going to get on my knees and beg for you, Cela."

"No, that's my job, right?" I bit back, hot tears burning my lids.

"Apparently not," he said, the bitter smirk the final dagger in this disaster of a morning.

I turned on my heel, before I did something stupid—like cry or throw a blunt object at his freaking head. "Thanks for the tour."

I collected myself in the few steps to the door as best I could and strode out his door, offering a quick good-bye to Lindy and heading straight for the elevators. As I rode down to the lobby, every part of me was shaking—with anger, with grief, and with utter frustration. When

I had said I needed time, Foster had looked at me like he'd already known it was coming. Like I'd been some forgone conclusion he was waiting out. I hadn't been breaking up with him. I'd only wanted to be honest. But he'd cut me off so quickly it was like I'd never meant anything at all.

I'd stayed here for him. I'd taken the risk and put everything on the line.

And then at the first sign of strife, he hadn't fought for me. Not one bit.

I walked through the lobby, only half hearing the receptionist inform me that the cab should be there in about ten minutes. I plunked myself on a bench near the front windows, wishing I could close my eyes and teleport back to my place. Hell, maybe I should teleport all the way back to graduation night and just stay inside and drink alone.

Unfortunately, no portal to the past or wrinkle in the space-time continuum appeared to save me as I sat there. And of course, the cab was late. Twenty minutes and the receptionist let me know the driver had gotten a flat and was sending another car this way. I pinned a polite smile to my face but groaned inwardly. Dallas wasn't a place to have a lot of cabs rolling around anyway, especially outside of downtown, but I could've walked home faster than this. I should've just called Bailey.

A car pulled up a few minutes later, drawing my gaze upward, but it wasn't a taxi. The shiny black Jaguar pulled into an empty spot, and a tall blonde stepped out. She seemed to move with utter confidence as her knee-high boots clicked purposely over the pavement. The runway-style walk caught the attention of a guy heading out to the parking lot, and he did a full one-eighty turn to watch her after she passed him.

I couldn't help but watch, dread sinking and settling in my stomach. The woman perched her sunglasses atop her head, revealing kohl-lined blue eyes that appeared to be evaluating everything in their path, and stepped inside the main doors. The air seemed to part for her as she made her way to the front desk—like even oxygen was taken aback by her presence.

"Good morning, Ms. Avery," the receptionist said, as if she interacted with the woman all the time. "Love that handbag."

The woman returned the greeting with warmth, then cocked her head toward the elevators. "Is Ian ready? I know I'm a little early."

Ian.

I wanted to vomit right there on the shiny marble tiles. This was the woman he was going to have lunch with, and she called him Ian. A name, which by his own admission, was only used at one place and for one purpose.

I turned away, closing my eyes. Part of me wanted to believe he wouldn't be that cruel, that vindictive. But as the footsteps of Ms. Blonde and Gorgeous disappeared into the elevator, and my cab finally pulled up, everything that had been bright and glowing inside me these last few weeks shriveled and died.

I sank into the backseat of the cab, feeling like roadkill. The last time I'd ridden in a taxi, I'd been sandwiched between Foster and Pike on the way to a night of no-strings fun. This time, I wrapped my arms around myself, stared out the window, and sobbed.

THIRTY-ONE

Monday morning I sat outside Dr. Pelham's office, watching her through the glass and waiting for her to finish a phone call. I'd spent the rest of the weekend after the fight with Foster holed up in my apartment, watching movies with Bailey and doing a chef's tour of the junk food aisle at the grocery store. It was pathetic. I'd never felt so damn shitty. It was like having the flu without the chest congestion and fever.

But Bailey had informed me that I had every right to be miserable and mopey for a few days. According to her, it was breakup law. However, she'd also laid down the edict that by today, I had to get my shit together because it would be the first day of my new beginning. New job. New me. And, hopefully, in a few weeks, new apartment. Because God knows I couldn't live next door to Foster anymore.

I hadn't seen him since the day at 4N. And there'd been no sound from his side of the wall. So either he was out of town or he was sleeping somewhere else. Probably with blond amazons who wore fuck-me boots. My stomach rolled. I forced myself to sip my coffee, even though it tasted as bitter as my mood.

Dr. Pelham seemed to sigh as she hung up the phone and frown lines framed her mouth. She glanced over toward the glass, meeting my gaze, then waved me in. I got out of my chair, taking a deep breath to put on my professional face, and went inside.

"Hi there, Cela," she said, shifting some papers around on her desk.

"Hi, Dr. Pelham, did you enjoy your cruise?"

She smiled, though it seemed a bit tight. "It was lovely. Thank you."

"Well, I know you're busy, but I just wanted to talk about the pos—"

"I got your email," she said, cutting me short and pressing her palms to the papers on her desk. "And I've been on the phone for the last half hour with Dr. Foreman."

"Okay," I said, a little unsure of what Dr. Foreman had to do with anything.

"When you didn't take the job before I left for my cruise, I gave Dr. Foreman the go-ahead to hire from the other candidates."

I stared at her, my thoughts going blank. "What?"

"Hon, last I had talked to you, you were planning to go home. And the position needed to be filled. If I had known you were truly considering it . . ." She shook her head, then pulled her reading glasses off and rubbed the bridge of her nose, clearly distressed by all of it. "There's no one I wanted more on my team than you. You've been a stellar intern. But another offer has already been extended and accepted. I can't undo it."

"Another offer," I repeated, the words falling from my lips like heavy stones.

"I'm so sorry, Cela," she said. "I will absolutely write any recommendations you need to apply other places if you plan to stay in town. I know that Dr. Murphy over at Banks Street Emergency needs a—"

"Right." I stood so abruptly that the gust I caused sent papers fluttering off her desk. "It's fine. I should've . . . it's my fault . . . I just didn't . . ."

"Cela," she said, standing, too, worry on her face.

I pasted on some smile that seemed to belong to someone else. "It's okay. Thank you, Dr. Pelham. For offering recommendations and for all that you've taught me. I'll let you know. I just . . . I need to take care of some things first."

She may have said something else, but I was already cruising out the door on automaton legs. I didn't stop, didn't go by the front desk to see Bailey. I just kept walking, straight to my car. By the time I stepped into the lobby of my building, I'd gone full numb, my thoughts locked in some suspended state. I was unemployed.

I had no job.

I had no Foster.

I had nothing here.

At the top of the stairs, I didn't even see Pike coming out of his apartment until I nearly bumped right into him. "Whoa there, doc."

I glanced up, mumbled a "Sorry."

"Hey," he said, putting his hand on my arm when I tried to walk past him. "You okay?"

"Fine," I muttered and tried to move forward again, but his hand stayed on me.

"Look, doc, I know Foster is being an asshole. Believe me. But don't give up on him yet. I think you two—"

"My job fell through," I said flatly. "This isn't about Foster. Can you please let me go now?"

Immediately, his hand lifted from me. I felt bad being a bitch to Pike. He hadn't done anything to me, but I couldn't handle talking to anyone right now, especially about Foster. "But I thought you had that job locked up."

"Yeah, well, not so much, apparently."

He ran a hand over the back of his neck. "Is there another position?"

"Yeah," I said with a bitter smile. "Back home."

"Oh, doc, you don't need to do that. I'm sure there are—"

"I have no job, Pike. No job means no money, no rent, no anything. I have a position waiting for me at home, a house, and my family. It's where I should've gone in the first place."

"But what about Foster?"

"What about him? I haven't seen him in days."

Pike stuck his hands in his pockets. "He's out of town."

"With Bret?" I asked.

Pike's brows went up. "He told you about *Bret*?"

"No, but you just did." My throat tightened until I could barely draw breath. I stalked past him and into my apartment, slamming the door behind me.

Screw. It. All.

I grabbed my cell phone and tossed my purse onto the kitchen counter. He answered on the second ring.

"Papá, it's me. Everything's wrapped up here. I'm coming home."

"Well, it's about time, *mija*."

Yeah. It was.

PART VII

Not Until You Believe

THIRTY-TWO

Foster shoved open the door to his apartment, feeling like he'd been put through a meat grinder, then stuck back together again. The weariness of days on the road and the scent of airport bars clung to him like some unwanted traveling companion. He tossed his keys on the counter and grabbed a beer out of the fridge.

Pike strolled into the kitchen, pulling a worn Toadies concert T-shirt down over his head. "Heh, well, look who it fucking is. He returns. All hail the King of Douchebaggery."

Foster shot Pike a murderous look. "Fuck off, Pike. I'm not in the mood."

"Oh you're not?" he asked with a sneer. "Well, you know what I'm not in the mood for? My goddamn friend who disappears and then doesn't answer his fucking phone for a week."

"I told you I'd be out of town. I wanted to be alone."

"Or with Bret."

He scowled. "She only hung around for the first part of it. We had some business to handle."

"Yeah, I bet."

Foster tipped back his beer, tempted to throw it just to hear the glass break.

"It wasn't like that." Though it almost had been. He and Bret had been friends for a long time and had fooled around off and on through the years anytime one of them got a little too drunk or a little too lonely. They weren't suited—both too dominant for the other—but an angry fuck between two control freaks could work out a lot of rage. And it had been in the back of his mind when he'd called her in for a last-minute business trip. He'd needed something—anything—to numb the pain he'd felt when Cela had said she couldn't be submissive.

But when it came down to acting on anything with Bret, he hadn't been able to drum up an iota of interest. He'd ended up sitting in a bar with her and getting shit-faced drunk while he told her all about Cela. Fucking ridiculous.

Pike sniffed. "It wasn't like that, huh? So you just paraded her in front of Cela to be a complete asshole."

"Cela? She doesn't know Bret."

"She knows you were out of town with her."

"*What?*"

Pike's jaw flexed. "And if you had answered your goddamn phone, I could've told you that."

"Fuck." He raked his hand through his hair, his head booming like a bass drum beneath his fingertips. "I'll talk to her. Apologize. I have a list of dick moves to make up for at this point."

"Yeah, well, good luck talking to her, buddy," Pike said, leaning back against the edge of the counter and crossing his arms. "She left a few days ago."

"What?" He stared down at his beer, trying to process that information. "Oh, right, her birthday trip. She'd mentioned that to me. I'll talk to her when she comes back. It'll give us both time to get our heads together."

Pike shook his head slowly, his expression making the hairs prickle on the back of Foster's neck. "No, man. That's not what I mean. She *left*. Like for good. Her job fell through."

Every ounce of alcohol Foster had consumed in the last week seemed to burn a path up his throat, singeing his insides and threatening to come out. "She moved *home*?"

Pike sighed. "There was no one here to convince her otherwise."

Foster sagged against the counter, his beer forgotten in his hand. Cela was gone. *Gone.*

"What happened between you two, man?" Pike asked, no sarcasm left in his voice. "One minute you're buying her a bed, the next she can't get out of town fast enough."

He rubbed fingers over his brow bone, massaging the spot where all the pressure was building. "I asked her to wear a Home Safe anklet."

"Ah, fuck, Foster," Pike said with a groan. "Just what every girl wants—a piece of jewelry her boyfriend can stalk her with."

"You know I wouldn't use it like that," he bit back, but he couldn't muster much fire behind it. Suddenly, he was tired, so very exhausted by it all. "I just wanted her to be safe."

"Uh-huh."

"But if it'd just been that, I'm sure we would've worked past it. It was more than the anklet. She told me she needed time, that she wasn't sure she could be submissive. It all started spilling out like it'd been bottled up the whole time, like she was just waiting for the opportunity to bail. It was Darcy all over again."

"Like Darcy? Fuck. That. Cela is nothing like that girl. Darcy wanted a rich husband who would indulge her with a pampered princess life. She was never really submissive. And when she figured out that you weren't going to magically morph into some Stepford husband she could control with a pout, she cut bait."

"Cela probably wishes I'd morph into something different, too," he said, the muscle in his jaw twitching.

"No, she knew who you were when she stayed in the first place. But she probably backpedaled because you freaked her the hell out," Pike said, making it sound like the most obvious truth in the world. "I saw that girl the first night with you. And I heard what happened the night you cuffed her to the door. Cela is *not* afraid of giving you control. But she *is* independent, and if you try to lock her down and treat her like a kid, she's going to feel smothered. For fuck's sake, you asked her to wear a homing device. You don't LoJack your girlfriend like she's your newest Mercedes."

"It's not a—goddammit, Pike." Foster did toss the beer this time, but managed to hit the trash. His head hurt, his chest hurt, and now he felt like an even bigger dick than before.

"Did you even manage to tell the girl you loved her before you laid the whole tracking device thing down on her?"

"What?" He looked at Pike like he'd grown an extra head. "Of course I didn't tell her that. We're not at that point yet, I don't—"

"Bull. Fucking. Shit," he said, jabbing his finger at him with each word. "I knew you were an asshole but don't be a liar, too. You had her apartment painted. You bought her a bed. You made her *pancakes*."

Foster threw his hands out to his side. "Again with the pancakes."

"You don't do that crap for girls you kinda like. You do it for the ones you are shit-faced in love with."

Foster simply glared back at him.

Pike pushed off the counter. "And for some unknown reason, she's got it just as bad. I mean, she had the chance at all this"—he swept his hand down and out—"and went for you. So the question is, what are you going to do about it?"

Foster wanted to punch something, and if he didn't walk away soon, it might be Pike. "Nothing. I don't chase women anymore. If they want to be with me, they are. If not, that's their choice."

He stalked past Pike, needing his dark bedroom and a dreamless night. And anything but this conversation.

"Coward," was the last word he heard before slamming his door.

A few hours later, still wide-awake, Foster slipped out of his room and into his roommate's. Pike was sound asleep on his stomach, all the covers kicked off. Making sure not to step on anything that would alert him, Foster stepped around the bed and grabbed what he needed off the nightstand.

———

The room was too quiet—oppressive. I stared at the ugly popcorn ceiling, mentally making a list of the things I needed to buy to make this room feel like home. I hadn't unpacked much of anything yet, and I knew I had my bedroom knickknacks tucked away some- where, but I had the urge to throw it all out and start fresh. I didn't want anything to remind me of my apartment back in Dallas. Not that this place could ever look like my apartment.

The 1970s decor my aunt had never updated was so awful it was almost back in style. Green carpet, faux wood-paneled walls, orange countertops in the kitchen. It even had a trash compactor, for God's sake—but no dishwasher. Because apparently, turning trash into a cube was way more important than having something that washed dishes.

But it was free and it was available when I high-tailed it here a few days ago, so here I lay. And really, I didn't care at this point. I just wanted to keep moving forward so I wouldn't have to think. I'd kept myself busy with moving related things for a few days, and tomorrow was my first official day at the clinic. As long as I didn't stop, I was okay. Mostly.

But nighttime sucked. My cable and wireless hadn't been turned on yet, so all I had was an empty, quiet house, some stale smell I couldn't seem to light enough candles to cover, and my thoughts. I rolled onto my side, determined to force myself to sleep, but the ding of my cell phone broke through the silence. I flipped back over to reach for my phone, my heart leaping a little bit, as if it had muscle memory from the last time I'd received a late-night text. But of course, this wouldn't be like that one.

I hit the button on my phone, expecting to see a text from Bailey. She'd been checking on me like I'd just gotten out of rehab and she was my sponsor. But the name staring back at me was definitely not what I expected.

Pike.

Move go ok?

I shifted fully on my side, propping my head up with my hand and typed back. It was sweet of Pike to check on me, but even seeing his name sent a cymbal crash of sadness and longing reverberating through me. Already, it felt like Dallas and everything I'd left there existed on some other planet I no longer had access to anymore.

Survived.

Good.

U realize it's almost 1am, right?

Sorry, did I wake u? (Musician hours)

No. My new place is too quiet & possibly haunted with the spirits of Charlie's Angels or The Brady Bunch.

Scary. *Sends exorcist*

I smiled, some of the pressure that'd been crushing me for the last week easing with the relaxed banter.

Not sure the power of Christ would compel them. How's Monty?

Hardheaded & dominant. Like someone else we know.

I stared at the blinking cursor, a sharp pain digging right through the center of my chest and burrowing deep. I didn't want to talk about Foster. Couldn't. I was barely keeping myself together as it was. But before I could think of how to respond, my phone dinged again.

He came home. Nothing happened w/ Bret.

I rolled onto my back, finding it a challenge to draw in a full breath— the elephant-sized weight of everything pressing down on me again.

None of my business.

If ur not happy there, u should come back.

My job is here.

Even if my heart wasn't.

U know he would cover u while u looked for another job. Even if u aren't together. He'd take care of u.

I let the phone sit against my chest as I stared up again, the flecked ceiling blurring with fresh tears. Of course he would. And that was part of the problem. It took me a full minute before I could even attempt a response. I lifted the phone.

I don't need to be taken care of.

I just needed Foster. Not as a bodyguard or a parent or a master. Just him.

But being with Foster meant being with his dominance—all parts of it—and if I didn't think I could live that way long term, it wasn't fair for either of us to drag it out.

I'm happy here.

Lie.

This time it was Pike who took a while to respond. I shifted back to my side, wondering if he was going to say anything else when the final text came.

I'm glad ur happy. U deserve to be. Good luck w/ everything.

There was nothing else to say back to that except thanks and good-night. Continuing to lie to him would only make the yawning crack in my heart spread wider.

"Yep, that's me," I said aloud to my empty house, my voice hoarse with tears. "So freaking happy."

I tossed my phone onto the nightstand, curled up around my pillow, and tried to pretend it didn't hurt so bad.

THIRTY-THREE

ONE MONTH LATER

"Marcela!" My father's voice boomed from the other room, echoing through the hall.

"Coming." I sighed heavily as I scrubbed my hands. I was so not in the mood for that tone. I'd already had two emergencies this morning, plus had been faced with a devastated family when I'd had to put down their beloved fifteen-year-old tabby. The only thing I wanted right now was to take a lunch break and get a MexiCoke from the store next door to drown away my stress with cane sugar.

But I dutifully headed to my father's office. I leaned against the doorjamb. "Yes, Papá?"

"What is this crap?" he asked with a scowl. "I told you what to order for the Whitcombs' Rottweiler."

I nodded at the little tube of ointment he was holding in his hand. "That's a better treatment. It works faster and he'll only need a few doses instead of two weeks of applications to clear up the rash."

"Just because it's the newest, fanciest cream doesn't mean it's better," he said, tossing it onto the desk like it had dirtied his fingers.

"I realize that," I said, trying to keep my patience. "But in this case, it is better. Plus, he's my patient now. I make the call."

My father looked up, his glare holding warning. "Order what I told you to order. I still make the final call in this practice. And I don't need my clients spending more just to get a brand name when something else works."

In the past, that quelling look alone would've sent me cowering. But the more I worked with him, the more I was realizing how much of a bully he could be. And when we were here, I was supposed to be his co-worker first, daughter second. Not the other way around. I crossed my arms over my chest. "Would you bark an order like that at me if I were some other doctor you hired?"

One bushy eyebrow lifted. "Yes, Marcela, I would. I am training you how I want this practice to be handled. Our clients expect a certain kind of service and when I retire, I want to insure that we continue to do that. And I appreciate that you learned some different techniques in school, but you need to remember who has the decades of experience here."

Like I could ever forget. "Yes, Dr. Medina."

He frowned. "Don't be smart, Marcela."

"Sorry. I've been told I have a problem with that," I said, remembering the playful way Foster used to call me smartass and the amused glint that would light his eyes when I'd spar with him. I turned on my heel, trying to tamp down the surge of loss that greeted me over the memory.

Two, my mind silently made the hash mark.

I was getting better. Already lunchtime, and it was only the second time he'd crossed my mind today.

I grabbed my purse and headed out of the clinic to get some fresh air and food. There wasn't much to do in Verde Pass for lunch, and I knew my mom would probably have something cooking since my dad went home daily for lunch. But a Mexican Coke and a chicken salad sandwich from the shop next door sounded way better than listening to my mother wax on about so-and-so's son and how I should make a point to get to know him better.

I stepped inside the Sip 'N Shop, the little bell announcing my arrival, and gave a quick wave to J.C., who covered the shop for his dad during the day. I bought what I needed, then took it outside to one of the picnic benches. The temperature was in the triple digits again today, but I couldn't bear to be inside much longer. Plus, the shade trees arching over the tables and the faint breeze provided a sliver of relief.

And apparently, I wasn't the only one who'd had this plan for lunch today. Before I finished unwrapping my sandwich, a shadow crossed over the table. I glanced up and smiled. "Fancy meeting you here."

Michael Ruiz, now Dr. Ruiz the dentist, slid onto the other side of the picnic table. "Well, I've heard this is the hottest spot in town."

I took a sip of my Coke, the bottle sweating against my palm. "It definitely is hot."

Michael pulled a bottle of water from his bag. When we'd dated in high school, he'd had a Mountain Dew addiction, but apparently dental school had scared him off the hard stuff. "Hey, I'd be willing to take you to some place fancier, you know, with air conditioning and stuff, if you'd ever let me. I've heard the Subway has an excellent charcuterie platter."

I smirked as I peeled the crust off my sandwich. Michael asked me out pretty much daily these days. I'd told him I was coming off a breakup and wasn't ready to start dating again, which he'd respected. But he hadn't stopped joining me for lunch to keep me company. I appreciated that he wasn't putting pressure on me about it, just being a friend to me when I really needed one. But I knew that he would prefer it was more than that.

Bailey had told me to give the guy a break—well, after I'd told her he was a doctor and had sent her a photo of him so she could verify he was of acceptable hotness. She was of the "get back on the horse" mind-set, but the thought of going out with anyone held about as much appeal as watching a *CSI* marathon with my dad—which, incidentally, was what I'd done last weekend.

"I'll keep that in mind," I said, hoping it came across light and not like a jab.

He pulled the butcher paper from around his sandwich, but his dark eyes stayed on me. "Want me to stop asking?"

I sighed, elbows on the table, sandwich in hand. Michael had always been sweet to me. When we'd dated, we'd never gotten too serious, but I'd always known he was an inherently good guy. He'd be the type to take it slow, to be polite no matter what, and to yield to my preferences on where to go and what to do. He was everything on paper I'd always thought I wanted—good-looking, hardworking, and a guy my parents would be happy to see me with.

He was an obvious choice, and I already knew we got along and that

I'd have fun with him. I'd said no over and over again in ten different subtle and polite ways. But as I peered at him there across the table, I started to question my reasons. The stuff that had been holding me back was beginning to look more and more ridiculous—silly, romantic notions that belonged in movies, not real life.

Maybe I didn't need that *thing*. Whatever that thing was that I used to feel when I looked at Foster. In the end, that intensity had only led me straight to a heartbreaking dead end anyway.

Time to change gears. Reboot. Get with reality.

I reached out and put my hand over Mike's. "Don't stop asking."

His mouth curved. "I'm good at being patient."

"Thanks, Mike."

Later that night, as I sat on my living room floor unpacking boxes and eating a microwaved potpie, I was still ruminating over my conversation with Mike when I came across a little silver piece of jewelry that I'd tossed into one of the boxes. I pulled the anklet out of the pile of stuff, the sound of the *Big Bang Theory* rerun on the TV fading into the background, as I held it along my palm. Such a small thing—a little length of silver. But it'd been the lynchpin that had blown everything up between me and Foster. That day in the office, I'd dropped it in my purse in my haste to get out of there as soon as possible. But now it was here, opening up the wound that I was working so hard to close.

He'd wanted to protect me. That's what he had said. And to mark me as his.

The memory made tears knot my throat. *His.*

I'd been so ready to start something with him, so open to the possibilities, but that simple word had scared the hell out of me. He'd looked so serious, so sincere. And I hadn't wanted to promise him something I wasn't sure I could give. And I definitely couldn't imagine wearing something that could be tracked. Visions of my teen years had flashed before me—trapped, monitored, ruled over. It would've been the wrong move. I wouldn't have been able to handle it long term. And it would've hurt us both more in the long run.

I couldn't be his submissive. It wasn't me.

But the thought wrenched something sideways inside me, making me press my forehead to my knees. Who was I kidding? I didn't know who I was. I didn't have a freaking clue. During the day, I fought constantly to make my own path at the clinic, do things my own way. I'd stood up more for myself since being back home than I ever had in my life. But at night, when the place got quiet and my mind drifted to memories of Foster, I couldn't help but let myself fall back into the fantasies we'd shared, times when I had no control at all. I replayed them in my mind like some addict needing a hit—just one more time, one more time . . . And when that wasn't enough, I'd create new ones, weave even dirtier, more sordid scenes for us to star in.

I didn't know how to reconcile that girl with the other. How could I be both?

I stared down at the anklet, running my thumb along the metal, which was now warming from the heat of my hand. The latch was some type of screw design, and I found my fingers slowly turning it. The anklet fell open, and without knowing why, I reached down and fastened it around my ankle. The silver pressed against my skin, sliding over the delicate bones there. And the sight of it—his mark—locked around me sent burning tears to my eyes.

I could imagine Foster there, kneeling down and looping the jewelry around my ankle, pleasure in his eyes. The word *mine* on his lips. His mouth kissing up along my calf, my thigh, my eyes going hot with intent as he whispered all those dirty, tempting things he was so good at saying. The image warmed me from the inside out, making a flush creep over my skin.

Unconsciously, I pushed up from the floor and clicked off the TV. I lowered myself onto the couch, closing my eyes and letting the fantasy run, sinking into it. Foster always had such a slow, deliberate way of kissing every part of me, his mouth leaving trails of heat on my skin. Without thinking too hard about what I was doing, I let my body and the images take over. My hands slid up my stomach beneath my shirt, and I cupped my breasts, imagining it was his big hands instead of mine. The feel wasn't quite right, my touch too soft, too feminine to be his. So I pinched and plucked at my nipples like he would've, making sure to do it hard enough to cause a snap of pain. Yes, that was better. I sighed softly, opening my eyes briefly to see the silver glinting against my ankle.

Moisture and heat gathered between my thighs, the sight of jewelry pushing some lever inside me. I let my eyes drift shut again and trailed my hand down my stomach. Foster liked to tease me, to move his fingers along my folds but not quite stroke my clit yet. And his touch was always so sure, like he knew exactly how to bring me right to the edge and hold me there, hanging by my fingernails. I imagined him lowering his head between my legs, my arms tied above me, and the feel of that five-o'clock stubble moving against the tender skin of my thighs—the abrasive, *scritch-scritch* sound that made.

In my mind's eye, he was there with me, calling me angel and whispering lovely, filthy things to me. My fingers moved inside me, my hips rocking against the stimulation. I moaned in the silent house, lost to the fantasy and to the man who I'd never touch again, and came hard.

Slowly, my breath returned to me, and I blinked out of the haze of the dreamland—my heart still pounding but my body cooling. My living room came back into view. The boxes. The ugly walls. The emptiness. Despair rolled through me.

I pushed myself off the couch and dragged myself into the shower, sitting on the floor of the tub and just letting the hot water pound against me.

Afterward, when I caught a view of myself in the bathroom mirror, I barely even recognized the person staring back at me. I'd changed out of scrubs into pajamas, but other than that, I didn't look much different than when I'd woken up this morning. No makeup. Hair hanging limp around my cheeks. It was the face of a girl who had totally given up on being presentable.

I stared at my reflection, my hands gripping the edge of the counter. Was this what my life was going to be? Sitting around in my half-unpacked, *That '70s Show* house, fantasizing about some guy who I hadn't talked to in over a month? I'd become a goddamn cliché. All those times I'd rolled my eyes at movie heroines who ended up on their couch with a pint of Ben & Jerry's, watching Lifetime network, and now here I was. The only thing different was that I'd chosen Hungry-Man potpie instead of Ben & Jerry tonight. Pathetic.

I flicked the light off, getting rid of that girl in the mirror, and strode into my bedroom, grabbing my phone off the charger. Enough of this shit. I scrolled through the numbers, looking for the one I needed, then hit Call.

"Cela?"

He was clearly surprised to be hearing from me. But before I lost my nerve, I let the question fall from my lips. "What are you doing tomorrow night?"

"Why do I have the feeling you're going to tell me?"

"I'm saying yes, Michael."

I could hear his smile over the phone. "That's the best news I've heard all night. Pick you up at seven."

"I'll be ready."

And hopefully, I would be.

THIRTY-FOUR

Sixty-seven, sixty-eight . . .

Foster counted in his head as he lowered back down to the floor for another push-up. Sweat slid down his neck and bare back as he repeated the motion again and again. The numbers ticked off in his head as he breathed through the count. A flash of Cela tied up in the garden came to him. Fuck.

Seventy-three.

That night she had counted aloud for him, her tawny skin glistening with the exertion of receiving the stings of his crop. But she'd been counting down. Not up. Not like he was doing. This had nothing to do with that day. His cock stirred. Fuck. Fuck. Fuck.

Eighty.

He lifted one foot off the ground, trying to increase the difficulty of the push-ups and block out any thoughts of her. Music blared in the background, his new neighbor probably hating him already for all the noise.

Eighty-one.

She'd wanted to come so bad that night, she'd fallen to her knees and would've begged him for it, would've given him those doe eyes and pleaded. He'd wanted to break his plans that night. He'd wanted to spread her right out in that bed of flowers and fuck her until everyone inside the restaurant heard her scream. He gritted his teeth as his cock went from intrigued to full, throbbing hard-on.

Refusing to relent, he pushed through to hit one hundred. Afterward, he rolled onto his back, his stomach rising and falling with exertion, but the ache in his dick not relenting. He tucked his hands behind his head and with a locked jaw, started a round of sit-ups. He would not fucking give himself the satisfaction of thinking about her and jerking off. If he wanted to get laid, he could damn well go find a willing partner.

But he knew it was an idle notion. He wouldn't do it. He'd gotten in his car to drive to The Ranch more than once since Cela had left, and he hadn't been able to put the key in the ignition. He was in fucking love. Love!

A goddamn disaster considering that the object of those affections was currently hundreds of miles away, happily moving on with her life. She didn't want what he had to offer. And as much as he cared about her, he couldn't give her what she was seeking. If she wanted a traditional, vanilla relationship, he couldn't be that for her. It'd be like asking a gay man to go straight. His dominance was part of him, and neither of them would be happy if he tried to shut that part of himself off.

Six. Seven.

His hair was damp, falling in his eyes as he did more crunches. In his direct line of sight was the bed he'd bought for her. And of course, now every time he looked at it, he saw her there, kneeling on the white covers, knees parted, head tilted back as she touched herself for him.

Son. Of. A. Bitch.

He rolled up off the floor and stalked into his bathroom, turning on the shower. He grabbed an empty cup and filled it with water from the sink, gulping it down as he caught sight of himself in the mirror. He looked like a crazed version of himself. His face and chest were shiny with sweat, his cheeks flushed, and his dick hard.

He tugged off his shorts and stepped into the shower. The water hadn't fully warmed yet and it hit his skin with a shock. But even the chill wasn't going to vanquish the driving need demanding his attention. His erection was still hard as steel. Fuck it. He grabbed the soap from the holder on the wall and slicked his hand. Might as well get over the inevitable. He was past the point of being able to will the thoughts away. He braced an arm against the shower wall and pressed his forehead against it. His other hand grasped his cock with a rough, almost angry grip. He'd never had the chance to take Cela in the shower, and he let his mind go there now—water dripping over her curves, that dark hair curling and clinging to her shoulders, the swells of her ass tucked against him as he slid into her from behind.

His fist moved along his cock, imagining her heat and the sweet sounds she made when they made love. Yes, love. He'd tried to convince himself it had been something else, but from the very beginning, it'd been different with her. Sweeter. More intense. More important.

He angled away from the water, letting it only hit his back and tightened his grip as he fisted his shaft. The pad of his thumb moved over the head, swiping at the pre-come glistening there. If she were here, he'd bring his thumb to her mouth and watch her suck his taste from his skin. She was such a vixen when she let go, let her inhibitions fall away. He'd hoped she'd be the one, the girl he could cherish and pamper but who would also crave playing on the edge with him, the one who would give herself into his keeping and care.

He could imagine her giving him hell with that smart mouth, then dropping to her knees and bringing him to his. That soft, yielding look in her eyes, that giving, plush mouth.

With that image, every muscle in his body seemed to tighten and pleasure raced down his spine. *God, Cela.* Hot streams of his release splashed against the tile and coated his fist as he pumped into his hand, riding the last wave of orgasm.

After a few more ragged breaths, he rinsed, turning the water to searing hot, then toweled off. Too exhausted to even bother digging through the basket of clean laundry for boxers, he headed to bed and got in naked. As he reached to turn off his lamp, he noticed the light on his phone indicating new emails. "Fuck 'em, they can wait 'til morning."

But after he clicked off the light and tried to close his eyes, he couldn't help himself. What was it about new email that was so hard to ignore? It couldn't be anything good. Just more work. But he found himself reaching for the damned phone anyway. He unlocked the screen, noticing the new email was to his personal account, not his work one. Odd. He rarely used that account.

He opened up the screen, frowning at the subject line. *Your Home*

Safe purchase has been activated. What in the hell? It was the standard auto-send email customers received when they activated one of their products. Why the hell would he be getting that in his personal . . .

He sat up.

Quickly, he tapped to open the full email and scrolled down. *Your Home Safe anklet was activated at 9:34pm CST in Verde Pass, TX.*

He stared down at the screen, something like hope growing in his chest, snaking through him like a vine. Cela had kept his bracelet. And the only way to activate was to open it and close it. Had she put it on?

Weeks had passed since she'd left. He'd texted her that first night under the guise of being Pike, and she'd made it rather clear that she was staying and moving on. What would make her pull out his gift now? Unless . . .

Unless she was thinking about him.

He flipped the covers off and got out of bed, heading straight toward the living room. Pike was laid out on the couch playing some video game while Monty dozed at his feet. He looked over when Foster strode in.

"Dude, what the fuck?" He put his hand out as if to shield himself. "You're going to traumatize Monty."

Foster glanced down, realizing he'd walked out naked. But at the moment, he could give a shit. "I need your help."

Pike smirked. "Man, I'm flattered, and I know you're hard up, but I'm really not into you that way."

Foster wished he had something to throw at him. He grabbed a blanket from the back of the couch and tied it around his hips. "Would you shut the fuck up and listen?"

"All ears."

"I need your car for a few days."

He paused his game. "Do what?"

"I can't sit around anymore. I need to know if she's happy. I need to know if there's still a chance."

Pike's questioning look morphed into a sly, victorious smile. "'Bout damn time. But what exactly would you need my car for?"

He shrugged. "I'm not going to bust into her life and shake things up if she really is doing well and is happy there. I don't want to cause her more hurt. So I'm going to do a little recon first and I need her not to recognize my car. I'd get a rental, but I want to leave first thing in the morning."

Pike sat up at that. "Hold up. You're going to *spy* on her? You really are the crazy, stalker ex-boyfriend."

"Maybe I am."

He grinned. "For the record, I kind of like this crazed, in-love version of you. Way more fun. Just don't fuck things up this time."

"Well, that's not the plan."

"How are you going to find her? I mean, small town or not, it's still a whole town."

Foster walked over to the coffee table and swiped Pike's keys. "You don't want to know."

"Ah, hell."

Foster headed back toward his bedroom, but not before he heard Pike mutter, "Yeah, he's going to fuck it up."

―――――――

I sat at the small, scarred table sipping my drink and enjoying the band who was playing at the Rusty Wheel tonight. I'd never been a huge fan of country music, but the acoustic set had a certain charm. And Michael seemed to be thoroughly enjoying it, singing along to the music and sending me a smile every now and again from beneath the brim of the cowboy hat he'd worn tonight. He had a nice voice. I'd never noticed that about him. It was probably very soothing to his patients when he was yanking teeth out and such.

This was the third time I'd been out with him this week, and each time it'd gotten more and more comfortable. He didn't make my stomach flip over when he looked at me, but he was fun. And it sure was better than being mopey girl in my house. When antidepressant commercials start to look upbeat, it's time to get out.

Michael leaned over, draping his arm over the back of my chair, and spoke against my ear. "Dance with me?"

"I'm not very good at the two-step," I said, cocking my head toward the other couples out on the floor.

"Just follow my lead. You can do that, right?" he asked with a good-natured wink.

I smirked. Oh, if he only knew. "Sure."

I let him take my hand and lead me onto the dance floor. With a smile of encouragement, he pulled me close, his hand at my back, and guided me into the flow, counting the steps for me. "Quick, quick, slow."

He was a confident dancer and easy to follow, so I kept up pretty well. We moved around the floor, keeping the circle pattern that everyone seemed to be following, and I found myself enjoying it. Quick, quick, slow. Quick, quick, slow. Apparently he thought I was catching on quicker than I actually was though, because he moved to try to spin me. Not expecting the changeup, I missed the cue and turned the wrong way, almost twisting his arm out of its socket in the process. He let go of my hand and my momentum carried me into the next couple.

Michael barely rescued me before I took us all down. I grabbed for his arm, half-panicked, half laughing. He dragged me against him, laughing as well, eyes sparkling. "Whoa, there."

"Sorry," I said, hands still curled into his biceps as he moved me out of the flow of dancers and off to the side. "Awkward girl plus beer. Bad combination."

"No need to apologize. I like awkward. And sloshed is just a bonus."

I snorted. But he pushed my hair behind my ear, looking down at me with a smile that went from humor to something else. And I knew that look. I didn't have a ton of experience, but no one could mistake what his intention was or what was about to happen. I opened my mouth to say something, but it was already past the point of no return.

Michael leaned in and pressed his lips to mine, cradling my head in his hands, and kissing me with a tender reverence I didn't deserve. I was frozen for a moment, unsure what to do or how to react. But my mouth moved on its own accord, answering the kiss, even as my mind was spinning in every direction. He tasted like beer and peanuts and faintly of mouthwash. And none of what he was doing was bad, but it was all . . . wrong.

My hands slid up to his chest and pushed gently. Instantly, he eased back from the kiss, respecting my subtle signal. He gave me a sheepish smile. "Sorry, probably too soon, right? I lost myself there for a moment."

"It's okay," I said, looking down, a sadness eating away at my insides. "I'm just . . . not quite ready for that yet."

Or maybe ever. Not if it felt like that. Maybe I hadn't been overreacting when I thought I'd never experience anything like Foster again. I craved the fire that happened every time we'd touched, that must-have-more passion. Maybe it could grow with Michael. Maybe I needed to give it time, give us both a chance.

"Hey, there's no rush or pressure from me, all right?" he said, taking my hand again. "I'm not on some predetermined timeline."

"Thank you." He led me back to our table and ordered another round of drinks, but my heart wasn't in the music anymore. Or the date. After a few minutes, Michael seemed to be just as content as before— not perturbed or offended by my brush-off. He really was a good guy. I glanced at my cell phone to check the time and made a show of yawning.

"Getting tired on me?" he asked, bumping my knee with his.

"Yeah, I had a surgery first thing this morning and another tomorrow. Mind if I call it a night?"

"Nah, not at all," he said, moving to get up.

I put my hand on his arm. "You're fine. Stay. I know you have tomorrow off and that you love this band. My car is right out front."

"You sure?" He frowned. "Are you okay to drive?"

"Yeah, I'm not that much of a lightweight." I offered a smile and gave him a quick hug, thanking him for the night.

Outside, the summer air was muggy and warm, heavy with an oncoming rainstorm. But it was nice to get out of the smoky honky-tonk. The parking lot lights were blinking on and off with a loud buzz, giving the lot a strobe effect, but the moonlight was enough to help me find my car.

I put my hand into my purse to grab my keys and heard the shift of gravel somewhere behind me. I turned my head, on full alert. Verde Pass wasn't exactly the crime capital of the world, but I wasn't stupid enough to think bad things didn't happen here. I didn't see anything behind me, and I turned back around, rubbing the sudden chill off my arms. I had the sense that I wasn't alone, that I was being watched. But a second later, the front door of the Rusty Wheel swung open, and a loud, rowdy group spilled out, instantly lifting that strange feeling I'd gotten. Quickly, I hit the fob to open my car and climbed inside, thinking in the back of my mind how Foster would've never let me walk out into a parking lot like this alone.

He wouldn't have let me dismiss him so easily like I had Michael. It wasn't fair for me to hold that against Mike. I had wanted him to stay behind, but still, the thought niggled at me like a rock in my shoe. I didn't need to be taken care of. I was completely capable of managing things myself. But I couldn't deny that part of me missed being . . . handled.

Foster had made me feel like I was something precious, something to be guarded.

Part of the time that had driven me mad.

But right now, as I drove home in the dark, still wearing that stupid ankle bracelet because I couldn't bring myself to take it off, I felt . . . adrift.

THIRTY-FIVE

Foster sat in Pike's car in the dark, not sure what he was more ready to do, punch something or throw up. He'd snuck into the damned cowboy joint, knowing he shouldn't watch, but unable to stop the perverse need to see for himself. He'd tracked down Cela two days ago with the anklet and had been watching her, waiting for the right time to approach her.

He'd never planned to stay in the background this long. But he also hadn't planned to find Cela dating someone. He should've assumed it was a possibility. It's not like they had talked since he'd won the Asshat of the Year award in his office that day. But part of him had hoped that maybe she was having as hard a time moving on as he was. Dating hadn't even been a possibility for him since she'd left. But here she was out on another date with Mr. Teeth. Who the fuck smiled that much? The guy seemed to have permanent hooks holding his mouth up. No doubt because he figured he was getting closer and closer to working his way into Cela's life . . . and bed.

Foster rubbed the back of his neck, tension gathering there at the thought of someone else touching Cela. He'd almost convinced himself that Cela was just friends with the guy . . . until tonight. Watching that fucker put his hands on her and kiss *his* woman had inspired murderous thoughts in Foster and had almost launched him into an unprovoked barroom brawl. But he'd held himself back, not wanting to embarrass Cela or cause trouble for her. She wasn't doing anything wrong. She was simply moving on.

Without him.

And really, if it was that easy for her to go on with someone new, maybe everything Foster had read into their relationship had been bullshit anyway. He'd *wanted* it to be her. He'd wanted Cela to be that girl for him. But maybe he'd laid all that expectation on her and then only saw what he wanted to see. He'd done it before with Darcy. And even with his parents early on. When it came to relationships, he saw what he hoped for instead of what really was. And if Cela could be happy with some vanilla dentist who didn't even bother to walk her out to her car, then he couldn't do a damned thing about it.

The kind of relationship he wanted with her wasn't the type you persuaded someone into. You were either wired for it or not. And if she could walk away from it and not look back, that said everything he needed to know.

Of course, that hadn't stopped him from following her home to make sure she got in okay. God, he was pathetic. He could now add creepy stalker to his list of attributes. What the fuck was wrong with him?

She was on the phone when she turned her car into her driveway, but waited until she ended the call before getting out. When she climbed out, she had her keys in her hand and peeked over her shoulder, quickly checking the perimeter. That brought a touch of a smile to his lips. Good girl. If nothing else, he could take comfort in knowing that she was being more aware now, looking out for herself.

Foster watched from his spot across the street a couple of houses down, drinking up the last view of her as she headed up the steps in her painted-on jeans and cowboy boots. Her hair hung loose along her back, and he remembered what it had felt like to wrap around his fingers. A pang went through his chest as she unlocked her door and slipped inside.

It'd be the last time he'd lay eyes on her.

Because as much as he wanted to bust her door right down and beg for another chance, he wasn't going to disrupt her life like that again. She seemed to be doing fine without him. He took a long breath, daggers of regret knifing through him, then shifted forward to turn the key in the ignition. But a loud rap on the window had him jumping in his seat.

He turned to the left to find himself face-to-face with the barrel of a shotgun, the butt of it against the glass. "Fuck."

He ducked down on instinct, his mind whirling.

"Get out the car," a low, exceptionally calm voice said through the window.

"Motherfucker," he muttered, grasping for any possible escape route. If he were in his car, he'd have a gun in the glove box. But Pike wouldn't have anything—the guy had hated firearms since the days his dad used to wave one around for effect while he was shit-faced. Left without much choice, Foster put his hands up to indicate he was cooperating, then reached for the door handle.

Whoever was on the other side backed up to make room but kept the gun steady and pointed right at him. Foster pushed the door open and climbed out slowly, hands up, hoping it was just a carjacking. Pike would be so pissed, but Foster could replace his car. He silently thanked God that Cela had already gone inside or this could be her with the gun pointed at her head.

The man on the other side of the shotgun was older and shorter than him and seemed to be wearing . . . *pajamas*? But the dude had a determined look in his dark eyes, so Foster wasn't going to attempt to overtake him unless he had to.

"Is there a problem?" Foster asked carefully, beginning to wonder if this was just some neighbor protecting his property line or something. Maybe he'd parked his car too high on the curb and hit a flower bed. Texans could be touchy about that shit.

"Yes, there is," he said, accent thick and tone terse. "Mind telling me why you're lurking in the dark watching my daughter? And don't try anything stupid. I've already called the police."

Oh, shit. Pieces fell together in a quick jumble. *The dad.* Foster closed his eyes for a moment. Okay, so not a carjacker or criminal. At least he wouldn't get shot tonight. Well, probably not. "I'm so very sorry, Dr. Medina. I'm no threat. I'm a friend of Cela's."

His eyes narrowed. "A friend who sneaks around in the middle of the night spying on her like some cockroach?"

Rapid-fire muttering in Spanish punctuated the statement. Foster wasn't one hundred percent fluent, but he picked up a few choice names including pervert and bastard.

Damn, how was he going to explain this? The truth wasn't exactly good news. "My name is Ian Foster. I'm a friend of Cela's from Dallas. A neighbor."

He tilted the gun and gave Foster the hairy eyeball.

"And an ex-boyfriend," he said finally, realizing the man wasn't going to take any bullshit answer.

More Spanish and a look of utter distaste from Cela's father. "Shut up and stay where you are."

Sirens cut through the night, and Foster tilted his head back. Fan-fucking-tastic. So much for being covert. For the first time he wished *he* had a safe word—anything that would get him out of this mess.

A few minutes later, he found himself face-to-face with a cop who was not in the mood for niceties. Cela's father had stepped aside and put the gun down, but he clearly was going to stick around for the show. Foster glanced over at Cela's house, wondering how long it'd be before she saw the flashing lights and peeked out her window. Nothing like a heaping dose of humiliation served up hot. And he'd suffer it in front of her family no less. Terrific.

"Mr. Foster, do you mind explaining to me why this car is registered to someone else?" the cop asked, gripping the car's registration in his hand and holding it up for Foster to see.

"Pike's my roommate. He let me borrow the car."

"Borrow?" the cop frowned like he wasn't familiar with such a progressive idea. "Turn around, Mr. Foster."

"For what?"

The cop pulled out his handcuffs and gave Foster the don't-mess-with-me face. Fucking hell. Foster turned around, handcuffs going over his wrists. Click, click. "I'm just going to put these on until we get this sorted out."

That's when the door opened across the street. Cela peered out, the red and blue lights flashing over the shorts and T-shirt she'd changed into. Her head turned toward her father, who was leaning against a tree with arms crossed and a fierce expression. He noticed his daughter and waved a dismissing hand. "Go inside, Marcela."

"What's going on?" she called out.

"I said go inside," he barked back.

Foster's eyebrow lifted. He had an idea of how *that* tone would go over. He could almost hear Cela gritting her teeth. As expected, she stalked across her yard and toward her father. Heh.

"What are you smirking about?" the cop snapped.

Foster's gaze slid back to the cop. "Nothing at all, officer."

But he had no doubt the cop heard the heavy sarcasm in Foster's voice. Foster was about done putting up with this crap. There was no avoiding Cela knowing now, so he had no reason to continue playing nice.

"I suggest you wipe that look off your face then," the cop said.

"Well, *I* suggest that you take me out of these handcuffs. You haven't placed me under arrest. I haven't threatened you. And I was parked on a public street, not bothering anyone when a gun was pointed at my head. If anything, I'm the victim here. So you can either unlock these or I can make a call to my lawyer."

"*Foster?*"

Cela had made her way across the street and was now staring at him, mouth agape.

He gave her a sheepish smile. "Hi."

She blinked, like she hadn't understood his greeting, then seemed to snap back into place. Her gaze slid to the handcuffs then back to him and the cop. "What the hell is going on?"

"Your father found this man watching your house," the cop explained in that I'll-take-care-of-this-little-lady tone. "But don't worry, we have it under control. Your father kept him contained until I got here."

She glanced at her father, then to the shotgun lying next to the tree, and her eyes widened with horror. "Oh, please tell me you didn't."

Her father pointed Foster's way and went into a heated explanation in Spanish. Cela snapped back at him with just as fiery of a response.

"Hey, it's okay," Foster said, not wanting to cause problems for her with her family. "It was my fault. I came down here to see you, then decided not to bother you. I'm sure it looked suspicious."

She swiveled her attention his way. "I'll deal with you in a second.

And I don't care what you looked like, he doesn't get to threaten people with a gun." She looked back to her father. "What if he had been a real criminal, Papá? He could've hurt *you*."

"I can handle myself," her father said petulantly.

"And so can I!" She looked to the heavens. "When are any of you going to get that through your heads? What were you doing? Waiting for me to get home tonight?"

Her father's gaze flicked away.

"Oh my God, seriously? I'm twenty-three-years old. What would have happened if I'd brought my date home? Would you have banged on the door and pointed a gun at him, too?"

Foster's jaw clenched at even the mention of her date going home with her.

Her father didn't answer, which was answer enough. She turned her head Foster's way again, cheeks flushed with anger. "For God's sake, get him out of those handcuffs, Will. He's not some criminal."

Will didn't look pleased with the order, but he complied. Foster watched Cela as the cop went to work on the cuffs. She was so beautiful standing there, cheeks pink, eyes wild. As his gaze drifted downward over the clothes she'd put on for bed and her bare legs, he caught sight of a glint of silver in the glare of the streetlight. His anklet. Even after everything, she was wearing his gift. Something turned over inside him. He lifted his gaze to hers, and he knew she was aware of what he'd seen. Heartbreak sat there heavy in her eyes, taking the breath from his chest.

Foster rolled his wrists once they were out of the cuffs and stepped onto the sidewalk but didn't take his eyes off Cela. Behind her, he could see other neighbors drifting out now, gawking. And a lady he assumed to be her mother was standing out on the porch of the house directly across from Cela's. He shook his head. "I'm really sorry about all this."

She crossed her arms over her chest, *why?* all over her face, then sighed. "Come on."

Before he could ask her what she meant, she spun on her heel, walked around to the passenger side of Pike's car, and opened the door.

"Marcela, you can't mean to go somewhere with this man," her father sputtered as he moved forward. "It's past midnight and look how you're dressed."

She glanced down at her T-shirt and boxers and laughed mirthlessly. Foster had a feeling she was thinking, *If you only knew.* "Good night, Papá."

She climbed in the car and slammed the door. Dr. Medina sent Foster a touch-my-daughter-and-die glare his way, but Foster wasn't going to wait around for the man to grab his shotgun again. He snagged the car registration off the top of the hood and pulled open his door. "Sorry for the trouble."

Without waiting for a response, he got into the car and shut the door. He gripped the wheel, still trying to process how he'd gone from saying good-bye to Cela for good to having her in his car. He turned her way. "What now, angel?"

"Just drive," she said, staring out the front window.

"Yes, ma'am."

THIRTY-SIX

I must be hallucinating. That was my first thought as I rode away from my shotgun-wielding father and realized I was now sitting next to Foster—Foster, who lived hours away from here and hadn't spoken to me in over a month. Maybe someone had slipped something into my drink at the bar, and I was now passed out in the parking lot of the Rusty Wheel.

"So, you're here," I said, showing my penchant for brilliant conversation starters. Not that one really knew how to start a conversation when you found your ex-boyfriend being arrested in your front yard.

He gave me a sidelong glance, as if he were half-worried I'd come to my senses and jump out of the moving vehicle. "I am."

"And my father almost shot you," I said, going down the list of things I needed to establish before processing anything else.

"Well, I don't think he would've really shot me. But yes, he threatened me with a gun, which I can respect—he thought I was a danger to you."

I turned to him then, allowing myself to fully drink in his presence there. God, even my imagination hadn't done him justice. He looked tired and his stubble was way past five o'clock, but every muscle fiber in me seemed to strain toward him, wanting to wrap myself around him. But that's not who we were to each other anymore.

I glanced away, staring out at the reflective yellow line at the center of the road. "Are you a danger to me?"

"Cela." He said my name with an ache in it.

"No, I'm serious," I said, pulling my self-preservation armor around me, locking out the part of me that only wanted to remember the good stuff, the part that didn't want to remember how mean he'd been the last time I'd seen him, how much he'd hurt me. "Why are you here? What were you doing on my street at midnight?"

He blew out a long breath and took a turn into an empty Home Depot parking lot, cutting off the engine. He focused on the empty, orange building in front of us. "I was here to see if you were doing okay, to make sure that when you told me you were happy here, that you really were."

I frowned. "When I told you I was happy here? Foster we haven't talked since—"

"It wasn't Pike who texted you."

I stared at his profile, not even sure what to do with that information. "Why would you do that?"

He faced me finally, his blue eyes almost black in the dark interior of the car, but I could see the remorse there. "I needed you to know that nothing happened with Bret. And I had to hear from you that you were okay. You had decided to stay in Dallas for more reasons than to be with me, and I felt responsible for chasing you back here."

I sighed. "You didn't chase me back here—at least, not totally. They gave the job to someone else. I didn't have anything to stay for anymore."

He leaned back in his seat, running a hand over his face. "I fucked everything up. I'm sorry. I told you from the start that you could slow down or back out at any time, and then when you did, I acted like an asshole. You didn't deserve that."

I pulled my legs onto the seat and sat my chin on my knees, feeling cold despite the warm night. "No, I didn't. And when I saw that blonde walk into your building, I wanted to throw up, Foster." I turned my head to face him. "All I wanted was time to think, and you called up another girl before I was even out the door."

He looked my way, expression pained. "I can't even tell you how sorry I am for that. Nothing happened with her. I promise you. Bret is the private investigator I hired to keep digging up leads on my sister's case. We're friends. That's it."

"Friends who've slept together," I said flatly.

He grimaced.

The wordless answer was like a two-by-four swinging right into my gut. I looked away, clenching my jaw to keep stupid tears from appearing.

"But that was in the past, a long time ago. And nothing was ever like . . ."

"Like what, Foster?" I asked, needing him to finish that sentence, needing to know why he was here, tearing open this wound again.

"Are you happy, Cela?" he asked abruptly.

The question caught me off guard. "What?"

"The last thing I want to do is make this worse. And even though it was killing me not to talk to you, I was going to leave you alone, let you move on with your life. But then I got an email telling me you'd activated my anklet, and . . . I just needed to know for sure. Needed to see. Are you happy? Is this where you want to be? Work? Is that dentist who was kissing you tonight the kind of guy you want to be with?"

"The dentist . . ." My jaw went slack. "You *followed* me on my date?"

He rubbed a hand over the back of his neck. "Yes. And I'm not going to make excuses to justify that. It was completely out of line. I know that. I'm acting like a crazy person. But my questions still stand. Are you happy here? Is this what you want?"

"Why do you care?" I asked, still in shock that he'd followed me. That he'd watched me kiss another guy.

He reached out and grasped my chin with gentle fingers, drawing my gaze to his intense one. "I care because if you're happy, if this is what you want, I will drive you right back home and never bother you again. I will let you go."

I blinked, the tears blurring my vision now.

"But if you're not, if there's even part of you that misses me half as much as I miss you, a part that lies awake at night and can't stop thinking about how things were with us, then please God, tell me. Because I'm fucking miserable, Cela."

I closed my eyes, unable to bear the weight of his stare, his words. My airway seemed to narrow to a pinhole. "Foster . . ."

"And I wish I could tell you that I'll change everything. Especially after tonight, I can see how the dominant stuff would scare you off. I know I can be overbearing and high-handed. And I can be fucked up and paranoid about stuff sometimes. It's a lot. And I would fix it if I could, but I don't know how to be any other way."

I couldn't look at him. It was all too much. Having him here, hearing his voice, the sharp edge of sadness in his words.

"All I can tell you is that I never intended to lock you down or take away your independence. Your strength and stubbornness are part of what draws me to you. Even with the whole anklet thing, it was never a desire to keep tabs on you or intrude on your privacy. I just . . . I was falling in love with you, and it inspired every ounce of my protective streak."

My eyes snapped open, my heart jumping right into my throat and the word *love* getting tangled in my synapses.

"I couldn't bear the thought of something bad happening to you, of losing you." He cradled my face in his palms, every line in his expression etched with regret. "And I lost you anyway. Because I'm an idiot. I chased you away before we even got a real chance."

Moisture tracked along my cheeks. I said his name again, unable to put my thoughts in the right order.

"Are you happy, Cela?" he asked again, his own voice knotted with emotion now. "That's all I need to know."

I leaned forward, letting my forehead press to his. Everything felt so heavy all of a sudden—the move, my job, leaving Foster, dating again, trying to figure out what the hell I wanted out of my life. I wanted to curl in a ball and be back in my dorm freshman year when everything was simple and laid out and obvious. All possibility. No reality. "I don't know what I am anymore. I'm lost."

"Oh, angel," he said softly. "I know what you mean."

I pulled back and rested against my seat, the nearness of him too much to take for my wrung-out system. All I wanted to do was crawl into his lap and let him tell me everything was going to be okay. And that was exactly what always freaked me out with Foster. I didn't want to be weak and need someone else like that. "I'm scared of how I feel when I'm with you."

"What do you mean?"

"Did I ever tell you that my mom used to be a painter?"

He shook his head, leaning back in his own seat, giving me space.

"She was. She had a lot of talent and even got a scholarship to a school in New York. But she was already dating my dad, and he had a full ride to UT in Austin. She couldn't get into the university because, though she was a brilliant artist, she sucked at things like math and science and didn't have high enough scores. So she just gave it up for him, got a receptionist job in Austin and dedicated her life to being his wife. And they love each other, I know that. But she isn't her own person anymore. He makes the decisions. She follows them. I know it tore her to pieces when he kicked my sister out, and she didn't stand up to him. She didn't stand up for her own daughter. I love her with all my heart, but I *cannot* become her."

Foster's mouth curved downward. "Baby, I hear what you're saying, but you have to realize that you are so far from being at risk of that happening, it's not even funny. You are tough and independent and hardheaded."

"But when I'm with you, all I want to do is give in," I fired back. "I fall to my knees willingly, I step past lines I never would've considered walking over, and I have this thing, this desire to please you, that scares the living shit out of me. I haven't gone a day without thinking about you, Foster. And tonight, even after I *told* Mike not to walk me out, I found myself annoyed that he didn't. I missed your crazy overprotectiveness. How messed up is that?"

A ghost of a smile touched his lips. "Did you just say you missed my crazy?"

I stared at him for a long second and then laughed some weird, tear-clogged laugh. I put my hands over my face. "Goddammit. I *do* miss it. What the hell is wrong with me?"

"Cela," he said, tugging one of my hands away from my face. "There's nothing wrong with you. All of that stuff doesn't mean you want to turn into some robot wife. You have a submissive side to you—a beautiful, dead-sexy desire to please. But the only time that's dangerous or wrong is if you put it in the hands of someone who is going to exploit it. I would never want to change you or get in the way of your career or dreams. And it's okay to want to be taken care of or protected sometimes. No one should have to take on the world all alone all the time."

I looked at him. How many times had I imagined his face these last few weeks? How many times when I'd curled up at night had I wished he were there next to me? And though I liked Mike, I knew in my gut it was only friendship. When he'd kissed me tonight, there'd been none of that fire that was there when Foster simply brushed his lips over mine. Even just sitting here in the car with him had this hum of electricity moving through me.

But there was so much to think about, so many decisions already made. My job was here, my dad was counting on me. I had a house now. And Foster had said it himself, he was who he was. I either had to embrace his personality and dominance fully and accept what that brought out in me, or it'd never work.

I reached out and took his hand. "I don't know if I'm going to have all the answers for you tonight. All I can offer you is honesty."

"That's all I'm asking, angel," he said, lacing his fingers with mine.

"I've missed you so much, I can barely breathe through it sometimes," I admitted. "When I lie in bed at night, it's you who's on my mind. And I'm wearing this anklet because I wanted to feel close to you again, and I can't seem to take it off."

He closed his eyes, his chest expanding with a deep breath, and brought my hand up to his mouth, brushing his lips over our entwined knuckles.

"And I'm not unhappy, but I'm not happy either. I haven't been happy since that last morning I woke up next to you."

His gaze met mine, naked emotion swirling in those blue depths. "Ditto."

"And there's a lot we need to talk about and consider. But it's late, and it's already been a long night for us both."

He sighed, his expression turning resigned, and let go of my hand. "Right. Plus, I'm sure if I don't take you home in the next ten minutes, your dad will probably send out a search party. Last thing I want is to cause you more trouble with him."

Foster lifted his arm to turn the key, but I put my hand over his, stopping him. "I don't want to talk anymore tonight. But I don't want to go home either."

He turned his head, brows knitted. "What?"

I wet my lips, the yearning that'd been building over all these weeks filling every pore of my body. I knew it probably wasn't fair to ask, but I was done overanalyzing things tonight. Even if I didn't know what the future would look like, right now I needed this. Him. "I don't want either of us to face the world alone tonight, Foster. Let me stay with you."

Awareness flickered over his features, like streetlamps blinking on, and I saw my own yearning reflected back in him. He gave a quiet assent and turned the ignition.

Tonight, we wouldn't be alone.

THIRTY-SEVEN

We didn't speak on the drive to his hotel or on the way to his room. We simply held hands, our fingers twined tightly together. And during the climb in the elevator, he watched me, much like he had that first night riding up to that hotel room. But this time I wasn't trying to hide anything from him. This was me, stripped down to the studs, no walls to protect me.

When the door shut behind us in his room, he flipped the lock and turned to me. Everything was there on his face. He pushed my hair behind my ears, looking at me like he was afraid I wasn't real, like I'd disintegrate and sift between his fingers like sand. His thumb traced my bottom lip. I shuddered beneath the simple touch, my heartbeat loud in my ears.

Then his fingers were tangling in my hair as he bent my head back and brought his mouth down to mine. His lips were tender at first, gentle—like an innocent first kiss. But when I parted mine and touched my tongue to his, the wall of the dam broke. He banded an arm around my waist and dragged me against him, his tongue twining with mine and his fingers tightening against my scalp. The roughness of it sent sparks racing along my nerve endings, electrifying every point of contact between us. I moaned into the kiss and wrapped my arms around his neck.

God. This. In the loneliness of the last few weeks, I had tried to talk myself out of how good things had felt with Foster, had tried to convince myself that I'd exaggerated it, that my memories were embellished. But having his body pressed against mine, the command of his kiss liquefying every ounce of me, I realized that, if anything, even my most vivid recollections paled to the reality.

He broke away from the kiss, both of us breathless, and put his hands on my shoulders, his gaze flaring with heat. "If you want me to stop, now's the time to tell me. Because if I keep kissing you, I'm taking you to that bed and not letting you out of it until tomorrow."

I curled my fingers into the waistband of his jeans, pulling us together again. "I want this. I want *you*. And I don't need some vanilla, PC version. No matter what happens, I would never ask you to change."

His lips pressed together as he watched me, and something seemed to lift from his expression. Soon, that wicked smile of intent that I loved so much graced his mouth. He slid his hands down my sides, found the hem of my T-shirt and tugged it over my head, then made quick work of my bra. His hands cupped my breasts and teased, cajoling soft, needy sounds from me. "I haven't been able to think about anything, angel, except you since you left. I've tried everything to distract myself, but no matter what, when I close my eyes, there you are."

He backed me toward the bed, but I put a hand to his chest. "Tried everything to distract yourself or every*one*?"

He growled and lifted me off my feet. "Angel, I haven't even been able to look at another woman. You think I would fuck someone else, then come looking for you?"

"Well, I don't know—" He tossed me onto the bed and I bounced with an *oof*.

"You should have more faith in me." He sat on the edge of the bed and dragged me onto his lap to straddle him. "The only thing that has seen any action is my fist because I couldn't stop thinking about you, picturing you like this."

His mouth closed over one of my nipples and pleasure arced through me. I braced my hands on his shoulders and let my head fall back as I imagined him taking himself in his hand, sliding those long fingers over his cock. Damp heat pressed against my cotton panties as he moved to the other breast.

"I'm sorry," I whispered.

He lifted his head, drawing my attention back to him. "What about you? I won't hold it against you if you did. I'm the one who pushed you away."

I frowned. "Wouldn't hold what against me?"

"If you slept with the dentist," he said, his tone belying how totally un-okay with it he'd really be about that.

I blanched. "God, Foster, no. Tonight was the first time we even kissed."

He closed his eyes briefly in a thank-God way, then lifted his lids, his gaze intent. "I wanted to beat the shit out of that guy for even daring to touch you. Took everything I had not to interrupt."

"He's a good guy." I leaned down and kissed his brow. "But he does nothing for me. You"—I grabbed his wrist and brought his hand downward, slipping his warm fingers inside my shorts and panties—"do this to me just by looking my way."

He groaned as his fingers parted my folds and found wet heat. "I love how fucking bold you're becoming. So sexy and confident."

"You make me brave." I rocked against his hand, the stimulation like sweet fire licking up my body.

He slipped his fingers from my panties and swiped them over my lips, spreading my own taste there, then took my mouth in another heated kiss. I threaded my fingers in his hair and scooted forward, dragging myself along his erection. Everything inside me was already coiling tight. It'd been so long since I'd touched him. I felt starved— each breath, each touch providing the sweet sustenance I'd been craving.

He pulled back from the kiss, his eyes almost black in the soft lamp-light of the hotel room. "God, I've missed you."

I brought my hands to his jaw, feeling the stubble beneath my fingertips. "Every night I'd crawl into bed to try to sleep, but then I'd remember this, you, and my body would go so hot."

His grip tightened on my thighs. "Did you touch that pretty cunt of yours?"

"Even when I promised myself I wouldn't," I admitted, the old flush of embarrassment still rising to the surface at the confession and his crude words.

"Mmm," he said, the sound rumbling through his chest. "And what did you imagine I was doing to you, my angel?"

I bit my lip but refused to let my bred-in shyness rear its head again. "I imagined rough things, your dominance, you tying me up. My skin would actually tingle when I'd imagine your hand or your flogger coming down on me."

The look that crossed his face was almost one of anguish. "Christ, Cela, you're killing me."

The open honesty on Cela's face was enough to wring the air from his lungs. All the times they were together, Foster had always wondered if maybe she'd only been going along with things to please him, to be experimental. But to hear that not only had she missed him, but had also fantasized about his binding her and bringing her pain, made his heart want to grow wings and zoom right out of his chest.

He knew he had to be cautious. She said she didn't have answers tonight. There was still a very real possibility that she could walk away from him. But if he'd had any doubts whether or not she was truly wired for being submissive, he didn't now. She craved what he could give her. And God knows, he ached for her.

He pushed her dark hair away from her face. "Turn around and lie across my lap, angel. I don't need you imagining anymore."

Her eyes went half-mast and she eased off his lap, turning to lay herself prone across his knees. Her muscles were already starting to loosen, her mind sinking into the moment. When he had her in position, he tugged down her shorts and panties, leaving them at her knees. Fuck, she was beautiful—full breasts pressed against his thigh, hair hanging down to brush the floor, and the feminine curve of her back and ass there like a feast for him.

He rubbed a hand along the globe of one cheek, enjoying the silky-smooth skin, then he raised his hand and gave it a swift smack. She reared up, her breath catching, and his cock pressed against the fly of his jeans. The bright pink, five-fingered image appeared on that golden skin. He'd never be able to describe to her what that did to him, to see his mark on her, to know that she craved both his softness and his sting, but it was almost religious for him. He brought his hand down again on the other side and inhaled her reaction—the soft cry, the scent of her arousal drifting upward, the surrender in her stance.

"Give me a color, Cela," he said, rubbing his palm along the place he'd hit.

"Green," she whispered, squirming a bit beneath his hold. "So very green."

He smiled. How far she'd come. From being embarrassed about the smallest desire to begging to be spanked. He couldn't ever remember seeing something as sexy as this woman taking ownership of her desires. He spanked her with a little more oomph this time and she quivered against him.

Confident that she was totally with him now, he worked her over, darkening her ass and the backs of her thighs with a pattern of red marks. Her skin began to glisten with sweat, and her moans turned into breathy, desperate whimpers. He drew his hand down and between her legs, finding her soaked and hot with arousal. "You need to come, angel?"

"Yes, please, sir," she said, pushing up on her toes to grind against his fingers.

He lifted her up and rolled her onto her back on the bed. She looked up at him with glazed eyes, her cheeks flushed. He knelt on the floor and tugged her panties and shorts fully off. "You have my permission."

He undid his belt buckle and the fly of his pants, his erection demanding to be freed from its denim prison, and he draped Cela's legs over his shoulders. The soft, pink folds of her pussy spread before him, swollen and glistening with her arousal, and he had to hold back the groan. He fisted his cock at the base, trying to tame the need building in him. He wanted to take his time and savor this, savor her.

He dipped forward and laid kisses along her inner thighs, giving her a quick little pop on the hip when she wouldn't be still. She huffed her frustration, making him smile, but she made a decidedly different noise when he ran his tongue along her center. Her fingers curled into the comforter, and her hips rocked forward. He closed his eyes, relishing her tart taste and the sweet scent of her desire. He loved how shameless she was, arching against his tongue and making all those soft, throaty noises.

He eased two fingers inside her, the heat of her making his cock throb, and ran the tip of his tongue around her clit before sucking it between his lips. She groaned, and he pumped his fingers inside her, working her with his mouth until he could feel her pussy tightening. He curled his fingers inside her, finding the spot he knew she needed, and a sharp cry broke through the room. She writhed against the bed, and he held her to his mouth with his free arm, helping her ride the intensity when her body's instinct was to pull away.

Her strangled cries were like sweet music seeping into his bloodstream, making his body throb in time with her sounds. When he could tell she couldn't take anymore, he backed off, rubbing his cheek against her thigh and talking to her in soft tones. "Beautiful, angel."

She reached for him, dragging her nails along his scalp and sending hot shivers through him. "I need you, Foster. Please."

"Greedy little girl, aren't you?" he teased, as he pushed himself off the floor, shucking off his clothes and lowering onto the bed.

Her eyelids fluttered open and she gave him a slow smile. "If I wasn't high on afterglow, I would totally be offended at that."

He grinned as he crawled over her, bracing himself above her. "Then I'll just keep you in a constant state of arousal so I can say any filthy, offensive thing that comes to mind."

She ran her hands along his chest, openly exploring every dip and valley. "That won't be hard. You seem to have that effect on me."

He loved how she touched him so hungrily, like each part of him was a revelation. "Feeling's mutual, gorgeous."

He leaned down to kiss her as he positioned himself at her entrance, no longer in the mood to be patient. The moment he sank into her, all felt right with the world again. His woman wrapped around him, her taste on his lips, and her heartbeat pounding against his chest in time with his.

No. Not *his* woman, he corrected. Not yet. But he was going to try his damnedest to make it so.

Unable to resist, he grabbed her wrists and pinned both of them above her head as he rocked into her. She surrendered willingly, her eyes catching his and holding the gaze as he slid deep. And in that moment, he didn't need her words to know. He affected her as much as she did him. There was something there that he'd never experienced before with anyone else. Even when he thought he'd been in love with Darcy, he hadn't felt that rip-through-your-chest-and-tug-out-your-soul feeling like he did when he looked at Cela.

Cela shifted below him, her eyes blinking closed and a flush creeping over her neck. She was so close again already. The passion in her was right there at the surface, bursting through with almost no coaxing. He could spend forever discovering all the ways to bring her right to the edge of her pleasure and then tormenting her until she came apart beneath him. He reached down with his free hand and grabbed her hip, tilting her upward and moving inside her at the angle he wanted.

Sweat glazed both their bodies as he relentlessly pumped into her, knowing that his girl responded better to a nice, hard fucking as opposed to slow, sweet lovemaking—the virgin had grown into the vixen. And he couldn't get enough of her and how ravenous she was for him. It made him feel powerful and wanted. Like a man. Like *her* man.

"God, Foster, yes," she murmured, talking out of her head now, so close to breaking apart.

He increased his pace, the sound of skin slapping skin mixing in with her throaty whimpers, and all his muscles began to tighten. Her crossed wrists thrashed restlessly beneath his tight hold as she raced up the hill again.

"Come for me, angel," he said, his breath sawing out of him now.

Her head tilted back into the pillows, exposing the long length of her throat, and a low, glorious cry filled the room. He sank forward, going straight for the spot where neck met shoulder, the creamy skin beckoning him, and bit down. Her moan turned guttural, and he released her wrists. Her hands clamped on to his back instantly, her nails digging into his skin, and the nip of pain sent his own orgasm thundering down his spine. Pleasure exploded through him, and he groaned as everything went white behind his eyes, filling her with his release.

Later. Seconds? Minutes? He didn't know or care, they both got out of bed and took a long bath together in the hotel's Jacuzzi tub. Neither of them seemed in the mood to talk, both content to bask in the quiet of each other's embrace. He knew she had a lot on her mind. So did he. And he wasn't going to push her for anything more tonight. He'd already gotten way more than he had ever anticipated. The look she'd given him when they'd joined together could keep him surviving on hope for a while longer.

But when they both climbed under the covers, and he wrapped his arms around her, he couldn't help but say what had been sitting there on his chest all night. He pressed a kiss to her bare shoulder. "I'm in love with you, Cela."

The stiffening of her muscles was slight, but he didn't miss it.

And that worried him more than anything had all night.

Even more than the fact that she didn't say anything back.

PART VIII

Not Until You Love

THIRTY-EIGHT

I woke up groggy and disoriented, a loud sound filling my ears and the bed jostling. I rolled over to find Foster groping around the hotel room in the dark and cursing.

"Who the fuck would call this early? And where the hell is my phone?"

I wrapped the covers around me, the chill of the room raising goose bumps on my skin, and climbed out of bed, dragging the sheet with me. "I think it's over here on the desk."

I grabbed it for him, but it'd stopped ringing by that time.

"Dammit," he said from the other side of the room.

I peeked over at the clock. A little past five. Calls this early were never good. For me it usually meant a panicked family and an injured pet, but I had a feeling someone calling Foster this early would be even more ominous.

"Does it say who it was?" he asked, fumbling around for the lamp.

I flipped over the phone and hit the button to illuminate the screen. Ugh. Bile burned the back of my throat. I tossed the phone on the bed. "Yeah. It's Bret."

"Bret?" he said, the lamp flicking on, lighting his stricken face. "Shit."

I pulled the sheet tighter around me, my chill no longer related to the overactive air conditioner. "I'm going to go shower, so if you need to call her back, you'll have some privacy."

If he caught the biting edge to my tone, he didn't acknowledge it. Instead, he was already moving toward the phone, probably not even hearing me.

"Right," I said under my breath. Guess when *she* called, the whole world needed to stop. I turned on my heel and headed to the bathroom before the ugly jealousy could cause me to say something I'd regret.

As I stood under the stream of hot water in the shower, I tried to pull myself back together and *not* picture Foster in bed with that blond knockout. He'd said Bret was a colleague and a friend now, not a lover. If she was calling, it probably wasn't for a booty call. My logical brain knew that, but my completely irrational heart wasn't hearing any of it.

He'd told me last night that he *loved* me. I still couldn't fully digest that turn of events. My cognitive functioning had frozen when he'd said the words. In a lot of ways, it'd been everything I'd wanted to hear. Being with him last night, feeling his touch, had only solidified how strongly I felt for him. And maybe I had fallen in love with him, too. But I had no idea if that was enough. I had moved my life here. And a relationship with Foster meant a certain kind of lifestyle that my brain and body were at war over.

I couldn't—wouldn't—say the words to him if I wasn't going to be able to back them up with a commitment. I didn't want to be another hurt in his life.

By the time I stepped out of the bathroom, Foster was fully dressed and tossing clothes into his suitcase. Any remnants of my jealous bitch side shut her mouth and concern flooded me. "What's going on?"

He turned to look at me, face drawn. "Bret said she found some information about my sister's case and had to go to the FBI with it. They wouldn't let her give me the details over the phone. I have to get back to town."

I wrapped my arms myself. "Of course. Is there anything I can do to help?"

He walked over to me, taking my face in his hands, and pressed a quick kiss to my lips. "You can forgive me for leaving before we have a chance to talk things out."

"Done," I said without hesitation. We could deal with the complicated tangle of our relationship another day. "She didn't give you any indication of what type of news this was."

He went back to his packing, his movements efficient but his shoulders stiff with tension. "Well, there really is no good news in this. I'm not naive enough to think Neve is just going to reappear one day. But if we could find out what happened, who took her . . . I may be able to provide some closure for my parents. Some peace. They've spent every day since she went missing dedicating their lives to the cause."

"So have you," I said gently.

He peered back over his shoulder at me. "I owed that much to her. If I had done what I was supposed to that day, she may still be around."

"You were a kid, Foster," I said, coming to sit on the edge of the bed. "You weren't old enough to be responsible for someone else."

His jaw twitched. "I just need to be able to tell my parents—we got him or them or whoever was involved. Maybe once there's some justice handed down . . ."

"They'll forgive you?" I asked, my heart heavy for him.

He zipped up his suitcase and stared down at it, his expression grim. "No, angel, they'll never do that. How could they? But maybe they'll at least be able to move on."

The lonely ache in his voice—that of a kid still looking for love from his parents—made my chest hurt. But I knew there was nothing I could say to make him feel better. That wound was one only his mom and dad could heal. I hoped for his sake that they would mend that bridge.

"Will you call me and let me know how things go when you get a chance?"

A brief smile touched his lips and he cupped my cheek. "I won't have to. As soon as I take care of this, I'm coming right back down here so we can really talk."

"Okay," I said returning his smile.

"Just tell me one thing."

I leaned into his touch. "What's that?"

"Tell me I have still have a shot, angel."

I closed my eyes, knowing the truth in my heart even if I couldn't quite face it yet. "You've still got a shot."

He grinned fully now and laid a soft, toe-curling kiss on my mouth. "I love you, Cela."

"You keep saying that," I teased, trying to lighten the impact of the words.

"I keep meaning it." He gave me another quick peck, then grabbed his bag. "Come on, I'll drive you home."

"All right." I went to grab my things but then realized I had no things. I'd basically gone out in my pajamas last night. No phone. No purse. Just my keys. Then the rest of that reality hit. "Shit."

"What's wrong?" he asked, pulling the door open.

"Remember how angry you got when I didn't check the peephole?"

"Yeah," he said cautiously.

"Well, that is going to look like a trip through the daisies compared to how livid my father is going to be when I get home."

He wagged a finger at me. "Ooh, someone's getting grounded."

I swatted his arm and laughed. "Shut up."

He put his arm around my shoulders. "See, at least when I punish you, you get some fun out of it."

"I'll add that into your pro column."

He gave me a squeeze. "Good, I need all the help I can get."

I leaned into him and sighed. Being there with his arm wrapped around me again was like finding my comfortable corner in the universe. Something inside me smoothed out when I was with him. He thought he was the one that needed help. But really, it was me who was in trouble.

Because if I followed my head, I had a feeling I'd never find anyone who made me feel this way again. And I would always wonder what could've been if I walked away from him.

But if I followed my heart, I was going to alienate the people who meant most to me in the world.

Either way, someone's heart was getting broken.

———————

Foster dropped me off with a promise to call me and to be back as soon as he could. I kept the good-bye brief and chaste, knowing that my parents were probably crowded up against the blinds in their house, spying on us.

But when I opened my front door, I realized the truth was even worse. My father was sitting on my living room couch, drinking a cup of coffee and staring out my front window. He'd at least changed out of his pajamas from last night into a pair of jeans and a Rangers T-shirt, but otherwise didn't look like he'd slept or shaved. He didn't look my way.

"Papá, what are you doing here?" I asked, too tired to even get angry that he had a key.

"Are you okay, Marcela?" he asked, still staring out the window. "Did he hurt you?"

I blew out a breath and dropped my keys onto the table by the door. "Of course not. Foster's a friend and a good guy."

"A friend who you take off with wearing next to nothing. A friend who doesn't bring you home until morning." The quiet anger rumbled beneath his words.

"Papá, I was dating Foster in Dallas. We were in a relationship. Maybe still are."

He turned to look at me then, lines of strain around his eyes. In that moment, I felt bad that he carried that stress, that he felt the need to watch over me so closely. I saw the age there, the wear of years gone by while I'd been away. "Is he why you were delayed moving back home?"

I shifted on my feet, my gaze flitting away. "Yes."

"And what are you going to do now, Marcela? Did he come here to try to bring you back?"

I hugged my elbows, folding in on myself, the fear of admitting the truth to my father making a shiver go through me. But what else could I do? I'd lived my whole life trying to land on the right squares of hopscotch so I wouldn't get ejected from the game, wouldn't disappoint my family. But if winning that game meant never taking a risk, never following my heart, then I guess I was finally prepared to lose. "I think I love him, Papá."

A black cloud seemed to eclipse his expression, chilling the temperature in the room. He stood. "Go change clothes. We're going for a ride."

I straightened. "What?"

"If you still have any respect for me, you will do as I ask and come with me."

I clenched my teeth together, wanting to tell him that I was tired and wasn't in the mood to go anywhere, but a lifetime of good behavior was too deeply ingrained. I couldn't disrespect my father. "I'll be down in a few minutes."

———

An hour later we were pulling up to a spot I hadn't been to in years, with a sack full of breakfast tacos and tall cups of coffee. The view through the windshield made nostalgia wash through me, dragging me backward in time. I glanced at my dad, waiting for an explanation. He hadn't said much of anything the entire drive out here.

He nodded at the grease-stained paper bag. "Get our breakfast. Let's see if our spot is still there."

I grabbed the bag and got out of the car, my tennis shoes hitting the packed dirt of the makeshift parking lot. In front of me stretched a line of trees that marked the entrance to the nature park. A Don't Feed the Animals sign sat askew on a wooden post. I could still see myself at eight, carrying my backpack on my shoulder and walking past that sign, ponytail swinging. Back then, my dad had tirelessly fed me information and answered my endless questions while we traipsed along the trail. What kind of bird is that? How do raccoons always manage to break into the Dumpsters? Where do the squirrels hide all those acorns? Why do armadillos look like that?

This had been our no-one-else-allowed place. No Mom, no Luz, and no Andre. Not that any of them would've wanted to come anyway. Neither of my brothers nor my sister had ever shown a real interest in animals or my father's job like I had. And Mom was about as outdoorsy as a houseplant. So this place had been sacred to me back when I thought my father was the best man in the world and time spent with him was a special privilege.

Sadness settled over me as I followed my dad down the path, passing the old sign. The place hadn't changed. The trees had gotten bigger and the underbrush more tangled. But the scent of wildflowers and morning dew still hung in the air. The hum of life buzzed around us, as if the bees and dragonflies were excited that we'd finally returned. It was all so familiar. Comforting. But as I looked ahead at the back of my father, his gray hairs now more prominent than the inky black of all those years ago, his proud gait a little hunched, a sense of loss filled me. Everything has stayed the same except us.

Life had tarnished that dappled sunlit photograph of a doting father and the daughter that worshipped him. The long afternoons of discussing the wonders of nature and the animal world had shifted into butting heads and growing distant. I didn't even know who those two people were anymore.

Papá stopped at the small clearing where two picnic tables had sat for as long as I could remember. He set down our coffees and bent over to check beneath the tables. A smile touched my lips. I didn't have to ask what he was doing. Ever since the day I had a very unfortunate encounter with a pissed-off yellow jacket, my dad had always checked for nests before we sat down.

He stood and patted the top of the table. "All clear, *mija*."

"Thanks." I set the bag down in the center of the table and climbed onto the bench. "You want the brisket or the chorizo?"

"Give me one of each. I haven't had them in a long time. Your mamá has me drinking smoothies in the morning. *Green* ones."

I cocked an eyebrow at him, having a hard time imagining him drinking such a thing. "Do they have bacon in them?"

He laughed. "I wish. She puts kale. Have you ever heard of such a thing?"

"I think I'd rather eat a salad." I unwrapped two tacos for each of us, spreading the paper out on the table.

We ate for a few minutes, the chirping birds providing the soundtrack, and I began to wonder if we were going to share the whole meal in silence. But as soon as my dad polished off the brisket taco, he took a long sip of a coffee, then pinned me with his patented don't-lie-to-me look. "So you think you're in love."

I picked at a piece of egg that had fallen onto the grease-speckled paper. "I think I may be."

"But you were out with the Ruiz boy last night before Romeo showed up?"

I frowned. "His name is Foster. And yes, I was, but Michael and I are only friends. I was out with him . . . trying to forget about Foster."

He balled up the wrapper from his first taco and tossed it in the bag, his thick brows low over his eyes. "I see."

I huffed a breath and peered out toward the trees, not sure what to say to my dad to make him have any sort of understanding.

"You know," he said, following my line of sight, "when we used to come out here, I'd break the rules and feed the animals."

I turned to him. "What? No, you didn't. You were always careful. You told me we couldn't mess with their natural diet."

He shook his head. "I would carry dried corn in my pocket to drop along the way so that you'd get to see the animals." He smiled warmly, and I could tell he was looking back in time, seeing the past like I had a few minutes ago. "Your little face would light up anytime you saw the simplest thing—a squirrel, a robin. The few times we saw a deer, I thought you were going to explode with excitement. I couldn't bear the thought of us making a trip out here and you not getting the chance to see anything."

"Papá," I said, the admission touching me. "I always thought that we were lucky, that the animals happened to like us."

He looked at me then, his dark eyes a little glossy. "We were lucky, *mija*. We had a happy family then. I had kids who were on the way to making good lives for themselves. And I had you, who by some miracle, liked the same things I did and wanted to walk in my footsteps. I didn't want anything to touch that bubble."

I tucked my hands in my lap, food forgotten.

"But I let you all down," he said, staring back out at the forest. "I was cocky to think nothing would change. I thought I'd done my job well and all would be fine. But as you all got older, everything changed so fast. All of a sudden, I didn't know how to connect with you in the same way. I became someone to argue with instead of someone you came to with your problems. And I didn't know how to handle that. I knew what dangers lurked out there in the world, the things that could derail good kids from their path. But even knowing it, I couldn't seem to stop it. Luz had so much going for her, so much talent, and look how she tossed that away. For a boy. For so-called love."

"She made a mistake," I said gently.

"We both did, and it ruined everything," he said, a bitter edge to his voice. "When I kicked her out, my happy family broke apart. Your mother has never truly forgiven me. She was already sad that Marco had decided to go into the military and was so far away. But losing Luz crushed her. She was never the same and neither were you kids. You began to see me as someone to fear, and Andre couldn't move away fast enough. I went to Luz a few months afterward, wanting to make amends and help her, but she was too angry. She said she never wanted to see me again—that I was the coldest, most horrible father she could ever imagine."

I blinked, the news a shock to me. Luz had never mentioned that he'd ever reached out to her again.

"I swore to myself then that I wouldn't let anything like that happen again, that I would make sure you and Andre didn't get off track." He shook his head. "And here we are again. All my adult life, I've looked forward to the day when I could work side by side with one of my children, when I could pass on the family business to you. I know I'm tough on you, but the last few weeks have been some of the happiest I've had in years. To see you so confident, so professional. I swell with pride every time I see your name on the door next to mine."

"Papá," I whispered, tears getting caught in my throat.

He reached out and laid his hand over mine. "I want you to be happy, *mija*. But I also want you to be successful and follow the dream you've worked so hard for. No man is worth giving that up for. Don't you think you can be happy here?"

I stared down at our joined hands, his big one swallowing my small one, and a desperate, aching regret pinged through me. No man was worth giving up my happiness for. Not even my dad. I slid my hand from beneath his and back into my lap. "Papá, I am so thankful for everything you've given me and all your guidance. I wouldn't be where I am without you. You've been a good father and mentor to me. And you need to know that I would never give up my career. I love what I do."

He nodded. "I'm glad to hear it."

I lifted my gaze to his. "But I don't know if I need to be doing it here."

"Oh, Marcela." He rubbed a hand over his forehead.

The anguish in his voice almost did me in. A big part of me just wanted to make it better, wanted to tell him what he hoped to hear. But I'd spent so long trying to be who he wanted me to be, and it wasn't fair for either of us for me to keep doing that. I wanted a good relationship with my dad, wanted to recapture the bond we used to have. But I knew that probably wouldn't be possible with our working together and living so close. He was who he was. Turning off that overbearing side would require a personality transplant. And the more he smothered me, the more I'd resent him.

And I could analyze to death my feelings for Foster and worry about the nature of our relationship and if it would last and on and on. But the truth of the matter was that I loved him. And maybe it would work. And maybe it wouldn't. But I wasn't going to spend my life playing *what if*. I wanted a life with passion and risk and not knowing what was around every corner. I wanted to be surprised.

And if I stayed here, maybe I could be content or even happy, but there would be no surprises. And there would be no Foster.

"I'm so sorry," I said, silent tears escaping. "I love you so much, and I know I'm breaking my word. But I need to make my own way, Papá."

His eyes held all the sadness and disappointment he'd never tell me in words. "I don't approve."

I nodded and let my gaze fall to the table, the words stinging.

"But I understand."

I glanced up.

He reached over and brushed my tears away with a napkin. "You will always have a place to come back to if you need it. Your mother and I will never ever turn you away. I wouldn't make that mistake again. I've lost one piece of my heart with Luz. I refuse to lose another."

"Oh, Papá," I said, a full-out weepy mess now.

"Also, you tell that boy that if he hurts you, the next time I'll shoot first and ask questions later."

I snorted some sort of half sob, half laugh, and took the napkin from him to wipe my nose. "Andre's already threatened him, too. Dating me is turning out to be a very dangerous gig."

"Is he a good man, *mija*? This Foster," he asked, his serious face back in place.

"Yes," I said, believing that down the depths of my being. "He'll take good care of me."

My dad smiled and got up to give me a hug. "That's all I ask."

I pressed my face into his shoulder, holding him tight, and let myself be that little girl again—the one who loved her father unconditionally and only saw the wonderful, spectacular parts of him.

For all his faults, my father had given me a good upbringing and a loving home. I would always love him, my family, and my hometown. They were part of the fabric of who I was. But now it was time for me to take those things and carry them forward.

Now it was my turn to live the life I wanted.

And that life started now.

THIRTY-NINE

Foster wasn't positive when he knew for sure. Maybe it was when Bret had called so early, and his normally tell-it-like-it-is friend hadn't been able to give him any information. Maybe it had been the guarded, too-high tone of her voice. But when she'd sent him a follow-up text telling him not to listen to news radio on his drive back to Dallas, he had no doubts left.

Either Neve's kidnapper had been discovered or Neve had been found. And if Bret wasn't talking, he knew that there was no happy news waiting at the end of this road. Not that he'd ever held out hope that Neve had made it through okay. Not after all this time. But he couldn't deny that a small sliver of him had held on to the notion that maybe she'd been kidnapped by someone who'd wanted a child and that she had been cared for. It'd been a stupid, illogical hope, but it'd always been sitting there nestled deep in his mind. Now there'd be nothing there except the despair of knowing she was gone, *really* gone.

By the time he pulled up to the building Bret had given him directions to, he'd gone fully numb from the inside out. A news van was out front, which would explain why Bret had told him to pull around back. He parked the car, took a few breaths, and headed inside like a man on his way to his death sentence.

The fluorescent lights inside pushed against his already edgy senses, and he got the impression of walking into a morgue it was so quiet and cold. Before he could make his brain function and figure out where he was supposed to go, Bret was striding toward him, her face drawn and pale. He couldn't remember ever seeing her without makeup. Dread so deep it took his breath moved through him, leaving icy trails in its wake.

"Hey, you," she said gently, giving him a quick hug. "I don't even want to know how fast you drove to get here."

"Just tell me," he said flatly.

In the distance, he saw an older couple huddled together on a bench in the hallway. The woman peered his way, a hollow look in her eyes. Eyes the same color as his. His mother seemed to look through him, then turned back to his father.

Bret put a hand on his shoulder. "We found the guy. We got him."

Foster took in a ragged breath, absorbing that information. It didn't feel nearly as good as he thought it would. He'd spent much of his life waiting to hear those words, but they didn't offer any solace. Not when he sensed what was to follow.

"And Neve?" he asked, the question like jagged glass in his mouth.

Bret gave his shoulder a squeeze and shook her head sadly. "I'm sorry, hon. She didn't make it past the second day."

Everything seemed to crumple around him, collapsing in until he couldn't even see in front of him. He leaned against the wall and sank to the floor.

I rolled my suitcase behind me, already feeling guilty for imposing when I knocked on the door. When I'd gotten in the car this morning, this had seemed like a wise idea, but now I was starting to wonder if I should've given it more thought. Or at least talked to Foster first.

But after three days of not hearing from him, I was done waiting around for my life to start. Of course, that rah-rah-you-go-girl pep talk had only lasted a few hours into my trip from Verde Pass. My internal cheerleader had fallen off the top of the pyramid and lost her pom-poms somewhere around San Antonio.

The door swung open, and my brother filled the doorway, smiling down at me. "Well, if it isn't my homeless sister."

I rolled my eyes. "Shut up. I'm not homeless. I have a house."

"Just not here," he pointed out.

"Not yet."

He stepped inside and swept his arm toward his loft. "Never let it be said that I don't help those in need."

I sauntered past him, rolling my bag behind me and wishing that Bailey didn't live in a dorm. I loved my brother, but I'd spent enough time under the same roof with him to last a lifetime. Plus, I didn't want to be in the way. They already had a pretty crowded household. And I'd gotten the vibe when I asked Andre if I could crash here for a few days that he was hesitant. I turned to Andre and did a mock curtsy and head bow. "I will forever be indebted, dear brother."

Jace, who was on the couch with his legs propped up on the coffee table and a game controller in hand, gave me a quick grin. "Hey, doll-face. Don't let that asshole make you feel unwelcome. You can stay here as long as you need."

"Did I say she was unwelcome?" Andre said, walking past me and tugging my ponytail before taking my suitcase from me. "My door is always open."

"Uh-huh," I said, not quite buying it.

He strolled off toward the stairs and the bedrooms on the second level. Jace paused his game and turned around, smirk in place. "You realize why he's freaked out, right?"

"Because me staying here is a pain the ass," I offered.

"Nah." Jace glanced up at where Andre had disappeared. "He knows you know about the three of us, but he's afraid of you *seeing* it. Knowing and witnessing are two different things. I think he's afraid the fabric of your very existence will split in two."

"Oh, come on. Seriously?" I frowned. "It's not like I haven't already seen him kissing Evan."

Jace tilted his head, giving me the come-on-now look.

"Okay, yes, it's going to be different seeing PDAs between the two of you. But seriously, I have no issue with any of it. I want him to be happy."

"Good, then we're going to get this shit out of the way right now, because Evan's out of town on a job for the weekend, and I don't want Dre walking around with his shorts in a knot."

I had no idea what he meant by that but had a feeling I wouldn't be wondering for long.

Andre came back downstairs a few minutes later. He crooked his thumb behind him. "I went ahead and set you up in my room."

"Oh, you didn't have to do that. I can take the couch."

"It's not a problem," Andre said quickly.

"But—"

"He doesn't sleep in there anymore," Jace supplied. "So really, don't stress."

Andre's gaze narrowed as he turned to him. "Jace."

"What?" Jace asked, all wide-eyed innocence. "It's not like she doesn't know."

Andre scraped a hand through his dark hair, and there may have been a hint of color in his cheeks. I had to bite my lip to keep from laughing. It was a rare day to see the great Andre Medina embarrassed.

"Let's just not go there, all right?" Andre said, his tone holding warning.

That's all it took. Jace was pushing himself off the couch and heading her brother's way. The switch from laid-back, fun-loving Jace to this version kind of took my breath for a second. I recognized that look. It was the look Foster gave me when he was about to issue a command. Oh, shit. A little shiver went through me—like my body knew how to pick up a predator in its midst.

Andre's dark eyes went a little wide as Jace stepped in front of him and clamped a hand around the back of his neck.

"J, don't."

But Jace was already leaning in to kiss him. The sight of the two of them was a little hard for my brain to process. Of course, I'd seen two guys kiss before. But not two I knew so well. Jace and Andre had been best friends for so long—bros, dudes. And both were about as alpha male as any guy could get. They fit into these certain boxes in my head. Boxes that hadn't included this. But it was hard to deny the sweetness there between them as Jace took the kiss and cajoled Andre into returning it. Soon, as if forgetting he'd protested a moment before, Andre relaxed into it, his hand going to Jace's hip and moving him closer.

When Jace finally pulled back, Andre blinked, seeming to come back into himself, then scowled. "Dammit, J."

"Now that the awkward is out of the way," Jace said, turning and heading back toward the couch with a pleased grin, "who's going to challenge me in Mario Kart?"

Andre peeked my way as if bracing for the impact of my reaction, but I was too busy smiling. "Wow, you guys are perfect for each other. I've never seen anyone shut *you* up, Dre."

Andre stared at me for a moment then matched my smile, his stance loosening. "Evan's pretty good at leaving me speechless, too."

I walked over to him and gave him a hug. "I'm happy for you. Really. We've both tried to live for other people a long time. Tried to be who we thought we were supposed to be. Frankly, I'm freaking sick of it."

He held me to him, putting his chin on top my head. "When you'd get to be so smart?"

"Well, I've always been smarter than you," I teased.

Andre huffed a laugh and leaned back from the hug, putting his hands on my shoulders. "True. So then tell me, why is my smart, imminently levelheaded sister back in town with no job and no place to live?"

I smirked. "Are you going to yell at me if I tell you it's for a guy?"

"Ian Foster," he said, his tone going a little grave.

"Yes. And don't give me that look," I said, jutting my chin upward. "I love him, Dre. And he loves me back. I don't want to walk away from that."

He blew out a breath and lowered his arms to his sides. "Well, I imagine if that's the case, he could really use you here with him right now."

My brows knitted. "What are you talking about?"

"You haven't talked to him?"

"No, he was going to call me. He had something to take care of, but I decided to come here and surprise him instead."

His frown deepened, increasing the foreboding vibes going through me. "Oh, Cela, I thought you knew. It's been all over the local news here."

My stomach dropped to my feet. "What has?"

"They arrested a child serial killer. They've pinned at least fifteen missing children cases on him from the last two decades all over the South. He confessed to the Foster girl's kidnapping, rape, and murder."

I put my hand over my mouth, horror bleeding through me and making everything go icy cold. "Oh my God."

"They interviewed the parents on TV for a minute last night, but I haven't seen Foster on anywhere. Even my precinct has been buzzing with calls about cold cases from all over the place who want to know more about this guy. The details of the crimes are pretty gruesome, Cela. I can't imagine what the family must be going through."

What Foster must be going through. His worst nightmare had come to fruition. Nausea rolled through me. "I need to go. I need to see him"

Andre nodded with sympathy. "Sure, okay, but be careful, baby girl. If he hasn't called you, there may be a reason. He may want—"

But I wasn't even listening. I was already retracing my steps back to the door and grabbing my purse. I made it out to the parking lot on high-speed autopilot.

As soon as I slid in my car, I picked up my phone and hit Dial. Pike answered on the first ring. "Doc."

"I'm in town. Where is he?" I asked without preamble.

"Thank fucking Christ," he said, his voice filled with relief. "He's at home, and I don't have a clue what to do with him. I've never seen him like this. He's shut down completely—like some emotionless, T-1000 version of himself. And he's talking about closing his business, saying it doesn't mean anything anymore. I can't seem to get any sense through his thick skull. And don't even get me started on his fucking parents. I feel horrible for what they've been through, but they've ignored Foster through all of this. Like he doesn't exist."

My ribs felt like they were cinching tighter, a corset of grief squeezing everything together and making it hard to breathe. "I'm coming over."

"Good. I'll take all the help I can get."

I made it to my old building in record time, my brain and body operating with a singular focus. Get. To. Foster. Pike let me in without a word and cocked his head toward Foster's bedroom.

"Did you tell him I was coming?"

"No. He just came home a little while ago from another meeting with the FBI and went straight into his room."

I took a shaky breath. "Wish me luck, then."

"You'll probably need it, doc. He hates the world right now and everyone in it."

"How could he not?"

Pike nodded grimly. "Yeah."

I set my purse down on the counter and headed toward Foster's room. He may hate the world, but I loved him. And I'd waited far too long to tell him that.

I knocked on the door.

FORTY

There was no answer on the first knock, so I rapped the door again.

"Fuck off, Pike. I'm busy."

I wet my lips. "It's Cela."

There was silence on the other side for a long few seconds. I started to wonder if he'd heard me, but then the door opened.

Foster stood there, clean shaven and put together on the surface, but when I met his eyes I saw the hollowness there. "What are you doing here?"

His tone was flat, and I had to swallow past the anxiety of barging in on him while he was going through all of this. Maybe I was overstepping, maybe our relationship was more of a fun, sexy thing, and I wasn't welcome into his world for the big things like grief and tragedy and loss. Insecurity made me want to shrink back, but I pressed on, clearing my throat. "I wanted to . . ."

"Say you're sorry? Offer your condolences?"

The words were sharp and his grip tight on the door, but I recognized this mode. The dagger eyes, the movements that seemed both like aggression and retreat wrapped into one. I'd seen it time and again with animals when they were injured. Even the sweetest, gentlest pet could turn into a fire-breathing hound from hell when it was hurt. Bad news for Foster was that I wouldn't be scared off by it. Those were the animals most in need of help.

I squared my shoulders. "I *am* sorry. So very sorry, Foster. But I came here for you. To help with whatever you might need."

He scoffed. "Help. Like there's anything anyone can do. She's dead, Cela. My beautiful, innocent baby sister, raped and murdered by that fucking monster." Utter anguish crumpled his features for a moment before he pulled his expression back to its hard edge. "All because I gave him opportunity. I took my eyes off of her, and he *took* her. So, unless you have a time machine to go fix that, there is no goddamned help to be had."

I closed my eyes, the despair of his words, the life sentence he'd assigned himself making me physically hurt for him.

"So, go home. It's not a good time."

He moved to close the door and I stepped forward, my hand smacking the wood as I blocked it from shutting, and strode past him. "Well, that's too bad because if you want me to leave, you're going to have to carry me out. And I may kick and scream. Just warning you."

He turned, his face going blank for a moment at my declaration, then annoyed. "What the hell?"

"You're grieving and you're angry. I understand that. But now's not the time to be alone."

"The hell it's not."

"I love you."

He stilled. "What? Cela, no, I can't deal with this right now . . ."

I didn't let that response deter me. I knew he loved me, he'd told me—even if he couldn't quite access that emotion right now. My gaze flicked toward the open door, a crazy idea popping into my head. Last time when he'd tried to push me away, I'd let him. He'd needed an outlet for his anger, his anxiety, and I'd left him to call some other woman.

No way that shit was happening again. I loved him. And that meant all parts. Even the mean side that came out when his hurt or fear took over.

I put my fingers to the top button of my shirt, slipping it out of the hole.

His eyes followed the movement of my hands. "What are you doing?"

I caught his stare and went for the next button. "I told you I'm here for whatever you need. I'm tough. Take whatever it is going on inside you and let it out on me."

"*What?*" His voice was a low roar.

"Flog me, spank me, fuck me. I don't care. Take all of that crap you have raging inside of you and let it out. Give me your anger . . . sir." I let my shirt fall to the ground.

"Put your goddamned clothes on, Cela," he said, raking a hand through his hair like a man on the brink. "You don't need to be around me right now. I don't trust myself."

I went for the button on my shorts and tugged them off, my heart-beat like a hummingbird's wings flapping against my ribs. "I do."

"You're fucking out of your mind, then." He glanced at the open door as if just realizing I was exposed if Pike walked by and slammed the door shut. "You think sex is going to fix this? Fix me?"

I discarded my bra and panties, my body quaking from the risk I knew I was taking. It was like taunting a caged animal who was ready to tear apart its next victim. I stood there stark naked in front of him and pulled my hair from the band that held my ponytail.

"No, I don't think sex will. But owning me might." I lowered to my knees. "Give me your worst, Foster. I won't say no. And I won't run away."

He laced his hands behind his head, and I could see the utter agony there, the struggle. "Don't say things like that. It's a lie. Everybody leaves, Cela. Everybody. Anytime things seem like they're going to be okay, life fucking blindsides you. And you'll be no different. Why should I deserve to have you anyway? I couldn't even take care of my own family."

My fingers curled at my sides, my whole being yearning to reach out to him and hold him, reassure him. But I knew that it would do no good. Every instinct inside me told me he needed an outlet for all this emotion, action not talking. "I'm not going anywhere, so I guess you're going to have to make me."

He stared down at me like I'd been replaced by some pod person. "Did you not *hear* me? Can't you see I'm fucked up right now? If I touch you, I'll *hurt* you. Get. Out."

On a surge of bravery and pure emotion, I pushed to my feet and shoved him hard in the chest—like I was picking some schoolyard fight. Surprise was on my side, and I managed to knock him back a step, his shoulder hitting the door. "I said make me."

He blinked, momentarily stunned into silence, then outrage leaked into those blue eyes. He grabbed me by the arms, his fingers like vice grips to the soft flesh there, and spun me until my back was against the door. His mouth came down hard against mine in a clash of lips and teeth. I gasped into the kiss and opened to him, still scared for what I may have gotten myself into but ready to help him exorcise the demons. Bruises and bites would heal. I could handle his roughness. But I refused to accept the coldness, the distance, the shutting down.

I'd fallen in love with a passionate, beautiful man, and I wasn't going to let that man be another victim of the killer who'd taken his sister.

Foster's kiss was hungry and violent and like nothing he'd ever shown me before. I could feel the fury and frustration rumbling through him. He released my arms from the death grip and tangled his fingers in my hair as he deepened the kiss, taking, taking, taking. I was breathless and panting when he finally wrenched away. "Make you, huh? You want my worst. You may regret that in a minute."

"No regrets, sir."

That seemed to make him angrier, his teeth clenching. Without finesse, he pushed me down to my knees via the tight hold he still had on my hair and unbuttoned his jeans with his free hand. I resisted the urge to grab for my head and rub my stinging scalp. "You think you can make it all better, angel? Think a good cocksucking can fix it all?"

The words were meant to be crude and ugly. He was trying to make me hate him, to make me leave, to prove himself right. But all I heard was that he'd called me angel for the first time tonight. And if he thought forcing me to give him a blow job was a hardship, he didn't know just how good a submissive he'd trained. My body was already responding to his commands. And I wanted nothing more than to offer him some sort of pleasure to break up all that torment he'd been suffering through.

I reached out, yanking down his boxers and pants, and smiled inwardly. Despite his anger and all of his protests, he was hard and proud, ready for me. Before I could lean forward to take him, he tightened his grip on my hair and guided his cock into my mouth, setting the pace, holding on to all the control.

I got the message. I was his to use however he wanted. He would offer me no kindness right now because I'd goaded him into this. Perhaps I should've minded that. Old me would've thought to object. But the move sent a buzz through my brain, activating all those lovely things that submission seemed to bring with it. I hummed with pleasure as the tip of his cock touched the back of my throat.

"That's right. Make those pretty sounds. You like being used like my whore?" Foster asked through gritted teeth. "Because that's what you're asking for right now."

The word *whore* would've cut me deep a few months ago. He knew that. And a rush of ire went through me. Hardheaded bastard. He was working really hard to run me off. But he wasn't going to win this battle. I didn't believe his bullshit. I lifted my gaze to his, determined, and rolled my tongue around the head of his cock, teasing and torturing. Seducing.

"Fuck." He pulled out and stepped back, his hand still in my hair. I smiled up at him, challenging him. His mouth thinned into a firm, pissed-off line. "Get on the bed. On your belly. We'll see how long you can hold that smile."

"Yes, sir," I said, quite demurely, embracing all the brattiness that I had in me. "You're not going to break me. You realize that, right?"

His eyes flared—part fury, part unfettered animalistic lust. "Oh, is that right?"

He grasped me by the back of the neck and marched me over to the bed, bending me over the side of it. His hand came down hard on my ass and thighs in a quick, vicious volley of smacks. I cried out, unable to hold back the reaction, but holding still nonetheless, refusing to show any weakness.

"You're so brave now, is that it? You think a few times with me and you can handle whatever I dish out?" He spanked me again, right on top of a fresh mark. I bit the inside of my cheek. "You have no idea what I'm capable of right now, have *no idea.*"

"I love you," I said softly.

"Goddammit, Cela. Stop saying that," he said, his voice strangled.

"No, sir."

He stalked off and I heard the closet door opening. I braced myself, knowing that I'd pushed him even further. I was playing with fire near a propane tank, and we both knew it. The air shifted behind me, a cool breeze coasting over my burning skin as he moved back in place. Then whatever he'd grabbed was coming down on my back—biting, wicked lashes. Something he hadn't used on me before, a belt of some sort maybe. *One! Two! Three!* I lost count after that, my thoughts blurring at the edges as adrenaline pumped hard through my veins.

I pressed my cheek into the sheets, my eyes starting to water. I couldn't tell if they were tears or not. I didn't care. I could feel the emotion behind every swing, the desperation channeling through him. Everything trapped inside him was pouring out into the blows.

Wham, wham, wham!

Finally, after what seemed like forever, I sensed the strength behind the hits draining. My skin was a raging fire—half-burning, half-numb. But everything else in me was soaring, endorphins flooding my system. I'd done this to push him to a certain place, but he was sending me to another edge of my own.

"Christ, Cela," he said, the belt dropping to the floor. His breath was labored. I could feel his stare heavy against me. He ran his hands over my abused back, first simply touching, then kissing. One spot in particular made me flinch more than the others. "Tell me you're still with me. That you're okay."

I reached back for him blindly, grabbing hold of his hand. Even that movement took all my effort. I felt . . . drunk. And so freaking turned on. "Very, very with you."

He moved his hand between my thighs, finding me warm and wet, and groaned. "So goddamned sexy. All this pain, and you're turned on. Spread your legs."

I made the effort, but he had to help me most of the way. I was still bent over the bed in the prone position and really had no energy to move anywhere else. There was the shifting of fabric as he apparently shucked the rest of his clothes, then his palms were spanning my hips. Without preamble, he pushed into me.

I groaned at the feel of him filling me, of my body clenching around him. He buried deep, a tremble going through his hands where he held me—like he was drowning in the sensation as much as I was. The last of my will slipped away. I was truly his in that moment, whatever he wanted to do with me, I was in.

He eased back and thrust into me again, hard, his thighs hitting the backs of mine, reactivating the burn there, but also rocking my clit against the edge of the mattress—a killer combination. I whimpered into the sheets. "I know it stings and that I should be softer with you right now. But I need to fuck you, angel. You understand?"

"Yes, sir."

"You told me I owned you tonight, and I'm going to take you at your word," he said, strain in his voice as he rocked into me with a steady, rough rhythm. "Tell me you're mine."

"I'm yours," I gasped, release thundering toward me, the stimulation to my clit and the rushing endorphins almost too much to take. "All yours."

"That's right," he said, his words labored. "Give me your pleasure. Show me how much you like me using you."

My nails curled into my palms, every molecule in my body starting to quake, but I was trying to hold out as long as possible. "Foster . . ."

He caught hold of my wrists and pulled my arms behind my back, holding them at my tailbone, as he continued his punishing rhythm. I could do nothing but receive him and every bit of pleasure he was wringing from me. Sweat dripped down my temple, and with nothing to hold on to, I fell apart.

Wretched cries tore from my throat as every part of my body seemed to become laced with lightning—the sensitized skin on my back, my clit against the pressure of the bed, and the delicious fullness of being utterly, brutally taken by Foster. Tears leaked out my eyes mingling with the salt and sweat, and everything went hazy.

Foster let out a slew of filthy, dirty epitaphs and then let loose a grinding, primal groan as he buried himself to the hilt and spilled inside me, his hold on my wrists tightening until my fingers started to tingle.

When we were both gasping for breath, drifting down from our orgasm, he released my hands and draped himself over my back. All of my muscles seemed to give out and merge with the bed. I wasn't sure I'd ever be able to get them to function again.

Foster kissed my temple, my hair, his body blanketing me with heat that was both a blessing and a curse. Blessing because I couldn't seem to stop shivering, but curse because now that the orgasm was fading, the pain from the belt was setting in.

After a few long seconds, Foster pushed up on his forearms. "Sorry, angel. I'm probably smothering you."

"Mmm," I mumbled, too spent to form actual words. My mind still seemed to be sparking in fits and starts—aftershocks.

Foster lifted himself from the bed and pulled out. A rush of liquid heat came with him, sliding down my thighs. I knew I should probably get up and get a towel or something—vaguely, in the back of my mind I registered that these were new sheets. But something about having the evidence of what had just happened marking me seemed sexy and dirty in the best way.

"Motherfucker," Foster said, the harsh word cutting through my afterglow.

"What's wrong?"

"I'm sorry, angel." Foster touched a spot on my shoulder and I flinched. "I fucking drew blood."

I turned my head to look back at him. His fingertips were smeared with blood. He glanced down his chest, finding a streak of red there, too. When he looked over at me, regret morphed his features. I let my head sink back into the bed. "I'm sure I'll live."

"Goddammit," he said, obviously more disturbed by this turn of events than I was. "I just—fuck—what is wrong with me? You taunt me and I unleash on you, trampling over limits we haven't even discussed. I should've never—"

"Don't you dare take a second of this back," I said, cutting him off with what little energy I could muster. "Or I will personally kick your ass—well, when I have the ability to move again. I told you to do what you wanted. And you did. Now you're just raining on my afterglow."

He let out a long, belabored breath. "Don't move. I'm going to get you cleaned up and then there's a bathtub with our names on it."

An hour later, I was curled up in Foster's bed, mellow and sated. He'd gently cared for me, bathing me, then treating the spot where the skin had broken and rubbing salve on the rest. Two ibuprofen had been swallowed down, the curtains had been drawn tight, and now I was ready for a nap. But even though his back was to me, I could sense Foster's restlessness.

We hadn't talked much after sex, and I was trying to leave him be. I'd pushed enough today. But there was also no way I was going to drift off, knowing he was still so tense next to me. I reached out and touched his hip. "You okay?"

He didn't respond at first, but then reached back and laced his fingers with mine. "I don't know what I am, angel."

"That's understandable. I can't imagine what you've been through these last few days."

He pulled my hand off his hip and drew it around his front side until I was almost spooning him. He traced my knuckles with his fingertip. "I thought I would feel better once I knew. I thought it would help."

I pressed my lips to the back of his shoulder.

"But knowing all that happened to her . . ." A shudder worked through him. "I can't even . . ."

"Try not to think about that stuff," I said softly. "Remember her as she was."

He drew me even closer to him, like he was holding on to a ledge. After a deep breath he said, "You know, earlier that same year, I got the flu for the first time. God, it was awful. I didn't think I'd ever feel good again. That whole week was so miserable."

I stayed quiet, not sure where he was going, but knowing that talking was moving in the right direction. I'd listen to him all day and night if that could make him feel better.

"My parents had warned her to stay out of my room, told her she'd get sick, too. But Neve didn't listen. She would sneak into my room each morning before kindergarten and try to cheer me up. 'I don't want you to be sad no more, E,' she'd say in that perky little voice of hers. That's what she called me—E. She thought Ian was too long." His voice caught, and it took a moment before he continued. "One day she dressed up in her dance class outfit and sang Debbie Gibson songs, another she cooked me my favorite dinner with her play food since I couldn't manage to eat any real meals. She was like this joyous tornado of glitter and giggles."

Tears stung my eyes. "She sounds amazing."

"She was," he said, his voice pained. "And that horrible day later that summer, I told my bubbly little sister to go away, that she was annoying me. All she wanted to do was spend time with me and my friends, and I treated her like she was a brat. That was the last thing she heard from me before . . . before she was, God . . ."

"Oh, Foster," I said, my heart ripping in two for him, for his family, for that bright little girl who the world would never get the privilege of knowing. "Don't."

His body began to jerk with hard sobs. "I led her right to him, right into his sick fucking hands . . ."

I tightened my hold on him, my tears dripping and sliding down my cheeks, as Foster broke apart. "No, Foster, not you. Him. That sicko. What happened wasn't your fault, baby. It was *his* fault."

Foster shook his head against the pillow, but he was past words now. Everything that had been locked inside him seemed to rush out in a deluge. His body wracked with the force of his grief. I grabbed hold of him and rolled him over, wrapping him in my arms and holding him against me. He didn't fight it. Gone was the bravado, the tough man, and all that was left was the little boy who'd made a simple mistake and suffered the worst of consequences, a boy that'd been abandoned by his parents for it.

I cried silently with him, his pain becoming my own, and didn't let go.

I would never let go again.

FORTY-ONE

Foster scanned through his email, not feeling very motivated but at least feeling somewhat human again. Cela had refused to leave his side for the last week and had even helped him make it through his sister's memorial service. At first, he had protested her going, but trying to talk her off that was like trying to talk a brick wall into crumbling. And in the end, he'd been happy to have her there.

His parents had attended and they'd talked with him briefly—like a vaguely polite business relationship—but Cela hadn't let them get away with the brush-off. She'd cornered his mom and dad, telling them how sorry she was, of course, but also sharing how inspired she was by 4N and Foster's work for missing children. She'd thrown in a few, "You must be so proud of the man he's become" type comments.

It'd made his parents visibly uncomfortable, and he'd even caught a flash of regret cross his father's face. But, to his surprise, his mother had really *looked* at him for the first time in years, her blue eyes holding remorse for so much time lost, and said, "I am. More than he knows. Foster has probably suffered more than any of us for all of this."

It hadn't been an apology, but the acknowledgement had closed some gaps inside him. No matter what he'd done, what mistakes he'd made. He hadn't deserved to be left behind. No child deserved that.

Cela stepped up behind him, laying her hands on his shoulders and dragging him out of his thoughts. She leaned over to peek at his laptop. "What'cha working on?"

"There are some buyers interested in the company. I'm setting up meetings."

"Still stuck on that, huh?" she asked, her opinion clear in her tone.

He sighed. He'd come a long way in the last few days, but he still didn't think he could spend the rest of his life running 4N. He'd started the company for Neve, and now every day he went in, he'd be reminded of how he'd failed her. How he'd never be able to help her or add a gold "found" plaque beneath her photo on the wall. It all seemed so . . . pointless now. "I think it's for the best."

"Can you take a break from it?" she asked, stepping around him and sinking onto his lap. "I thought all three of us could bust out of these walls and go out tonight. Pike has tickets to a swanky record release party."

He frowned. "I don't think I'm ready for any parties, angel."

"Come on," she protested. "There will be alcohol and we can get all dressed up. It will do you good to get out for a while. Plus, I have a dress Bailey lent me that shows *a lot* of leg."

The pleading look on her face was more than he could handle. So much for the dom having all the power. One look like that and he was fucking toast. He pushed her hair behind her ears and cupped her face. "Fine. But only because you promised me leg."

She laughed and kissed him. "Good. Now go put on a suit, so I can drool over you all night, too."

He smiled, even with all the sadness still sitting on his shoulders, Cela could manage to cheer him up. "You're getting mighty bossy, slave girl."

"No worries. You can punish me later."

"Brat."

"You know it."

Cela was way too excited about this party. Foster was trying his best to be peppy, but really, he'd been to these record shindigs with Pike before and had never been all that impressed. Hopefully, he and Cela could have a few drinks, stay for an hour, and head back home.

Pike had lined up a limo and had asked Cela's friend Bailey to come with them. The girl seemed absolutely beside herself sitting next to Pike—her hands constantly smoothing the material of her dress, and her gaze regularly sneaking over to her date. Pike had told Cela he'd made it clear up front that he was only taking Bailey as a friend. Cela didn't seem bothered either way, but Foster knew Pike wasn't going to mess with a friend of Cela's—especially one so young and starstruck. Even he had his limits.

They pulled up to the place where the event was being held, and Foster was surprised to see the grand entrance of Hotel St. Mark through the window. He nodded toward the building. "Hey, look at that. What are the chances?"

Cela just smiled and grabbed his hand. "Ready?"

"As I'll ever be."

They climbed out of the limo and headed toward one of the ballrooms. The hotel, of course, looked the same as it had when he'd taken Cela here that first night, but God, so much had changed. He'd sauntered into that hotel that evening looking for a fun, kinky night with his sexy neighbor. Never would he have guessed he'd end up here again with Cela on his arm as his girlfriend.

Cela guided him through the lobby toward the back of the hotel, where the ballroom was located, but before they stepped through the doors, she turned and gave him a quick kiss. "Just remember, if you want to be mad, take it out on me later. But right now, I need you to smile."

"What?"

She tugged him through the door and into a room buzzing with people. He was still trying to process what her cryptic comment meant, when he saw the large banner above the stage on the far end of the room. *132 Lives Saved—Thank You, 4N!*

He froze, his feet fastening to the floor. "What the hell is this?"

Pike stepped up behind him, clapping a hand on his shoulder. "Welcome to your party, bro. You're a hero."

Heaviness landed in the pit of his stomach. Hero. That was the last thing he was. "Cela . . ."

She bit her lip, her expression anxiously expectant. "Remember, *smile*. You can make me pay later."

He ran a hand over the back of his head, fighting the urge to stride right back out. But before he could say anything else, his assistant, Lindy, hurried over to him like a whirlwind of fluttering hands and smiles. She threw her arms around him. "I'm so glad you came!"

On autopilot, he hugged her back. "You knew about this?"

She stepped back, smiling sheepishly. "Maybe? The staff has wanted to put together an event for a while. A lot of the families want to thank you. So when Cela called me to see if we could put something together quickly, I sort of made everyone work overtime to make it happen."

He peeked over Lindy's shoulder toward Cela. Everything in her stance belied her nerves. She'd gone through all of this trouble, and now she was afraid he was going to bail. He sighed, frustrated that this was happening but unable to let Cela or his staff down by being an asshole about it.

He forced himself to smile, the motion straining his face. "Thanks, Lindy. Y'all really shouldn't have gone through the trouble."

She crossed her arms and eyed him. "Yes, we should've. You built this company, and you need to accept the impact it's had. Now, go sit, eat and drink. The presentation is about to start."

"Presentation?" But Cela and Pike were already ushering him to a table without answering his question.

He felt like a piece being moved on a chessboard, everything out of his control. The whole experience was unnerving. But what else could he do at this point? Cela had thrown him into the deep end without an escape route. He ordered a stiff drink before his ass even hit the chair.

And he would need that liquid fortification, because a few minutes later, the lights went down and a video screen lowered on the back wall behind the stage. Music filled the cavernous ballroom, and Cela reached out and grabbed his hand. Familiar faces began to light the screen in time with the wordless music. One by one, every person who had ever been found because of one of their products appeared on the screen. Happy, smiling faces of two little boys running through the park, a little girl with a tiara on, the wizened smile of an elderly man who'd been found after wandering off, footage of news stories showing families reuniting when they found their loved ones.

Words appeared on the screen between the photos.

Every day . . . over two thousand children go missing.

Every day . . . families grieve for loved ones they'll never see again.

Foster's throat felt like it was stuffed with fiberfill, his chest going tight.

Every day . . . hope is lost.

But not for Mackenzie Osbourne in Cedar Rapids, IA.

Not for Jayden Kennedale in Biloxi, MS.

Not for MaryLou Wallace in Waco, TX.

Because people like Ian Foster and the staff of 4N refuse to accept that there's nothing we can do.

A video of the Kennedales came on, Jayden in the middle with a toothless grin. Jayden's mother began to speak. *"The day Jayden wandered off in the mall was the most terrifying day of my life. In a flash of seconds, I saw my whole world collapsing in on itself. I'd taken my eye off of him for one moment, and he was gone. My baby was gone and it was my fault."* She swiped at tears through a wavering smile. *"I'm not sure what made me buy that Home Safe wristband a month before. I live in a quiet town, low crime. It seemed kind of silly and paranoid to have such a thing. But Neve Foster's story affected me, and I bought one. If Jayden hadn't been wearing his that day, I know we would've never seen him again. I will never be able to repay Ian Foster and 4N for what they've given me. You saved us all."*

Foster's lungs constricted as another family came on giving more heartfelt testimony. He looked to Cela, who was swiping at tears. She turned his way and offered him a tentative smile as if to say, *See how amazing you are. This matters. You did this.*

The meaning behind that look hit him right in the sternum. It was like warm rays of sun shining on his face. For the first time ever, he felt it—truly felt it—by seeing himself though her eyes. He'd made a difference. Maybe not for his own family. He could never make things better for Neve. And nothing would ever bring her back. But he could honor her with this. Every person who came home safe with a 4N product was because of her, a tribute.

As he listened to story after story, and as families came up to him to thank him after the video presentation was over, everything that had been wound so tight for so long seemed to loosen and unknot inside him. This mattered.

And Cela had shown him that. She'd done this for him. Everyone else had let him get by with his bitterness and hardened front, but she hadn't accepted the bullshit. She'd pushed and pushed and stood up to him, had even taken the brunt of his wrath the night she'd refused to leave him alone to wallow. She'd bled for him.

The woman was more than he could have ever dreamed of or asked for. She was perfect. And she was his.

He exchanged hugs and good-byes with the last of the families who had stopped by to thank him, and then scanned the room for Cela. She'd stepped away when people had started to come over to talk with him, but he didn't want her anywhere but at his side. He caught sight of her across the room with Bailey, both of them chatting with Lindy. Cela's dark hair gleamed beneath the soft lighting in the room, and as promised, the short black dress she wore revealed just enough to drive him mad. If he hadn't known her, his eyes would have been drawn her way regardless. Without letting her see him, he slipped out the door to take care of something.

When he came back, she hadn't moved from her perch, but had added a glass of champagne to the mix. As if feeling his eyes on her, she glanced his way and sent him a *still mad at me?* quirk of her eyebrows. Inwardly, he grinned, but he kept his expression stern as he made his way over to her. When he reached the group, he grabbed her elbow and drew her next to him. "Excuse us, ladies, Cela and I have a lot to discuss."

Lindy put a hand on his arm. "You're not mad, are you?"

He sent her a quelling look. "Not at you."

Cela gave Bailey a *ruh-roh* expression as she handed over her champagne glass to her friend, but he winked at the girl over Cela's shoulder. Bailey bit back a smile. She gave Cela a little wave. "I'm going grab more of those puff pastry thingies."

"Good idea," Foster said, tugging Cela away.

She glanced back at her friend. "Is it just me or did she just throw me to the wolves?"

"Wolf," he corrected.

Cela eyed him, as if still trying to figure out if he was truly mad or screwing with her. "Where are we going?"

He didn't answer as he guided her out of the party room and toward the bank of elevators. As if they'd been waiting for Foster and Cela's arrival, the gold gleaming doors spread wide. Foster dragged her inside.

As soon as the doors slid shut, he crowded her against the wall, banding an arm around her waist. She let out a little squeak of surprise, and he pressed his forehead to hers, holding her eye contact. "Last time we were in this elevator, I was so desperate for you, I went against my better judgment. I could tell you were holding something back, and I took you to that room anyway."

"Regret it?"

He lifted his head and smiled down at her. "It was the best fuckup I've ever made."

She stared up at him with those big, brown eyes, her lips curving.

He cupped the back of her neck. "And all this time I've made you conform to me. What I want, what I thought I needed, what I prefer. I insisted you fit into this one box of ideal I'd made up."

"Foster."

"And I know we haven't talked about it since everything happened, and I know you've got a lot on your plate back home. But I'm telling you right now. I will do whatever it fucking takes, Cela. Vanilla. Kinky. Neapolitan. Staying here or moving south. I don't care anymore. All I want is you. And whatever way I get to have that, I'm willing to do."

Her fingers curled around the lapels of his suit jacket, and her eyes went shiny.

"Just tell me what you want, and I will make it happen."

The elevator doors dinged, opening to the top floor again. But unlike all those months ago, there was no doubt behind her smile, no fear. She pushed up on her toes and kissed him softly. When she pulled away, what he saw there nearly brought him to his knees.

"I want you to take care of me," she said, her gaze steady on his and her hand pressed over his pounding heart. "As long as I get to take care of you back. Sir."

Joy streamed through every cell in his body, lighting him from the inside out. Foster lifted her off her feet and carried her toward the hotel room. Last time they were here, she'd given him her virginity.

Tonight, he'd give her his heart.

EPILOGUE

CHRISTMAS EVE

The riding crop hit Cela's sweat-glazed skin with a satisfy-ing thwack, a nice hard hit at the end of a quick round of lighter blows. Cela's head tipped back on a moan, the chains holding her arms above her clinking. *Beautiful.* Foster lowered the crop to his side and stepped back, relishing the sight of that thick dark hair sliding back over her shoulders and dancing along the marks he'd made, *his* marks.

His angel was flying high. He could see it in the sway of her body, the slack in her muscles. Desire burned hot in his veins, urging him to take her, but he channeled his patience. He wanted to savor her, espe-cially considering the risky Christmas gift he had planned. If tonight didn't go the way he hoped, he may not have this privilege again—a thought he couldn't even bear to let fully form in his head right now.

The glow of the fireplace flickered in front of her, sending shafts of orange light dancing along the walls, changing a room that had once held so much coldness for him to one full of warmth and beauty . . . love. He ran his palm along Cela's back in a gentle caress, feeling the heat of her skin, the raised welts. She shivered beneath his hand and leaned into his touch. Everything in her reactions said she wanted more, but he knew that was her endorphins and need for release talking, her descent into subspace complete. He'd already worked her over for longer than usual, and he could sense she was close to begging.

But he hadn't been able to resist pushing her. She didn't know it, but tonight was a cleansing of sorts for him. He'd driven the long way to get here with Cela in a blindfold. She was under the impression he'd taken her to one of the cabins at The Ranch, but they were somewhere decidedly closer to home.

Foster set the crop down on a side table and wrapped an arm around Cela's waist before hitting a button on a remote he'd secured to his belt. The chains attached to the ceiling lowered with a soft grind. He smiled, enjoying the addition to the newly remodeled house. Where his mother's precious antique chandelier had once been, he now had recessed lighting and a hidden compartment for restraints. Cela sagged into his hold, and he laid a brush of a kiss along her shoulder. "Still with me, angel?"

"Yes, sir," she said, her breath choppy behind the words. "I'm just so . . . I need . . ."

"Shh, I know, baby," he soothed as he helped ease her arms down to her sides and unlocked the leather cuffs. "I need you, too. So much."

When he stepped in front of her, she raised her face to him, and he could imagine those soulful eyes behind the blindfold, the trusting, full-surrender way she looked at him in these moments. He cradled her face, his heart squeezing in his chest at the sight of her. He already loved her too much—the power of it almost painful.

He laid a kiss on her mouth, her lips parting and taking him in as if she were parched and he would provide the water. She tasted of cinnamon and nutmeg, like the cookies she'd baked this afternoon, mixed in with the earthy flavor of raw need. He tucked his hand behind her, supporting her head, and then let his other hand drift downward over her bare belly and to the smooth skin beneath. He deepened the kiss as he found her wet heat.

She sighed into the kiss as he slipped two fingers inside her, stroking her with enough pressure to make her shudder but not enough to send her over. Her body clenched around his fingers, a hot, slick fist that made his cock throb against his zipper. A groan of pleasure escaped him. "You're so ready for me, angel. I love how wet and desperate you get when I'm rough with you. I can't imagine anything sexier."

"It's all your fault," she said, smiling as she pressed her forehead against his. "I used to be such a good girl."

He grinned. "Oh, you're still very, very good, my Cela."

He dragged his hand upward, streaking her belly with her own arousal, and then cupped one of her breasts. The small metal clamp he'd placed on her nipple glinted in the firelight. He brushed a thumb across the hard point, and she gasped.

"So pretty." He lowered his head and licked the tight, swollen nub, eliciting a desperate mewl from her.

"Oh, God, please," she begged. "I can't take anymore. Going to lose it."

"You can take it. And no, you won't. Not until I tell you," he said, his tone firm. He sucked the other nipple into his mouth, grazing his teeth over the tip.

"*Fuck*." Her back bowed, and she pressed into him, near writhing.

He smiled as he released her breast. When his sweet-mouthed girl started cursing, he knew she was barely clinging to her edge. He pushed her down to her knees and onto the thick carpet. "On your elbows, angel. I want that pretty view while I fuck you."

Without hesitation, she went down onto her elbows, spreading her knees and presenting him with the sexiest Christmas gift he could imagine—the golden slope of her back, his marks coloring her skin, and her arousal glistening in the dancing light. Her submission, fully and unselfishly given. God, he wanted her. Not only in this moment. Not only tonight. And not only in his bed.

But right now he couldn't let himself think that far. Right now he needed to do the one thing he'd been waiting for all night—claim the woman he loved.

***

I pressed my palms to the floor, my fingers curling into the unfamiliar carpet. Every molecule in my body seemed to be vibrating, like one wrong move and my existence would simply disintegrate into a mass of amorphous energy.

Foster had spanked me and hit me with the crop so many times, my skin tingled like there was electricity skating over it. I'd come once already, but since the initial release he'd brought me to the brink of orgasm at least four more times, licking me, touching me, and teasing me with a vibrator. My thighs were damp with my need, and my sex was throbbing, the pressure building past anything I'd ever experienced before. If he made me wait too much longer, madness or violence was a distinct possibility.

But Lord, I loved every minute of this. Being under his hand was like experiencing life on a different plane. Every color was brighter, every sound amplified, every touch like sparks. I wished I could pull off the blindfold and look back at him, see that dark power that rolled off him in these moments. But tonight I sensed he needed the shield of the blindfold more than I did. There'd been a quiet intensity about him all day.

Tonight was more. But how exactly I wasn't sure.

I listened as Foster unzipped his pants and divested of his clothes— the room silent except for the popping logs in the fireplace. Then his hands were on me, spanning my hips, caressing me. He moved his palms along the curve of my ass, gently spreading me. "You have no idea how much I like seeing my marks on you, angel, what it does to me."

I let the small of my back dip low, lifting myself to his touch, loving the grit in his voice, the strain.

Breath tickled my damp sex and then his mouth was on me, tenderly licking along my sensitive folds. My body shook under the simple touch, orgasm coiling in me, ready to break free. But I forced it back, breathing deeply through my nose and rocking against my forearms. "Please."

He laid a wet kiss on my center, letting his tongue slide inside me, once, twice, then pulled back a second later as if knowing exactly how far he could push me without sending me over. "Such a patient girl. I think you need to be rewarded for that."

I sighed into the rug as he shifted behind me, my whole being readying for what I'd been dying for all night—Foster on me, inside me, overwhelming me. But instead of the head of his cock pressing against my cleft, the slick tip nudged my back entrance. I stiffened in surprise.

"Easy, angel," he said in that low, soothing voice of his. "We've been working up to this. You're ready tonight."

"Oh, God," I moaned as he rubbed the head over my pucker. He'd been teasing me back there, occasionally slipping a finger in or a small plug, but never had he tried to enter me. I'd been half-intrigued and half-terrified of it for a month now.

"You trust me?" he asked.

"Yes, sir," I said without hesitation.

"Then just breathe and push back against me. Your body will let me in."

"Okay," I said, sounding more confident than I felt. I did as he said, fighting hard not to brace myself and tense. I knew that would make it hurt. The head of his cock pressed against my ass, and I widened my knees. Resistance pushed back against him, and it felt like there was no way all of him was going to ever get past it, but then I took a deep breath and the thick head breached my entrance. A snap of discomfort went through me, the invasion so foreign, but then the lubricant went to work, easing his way, and he sank inside me. My eyes almost rolled back in my head with the intensely intimate feel of it.

"Fuck, you feel so good," Foster said on a groan, rocking into me oh-so gently. "So fucking perfect, angel. I'll never get tired of this, of feeling you around me, every part of you being mine, experiencing how beautiful you are when you let go."

Neither did I. And I couldn't imagine ever tiring of his touch. I'd worried early on that the thrill of this kind of relationship would wear off. That the dynamic could get old after the initial intrigue faded. But being with him like this was my escape. Even if I'd had a day of work at the ER vet clinic that had made me want to take up heavy drinking, I could go into this sacred space with Foster and all of that would fade away, leaving only the two of us.

I loved it.

I loved *him*.

Though I hadn't had the guts to admit how desperately yet.

He thrust into me again and I bit my lip, the sensation edgier and more intense than regular sex. Need built in me like a tsunami—looming there. I fought hard to hold back the tide, my fingers aching from my grip on the rug. But I knew I had only seconds of resistance left in me, especially with this bombardment of new sensation. It was too much, too good, too sweet. Foster slipped a hand onto my belly, angling me just right, brushing over my clit. The move seemed to send fire into my blood. I whimpered into the carpet, my brain going fuzzy with half-formed thoughts and fully formed desperation. "Foster, I can't . . . please, sir."

"Go for it, baby. Let me feel you come around me," he said, his voice belying his own dwindling control. He draped himself over my back, and reached around to remove the clamps.

The blinding rush of sensation returning to my nipples shot through me like lava, making me scream and collapse to the carpet, my arms trapped beneath me. Orgasm rumbled on the heels of the pain, bursting through and crashing over me. Sounds I didn't know I was capable of dragged from my throat.

"That's it, angel. Let it all go." Foster didn't break stride. He thrust into me with long, steady strokes, his body blanketing mine and stealing my breath in the best way possible.

I was pinned beneath him, writhing, helpless, his weight and motion dragging me against the shaggy carpet. The soft fibers teased my skin, tickling my clit and sensitized nipples, driving me past the point I thought I could take. I clawed at the edge of the rug, my noises and movements turning animalistic, primal. I couldn't stop it, couldn't do anything but let him have me.

Foster braced his forearms next to my head, and he rocked deep into me, his muscles tightening, his breath ragged in my ear. He was right there with me. Beyond control. Beyond restraint. Then his low, guttural moan twined with mine, and he was pulsing, his hot release jetting inside me.

And for that suspended moment, we were one—two bodies fused in the heady bliss of shared ecstasy. Two hearts . . .

I closed my eyes and rode the last waves of pleasure. Then, when my spasms finally quieted, I laid my cheek against the carpet and did the only thing my body could manage—I succumbed to the exhaustion.

My mind was drifting, my body surrounded by warmth and my limbs languid and heavy, like floating in a sea of gooey caramel. Lovely. I attempted to nestle deeper into the sensation.

"Cela?"

The voice seemed to come from both far away and inside my head at the same time. Was someone calling me? My lips parted to respond, to ask who was there, but instead everything came out muffled and slurred.

"You awake, angel?" a familiar voice asked, the words soft.

Foster.

That pulled me from my dream state, dragging me back to the memory of what had happened tonight. I blinked, trying to clear the fog in my brain, and the flickering orange glow of a fire filled my vision. "Maybe."

Foster, who'd apparently been stretched out along my backside with his arms around me, shifted from behind me and sat up, tucking me back into the cozy corner of the couch. He smiled down at me, pushing my hair off my forehead. "I was starting to worry you weren't going to wake up until our flight in the morning. Your parents already think I'm some crazed, obsessive boyfriend who stole you away. They would really hate me if I caused you to miss Christmas."

"You have no idea," I murmured, adjusting myself so I could sit more upright. I was wrapped tightly in a blanket, though I had no memory of how I'd ended up that way. Subspace, for the win. "Plus, Andre would kill me if I bailed. He's going to drop the I-kiss-boys-too bomb on them."

"I have a feeling lots of spiked eggnog will be consumed over this holiday."

"Count on it. But hey, we should thank him. It will take some of the spotlight off of us." I smiled. "I'm sorry I fell asleep, guess I was more exhausted than I realized."

"No, it's fine. I put you through a lot tonight. I think your body finally waved the white flag."

I rubbed my eyes and glanced around, trying to get my bearings now that I didn't have a blindfold on. But when I looked to the left, I had to do a double take. A wall of windows overlooking the slope of a hill and a moonlit lake beyond spanned the far side of the room. *What the hell?* The Ranch didn't have any hilltop cabins. I peeked behind me, finding an archway to a large gourmet kitchen. And they definitely didn't have cabins this modern or this big. Confusion swamped me. I turned back to Foster. "Where are we?"

He glanced toward the stretch of windows. "We're in a place I never thought I'd come back to again—the house my family moved to after Neve disappeared. I own it."

I raised my eyebrows. "You own a house?"

"Yeah, have for a few years. My parents left it to me when they built their place in Florida."

I let my eyes drift around the room, over the expensive furniture, the beautiful stonework around the fireplace, the polished wood floors. The place was gorgeous and, from the looks of the shadowed hallways, huge. "I think you could fit your entire apartment into this room alone. Why haven't you used it?"

He sighed. "It's a great house and view, but the times I spent here were some of my roughest—lonely years. I basically lived here with a rotating herd of paid caretakers while my parents traveled doing their charity work and chasing leads about Neve."

I frowned, reaching out for his hand, knowing that, though his parents were making an effort to build some sort of relationship with him again now, there were still decades of hurt to heal.

"The last Christmas I spent in this house, I was fifteen. We had this monster-sized tree. It touched the ceiling and had hand-painted ornaments from Paris. It could've been in a showroom or the centerpiece on some TV holiday special. Beneath it were enough presents to fill a dump truck. From the outside looking in, the place looked idyllic, like every kid's dream. But if I hadn't invited Pike over, I would've spent Christmas alone. My parents had a benefit in New York for their foundation. Pike and I spent the night getting drunk on peppermint schnapps while burning wrapping paper in the fireplace to watch the flame turn colors."

The sadness that crossed his face made my heart hurt for him all over again. My parents may have smothered me, but at least I was never short on attention or love. Christmas at my house was so full of people, there was hardly space to sit down. "Oh, Foster."

He turned back to me then, a resigned smile. "It's okay. I'm not telling you this so you feel sorry for me. Just explaining why I've let this place sit. A big, empty house filled with those kinds of memories was the last thing I wanted."

"I understand," I said softly. "But why are we here now?"

Foster brushed his knuckle along my cheek, watching me, studying. Debating. He frowned. "You asked me a few weeks ago what I wanted for Christmas, and I told you nothing, that I had everything I wanted."

I leaned into his touch, giving him a small smile.

"But I lied," he said, lowering his hand.

That gave me pause, a little pinch of worry, I tucked the blanket more tightly around myself. "Oh?"

"Yes. I know we promised to be completely honest with each other."

I nodded.

"But I've been failing you on that these last few months. Because what I've really been wanting is something more than I've asked for."

I wet my lips, my stomach dipping a bit at where his words could be leading. "Okay."

I could hear him take a long, deep breath, as if he needed extra oxygen to say what he needed to say. "I promised myself I wouldn't put pressure on you, wanted to give you time to explore this kind of relationship because you were so new to everything. I told myself it was to protect you, but really, it was to protect me."

I frowned, not understanding.

"I think part of me was always still waiting for the other shoe to drop, for everything to fall apart again. For you to change your mind and move on."

The insecurity in his words tugged at me. "Foster . . ."

"But I can't help how I feel, how you make me feel. And I'm done being chickenshit about it. What I really want for Christmas is to have you by my side every night . . ."

My brows knitted. "I'm at your place almost every night, or you're at mine."

He looked down at our linked hands, brushing a thumb over my knuckles, then raised his face to me. "I don't want to just date you. I know we haven't been together that long, but I also know what's in my heart. And what I think I see in yours. I want more with you. I want everything, Cela."

I blinked at him in the muted firelight. His expression was as stripped bare as I'd ever seen it. Vulnerable. Nervous. The sight made it hard for me to draw breath. I was so used to seeing the confident and collected Foster that this side was a revelation. He'd left his armor at the door tonight.

Then his request finally registered. *I want everything.* My voice shook a little when I managed to get words out. "What are you asking?"

"Exactly what you think I'm asking. But I'm not going to get on one knee yet. Know that I will, and I'd marry you tomorrow if you'd have me, but that's definitely a decision I'm not going to lay on you yet. We've got time for a ring. But as a start, I'm asking you to live with me, angel—here. I've had everything remodeled and updated. I want to build a life here with you. And I want you to wear my mark of ownership."

I stared at him, struck speechless by the requests. *Live with me. Wear my mark. One day wear my ring.* My heart knocked hard against my ribs. He was asking me to move in, to be his—forever, putting himself out there in a way I knew had to be punching old fear buttons for him.

So many things zipped through my mind—the sheer gravity of the decision, the implications, the permanence. For all these months, we'd spent so much time together, but we'd still kept some space. We would sleep over at each other's place, but not every night. And though I wore a collar when we made trips to The Ranch, it was only on during scenes. It was as if we were both playing with parachutes, always anticipating that one of us might jump off the plane.

If I said yes, I knew this would transform, deepen to a level I couldn't even fathom. I knew what Foster craved from me—a craving I'd felt blooming within myself with each passing week we were together. *Owned.* When I came home after work, I'd become his, my submission a daily gift. Even though I had let myself imagine it, fantasize about it, it was a lot to process. But as I closed my eyes and pictured what that life would look like—Foster and me sharing a home, the two of us facing the world together, intense nights of being under his command mixed in with days of being surrounded by his laughter and love—well, I couldn't quite access any fear over that.

Instead, like water rising in a well, an overwhelming surge of happiness spread within me, filling every nook, and threatening to burst through my pores. I knew all too well the sense of loss I felt when he unlatched my collar at The Ranch or when we had to part for the night.

In the beginning, the idea of true submission to Foster had scared me, had made me worry about putting myself in another suffocating situation like the one I'd grown up with. But my parents had controlled me through guilt and shame, and had used my natural urge to make those around me proud and happy against me. They'd let their love and overprotectiveness of me overshadow what may have been right for me.

But in my heart, I knew Foster would never take advantage of my desire to please that way. He'd been the one cheering me on these last few months while I went through my tough ER position. The one who'd held me when I lost my first patient in surgery. He wanted me on my own two feet in the world—strong, capable, successful. But behind closed doors, he wanted me under his care.

And I could think of no place I'd rather be.

"Foster," I whispered.

He leaned over to the coffee table to grab something, then squared himself toward me on the couch. In his hands, he held a small, flat box. I stared down at it, my breath quickening as he flipped it open. Inside lay a delicate choker-style necklace with a silver pendant in the shape of . . . a wing.

"I promise this one has no tracking device involved."

My lips lifted.

"I want you to be mine, angel."

Tears coated my throat, but I held them back, not wanting to taint the moment by crying. I reached out to trace the curve of the angel wing. It was a piece of jewelry I could wear out—a day collar—and no one would know what it meant. But I would. I'd be wearing his mark. And the thought made everything go warm inside me.

"If it's too soon or too much or you're not ready or you think I'm crazy or this house isn't what you . . ."

I grinned and raised my fingers, pressing them against his mouth. "Shut up, Foster. Nervous rambling is my job."

He smiled beneath my fingertips, but the worry still hovered at the corners of his eyes.

Seeing his uncertainty only made me fall for him more. His hard, dominant side spoke to me on an elemental level, but that tenderness beneath affected something much deeper, filled spaces and corners inside me. I held his gaze, lowering my hand and told him exactly what I'd been feeling for months. "Don't look so worried. You remember I'm in with love you, right? Like, stupid, crazy, drawing-hearts-in-my-journal in love with you. I want it all, too. Forever, Foster. Us. Like this."

He was silent for a moment, as if he hadn't heard anything I said. But then all the starch seemed to leave him.

"Thank God." He closed his eyes, his tense posture fully deflating before he opened them again. "I love you, too. So much. And I know what I'm asking is a big step. I know it's a lot."

I leaned back against the arm of the couch. "Yes, it *is* a big step. And if we're sticking to the honesty rule, I can say that I've never imagined wanting a relationship like this."

He nodded, going a bit somber, like he was anticipating the gauntlet.

I reached out and brushed my fingers against his stubble. "Not until you."

The beaming smile that broke through that five-o'clock shadow of his was bright enough to rival the moon outside. I'd never seen such a beautiful sight. My man, shirtless and grinning, his happiness like pure light. And now I was going to get to wake up every morning to his face, feel that love around me, and be his.

I let the blanket slip off my shoulders, not wanting anything between us, and climbed off the couch. I eased myself down to my knees, all the while holding Foster's eye contact. Then I lowered my head and presented my neck to him, the submissive move making me feel more in control of my life than I ever had before. Finally, I was on the path of my own choosing. "Merry Christmas, sir."

"Merry Christmas, angel."

He gathered my hair to lay it on one shoulder, and I felt the quiver in his hand, the depth of emotion behind the simple caress. And when he fastened the choker around my neck, and the cool curve of the angel wing touched my collarbone, a soul-deep, peaceful calm settled over me, leaving no doubt as to where I most wanted to be.

Never have I ever . . . been this happy.

Dear Reader,

When I'm writing books, there are always characters who pop up that weren't necessarily part of the plan. Or maybe they were planned to serve a specific purpose for the story, but I didn't expect them to demand more attention. My first experience with that kind of character was with Jace in Crash Into You. *He was only supposed to be the best friend—that's it. Then he showed up and tried to steal the show. So I gave that bossy man his own book in* Melt Into You.

But sometimes there are more minor characters who arrive on the scene that catch my interest as well. Once again, I have no plan beyond whatever purpose he or she is supposed to serve in the current book, but then I find myself wondering—hmm, what's his or her story? And this is what happened when I first wrote Bret, Foster's friend and private investigator.

Here was this woman who was tough, beautiful, and confident, but who also had this on-again, off-again dalliance with Foster. I couldn't help but wonder where the chink in her armor was. Clearly, she didn't have it all figured out. So I began to wonder what would happen to her after Foster and Cela fell in love. What would it be like to not have her friends-with-benefits arrangement with Foster? How would that affect her? And why was she having that kind of relationship anyway when it was obvious she was a domme at heart and ultimately incompatible with Foster?

That's where the idea for **"So Into You"** *came from. I wanted to know more about this woman. And based on reader emails, so did you! So this is Bret's story. Now you can see what happens with her after the end of* Not Until You.

I hope you enjoy seeing her pursue her own happy ending.
Thank you and happy reading!

Roni

CHAPTER 1

Bret peered down at the man kneeling at her feet. His head was bowed, and the long, lean lines of his bared back were offering her a lovely view. Julian really was a sight to behold. Gorgeous. Strong. And deeply submissive. Any mistress here at The Ranch would be thrilled to have him offer himself to her for the night. In fact, she knew based on the looks she and Julian were getting that a few of the other dommes in the room would happily take her down for the chance.

He should be perfect for Bret. Especially when she'd come out here with the express purpose of losing herself in a scene so she could forget the horrible few weeks she'd had.

Julian could heal all. He would let her be as mean as she needed to be to purge the demons. But when she imagined leading Julian to one of the playrooms, she couldn't find it in herself to muster up any excitement. And going into it without full anticipation wasn't fair to the man so generously offering himself.

She sighed and leaned over to grasp Julian's chin. She tipped his face toward her, finding his expression open as he awaited her instructions. Eager, willing, and sexy as shit. Goddammit, why couldn't she get her head together?

"I would be lucky to have you tonight, Jules," she said, giving him a small smile. "But I'm not in the right headspace to top anyone tonight."

His dark eyes flickered with disappointment. "Is there anything I can do to help, Mistress? I could find ways to get you in the right mind-set."

She released his chin and sat back in her chair, her shoulders feeling heavy. "I'm sure you could, hon. But really, right now, all I want is a drink. Is it true that there's a secret bar here where you can get more than a beer?"

Julian's brow arched. "Only the employee bar, Mistress. A domme snuck me in there once. But they don't let you play after you've had more than one."

"I don't think I'll be playing tonight. Can you bring me there?"

He stood and put out his hand. "I'd be honored."

She placed her hand in his and got out of the chair, the thigh-high boots she'd donned for tonight already starting to hurt. She should've stuck with her favorites instead of breaking in new ones tonight. Julian tucked her hand in the crook of his elbow and led her toward the door.

"This way, Mistress." The guy clearly knew the layout of the place better than she did, guiding her without hesitation. And after a flight of stairs and three turns, he escorted her to an unmarked door at the end of a hallway. She could hear the clink of glasses on the other side.

"This is it," Julian said, releasing her hand. "It's not too fancy in there, but the liquor's good."

She reached out and gave his arm a squeeze. "Thank you, Julian. I hope tonight works out better for you than it has so far. If it's any consolation, I think half the women in the common room are going to cheer when you walk back in without me."

He gave her a roguish smile, proving he knew exactly how tempting he was. "I'll still mourn the loss of a night with you, Mistress."

She smirked. "Good answer."

"Would you like me to bring you in?"

"No, I know we're not supposed to be in there. I don't want to get you in trouble. You can leave me now."

He gave a little nod, thanked her, and headed back down the hallway. She watched him leave with a wistful sigh. Damn, the guy was as nice to look at walking away as he was straight-on. Why couldn't she get it into gear tonight?

She pulled her gaze away from Julian and turned to open the door to the bar. The room on the other side was a good size and lively with chatter and laughter. Ranch employees were scattered around in small groupings at the tables. Some had changed into street clothes. Others were still in their fetish wear from the night. The whole place had a jovial mood.

It completely didn't fit Bret's state of mind. She wanted to drink and wallow. Where were the dark corners to sulk in?

She scanned the crowd. A few faces turned her way, but before anyone could tell her that she wasn't supposed to be there, she headed toward the long bar where she spotted a familiar face. She slid into the spot next to the hulking dark-haired man. "This seat taken?"

Colby Wilkes turned her way and tipped the bill of his ball cap up a little to look at her. His hazel eyes narrowed as if he were trying to place her.

"Bret," she offered.

Colby absorbed that then nodded. "I thought you looked familiar. Foster's friend, right?"

"Right." She smiled, though hearing Foster's name sent a pang of melancholy through her. The main reason her month had been so horrible had been because she'd finally helped solved the murder of Foster's little sister. The news had been devastating to her friend, but also to her. She'd worked the case for a long time, and even though she'd known it would take a miracle to find the girl alive, she'd harbored hope for better news anyway.

Colby motioned for the bartender and asked Bret what she wanted to drink. When she'd put her order in, Colby took a sip of his bourbon and turned back to her. "How's he doing? I heard about his sister. I can't even imagine how hard that's got to be on him."

She blew out a breath. "He's doing all right. That girl he's dating seems to be helping him through it."

"Cela," Colby supplied. "I met her. Young but sharp. She seems good for him."

Bret frowned and accepted her margarita from the bartender. "Yeah, fantastic."

The words came out more bitter than she'd planned, and Colby—Mr. Dom Trainer—didn't miss it. His lips lifted at the corner. "Not a fan?"

God, she'd probably sounded like a bitch. Her friend had found the love of his life—apparently—and here she was gnawing on sour grapes. "It's not that. I have nothing against her. And God knows, no one deserves to be happy more than Foster. It's just . . . he and I had a convenient arrangement. We were good stress relief for each other when we needed it."

And it kept her from torturing herself as much at work with the guy she really wanted. The occasional night with Foster took the edge off.

Colby sipped his drink. "You're both dominant. How was that convenient?"

She shrugged. "I don't know. I mean, that's why we never tried anything serious. We couldn't be what the other needed long-term. But after a shit week, it was sometimes fun to have someone to spar with in bed, fight for the control."

Colby chuckled. "Angry sex."

"Yes," she said, laughing a little. "It can be therapeutic."

"Interesting choice for a mistress. A sparring partner is not an obedient one. Do you switch?"

She sighed. "No. I've tried to bottom. Not for me. But I do have a really bad habit of being attracted to guys who are super alpha outside the bedroom."

"Ah," Colby said, and lifted his hand to let the bartender know he wanted another drink. "That makes it tougher. Though, I know a number of subs here who fit that bill. I can introduce you to a few if you want."

"How do you know I'm looking?" she asked, stirring her drink.

He gave her a wry smile. "You're at the biggest kink resort in North Texas and are hiding in the employee bar to drink. Things can't be going well out there."

"I'll have you know that a very willing Julian was at my feet a few minutes ago. I just wasn't in the mood." She sniffed. "And what are *you* doing in here? Don't you play for fun after your shift ends?"

His jaw twitched and he looked away, letting her know she'd hit some mark. "Nothing's holding my interest tonight. Or any night lately."

She raised her glass. "Join the club, big man. Wanna spar?"

He peered over at her, amusement in those hazel eyes. "You wouldn't be propositioning me, would you, Mistress? Because this bar is strictly a no-cruising zone. And we both know I'm not your type."

She groaned and tilted her head back. Of course, she knew that. Colby had a reputation for being a nice, laid-back guy, but in the dungeon he was about as dominant as they came. He didn't spar. He owned. "No one's my type."

Well, except for one guy. One who she'd freaked the fuck out the only time she'd tried something with him. One who she was steadily avoiding tonight because she was feeling lonely and stressed out, and that's when she couldn't trust herself to play it cool around him.

"So why'd you turn Julian down? That guy doesn't hear 'no' too often."

She shook her head, feeling completely worn out all of a sudden, and took a long draw of her margarita. "I don't even know. He has everything I thought I wanted tonight."

"Does he?" Colby considered her. "You don't strike me as a woman who's confused about what she wants. You strike me as one who's avoiding it."

She stiffened at that. "What do you mean?"

He drummed his fingers along his glass, his gaze not leaving her face. Damn, this man was unnerving. Fucking doms and their looks. "I have a feeling you know exactly what you want, or maybe who you want. But for some reason, you're trying to convince yourself otherwise."

"Not true. I came out here tonight for a fun time and no one caught my eye. That's all."

"Yet, when I offer to introduce you to some subs that fit your qualifications, you don't take me up on it. Why is that?"

She pressed her lips together.

He released a breath and gave her a small smile. "Look, I'm not trying to give you a hard time. And believe me, if we didn't play for the same team, I'd be more than happy to wipe that grim look off your face tonight. But life's too short to pine for someone. If it's Foster you're trying to get over—"

Ah, so that's the vibe he was picking up. "It's not."

"Oh?" His brow lifted. "But it's someone then?"

Damn. She would suck at poker. She'd walked right into that one. "No comment."

He nodded and pushed his chair out from the bar. "My advice? Not that you asked for it. But pining is a masochistic activity with no upside. I see the kids at the school where I work spend years doing that shit. And I see people doing it here. Don't torture yourself. You want someone, go for it. If they don't want you back, lick your wounds and move on."

She crossed her arms. "And if he lives in the vanilla world?"

Colby stood and tossed money on the bar for both of their drinks, then gave her an appreciative up-and-down perusal. "You're a beautiful, tough woman who knows how to bring a man to his knees and make him love being there. If the man you want isn't into that, then to hell with him. You're a gift a lot of very worthy guys here would kill themselves to unwrap. Don't put yourself on ice for some dude who can't appreciate that."

She smiled at that. "Is your world always so black-and-white, Colby Wilkes?"

He shrugged. "I guess it is."

She crossed her legs and leaned back in her chair. "You say that, but just wait until you fall for someone. Shit gets gray real fast."

His eyes crinkled at the corners. "Well, if that ever happens, maybe I'll come to you for advice."

She laughed. "Yes, because clearly I have it all figured out."

He gave a little tip of his ball cap. "Go get 'em, Mistress. And be sure to let me know if the poor guy survives the takedown."

She grinned, feeling much lighter than she had when she walked in there, the combo of Colby and tequila an effective cocktail. "I'll be sure and do that."

But as Colby walked away and she finished off her drink, the off-handed suggestion churned in her head, becoming more a possibility than a joke.

Go get 'em.

Could she?

She'd spent the last year working alongside the object of her torment. She'd played by the rules. She'd kept her mind off Malone as best she could with trips to The Ranch and occasional nights with Foster. Besides the one ill-advised drunken night when things had gone too far with Malone, she'd kept it professional. And after Malone had freaked out after said night, she'd kept it *really* professional.

But maybe it was time to take a chance. She'd caught her business partner sneaking glances at her on occasion when he thought she couldn't see. He wasn't immune to her—even if he might be a little scared of what he'd found out about her that night.

And she was damn tired of walking on eggshells around him and pretending nothing had ever happened.

Maybe Colby was right. The time had come to fish or cut bait.

And right now, Bret was in the mood to catch a really big fish.

CHAPTER 2

Malone leaned forward in his desk chair, sandwich forgotten in his hand, as he scanned through the cell phone records of his client's husband. He let his finger slide over the lines of numbers. The same one kept popping up late at night when her husband was on business trips.

He set his sandwich down and typed the number into his computer, but it came up unlisted. Nothing new. Everything seemed to be unlisted these days. He grabbed one of the disposable cell phones he kept in his drawer and dialed the number. No one picked up. A generic computer-generated voice mail came on and didn't list a name. He sighed and ended the call.

"Uh-oh, you're wearing your strikeout face this early in the day? Maybe I should've worked from home."

Malone barely glanced up as Bret strolled into the office, too distracted by the case in front of him, but then had to do a double take when he saw what she was wearing. Normally, his business partner stuck to the basic, blend-in clothes of a private investigator, understanding that most of the time their job was to be invisible. But today Bret looked like a blonde pinup stepping from the screen of some retro film.

Malone let his gaze trace over her sleeveless white blouse, tight red pants, and heels that looked impossible to walk in. *Jesus.* He set his sandwich down and grabbed his bottle of water, his mouth stark dry all of a sudden.

Bret slid her sunglasses up to the top of her head and flipped her long, blond ponytail over her shoulder. "So what's up, bossman? Still hitting dead ends on the Wickersham case?"

He cleared his throat, trying to get his thoughts back in order, and adjusted himself in his chair. "Yeah. I know the bastard's cheating. I just can't get anything solid enough for his wife to use in a divorce case."

"He'll screw up at some point. That guy's smart but not that smart. You'll find something."

Malone's eyes tracked Bret as she dropped her purse and keys onto her desk, the one across the room from his. The view from behind was impossible to turn away from—flared hips, perfect ass, and long legs looking even longer with those heels. She bent over to grab a piece of balled up paper that had fallen onto the floor, and his tongue pressed to the roof of his mouth.

When she straightened, she peeked back at him over her shoulder. "Throwing things already today?"

"That trash can is just too far way."

She flashed her smile, and he knew he had to be wearing some dumb look on his face.

God knows she was always easy to look at, but today something seemed different about her. It wasn't just the clothes. For the last few weeks, she'd seemed so drawn and defeated. The cold case she'd worked on for her friend had turned out tragic, and he knew it had been weighing heavy on her. He'd tried to give her space, but he'd been damn worried. Now it was like sunshine had spilled into the room.

"You look fresh and spry today," he said finally. "Caught up on sleep?"

Bret perched on the edge of her desk and crossed her legs, looking like a queen atop her throne. "Not really. Had a late night actually. But it's a beautiful day outside, and I've had two cups of coffee already. So I'm raring to go."

Late night. He knew what that probably meant, because she definitely hadn't been out late working. He knew the cases she was on, and they always checked in with each other if they were doing nighttime surveillance. No, she'd gone to that place. The one where she . . .

Malone shook the thought from his head. If he let his mind go off and imagine what Bret did at that kinky resort, he'd end up getting pissed off, turned on, or both.

Fucking hell.

He'd had this talk with himself way too many times. He should know the drill. No matter how attracted he was to his co-worker, nothing could happen between them. Besides the obvious awkwardness it could cause at work, Bret was into stuff that he couldn't really wrap his mind around. He didn't judge her for what turned her crank. In fact, he'd spent way too much time thinking about their night together when she'd showed him a glimpse of that side of herself. But he was a man of simple needs.

A beautiful woman, a bed, and enough time to drive that woman wild was all he required.

"So what's on your agenda today?" he asked, dragging his thoughts back to the present before they could wander too far. "Are you all set up for the Collins job this weekend?"

"I called to get room rates. And I have good news and bad news."

He tilted back in his chair. "Lay it on me."

She got up and headed to the coffeepot, giving him an unencumbered view of how her hips swayed on those heels. And there were no panty lines in those tight pants. *Fuck me.*

"Good news is that it's a couples-only weekend," she said, pouring herself a cup.

Couples weekend? He grinned wide. "Hot damn. That's as good as hanging a guilty sign around Mrs. Collins's neck. What's the bad news?"

She glanced back at him. "Bad news is that it's a couples-*only* weekend. If I go solo, I'm going to stick out."

Malone frowned. "So find a date who wants a free vacation to Mexico and take him with you. Mr. Collins is paying us enough to cover the extra expense."

She gave him an oh-aren't-you-cute smile. "Mal, if I take a date with me to a couples resort in Mexico, he's not going to want to tag along as I surveil a cheating wife. This is a business trip. I should take my business partner."

He lifted his eyebrows. "You want *me* to go?"

They hadn't done a job together since . . . well, since the night he'd drank a little too much whiskey and embarrassed himself with her. "I don't think that's necessary. I have stuff here—"

"You have stuff that can wait a few days. And if we're both there, it gives us two sets of eyes. We can split up when we need to and have a better chance at getting what we need. This case is paying a lot, and you know we haven't given her husband anything worth a damn yet."

"Bret—"

"And this place is swank, Mal. Even if we're going to be working, I think we both could use a little sun and sand. It's been a bitch of a summer, and we've both been killing ourselves taking on extra cases. This job doesn't come with many perks, so we need to take them where we can. Don't you want a break? I definitely could use one."

Well, hell, when she looked at him like that, it was hard to shut her down. He'd seen how much she'd run herself down over the last few months, and the hopeful look in her eye was too much for him. He sighed. "Maybe I could move a few things around."

Her face brightened. "Do it. You know you need this as much as I do. Think of the margaritas."

"No margaritas," he said firmly. Last thing they needed in the mix again was alcohol. Not that liquid help was necessary to get himself in trouble with his siren of a coworker. One faulty step, and he'd fall in the pit. He ran a hand over his face. Three nights in a luxe resort on the beach with Bret Langdon? He may not survive the weekend. But he couldn't find the words to back out of it.

"Why are you so hard to say no to, woman?"

She grinned and gave a little bow. "It's a gift."

Of that he had no doubt.

He remembered how he'd felt that night on his knees for her. There hadn't been much he hadn't been willing to do to put that wicked smile on her face.

But he also remembered how he'd felt the next morning. And he never wanted to feel that way again.

Then he'd been a dick and lied to her like a fucking coward. Pathetic.

No way would he put either of them through that again. He would go on this business trip with her—keyword: *business*—and keep his thoughts and his hands to himself.

———

Malone was suffering. There was no question in Bret's mind as she bent down to dig through the bottom file cabinet. Those dark blue eyes of his kept sliding her way every few minutes, and his jaw had yet to unlock. She was kind of enjoying it.

She knew she'd thrown Mr. Stoic for a loop earlier. First with her outfit, then with her invitation. But she'd decided she was tired of playing this game with him. She had no idea how much he remembered of their one night together, but she suspected he remembered more than he was letting on. She'd never known the former solider to have a bad memory. The man could remember cases from years ago with amazing clarity. But what she didn't know was how he really felt about that night—about her.

She knew her preferences in the bedroom weren't for everyone. And she'd never want to push that on anyone. She'd already accepted that most guys weren't down with giving the power over to the woman in bed. And really, she hadn't expected Malone to be into it either. He was a guy who loved control. It was why she called him bossman even though they were technically equal partners in this business. The man had been a sergeant in the Army and pretty much went through life assuming everyone else was a soldier who needed guidance until they proved otherwise.

But that night, they'd both been loose-lipped from a rough night and too many drinks, and she'd seen a side of him that she hadn't been able to get out of her mind since.

That big, finely-sculpted body laid out on the bed before her, hands cuffed to the headboard. Those hard-to-read blue eyes as heated as she'd ever seen them. And the look on his face that said he was all hers in that moment.

Damn. Her body was already revving up thinking about it.

She straightened, smoothing her pants, then walked over to her desk, hoping her expression didn't reveal her less-than-PG thoughts.

She dropped the file on top of her desk and slid into her chair. Malone looked to be concentrating way too hard on his computer screen. She grabbed a piece of scrap paper, balled it up, and launched it at him. Without looking her way, his hand jerked upward and he caught the paper before it hit his head. Damn, the man had quick reflexes. He turned his face toward her, those dark eyebrows lifting. "Never give up, do ya?"

"I'll land one. I just need to catch you when you're more distracted."

He smirked. "Darlin', with you prancing around here in that outfit, I'm not sure I can get more distracted."

Well, then. She sat up taller in her chair and popped the collar of her blouse. "You like?"

"I'm breathing. And male. So, yeah." He shifted in his chair, those broad shoulders looking even more tense than they had a few moments ago. "Got a hot date tonight or something?"

She schooled her expression into impassivity. "No."

"Left it all on the court last night, huh?"

She smiled sweetly. She and Malone ended up talking like two bros more often than was probably healthy, but she knew this innocuous question wasn't simply making conversation this time. She'd gotten to him today. "Wouldn't you like to know."

He grunted and turned back to his computer as if he could care less, but she didn't miss the scowl that had crossed his face.

"Come on, Mal. Don't pretend like you're not curious. Everyone wants to be a fly on the wall at The Ranch—even the most vanilla souls out there wouldn't pass up the chance to peek inside those doors."

Malone's fingers banged along the keyboard—*click, click, click.* "I don't need to know your private business, Bret. As long as it doesn't interfere with your job, I don't care what you do with your personal time."

She pressed her lips together. God damn, he was a hardheaded man. "Of course, forgive me for being so *wildly* unprofessional."

He snorted. "Like that's ever stopped you before."

Oh, he had no idea how unprofessional she was about to get. She opened up the website for the Grand Riviera Resort on her computer and clicked through to the reservations and the special convention rates. She made a few selections and got a rush of nerves when the confirmation message popped up.

Thank you for reserving a room with the Grand Riviera. We hope you enjoy your stay in paradise.

Paradise.

Maybe it would be. Or maybe she'd completely humiliate herself and be looking to sell off her half of the business by Monday.

Either way, she'd deal with it.

She'd learned early on in life that the meek may inherit the earth, but they rarely got what they wanted. She'd spent her childhood and teenage years shrinking back, too scared to stand up for herself. She wasn't that frightened girl anymore, and she was pissed at herself for letting this situation with Malone go on so long. Like Colby had said, life was too short to pine.

Paradise, here we come.

CHAPTER 3

Malone's gaze followed the two men walking hand-in-hand through the lush, tropical-themed lobby of the Grand Riviera Resort. One was dressed in cargo shorts and a button-up top but the other one was shirtless and wearing the smallest bathing suit bottoms Malone had ever seen. And that wasn't all he was wearing. There was a very obvious leather band around the guy's neck . . . a collar. It was the second one Malone had seen since standing here in the lobby waiting for Bret to get their room keys.

Malone moved his attention back to his companion. He nudged Bret's arm when the front desk lady left for a second to get their welcome package. "Bret."

She glanced over at him with a smile. "Yes, dear?"

He gritted his teeth. She'd been calling him that since they got off the plane. *To stay in character,* she'd said. But he wanted to tell her that if she were his woman, the last thing she'd be inspired to call him was *dear.* It sounded so boring and lame. Like they were an old couple whose idea of excitement was doing crosswords while watching *Wheel of Fortune.* But hell, maybe in her eyes he was that boring. *Vanilla.* That's what she'd called him the other day. The label had annoyed the shit out of him.

"Is there some sort of convention or event going on here that I'm not aware of?" he asked.

She lifted a brow. She was good at that—the intimidating brow lift. Like a drill sergeant who somehow knew without seeing that you'd broken a rule. "What do you mean?"

He nodded discreetly toward the gay couple he'd noticed a few seconds before. The fully clothed guy was now talking to a hotel employee while the collared man hung back a few steps.

Bret peered over her shoulder, and a little smile touched her lips. She turned back to him. "There's not a gay event happening, if that's what you're worried about."

"I'm not—" Goddammit. A gay event was the least of his worries. "It's not that."

"No?" she asked. "Because you, Mr. Military Man, could certainly turn a few of their heads. I know you hate being the center of attention."

"I don't fucking care about that. But the guy's wearing a—"

"Here you go, Miss Langdon," the front desk lady crooned in her heavily accented English as she returned to her post carrying a black gift bag. A little silver symbol that looked similar to a yin-yang was embossed on the side of it. "This is included with your stay this week."

Bret took the gift bag. "Thank you."

"And the itinerary for all the different events and workshops is in here." She handed Bret a folder. "The beach by your cabana is private and has an open dress code."

Malone's brain snagged on that last bit. Open dress code? What the fuck was that supposed to mean? The niggling feeling in the back of his head was turning into a loud, bellowing shout.

Bret listened to a few more things the lady had to say then thanked her and took the room keys. She turned to him, all bright eyes and blond hair. "Ready, dear?"

"Bret, you keep calling me that and I swear—"

"Oh, shit," she said, cutting him off, her gaze homing in on something behind him. "Don't look now but our target is walking right this way."

Malone forgot what he was going to say, all focus shifting to the job at hand. They'd been trying to catch Mrs. Collins in the act for months now. Her husband was the nicest guy you could ever meet, and though he was obviously suspicious, Malone could tell the man was hoping against hope that his worries about his wife were unfounded. Malone felt for the guy. He knew what a shitty feeling it was to be cheated on by someone you thought you were going to spend your life with. He could still remember sitting in that car watching his now ex-wife, Margaret, as she led her lover into the house that Malone had paid for.

"Is she with someone?" Malone asked, keeping his voice low.

Bret stepped closer to him, probably to make it look like they were in some intimate conversation, but her blue eyes were shrewd as she watched their target over his shoulder. And in that moment, Malone couldn't help but notice how beautiful Bret was when she went into investigator mode. Bret could drive him nuts, tease him without mercy, and push his buttons, but she was as good of a PI as he'd ever seen. She could make herself invisible, play a role when needed, and dog a case relentlessly until she got exactly what she needed.

The girl didn't give up.

Bret wet her lips and leaned in close to his ear. To an outsider, it'd look like she was being flirty with him. His body wanted to react that way, too, when her breath brushed his neck, but he somehow kept his expression smooth. "She's alone, but is looking around the lobby, like she's expecting to find someone. We need to wait her out. I'm going to guide you against the wall a few steps behind you. Once you're against it, she's going to be in your view. Can you keep a bead on her while I make it look like I just can't wait until we get to the room?"

Malone nodded and cleared his throat. He knew this was going to be part of this weekend. Had prepared himself. Well, as much as he could. "Go for it."

She glanced up at him with those big blue eyes, as if checking that his expression matched his words. Then she slid her hands up his chest, the small gift bag swinging from one, and stepped farther into his space. He could feel the heat of her through his T-shirt and had to fight the urge to grab her and haul her fully against him.

"Here we go," she said softly. She gave him a little push with her hands, and he backed up the few steps until he felt the wall behind him. She set the hotel gift bag down by his feet. "You see her? She's in the white blouse and pink capris."

Malone was having a hard time pulling his attention away from Bret, especially when she let her hands drift lower, dragging her nails

along the sides of his abdomen. Fuck. He forced his focus to the bus-
tling lobby. Thankfully, the pink pants were hard to miss. "Got her."

Mrs. Collins did another scan of the lobby, brushed her hair off her
face with a little huff, and then rolled her suitcase toward the check-in
desk, making a beeline for the open spot he and Bret had just vacated.
Her heels clicked against the marble, her gaze swiveling back and forth
as she walked. Her attention landed on Malone and Bret.

Malone lifted his hand and wrapped it around the back of Bret's
neck, tilting her face toward him. He smiled down at her, giving her his
best bedroom eyes.

"Company?" Bret asked, her instincts always spot-on.

"Mmm-hmm." He let his fingers drift through the silky strands of
her hair, enjoying it maybe a little too much.

"Can you tell me if Stephen Miller has checked in yet?" Mrs. Collins
asked primly.

The front desk clerk frowned. "I'm sorry, ma'am, we can't release
guest information. Are you on the reservation?"

"No," Mrs. Collins said, clearly annoyed. She looked over her shoulder. "Oh, never mind, there he is."

Malone's attention swept toward the lobby, where a man in a linen
suit lifted a hand in greeting to Mrs. Collins. Bingo.

Bret smiled up at him, having obviously heard the conversation and
read the victory on Malone's face. "We got her?"

"About to." Malone dipped his hand in his pocket and pulled out his
phone. He quickly swiped it to camera mode and wrapped his arm
around Bret, aiming just so.

But right as he was posed to snap, Mrs. Collins glanced his way
again, eyes narrowing ever so slightly. Ah, shit. He and Bret had been
following her for over three months now. And there was a distinct possibility that the overly cautious Katrin Collins recognized him. He
always did his best to blend in. But Mrs. Collins's eyes had landed on
him once at the mall when he'd been following her. She'd given him a
once-over and an overly generous smile. He knew that kind of smile—
Hiya, sergeant. I'd love to thank you for your service. He'd turned into a
store, pretending not to have noticed.

But this lady wasn't dumb. She'd evaded getting caught in the act for months. And no one did that without being overly paranoid. He needed to act fast.

Malone peered down at the woman in his arms, changing the plan on the fly. "Kiss me and make it last."

Bret's eyebrows shot upward. But to her credit, she trusted him enough not to hesitate. She moved her hands up to cup his jaw, pushed up on her toes, and pressed her mouth against his.

The instant their lips met, Malone forgot what he was supposed to be doing. His eyes fell shut, and he gathered Bret tighter against him. Her body molded to his, and she made a little sound, her lips parting with it. Not considering what a bad idea it was, he let his tongue slide inside. She tasted like some fruity gum and . . . Bret. He could remember those hot, hungry kisses they'd shared that night, remembered how powerful the chemistry had been.

His grip tightened against the nape of her neck and his tongue stroked against hers with an urgency he couldn't help. He felt like a dehydrated man who'd found a spring. He wanted to mainline her. Her fingers slid into his hair and held tight, the hold possessive and needy. *Christ.* He had the urge to reach down and lift her up, wrap her legs around him, and carry her off somewhere to really do this. But when he shifted his other arm, he felt the phone still clenched in his hand.

Motherfucker.

That's when he remembered this wasn't a passionate, take-me-to-bed kiss with a lover. This was Bret and he was supposed to be getting a shot of their target. He could hear Mrs. Collins and her companion still talking with the front desk attendant. Still time.

Malone kept his lips moving, but found the button on the side of his phone with his finger. Dragging the phone higher up Bret's back, he clicked as fast as the thing would let him, shifting the phone position a little each time, hoping against hope that he'd grab a usable shot.

But when Bret nipped at his bottom lip, he lost all hope of concentrating on the job. He gave his full attention over to her and kissed her like she was the last woman on earth he'd ever get to kiss. But when he groaned into it, she broke away, leaving him gasping.

Her eyes were unreadable when she looked up at him, but her lips were puffy and wet and perfect. "Did it work?"

The kiss? Oh yeah, that had worked. He could feel it working right now behind his goddamned zipper. But he knew that wasn't what Bret was asking. He looked over to the desk and Mrs. Collins was gone. "I hope so. I snapped as many photos as I could, but I was doing it blind."

Bret peeked over her shoulder. Another couple was stepping up to the desk, and the woman sent Malone and Bret a knowing smile—one that said she'd seen their little show. "Hard to not get caught up in it all this weekend, huh? It's like they put something in the air."

Bret laughed, the sound light and airy. "I know what you mean. I can't keep my hands off this one."

The woman gave Malone an appraising look. "Can't blame you there."

Malone knew the surprise had to show on his face when the woman openly checked him out. The guy she was with didn't bat an eye.

"Are you two doing any group activities while you're here?" the woman asked.

Bret turned and took Malone's hand, coming around to stand beside him. "I think I'm keeping him all to myself for the weekend. But maybe we'll see y'all around."

The woman smiled good-naturedly. "I'm sure we will. You guys have fun."

"Same to you," Bret said.

And Malone didn't miss that the woman hadn't talked to him directly at all. He was like a piece of furniture they'd been discussing. Bizarre.

Bret gave his hand a squeeze. "Ready to check out our cabana, baby?"

Baby.

He smiled. Well, at least the kiss had shown her he was no fucking *dear.*

"Lead the way."

Something flashed in her gaze—worry? But whatever it was, she covered it quickly with a bright smile. "Gladly."

CHAPTER 4

Bret was a pro at keeping her cool. But on the way to the cabana, she felt anything but. Up until this point on the trip, she'd kept her poise. She'd prepared herself for how very wrong this could go—had accepted the calculated risk. But now the man strolling beside her had unraveled her with that damn kiss. Now she knew for sure that if this blew up in her face, she wouldn't walk away unscathed. That kiss had reminded her of every single thing that had been wrong with her hookups over the last year.

Malone lit a fire in her that no one else did. Even her encounters with Foster didn't light up her switchboard like that. This man did something to her. And now that old dread of rejection was pulsing in her gut. Because there was a very high probability that when Malone found out why she'd really wanted him here this weekend, he was going to go right back the airport.

"Hot damn," Malone said from beside her as he swiped through the pics on his phone. "I got one."

He showed her the screen. On it, Mrs. Collins's companion had his arm around her and his hand parked on her ass. Her face was clearly recognizable in profile. Bret grinned. "Score."

"Bigger score than you think, darlin'." He swiped his thumb across the screen a few times then stopped.

Bret stopped walking and took the phone from him, angling it out of the sunlight to make sure she was seeing what she was seeing. "Is that—?"

"Our illustrious state representative Ted Dower? The one who Mr. Collins is always disparaging in the paper? Why, yes, it is."

"Holy shit. No wonder she's been so stealthy." All this time she'd been having an affair with the man her political reporter husband was trying to bring down.

"Stealthy and gullible," Malone said.

"Right?" Bret handed the phone back and shook her head as they started to walk again. "I hope the woman hasn't convinced herself that this is some love match. The guy's obviously getting his rocks off by fucking the enemy's wife. He probably reads those news stories Harry Collins writes while the man's wife is sucking him off."

Malone sniffed.

"What?"

He smirked. "Nothing. You're just such a delicate southern belle sometimes, it overwhelms me."

Her jaw snapped shut, and even though she knew Malone hadn't meant it maliciously, the barb landed square. She knew she had a locker-room mouth and a tomboy mentality. Growing up with three brothers hadn't given her a chance at delicate southern belle. And she didn't want to be that anyway. Fuck delicate. But hearing it from Malone stung more than it should.

"Sorry, I left my parasol and hoop skirt on the plane. I'll try not to offend your *gentlemanly* sensibilities in the future," she said peevishly as they turned onto the boardwalk that led to the private cabanas.

They walked for another few seconds, the cabanas coming into view, and she could feel Malone giving her the side-eye. He sighed. "Come on, Bret. You know I'm only teasing. I'm used to how you are."

"How I *am*?" She bent down to slip off her sandals before they took the last step down to the beach. She couldn't even enjoy the pristine ocean view. "And how is that, exactly?"

He grimaced at her tone as he kicked off his flip-flops and leaned down to grab them. "Come on, you know what I mean."

She stepped in front of him and turned, blocking his way to the beach. "No, maybe I don't. Maybe you should inform me so that we're on the same page."

She knew she was turning on the bitch switch, but she couldn't help herself. All the stress and nerves for this trip were coalescing into a ball of confused emotion and defensiveness.

He sighed and ran a hand through his hair, looking supremely uncomfortable. Those wary eyes of his reflected the bright blue skies above and turned them stormy. He gestured toward her. "Seriously, Bret? You know how you are. You hone that image. At work, you're the badass girl who dares people to mess with her. At night, you're the untouchable siren who makes men beg for the privilege of being with you. You can be goddamned intimidating and you like it that way. You want people to be a little scared of you."

She swallowed past the lump building in her throat. "It's not that."

"No?" He shook his head and scoffed. "Take this trip for example. You don't tell me a goddamned thing about it. Then we show up and there's clearly some kinky convention going on here, and we're staying on what I'm assuming is a nude beach, and you want to leave me wondering. Obviously, you're trying to freak me out or pay me back for what happened last summer."

"You think I'm out for *revenge*?" she asked, louder than she intended. He lifted a brow.

"Jesus, Malone. Glad you think so highly of me."

"Well, goddammit, woman, if that's not the case, then what the fuck are you trying to do? Why wouldn't you just tell me what's what here before we came? I'm a big boy. I can handle some X-rated resort. God knows I've seen it all in this job. I'm not some blushing virgin. But there's nothing I hate more than being in the dark and looking like the only dumb asshole who isn't in on the secret."

She put her hand to her forehead and released a long breath. "Fine. This isn't just a couples weekend. It's an adults-only resort—an anything goes place. And yes, there is kink here if you want it. I signed up for that package—hence the little black bag."

He stared at her for a long moment. "Why would you do that?"

Why, indeed. She waved a dismissive hand. "Never mind. It doesn't matter. Can we just get to our room? I'm tired and cranky, and all I want to do is lie down."

Deep frown lines appeared. "Bret—"

But she was already turning on her heel and stalking through the sand in search of cabana number fourteen. The bag of what was sure to be kinky swag swung in her hand, mocking her and her ridiculous plan. This had been such a bad idea.

She was doing that thing she did—trying to fit square pegs in round holes, trying to make life adjust to what she wanted instead of accepting what was. The world is what you make it—yeah, that was bullshit. The world was what it was, and you had to find a way to wedge yourself into a place that didn't hurt too much. She'd never fit in quite right. And here she was trying to shove a perfectly decent man into a spot that wasn't shaped like him.

Maybe they should just take a nap and then turn around and go home. They had a photo good enough to give Mr. Collins. Job done. No need to drag it out. They had no place being here this weekend. She'd be frustrated, and Malone would be uncomfortable. Even the spectacular beach view couldn't fix that.

She found their cabana, which was a cute blue stucco hut with a thatched roof. It was rustic on the outside, as the resort boasted their eco-friendly accommodations, but she knew the inside would be built for luxury. She put the key in the lock and pushed the door open. Sure enough, the inside was all buttercream-colored walls, dark wood furniture, and panoramic beach views. Against the back wall there was a big four-poster bed with fluffy white linens and wispy sheer material strung from the posts.

Beautiful. Sexy. Romantic.

Useless.

Malone, who'd only been a few steps behind her, stopped in the doorway. "Wow. This is—"

"Expensive," she finished, dropping the black bag and her purse on the couch in the living area. "We can check out in the morning and save Mr. Collins the expense of another two nights. We have what we need."

"Wait, what?" Malone said, shutting the door behind him. "We just got here and now you want to leave?"

"We came here to work. We have the pictures. We're done."

Malone's expression darkened to thunderstorm status as he looked at her. "So that's how you're going to play this?"

She crossed her arms. "Who said I was playing anything?"

"You're not playing—" That seemed to snap what little patience he had left. He stalked forward and she backed up a step, her thighs hitting the couch. He pinned her with that gaze of his. "Why did you bring me here, Bret?"

She wet her lips. "To work."

His eyes narrowed. "Try again. Why did you bring me here?"

Her heart was beating way too fast. She'd never seen Malone look so on the edge. "It really is couples only."

"No, Bret." He grasped her wrist and pulled her closer. "Stop with the bullshit. *Why* did you bring me here?"

"Fuck, Malone. You seem to have it all figured out, so why don't you inform me?"

"Because I need to hear it from you," he said, his voice going low, challenging. "Come on. Say it. I've never known you to be a coward."

Well, that just pissed her off. She stiffened her spine and sent him the look she knew had cowed many a submissive at The Ranch. "Fine. You want to know? I brought you here because I'm stupid. Because I thought if maybe I got you away from the office, we could be real and deal with what happened last summer. Because if you want to talk about bullshit, let's do that." She poked a finger to his chest with the hand he didn't have a hold of. "Bullshit is waking up the morning after to a guy who's claiming the drunk defense and pretending he doesn't remember what happened. Bullshit is him forgetting that at least while it was happening, he liked it. That the girl who did those things with him, *to* him, wasn't fucking taking advantage of some poor, defenseless, drunken soul. You know what that feels like, Mal? To take a chance and show some secret part of yourself to someone you care about and have him pretend like he doesn't even remember?"

He winced. "Bret—"

"I mean, at least have the balls to own up and tell me it wasn't your thing or that you're just not into me and be done with it. But pretending like it never even happened—"

"I couldn't—" His grip on her wrist tightened, drawing her an inch nearer. "I couldn't tell you that."

They were too close now. She could smell the soap he used and was having trouble concentrating. "Yes, you could've. You said it yourself—I'm tough. I can take it."

His jaw flexed. "I couldn't tell you those things because I'm not sure they're true."

She met his gaze at that. "What?"

He blew out a breath and released her wrist. But he didn't move away. "I do remember that night, Bret. Believe me. If put on a witness stand, I could detail the events blow by blow."

She smirked. "Well, there *was* blowing involved."

He gave her a warning look, but humor softened some of the tension in his face. "Yes, I remember that part particularly well. But I can't lie. That whole night confused the shit out of me. It was hot and intense, and if I think about it too long, it drives me to distraction. Sometimes I can't even look your way in the office without it coming to mind. But I also know you only gave me a glimpse of what you're into. And I'm not scared of you, but your world intimidates me. I don't know the first thing about how to navigate it. I'm used to knowing what I'm doing with a woman." He raked a hand through his hair, looking a little lost. "But I have no idea what the fuck I'm doing when it comes to you."

She stared at him, knocked off balance by his confession. "What would you do if I was any other woman you were attracted to?"

His eyes met here. "Like right now?"

"Yes."

"I would kiss you until neither of us could see straight and then toss you onto that bed over there. But I'm not going to do that."

"Why not?"

"Because I'm not taking you to bed again if I know I can't be the kind of guy you need. I don't want another one-night stand with you. It's not fair to either of us. The one we had has already done enough damage to our friendship. We can't keep playing this game."

She nodded. On that she agreed. "You're right. I'm sorry. This whole thing was a bad idea from the start."

"No." He put his hands on her upper arms, making her look up at him again. "This was the right idea."

"What?"

"I'm tired of wondering if that night was a fluke or if there's more to it. It's driving me fucking crazy. *You're* driving me crazy."

"But—"

"The other day when you walked into the office and told me you'd had a late night at that place you go to . . ." He shook his head. "I couldn't block out the image of what you must be like there. And I found myself not just curious, but damn jealous of whatever lucky fucker had caught your attention that night."

She bit her lip to hide her smile and looked down. Little did he know the only one on her mind that night had been him.

He put his fingers beneath her chin and tilted her face up toward him. "I can't stand here and make you promises because I don't know if I can be what you need. But tonight . . . I'm willing to try."

She blinked, the offer taking her by surprise. If anything, she'd expected him to try to sway her to his way of doing things. "You're . . . you're willing to try submission?"

He cupped her face with his hands, his eyes searching hers. "You were a siren that night, darlin'. Drunk, sober, or anywhere in between, I wouldn't have been able to resist you. I can't even tell you how that image of you looming over me with that look in your eye has haunted me. I go hot just thinking about it."

"Yeah?" she said, hearing the hope in her own voice.

"Yeah." He gave her a wry smile. "You don't even want to know what my computer search history looked like the few weeks afterward. I wanted to find out as much as I could about where you were coming from."

A flash of horror went through her. "Oh, God, you googled *kink*?"

He chuckled and pressed his forehead to hers. "I did. And let's just say there are some things that can't be unseen."

She laughed, her mood lifting as she imagined the things that had probably come up in that search and Malone's reaction. "Jesus, no wonder you're so terrified. If it makes you feel any better, I'm not out to do hard-core torture on your man parts or anything."

He lifted his head and grimaced. "Happily noted."

"But I do like the power, Mal," she said, not wanting to sugarcoat things. "And some of the pain stuff. And I'll want to tie you up eight ways to Sunday."

The flare of interest in his eyes was hard to miss. "I guess it's okay that I don't fully understand why hearing you say that makes me hot."

She smiled. "You don't always have to have an explanation for everything, soldier. Sometimes things just are. And sometimes they aren't. If we do this, I only ask for one promise from you."

"And what's that?"

"That when it's all over with, you're honest with me. And if we're really not compatible like this, we close that door for good. I'm not a masochist, and neither of us deserves that kind of torture."

"Deal." He cupped her jaw and leaned down to kiss her, but she lifted her hand and put her fingers against his lips before he got there.

"Not so fast, soldier," she said, giving him a pointed look. "You're going to have to earn that kiss this time."

He lifted his brows, but then it clicked. He gave a little nod, and she lowered her hand. "Then I guess you'd better tell me what to do . . ."

"Mistress," she supplied.

His gaze sparked at that. "Of course, *Mistress*."

The way he said it with that slow, sweet southern drawl promised so many kinds of sin that she didn't even know where she wanted to start.

All she knew was she wasn't going to rush this. Tonight might be her last time with Malone. There were no guarantees that he'd be into it. But she certainly could make sure neither of them would forget it.

CHAPTER 5

Malone had never seen so much flesh all in one place before. The mixer Bret had insisted they go to after dinner was packed with people who were wearing every type of fetish wear he could imagine—and some he definitely wouldn't have been able to imagine. As views went, it was definitely an entertaining one. But hell if he could focus on any of it. Not with Bret sitting next to him.

Bret had changed out of her flowery sundress and into a snug black skirt, a red blouse, and knee-high leather boots. As outfits went, it was something she could get away with in public. In fact, she'd gone to dinner wearing it. But goddamn, Malone hadn't been able to stop staring like a fool. She was always beautiful, but seeing her in that outfit with her blond hair pulled back into a long ponytail and her makeup more pronounced had created images he couldn't shake from his head. This was her version of lingerie. This was her uniform. And something about the clothes shifted not just her look but her attitude. Mistress Bret.

The last time they were together had been spontaneous. She'd shown him a peek of this side of herself, but never had he seen her in full mistress mode. It truly was something to behold. His funny, laid-back business partner was even more of a siren than he'd imagined. And if the looks they were consistently getting from others attending the party were any indication, he hadn't been the only one to notice. He tended not to be the jealous type, but every man who looked Bret's way with hopeful eyes had Malone wanting to throw down and stake his claim.

Bret reached for his hand beneath the table and gave it a squeeze. "Doing okay over there, soldier?"

He sniffed. "Just trying to talk myself out of beating the ass of that dude who keeps making laps in front of us and sending you those *how-you-doin'* looks. Can't he see I'm sitting right here?"

Bret laughed softly. "Well, he *is* being more bold than he should, but the two of us might be confusing him. He probably thinks we're both dominants looking to hook up with someone tonight."

Malone frowned. "Why would he think that?"

She shrugged and adjusted her ponytail. "Because you're not wearing anything indicating you're my submissive. And you're sitting there, looking all bad-ass-in-charge."

He glanced down at his crossed arms and wide-kneed position. And, of course, he hadn't worn anything outrageous. Dark jeans and an army green T-shirt were about as wild as he got. "If you're expecting me to parade around in vinyl and assless chaps, this is going to be a short night."

She snorted and gave him a come-on-now look. "Mal, despite what you may think, I want to do this with you because you're *you*. I'm not trying to change you into something you're not. And assless chaps you are not. Though, I do own a pair for me."

"You—Ah, fuck," he said, that image burning up his brain. This woman was going to be the death of him. He was never going to be able to think a non-X-rated thought again. "And what's a guy got to do to be granted that gift from the gods?"

Her lips curved. "Be a very good boy."

He leaned forward, giving her his own slow smile. "I bet I can be the best."

She arched a brow. "Is that right?"

"You know I don't make a habit of doing things halfway."

She considered him, the wheels obviously turning. "Well, in that case, I do have one thing I'd like you to wear for me."

The comment caught him off guard, but he nodded. He didn't make wagers he couldn't pay up on. "What's that?"

She reached into the bag she'd brought with her and pulled out a simple strip of black leather—a collar. She set it on the table between them. "I'd like to make everyone aware that you're mine for the night, so that they back the fuck off—especially that chick two tables over."

"What?" He turned his head toward the crowded room. "Who?"

"In case you haven't noticed, there've been a few people looking your way, too." She cocked her head to the left. "The pretty redheaded sub over there has been eyeing you for the last ten minutes. If you walked over to her table, she'd probably happily get on her knees for you. She thinks you're a dom."

He surreptitiously peered that way. And sure enough, the woman in question was looking right at him. When she realized he'd caught her, her lashes lowered and she smiled—a pretty, come-hither expression.

It did nothing for him.

He turned back to Bret and eyed the collar on the table between them. He certainly wouldn't stand out wearing it here. And really, if the collar declared to everyone that he belonged to Bret tonight, he was okay with that. He had no interest in anyone else, and he'd never been one to give a fuck what other people thought of him anyway. It'd also show those bastards trying to catch Bret's eye that she'd already made her choice this evening. There'd only be one man taking care of her, and that was him.

He picked up the collar and placed it her hands. "Make me yours for the night, Mistress. I don't want anyone's attention but yours."

The way Bret's eyes sparkled with pleasure at his words was reward enough. He'd made her happy. And damn, that felt good.

She smiled and lifted the collar to his neck. She took her time fastening it, letting her fingertips trail over his Adam's apple and throat, before buckling the collar in place. Then she leaned forward and brushed her lips against his ear as her hand slid on his thigh. "Now you're mine, soldier."

He closed his eyes as a fresh rush of desire flooded him, and swallowed hard. "Yes, ma'am, I am."

And he was. Without reservation this time. He'd signed up for this poker game. And he was officially all in.

He'd worry about the aftermath tomorrow.

───────

Bret had taken a risk bringing Malone out to the kink party at the hotel. She knew this wasn't his world, and so much all at once could be overwhelming and uncomfortable for him. But she hadn't wanted to dress up things too neatly for him. Plus, she wanted him a little off balance from the start. He was so used to controlling the situation that she had to show him he was subject to her whims tonight.

And maybe part of her had needed to see how he'd react. She liked being part of the kink community and needed to show him that this wasn't always a behind-closed-doors thing for her. Sometimes there was nothing hotter than watching others, or having them watch you.

But she had no intentions of sharing any part of her and Malone's night with other people this time. She wanted Malone all to herself. And though she had a sadistic streak, she'd never put such a proud man through his first scene with anyone watching. She wanted him to trust her and let go. She wanted to see what was there when the nerves washed away and the desire took over.

But she hadn't let herself hope that their little outing would go this well. Malone had been on guard the whole time, not out of discomfort, but he was in protective mode. The looks he'd given some of the other guys had made her smile. She didn't need the bodyguard, but it was damn endearing to see him warning other subs off when they even dared a glance her way.

And then, to her amazement, Malone had agreed to wear a collar for her. Seeing the broad-shouldered, tough military man wearing a sign of her possession had something much more potent than desire moving through her—especially when he showed no signs of being ashamed. The sub that had been trying to catch her eye since they arrived had looked hella surprised when Bret had fastened the collar on him.

Malone had given the guy a look like, *Yeah, that's right, motherfucker. I'm hers.* Bret had to bite back her grin. Malone was kind of irresistible when he went all junkyard dog.

But now she was ready to have him to herself, and desire and anxiety were coursing through her in equal measure. She didn't want to admit to herself how badly she wanted this to go well. She'd known long before now that her attraction to Malone went beyond her urge to take him to bed. She cared for this man. He meant something to her.

And even though she trusted both of them to be grown-ups about it and maintain their friendship if this didn't work out, she knew there would be consequences. Things would change whether they wanted them to or not. And the door she'd left cracked open for the past year would be officially sealed tight.

Malone shifted next to her. "What's on your mind, darlin'? You look a million miles away."

She turned his way and offered a small smile. "Sorry. I'm not, really. I was just thinking it's about time we headed back to our cabana."

His expression shifted to surprise, then concern. "I thought this thing didn't get down to business until after eleven. Something wrong?"

The fact that he looked worried that she was about to call the whole thing off gave her the boost of confidence she needed. He was here willingly. She'd coerced him into this situation by getting him on this trip, which hadn't been the best plan, but now he was here on his own volition.

"No, soldier," she said, trailing her fingers over that dark stubble of his. "Everything's very right. But I never planned to play publicly with you. Not for your first time, at least."

He gave a little nod, though there may have been a shade of relief on his face.

"And if I have to sit here another hour without touching you, I'm not going to make it."

The corner of his mouth lifted into wry male satisfaction. "I can be quite irresistible, Mistress."

She snorted. "And wildly humble."

"Yes, ma'am."

She pushed herself out of her chair and leaned down to brace her hands on the arms of his. She knew the angle afforded him a view down her blouse. "Cocky subs get more beatings, soldier. May want to watch that mouth of yours."

His gaze lingered on her cleavage for a moment, then traced up her throat until he met her eyes. "I have a high tolerance for pain, Mistress. And I have a feeling when it's delivered by someone as gorgeous as you, I could take most anything if it means I get to make you feel good later."

The boast sent warmth coiling low in her. She smiled and got a hairsbreadth away from his lips without touching him. "Oh, don't worry. I'll make sure you make me feel very, very good. Take me to my room, soldier."

CHAPTER 6

Malone had the hard-on from hell by the time they made it back to the cabana. And it was taking every ounce of his self-restraint not to make a move on Bret. Taking the lead with a woman was what he'd always done, and Bret looked so damn tempting strutting in front of him. But part of him was anticipating the challenge of balancing on that edge of desire.

He'd always enjoyed the game of walking that tightrope. He'd learned to savor that feeling of being right on the verge of no return. It allowed him to take his time with a woman since there wasn't that rush to the finish line. And he was good at teasing a woman to her own brink and maintaining his composure. But now the tables were going to be turned. He'd be the teased, the toyed with. The front of his pants tightened further.

Thank God it was dark out and the only lights were the small ones guiding their way on the boardwalk, because otherwise he'd be sporting wood for God and all His creatures to see.

Bret peered back over her shoulder. "Still with me, soldier?"

"You couldn't shake me off your trail if you wanted to now." He liked how she called him soldier. He'd heard some of the other dominants addressing their partners at the party—boy, sub, slave. He would've let Bret call him what she wanted, but he liked that she called him something that made him feel both knocked down a peg and proud at the same time.

And really, the simple term was helping him wrap his head around this better. That first night with her, he'd felt awkward and a little ashamed that he'd played the subservient role. But this power dynamic wasn't so different than what he'd experienced in the army. The military was about hierarchy, and just because you deferred to your superiors and showed them respect didn't mean you were weaker or less of a person. And in the service, he'd felt pride in all the roles, from the time he was a private to when he was the sergeant calling the shots.

He was very good at giving orders. But he also had been excellent at taking them—something he was about to show Bret to the fullest of his ability. And he had a feeling these orders would be way more fun to follow.

They reached the cabana and Bret opened the door, sweeping her arm forward, indicating that he should go ahead of her. He stepped inside, the space lit only with a small table lamp, and was enveloped by the seclusion of it all. With the sun down, the room took on a whole different feel—cavelike in the best way. The waves were a quiet, steady roar outside the windows, and the air smelled like tropical flowers and the ocean. And the girl he'd been fantasizing about for longer than he could remember was the only other soul who would share it with him. He must've done something good in a previous life to deserve this night.

Bret locked the door with a loud click, and Malone turned around. She leaned against the door, her smile pure Cheshire cat. "Last chance to run, soldier."

He gave her a long up-and-down look, taking in every bit of the tantalizing sight in front of him, then met her gaze. "Darlin', how could I want to be anywhere else?"

"Good answer."

She pushed herself off the door and moved toward him with slow, purposeful steps, those sexy boots making her hips sway in the most provocative way, hypnotizing him. *Click. Click. Click.*

When she stopped right in front of him, he had to curl his hands at his sides so he wouldn't reach for her.

"Take your shirt off, then lace your hands behind your head," she said, her voice soft but the tone firm.

He did as he was told, tugging his shirt off and tossing it to the floor, then linking his fingers behind his head, putting himself on display.

She took a step back as if to admire the goods up for sale, her heated gaze traveling over his body like a branding iron. "You're very nice to look at, soldier."

"Thank you, Mistress," he said, the term now easily rolling off his tongue.

"All this nice muscle and tanned skin." She put her hand to his chest and drew her fingernails down his sternum, scoring him and sending goose bumps over his flesh.

He swallowed past the sudden lump in his throat.

Her hand lingered at his abdomen, teasing, her eyes asking the unspoken question—*Hmm, where should I touch now?* Her fingers traced the buckle of his belt, then when he thought he would die if she didn't touch him again, she lowered her hand to the length of his very obvious erection.

"And you're very hard." She scraped her nails over the distended part of his jeans and gave his cock a squeeze through the material.

He groaned at the bolt of sensation and closed his eyes. "You seem to have that effect on me."

She moved closer, pressing her body against his, but keeping her hand cupped over his cock. "Good. I plan to keep you that way. You're not much use to me otherwise."

Her palm slid away, and he had to bite his lip not to groan again. The throb behind his zipper had increased tenfold from one touch. He might not survive the night.

Bret strolled over to the bed and tugged a long duffel bag out from beneath it. Malone breathed through the surge of desire and brought his focus back to her, letting himself enjoy the view of her bending over in that tight skirt. How many times had he forced himself to avert his gaze at work? And now here she was, letting him take his fill. Happy fucking day. She peeked over her shoulder, catching him in the act, and smiled.

"Subs are supposed to keep their gaze down unless I say otherwise, solider."

"Noted." But he didn't look away. He'd suffer the consequences.

"Lucky for you, I like your eyes and don't mind seeing them." She unzipped the bag and pulled out what he recognized as a flogger (thank you, Google), its long leather strips sliding along the side of the bag. "Not that it means you won't get an extra few hits for not following my order."

Malone's heartbeat kicked up a notch, his gaze locking on the flogger. "You brought equipment."

She shrugged, a little chagrined. "Guess I'm an optimist."

"Heh. Looks like I was a sure thing."

She gave him an are-you-serious look. "You're anything but a sure thing, Mal. To be honest, I don't think I've been this nervous with a guy since I was in college."

The little break in her armor warmed him. He loved that she was so tough, but it was nice to know he wasn't the only one with sweaty palms. "Don't be nervous, darlin'. Do what you do. I'm more than ready to see this part of you."

She let the strips of leather caress her hand as she watched him, her gaze going predatory, evaluating. "You really mean that?"

He wet his lips. The way she was looking at him had his blood rushing straight downward. "Yes. I want to touch you, Mistress, make you feel good. I want to hear what you sound like when you go over the edge. And I want to be the man who does that to you. You don't have to hide anything from me tonight, Bret."

If she was mad he'd used her name, she showed no indication. If anything, she looked a little speechless. But she quickly straightened her shoulders and nodded toward the bank of windows that faced the ocean. "Go over and put your hands on the window frame, then widen your stance."

"Yes, ma'am."

He strolled over to the window, a weird rush of adrenaline moving through him, and braced himself along the frame, presenting his back to her. The glass reflected his image, and he found himself gazing at this strange version of himself. He took a deep breath. Their cabana was set back a bit and tucked into the fauna, but if anyone was passing by on the beach, they'd see him here, wearing a collar, awaiting a beating.

He should probably care.

He didn't. After what he'd seen at the party, he was feeling pretty shameless already. But it was more than that. He wanted to give Bret his trust. He would do what she said because he knew she wouldn't do anything to purposely embarrass him.

The lamp clicked off behind him. It took a second for his eyes to adjust, but soon the white caps of the waves came into view and the room took on the silvery moonlight.

Bret stepped up behind him and pressed a kiss to the spot between his shoulder blades. "Now no one can see us, and you can enjoy the view."

"I wasn't scared of people seeing," he said, his voice low.

She slid her hands around his waist. "I don't want to share you, soldier. With anyone. You must bring out my possessive streak."

He smiled. "I like that."

"I don't remember asking you what you liked, soldier. But how convenient for you that we're on the same page."

He swallowed back the chuckle. Bret was always snarky, but hearing it in this context just reminded him how much he liked the woman, not just the mistress, not just the girl with the hot outfit and dirty thoughts. Bret was a force of nature in any role, and he loved that about her.

Loved.

He pushed the thought aside, afraid to chase that rabbit down the hole.

But he couldn't hold on to the thought for long anyway, because Bret's fingers found the button on his jeans and popped it free. He sucked in a breath as she dragged down the zipper and molded her body against his back. Her hand teased along the trail of hair that led down from his navel, and his cock flexed against his boxer briefs. He closed his eyes and breathed through the need.

But she wasn't done with the slow torture. Her hand dipped lower, and she wrapped her fingers around his erection. Her palm was cool against his heated skin, and it sent sensation straight down his legs and back up his spine. She kissed his shoulder and gave him a stroke. "Push your pants down to your ankles. I'm going to see how you handle a flogging. You need me to stop, you have the safe word I gave you. Correct?"

He clenched his teeth as she gave his cock another caress and then

ventured lower to cup his balls. She gave them a firm squeeze and he
lost his breath for a second.

"*Correct?*" she repeated

"Yes, Mistress," he said, his eyes wanting to roll back in his head
when she massaged him in her grip. "Red makes everything stop."

"Good." Her hand slid out from his waistband. "Pants down,
soldier."

He lowered his arms from the window and pushed his pants and
boxers to his ankles before quickly getting back into position. Naked,
bound at the ankles by his jeans, and about to get flogged by a beautiful
woman. Well, this trip had certainly taken an unexpected turn.

And if he had any worries about getting hit, his cock certainly hadn't
registered the fear. His body was all systems go for whatever his devious
co-worker was about to dish out.

He heard the clicking of her boots against the wood floor first, as if
Bret was pacing behind him, and he fought the urge to look over his
shoulder. But he didn't have time anyway because in the next breath,
the whooshing sound of leather slicing through air filled his ears. He
braced for it and the strips hit his back with a heavy thud. He let out the
breath he hadn't realized he'd been holding.

"Try not to tense," she said, and hit him again before he had time to
prepare. The blow landed solidly and he tightened his grip on the window frame.

"Pain from that hit from one to ten?" Bret asked, her tone steady,
focused.

His tongue swiped over his top lip. Both hits had been more a thud
than a sting, making him aware but not hurting per se. "Two and a
half."

"Good," she said. "I can make this feel like a massage or I can make
it feel like fire, depending on how I swing and where I hit. If you get to
an eight, you tell me."

"Yes, ma'am." He highly doubted Bret could swing with enough
strength to get him to an eight. He'd been shot in the leg in Afghanistan
and hadn't been able to get back to base for hours. He could handle a
flogging. "I'll be fine."

But the thought had barely crossed his mind when she changed her angle and striped the flogger over his ass with shocking force. The ends of the floggers tails snapped against his skin like sharp teeth, and his heels lifted off the ground as he absorbed the impact. "Jesus."

She sniffed. "Can't have you getting cocky on me. One to ten?"

He gritted his teeth. "Six."

In truth, his ass was on fire, but he could take much worse, especially when he pictured who was doing this to him, how Bret must look in her prim skirt and blouse as she wielded the flogger against him with that much force.

She hit him again, striping the other side, the sound of leather on skin echoing through the room. "Your skin turns a nice dark shade, soldier."

She stepped closer and patted a burning spot on his ass, then scored it with her nails. His cock nearly tapped his belly, he went so fucking hard. So much for pain being a turnoff.

She draped her arm over his shoulder and let the tails of the flogger dangle down and caress his erection. He glanced down his body, watching the strips of leather dance over the wet tip of his cock. For some reason, he found it wildly erotic to see her instrument of torture sliding over him with such a soft touch.

"I see you're still with me," she said against his ear.

He drew in a deep breath, inhaling the light coconut scent of her shampoo. "So with you."

"Good. Because I'm not done." She moved away again and he instantly missed her heat, that feel of her toying with him. But he wasn't left bereft for long because that's when the real flogging began. The first few had only been a prelude.

Now she was warmed up. The hits came hard and fast, as she swung the flogger against him in a steady pattern that left little chance for grabbing a thought in between. She mixed up the thuddy hits with the stinging ones, making his entire backside tingle and burn. *Thwack. Thwack. Thwack.* With every hit, he found himself settling into it more, anticipating it . . . enjoying it even. Every nerve felt alive and every hit seemed to send signals straight to his dick. He didn't understand it, how the pain could turn him on, but somehow it didn't feel like pain any-more. It felt like he was buzzing on the best kind of whiskey—loose-limbed, hot all over, and thoughts turning slow.

Bret landed a particularly sharp blow across the backs of his thighs and a moan slipped past his lips. His head sagged between his shoul-ders, and he arched back without thinking about it, giving her a better target.

"Very good, solider," Bret said, sounding a little breathless. "You look fucking amazing right now. Still with me?"

"Yes, Mistress," he said, his voice sandpaper rough.

"I should probably stop, but I can't seem to help myself right now. You make me want to indulge."

He grunted, hoping she wouldn't stop. He wanted to give her what-ever she needed right now. Indulging Bret Langdon was a perfect way to spend a Friday night. He was a very willing victim. He'd stand there all night if that's what she wanted.

She must've taken his response as assent because she started up the flogging again—this time marking a pattern from shoulders to thighs.

The sound of the straps hitting his skin mesmerized him, and soon he was humming with the sensation of it all—everything hot and sen-sitized and tingling.

Bret paused again and he could hear her exertion in the panted breaths behind him. God, he wanted to see her. Was she shiny with sweat? Flushed? Was this turning her on as much as it was turning him on?

"What are you thinking about, soldier?" she asked, still a little winded.

He cleared his throat, but his voice came out gravelly anyway. "I was wondering if you were wet, if you're as turned on as I am."

She didn't say anything for a few long seconds, but then there was that blessed clicking of boots. She moved beside him and grabbed his left wrist. She lowered his arm and drew his hand beneath her skirt. "Find out."

If she had said he'd just won the lottery, he wouldn't have been hap-pier than having the simple pleasure of touching her. He glided his hand up her smooth inner thigh and found the patch of silk between her legs. Man, what he'd give to see what she was wearing beneath that skirt. He nudged his fingers beneath the material and ran his fingers over her flesh, slick heat greeting him. He groaned aloud. She wasn't just turned on; she was soaked.

He stroked over her folds and found her clit, earning a shiver from her. "God, baby, I want you so fucking bad."

Bret's eyes went unfocused for a moment and her lips parted as he stroked her again. He could see how bad she craved his touch. But she grabbed his wrist and moved his hand away. "I didn't give you permission to take it that far."

"Please," he said, not above begging. "Let me make you feel good."

She licked her lips, and he could tell it was costing her something to maintain her patience. "You make me come, and I'll make you wait longer before you can."

He gazed down at her. "I can wait."

And he could. Right now, he wanted nothing more than to get her off. He wanted to see her lose it, wanted to make her melt.

Hell, maybe he was submissive after all, because he wanted to fucking serve her. And unlike last time, that urge didn't scare him.

The fear was gone. All that was left was Bret and what he was feeling deep in his gut. This woman was worth jumping out of his comfort zone.

"Please, Mistress," he said, sinking to his knees without reservation now. "Let me take care of you."

CHAPTER 7

Malone couldn't have said anything that would've gotten to Bret more. She was already beyond turned on from the way he'd handled the flogging. She had planned on not going too hard on him since it was his first time, but each time she hit him harder, she could see how into it he was getting, how he was settling into that zone and riding the high. When she'd checked in on him, his cock had been glistening with his arousal, and she'd nearly dropped to her knees right there to taste it.

The man was irresistible. The way that muscled back looked with all of her marks on it. The luscious curve of his ass. She wanted to take a bite, feel that firm flesh between her teeth. And the fact that he wasn't just not freaking out on her, but sinking into what looked like subspace had her ready to die with her own need.

And now he was offering to delay his own orgasm to take care of her. He was looking at her like a submissive looks at his mistress. Like his one mission on this earth was to bring her pleasure. And God, if he only knew how much pleasure he was bringing her already.

Those blue eyes of his were burning into hers and he lifted his fingers, still shiny with her arousal, to his mouth. He dragged his fingers between his lips, tasting her, then smiled. "Please. I need more than a taste."

Her tongue felt thick in her mouth. She reached down and cupped his chin, running her thumb over his damp lips. "This mouth of yours is beyond distracting. Stand up."

He rose to his feet, and she wrapped her hand around his neck to draw him down to her. When their lips met, his hands slid onto her waist, those long fingers spanning her hips, and he dove into the kiss like he was starved for her. Hungry, commanding, brimming with need.

She made a noise in the back of her throat as their tongues collided, her taste still fresh on his, and her fingers curled into the hair at his nape. Lord, but the man could kiss. She'd thought he'd sent her reeling earlier today with the kiss in the lobby. But this kiss was pure sex. What she hadn't allowed him to do yet with her body, he was doing with his mouth, showing her exactly how he would fuck her—long and slow and deep.

His erection pressed hot and urgent against her stomach, and she moved against him to rub herself along it. He groaned into her mouth, and she got the sense he was fighting the need to pick her up and toss her over his shoulder, caveman style.

This was getting away from her fast, but she wasn't sure she cared. With other men, she held the control tightly, everything structured. But with Malone, there was a wildness coursing between them that she didn't really want to tame. She wanted to flog Malone and tie him up. She wanted to wrangle that power and hold it in her palm, but then she also wanted him to break leash and take a run at her.

She broke off the kiss and shoved him away. "Get those jeans all the way off and get on your knees, soldier."

His eyes promised fire but he kicked off his boots and jeans in record time and lowered to his knees. God damn. This man on his knees could supply a thousand hours of fantasy for her. So strong, a hint of defiance in his eyes, but bowing to her will nonetheless.

She reached behind her and unzipped her skirt. The sound was loud in the quiet room, and she could tell she had Malone's undivided attention. When she shimmied the skirt down, revealing her panties and garters, he growled.

"Fuck, baby. You're going to kill me."

"What? These old things." She ran her finger along the sides of her thong. "I wear this to work all the time."

He grimaced. "I'm never getting anything done again ever."

She closed the distance between them, stopping just short of touching him. His face was eye level with her panties now. His eyelids went hooded and his nostrils flared. The palpable desire rolling off him was like the most potent aphrodisiac Bret could imagine. This is what she loved, that powerful feeling of being all that someone wanted in that moment. And the way Malone was looking at her went beyond that. He made her feel like a goddess.

"Tell me what you want, soldier," she said, her voice catching in her throat.

He wet his lips, his gaze holding hers. "I want to make you come, Mistress."

She put a hand to her hip. "And how do you propose we do that?"

His lips curled upward, that cockiness surfacing. "I propose you take these panties off and let me lick your cunt until you're screaming my name."

Well, then. The suggestion sent frissons of hot need straight downward. There was something about hearing Malone take the filter off, dropping the co-worker mode and telling her his filthy thoughts unedited. "You've got a dirty mouth, Mal. I like it. Let's see if it can back up the words."

She hooked her thumbs in the sides of her panties to tug them down and off. Malone's eyes followed her movements like a tiger tracking its prey. And normally she would stay standing, remain in the dominant position and hold him by the hair. But with the way he was looking at her, like he was about to devour her one slow nibble at a time, she worried her knees wouldn't hold up.

She hooked a finger in his collar and tugged a little. "Over to the bed, soldier."

He gave her a sly smile, like he knew exactly why she needed to sit. "Yes, ma'am."

When they reached the bed, she turned and sat down onto the edge of it. Malone sank back on his knees, thighs spread, cock standing proud, and that dusting of dark hair like icing on the most perfect cake. He was fucking decadent—a Greek god at her feet, awaiting his chance to rock her world. She couldn't wait to feel him inside her, to have him filling her and slaking that need that burned in those blue eyes.

But first she was going to indulge in that luscious mouth of his. She met his eyes and unbuttoned her top slowly, one button at a time, enjoying the growing strain on his face. She slid the blouse down her shoulders while his eyes tracked over her lacy bra, then she reached behind her and unfastened it. She tossed the bra to the side and ran her hands over her breasts, her gaze never leaving his.

He groaned aloud. "You're so fucking sexy, my head's going to explode."

She let her attention fall to his thick erection and pinched her nipples. "That's not the only thing that's going to explode."

His mouth lifted at the corner. "You're an evil mistress, but you're only making me harder."

She smiled, her confidence with him growing, and let one hand drift down. She spread her legs slowly and traced her finger over her mound, circling her clit. "I can torture you worse if you want. Maybe make you watch while I get off."

The tormented, hungry expression on his face was like the best drug. "Please, baby, let me take care of that for you. I promise I'm better than your finger."

Of that she had no doubt. And really, there was no way she was turning down his mouth for her own fingers. She moved her hand away and grabbed the back of his head, loving the feeling of that soft dark hair against her fingers. "You've been so good, soldier. I can't wait for you to show me how talented you are." She eased him closer and met his eyes. "Make me come, Malone."

She could tell the use of his real name did something to him, and for a moment their gazes held and it wasn't mistress and submissive or co-workers or anything else. It was Bret and Malone, sharing this intensely personal moment together.

She watched his Adam's apple bob in his throat, and the tender look in his eye threatened to break her wide open. For some ridiculous reason, tears tried to come to her eyes. "Bret—"

She broke the eye contact and gave his hair a tug, moving back into comfortable territory. "I'm waiting."

He blinked, as if shaking himself out of the moment, too. "Right, my pleasure."

The first touch of his mouth against her was a toe-curling shock to the system, her body so eager for him, she had to bite back the moan.

But he was only getting started. He gave head like he kissed—slow, hot, and thorough. And soon she found herself reclining onto her elbow, one hand still clinging to his hair like it was a life raft. "God, yes, that."

He hummed his response against her and sucked on her clit, teasing her with that clever tongue. Damn. She was usually good at stretching out orgasms and taking her time, but the man was lethal. He laved along her flesh, his pleasure in the act evident, and the effect was like sinking into a pool of warm water, all of her limbs softening and growing heavy.

No one was better at going down on a woman than an eager male sub. But Malone was putting the men she'd played with before to shame. He was covering every inch, every sweet spot, every delicious nerve ending. Her legs eased wider, and she found herself rocking against his mouth, using him and losing herself in the pleasure of it.

If he minded being used that way, he gave no indication. In fact, he seemed more into it the longer it went on, dialing up the enthusiasm. *Jesus.* Soon, she had to lie fully back, unable to support herself any longer, and he moved her legs over his shoulders and tucked his hands under her bottom to bring her up to him like a platter he was intent on licking clean. Her boot heels dug into his back, and that got him groaning again.

She smiled to herself. *Hello, you sexy masochist.* The man was perfect.

But her smile didn't last long because he slipped his tongue into her pussy and dug his fingers into the flesh of her ass before moving back up and taking her clit between his lips again.

"God, Mal." She lifted her head and glanced down her body at him, his hot gaze colliding with hers. His mouth was quickly devastating her, but those eyes were going to tear her apart. His lids went half-mast, and he pulled back for a second, his lips shiny with her arousal, then he drew his tongue over her in one long, flat stroke, never breaking eye contact.

Everything in her coiled tight, ready to break loose, and when he dropped down and sucked on her clit again, stars exploded behind her eyes. Her head tipped back and her back arched with her moan. Malone held her tight to his mouth, the speed of his strokes intensifying, and she began to shake with the force of her orgasm. It rolled through her in increasingly intense waves, and she fisted the sheets to keep from screaming out.

Malone made greedy sounds, not letting her get away, and she began to call his name over and over again. Not soldier, not sub, but Mal. *Mal, Mal, Mal.* In that moment, it was the sweetest syllable she'd ever heard. She said it until her throat felt raw with it. Until she had to tap out, slapping her hand against the bed and making pleas in between sharp breaths.

He released her, lowering her to the bed, and gently lifted her legs from his shoulders to set her feet on the floor. She sagged fully into the bed, panting. "Christ."

"I thought I was *dear* or *soldier*, but I'll answer to that, too."

She laughed, feeling giddy from the orgasm. "Shut up, smartass."

"Of course, Mistress."

She raised her head, finding him watching her with a satisfied smirk. He licked his lips, the simple move obscene considering what he was cleaning off, and she pushed up onto her elbows. "You're pretty proud of yourself, I see."

"I actually can't form thoughts right now. There's no blood left above my waist." He flashed his teeth.

She snorted. She liked that they could slip into casual joking mode in the midst of all this. There was an ease between them that she didn't find with lovers normally. She was usually strict with those boundaries. But with Mal, she didn't feel the need for any of those lines. "Well, how about we take care of that."

"Excellent plan. Your wisdom knows no bounds."

She sat up and put her hands on his shoulders. "On the bed, soldier. I'm ready to tie you up and give you your reward."

His expression shifted from lighthearted to let's-do-this in the space between blinks. "Yes, ma'am."

He got to his feet and strolled proud-as-you-please to the bed, then lay down and stretched out on his back, knees bent. He tucked his hands behind his head, completely relaxed in his nudity, and she couldn't pull her gaze away from all that lovely male flesh. He was hard everywhere he was supposed to be and blatantly aroused. She pressed her tongue to the roof of her mouth, her body already revving up again. "Touch yourself for me."

She knew he had to be dying for some stimulation, but he'd kept his hands off himself, proving he had iron-clad self-control. But now she wanted to see how he handled himself, how he took his own pleasure.

He wrapped his hand around his cock, those long, tanned fingers taking a sure grip, and gave himself a firm stroke. His belly dipped with the pleasure it must have sent through him.

"Mmm, very nice. Again," she said, walking over to pull a bottle of lube from her bag and offering him some. He held out his palm and she drizzled a few drops onto it—just enough to drive him crazy but not enough to give him all he needed. "Show me how you like to be touched, but don't let yourself get close to coming yet."

"Gladly." He followed her instructions, taking the slow path, and she found herself transfixed at the sight—his thick cock getting shiny with the lube, his thighs flexing, and his sac hanging heavy between his bent legs. So unapologetically masculine.

She had the urge to put her hands and mouth on every bit of it. Beyond that beautiful erection, she had a bit of a fetish for a man's scrotum, and his position right now was giving her a prime view. Really, there wasn't much about a man's body she didn't find fascinating. One of the dommes at The Ranch teased her that she was really a gay man in a woman's body because Bret so enjoyed every part of the male anatomy with unabashed enthusiasm. "Goddamn, Malone."

"What?" he said, his voice strained.

"You're a fucking sight."

"Back at ya, darlin'." His gaze slid down her body as his hand drifted low to fondle his balls before gripping his shaft again.

Lord, he was going to be the end of her. Whether he stuck around after tonight or not, their friendship was officially forever altered. She was never going to be able to look at him without picturing him exactly like this—shameless, sexy, *hers*. How the hell would she ever focus at work again?

She took a long, steadying breath, centering herself, and dug in her bag to get a length of hemp rope. Thank the kink gods for four-poster beds. She let the rope slide across her palm. "Put your arms out to your sides."

He eyed the rope but moved his hands where they were supposed to be. She slipped off her boots and walked over to the side of the bed, making quick work of securing him to the bed. Normally, she'd savor this part. She liked the bondage, enjoyed the ritual of wrapping someone in rope. But she'd lost most of her patience the minute Malone had started to stroke himself. She needed him beneath her now.

Malone watched with laser focus as she bound him, his gaze hopping from the rope to her face and back. He cleared his throat and shifted on the bed. "I love the look on your face right now. I can see how much this turns you on."

She moved to the other side of the bed and gave him a little smile. "Thinking how big of a freak I am?"

"If that's the case, then I must be one, too, because watching you is about the hottest thing I've ever seen. I'm a very willing captive."

The comment made something flip over in her chest. He was into this. Really into this. Whether he was truly submissive or just enjoying the novelty of it all wasn't clear, but in this moment, he was with her, totally on board. And she was ready to take full advantage of that gift.

She did the final knot on the rope and checked to make sure the binding wasn't too tight against his skin. "And what if I decided, instead of straddling you right now, I wanted to torture you some more?" She got onto the bed and climbed into the spot between his knees. She trailed her hands down his thighs "Maybe touch you in places you've never let a girl touch you before."

She let her fingernails gently score the underside of his testicles, not drifting to the forbidden zone, but making him aware of it.

He visibly swallowed. "Is that something you're into?"

She moved her hands up to grip his cock and his eyes fell shut. "I'm into a lot of stuff, Mal."

And that was the truth. If they decided to move forward with this for more than one night, he needed to know that she liked to push boundaries, experiment, explore.

She leaned down and licked the head of his cock. His spine arched, but he managed to talk through the rush of pleasure. "Once I trust someone, there's a lot I'd be willing to try."

She lifted her head to look up at him. "Yeah?"

He opened his eyes. "Yeah."

"You trust me?"

He lifted his bound hands. "I'll give you a hint."

She smiled—always the smartass—but hearing that he trusted her made her heart lift in her chest, especially when she knew Malone didn't give that out easily. That commodity, particularly with women, had gone up in flames courtesy of his cheating ex-wife.

"You haven't made me feel awkward or embarrassed at any point tonight," he continued. "I feel like there's this bubble around us that makes everything feel okay."

"A safe space," she said softly, feeling the same way. She thought she'd be much more nervous tonight, thought she'd be worried what Malone would think when she let her freak flag fly. But she hadn't felt any judgment or weirdness either.

He smiled. "Exactly. So do what you want to me, baby. If I'm not into something, I remember those words you gave me. You can trust me to use them."

Any final tension she might have been holding on to melted away. She guided her hands up his thighs and pushed herself up. "Well, right now, I know exactly what I want to do to you."

"Is that right?"

She climbed over him, lifting herself above him. "Definitely."

She pulled out the condom she'd tucked into her garter and opened the packet, then rolled it onto him, taking her time and enjoying his tortured groan.

"If you come before you get inside me, I really am going to beat you."

He chuckled, though it sounded strained. "No way is that happening. I may not be in control of much right now, but I'm in control of that."

She bent over him, still smiling, and leaned down for a kiss. His lips met hers with a slow, coaxing pace and she lowered her body, situating him at her entrance, teasing him a little. He grunted into the kiss, and she nipped playfully at his lip. "Still sure you're in control of that?"

"Fuck no."

She laughed and sunk down on him slowly, giving them both what they wanted, and this time she was the one to groan. He was so hot sliding inside her, his cock stretching her sensitized tissues as she took him deep. She closed her eyes and took a breath, savoring the feeling of being so full, so connected. With Malone.

The moment was a perfect snapshot in time. And when she opened her eyes, it only got better. Malone was looking at her with more than lust, more than male interest; he was looking at her like he wanted to make her his, like this was real and more than just a hookup to see how it went.

He was looking at her like this meant something to him. Like *she* meant something to him.

"Mal," she said softly.

He smiled, as if knowing she'd caught him revealing too much. "What, baby?"

"Tell me what you're thinking."

"I'm thinking I'm a dumbass for taking so long to go after what I wanted. I'm thinking I was a coward." He lifted his eyes to hers. "I'm thinking you're perfect . . . for me."

This time tears did prick her eyes.

"Now your turn. Tell me what you're thinking."

She shook her head and smiled. "I think I'm never ever untying you. You're staying right here forever."

He grinned. "Fucked to death by a beautiful woman. I'd die happy at least."

"So you're not regretting this yet?" she asked, rocking her hips and drawing out the pleasure for them both.

"Baby, all I'm regretting is that it took so long for us to get here. I won't be running this time. You'll have to chase me away."

She draped her body over him, brushing her lips against his. "Not a chance in hell. Now lie there, soldier, and take what I give you."

"Yes, Mistress."

The word had never sounded so right.

Their lips met, time slowed, and she made love to the man who she'd thought she could never have, the roaring waves outside no match for the intensity shared between the two lovers inside the little cabana.

She and Malone were together. It was only the beginning. But he'd be hers—and she his. She had no doubt.

No more pining. Colby had been right. It wasn't her style.

She'd taken control and found her corner of paradise.

The meek inherit the earth, but the bold get their man.

And Malone, well, he would get her heart.

Turn the page for a sneak peek at the next
Loving on the Edge book

NOTHING BETWEEN US

Coming Winter 2015

12:35 A.M.—SPRING

Georgia Delaune had never been particularly drawn to illegal activity. Or taking risks. Or, okay, fine—sexually deviant behavior. She was woman enough to admit what this was. So finding herself hiding in the dark, peering around the curtains of her second-story window with a set of binoculars, should've tipped her off that she was officially losing her shit.

But since moving into the house on Fallen Oaks Lane six months earlier, she'd known this moment was coming. Before now, she'd convinced herself that she'd only been catching inadvertent peeks and unintentional glimpses. Her neighbor would surely shut his curtains if he didn't want to risk being seen, right?

She groaned, lowered the binoculars, and pressed her forehead to the window frame. God, now she was blaming the victim. *He gets naked in the confines of his own home. A home that's on a treed corner lot with tons of privacy and a seven-foot-tall fence. How dare he!*

This was so screwed up. What if he saw her? He could call the cops, and she'd be slapped with some Peeping Tom charge—or Peeping Tammy, as the case may be. That'd be an epic disaster. Especially when the cops found no information on a Georgia Delaune. Plus, afterward, she'd have to move because there'd be no facing her neighbor again. Not after he knew what she did at night. And there was no way in hell she was moving. It had taken too much time, effort, and planning to find this spot, to finally feel even a smidgen of security and safety. These walls were her only haven, and she had no intention of leaving them.

But despite knowing the risks, when she saw a lamp flick on and light glow in the window of Colby Wilkes's bedroom, she found herself dragging a chair over to the window and lifting the binoculars to her eyes. It took a second to adjust the focus, but when the lenses cleared, the broad, wet shoulders of her dark-haired neighbor filled the view. Her stomach dipped in anticipation.

He wasn't alone.

She'd known he had friends over. She'd seen the group going in when she'd closed her living room blinds earlier that night. Two women and three guys, plus Colby. Later, she'd heard water splashing and the murmuring of voices, so she'd gone into her backyard for a while to listen to the distant sounds of life and laughter. That world seemed so foreign to her now. Being surrounded by people, having friends over, relaxing by the pool. She couldn't see anything from her backyard. Colby's pool area was blocked by the house and bordered by trees. So she'd lain in her lounge chair out back, closed her eyes, and imagined she was a guest at his party, that she was part of that laughter. And she'd also found herself wondering what would happen afterward.

Now she knew. Colby had stepped into his bedroom, obviously fresh from the pool with his dark hair wet and only a towel knotted around his waist. And he had company with him. One of Colby's friends, a tall blond guy who was also sporting a towel, had followed him in. And then there was a woman. She wore nothing at all. Georgia tucked her lip between her teeth, heat creeping into her face. She *so* shouldn't be watching this. But she couldn't turn away. She'd learned rather quickly that her dear neighbor, despite his affable grin, southern-boy charm, and straitlaced job, was a freak in the bedroom. Threesomes were only part of it. The man was dominant to the core. Considering her last relationship, that alone should've turned her off, sent her running. Guys who wanted control? Fuck, no.

But the first time she'd caught sight of Colby bringing a flogger down on a lover's back, Georgia had been transfixed. At the time she'd been completely stuck on her latest writing project. But after watching Colby drive a woman into a writhing, begging state, Georgia had gone into her office, opened a new document, and written until the sun had broken through the curtains the next morning. Before she knew it, her thriller-in-progress had taken a decidedly erotic turn. Thankfully, her editor had loved the new direction. So now Georgia, in her guiltiest moments, told herself these stolen moments at the window were all in the name of book research.

Yeah. Even her sleep-deprived brain didn't buy that one.

The guilt wasn't enough to make her stop, though. Especially now when Colby was grabbing for the knot on his towel. She held her breath. The terry cloth fell to the floor at Colby's feet, and everything inside Georgia went tight. *Holy heaven above.* She'd watched—oh, how she'd watched—but never before had she been able to see everything in such intimate detail. The binoculars transported her, took her by the hand and dragged her into that room with those strangers. Colby was right there in front of her—strong, beautiful, aroused. His hand wrapped around his cock and stroked ever so slowly, taunting her with unashamed confidence. No, not her. The woman. God, Georgia should look away. But need rolled through her like thunder from an oncoming storm, her fingers tightening around the binoculars.

The other man had stripped, too, and although he was gorgeous in his own right with his polished, camera-ready good looks, Georgia was drawn to the rough-around-the-edges brawn of her neighbor. Every part of Colby hinted at the wildness he hid beneath his surface—dark wavy hair that was a little too long, the close-cropped beard that shadowed his jaw, and a body that looked like he could bench-press a Buick. He was the opposite of the pressed and creased, Armani-clad businessmen she'd been attracted to in her former life. He was the guy you'd be wary of on first glance if you ran into him in a dark alley—the cowboy whose hat color you couldn't quite determine straight away.

Perhaps that was why she was so fascinated with him, despite the fact that he was a man who wanted what she could never give. She'd learned that danger often hid behind the gloss of an urbane smile and perfectly executed Windsor knot. Colby was none of that. But regardless of the reason for her mixed-up attraction, she couldn't stem the crackle of jealousy that went through her as the other man laced his fingers in the woman's hair and guided her to take Colby into her mouth.

The view of Colby's erection disappearing between the lips of some other woman was erotic. There was no denying that. But it also made Georgia's jaw clench a little too hard. She could tell, even from the brief moments she'd been watching, that this woman belonged to Colby's friend. They were a couple and Colby the third party. But it still activated Georgia's *He's mine, bitch!* reflex.

Georgia sniffed at her ridiculous, territorial reaction, and tried to loosen the tension gathering in her neck. *Sure, he's yours, girl. You can't walk down the street without swallowing a pill first, much less start something if he was even interested in the weird, spying chick next door.*

But she shoved the thought away. She didn't want anything tainting these few precious minutes. This wasn't about finding a hookup. Only when she stood at this window did she feel even a glimmer of her former self trying to break through. This was her gossamer-thin lifeline to who she used to be, to the capable and confident woman who would've never hidden in the dark.

Before long, the blond man eased the woman away from Colby and guided her toward himself, taking his turn. Georgia tilted the binoculars upward, finding Colby's face instead of focusing on the scene between the other man and his woman. What she found lurking in his expression wasn't what she expected. There was heat in Colby's eyes, interest for sure, but as she stared longer, she sensed a distance in those hazel depths. Like he was there with them but other . . . separate. Alone.

It probably was only because the other two were a couple. Or maybe it was Georgia's mind slapping labels on things to make herself feel better. But regardless, it made her chest constrict with recognition. She didn't know what was going on in his head. Or how seeing his friends together made him feel. But she knew loneliness. And for those few seconds, she was convinced Colby did, too. She pressed her fingertip against the cool glass of the window, tracing the outline of Colby's face. Needing to touch . . . something.

The glass may as well have been made of steel, the yards between the houses made of miles.

But she couldn't walk away. The night went on and there she sat, watching the three lovers move to the bed, the woman being cuffed to the headboard. The two men ravished her with hands and mouths and tongues. It was like watching a silent symphony, the arching of the woman's back the only thing Georgia needed to see to know exactly how these men were affecting their willing captive. The melancholy feelings that had stirred earlier had quickly been surpassed by ones much more base and primal. Georgia's body was growing hot and restless, her panties going damp.

When Colby braced himself between the woman's thighs and entered her, Georgia trained the binoculars on his face, unable to handle the image of him having sex with another woman. Her mind was developing quite the ability to focus on the fantasy and block out the unwanted parts. She only had a view of Colby's profile, but she watched with rapt attention as his jaw worked and his skin went slick with sweat instead of pool water.

Without giving it too much thought, she braced one elbow on the window ledge to hold the binoculars steady and let her other hand drift downward. Her cotton nightgown slid up her thighs easily. Somewhere her brain protested that this was wrong—sick and sad. She had a perfectly functioning vibrator in her bedside drawer. She had an imagination strong enough to fuel an orgasm without doing this, without watching the man next door screw another woman. But her starved libido didn't seem to give a damn about morals or ethics or pride right now. There was need. And a solution. Simple as that.

As Colby's lips parted with a sound she could only imagine, Georgia's fingers found the edge of her panties and slipped beneath the material. Her body tightened at the touch and the little gasp she made reverberated in the dead silence of the bedroom. Colby's head dipped between his shoulders, and Georgia imagined it was her he was whispering passionate words to. That deep Texas drawl telling her how good it felt to be inside her, how sexy she was, how he was going to make her come. He would be a dirty talker, she had no doubt. No sweet nothings from Colby Wilkes.

She closed her eyes for a moment as she moved her fingers in the rhythm of Colby's thrust—long, languid strokes that had a fire building from her center and radiating heat outward. It wouldn't take long. Her body was already singing with sensation, release hurtling toward her. But she wouldn't go over alone. She forced her eyes open, the binoculars still in her grip, and found Colby again. His dark hair was curling against his neck, sweat glistening at his temples. And she knew he had to be close, too. Every muscle in his shoulders and back had tensed. All of her attention zeroed in on him, and in her mind, the touch of her own fingers morphed into his—his hands and body moving against her, inside her.

Every molecule in her being seemed to contract, preparing for the burst of energy to come. Her breath quickened, her heartbeat pulsing in her ears. And right as she was about to close her eyes and go over, Colby jerked his head to the side toward the window. His heated gaze collided with hers through the binoculars—a dead-on eye lock that seemed to reach inside Georgia and flip her inside out. *He knows.*

But she was too far gone for the shock to derail her. Orgasm careened through her with a force that made the chair scrape back across the wood floor. She moaned into the quiet, the binoculars slipping from her hand and jerking the strap around her neck. The part in the curtains fell shut, but she didn't notice. Everything was too bright behind her eyelids, too good, to worry about anything else but the way she felt in those long seconds. *Enjoy. Don't think. Just feel.* The words whispered through her as her fingers kept moving, her body determined to eke out every ounce of sensation she could manage.

But, of course, the blissful, mindless moments couldn't last forever. Chilly reality made a swift reappearance as her gown slipped back down her thighs and sweat cooled on her skin. She sat there, staring at the closed curtain and listening to her thumping heart. Colby *couldn't* know, right? His gaze had felt intense and knowing because the binoculars had made him seem so close. But her window was dark, her curtains darker, and the moon was throwing off enough light that it would make the glass simply reflect back the glow.

But her chest felt like a hundred hummingbirds had roosted there, beating their wings against her ribs. She wet her lips and swallowed past the constriction in her throat. She had to look. Would her neighbor be striding over here to demand to know what was going on? Would he be disgusted? Embarrassed? Angry?

God, she didn't even want to think about it. She wanted to turn around, go to her bedroom, and hide under the covers. But that's all her life had turned into now—hiding. And though she couldn't fix that situation, she refused to create another one. So she forced herself to lean forward and peel the curtains back one more time, leaving the binoculars hanging around her neck.

What she saw made the hummingbirds thrash more. Colby wasn't in the room anymore. His friend was now with the woman in the bed, and both seemed totally absorbed in each other. Did that mean Colby had left and was heading this way to confront her? She was about to go to the front of the house to check the yard but then paused when she realized nothing had changed about the view. Nothing at all. If Colby had been concerned about a nosy neighbor, he hadn't bothered to close the curtains or warn his friends. Surely he would've done that.

She sat there, debating and worrying, but soon Colby returned to the bedroom. The man and woman had finished. Colby had on a pair of boxers and had brought clean towels in for everyone. He didn't look concerned. He didn't glance over at the window. He seemed perfectly relaxed as he helped untie the woman's hands, kissed her forehead in a friendly gesture, and then left his friends to sleep alone.

Georgia let out a long breath, sagging in the chair.

He didn't know.

She should stop taking this risk—throw away the binoculars, put a bookcase in front of this damn window, and stop while she was ahead.

But she knew she wouldn't. She would find herself here again.

Because if she didn't have her secret nights with Colby Wilkes, what was left?

Four walls, long days, and fear.

She needed this. She just had to made sure he never found out.

Roni Loren wrote her first romance novel at age fifteen when she discovered writing about boys was way easier than actually talking to them. Since then, her flirting skills haven't improved, but she likes to think her storytelling ability has. Though she'll forever be a New Orleans girl at heart, she now lives in Dallas with her husband and son. If she's not working on her latest sexy story, you can find her reading, watching reality television, or indulging in her unhealthy addiction to rock stars, er, rock concerts. Yeah, that's it. Visit her website: roniloren.com.